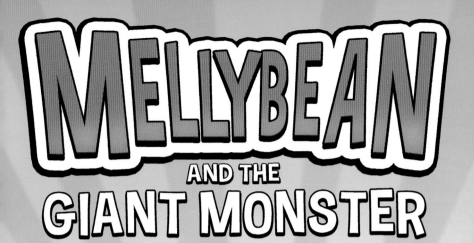

MELLYBEAN AND THE GIANT MONSTER

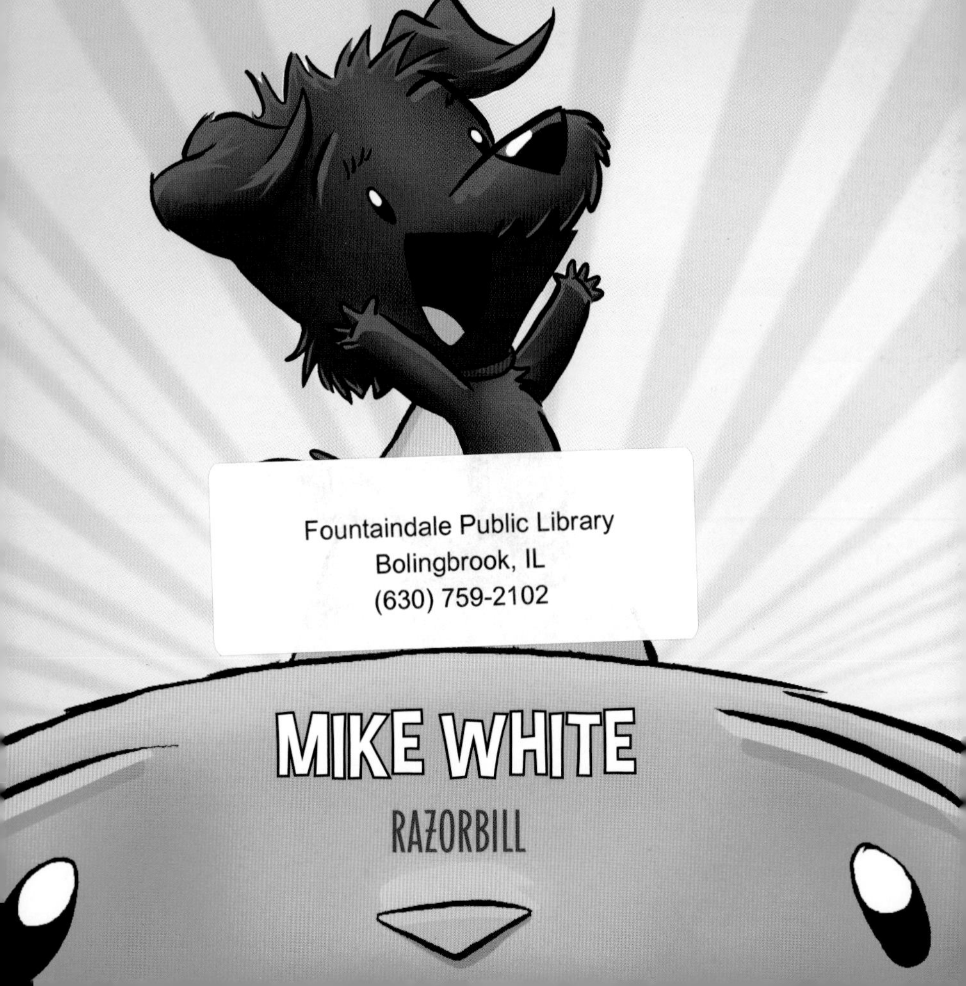

MIKE WHITE

RAZORBILL

RAZORBILL

An imprint of Penguin Random House LLC, New York

First published in the United States of America by Razorbill,
an imprint of Penguin Random House LLC, 2020

Visit us online at penguinrandomhouse.com

LIBRARY OF CONGRESS CATALOGING-IN-PUBLICATION DATA
Names: White, Mike (Children's author), author, illustrator.
Title: Mellybean and the giant monster / Mike White.
Description: New York : Razorbill, 2020. | Series: Mellybean; book 1 | Audience: Ages 8–12. |
Summary: While trying to bury a shoe in the backyard, a young dog who lives with two humans and three cats is transported to a world filled with magic, adventure, and one giant, grumpy monster.
Identifiers: LCCN 2020020473 | ISBN 9780593202807 (trade paperback) | ISBN 9780593202548 (hardcover) | ISBN 9780593205730 (kindle edition) | ISBN 9780593205747 (nook edition) | ISBN 9780593202791 (epub) Subjects: LCSH: Graphic novels. | CYAC: Graphic novels. | Dogs—Fiction. | Monsters—Fiction. | Adventure and adventurers—Fiction. Classification: LCC PZ7.7.W5415 Me 2020 | DDC 741.5/973—dc23 LC record available at https://lccn.loc.gov/2020020473

Manufactured in China.

ISBN 9780593202548 (hardcover); ISBN 9780593202807 (paperback)

1 3 5 7 9 10 8 6 4 2

Design by Mike White.
Colors by Valery Kutz.
Text set in Evil Genius.

Dedicated to:
Carol, Melody, Butternut,
Charlie, & Tugs

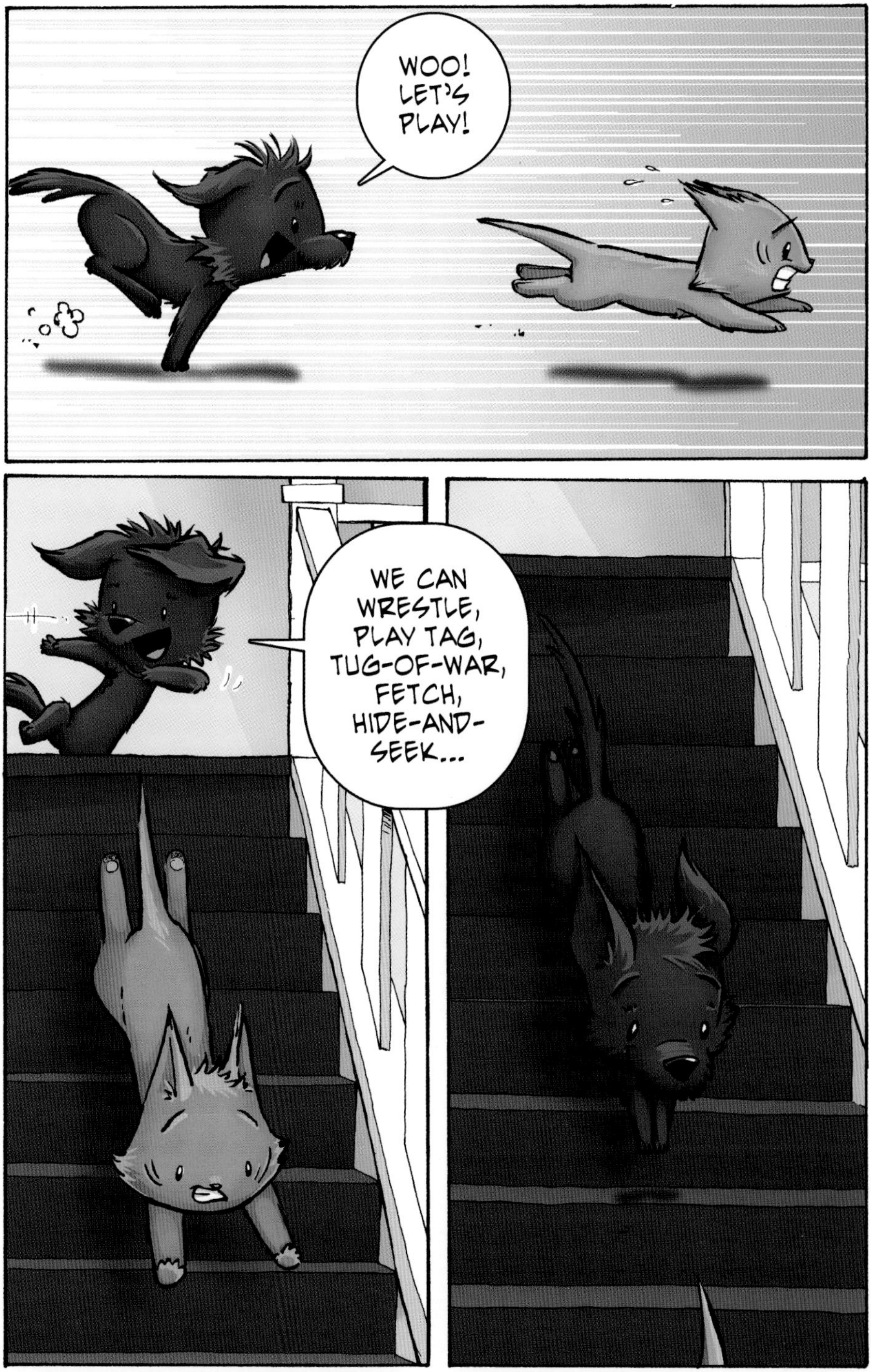
WOO! LET'S PLAY!
WE CAN WRESTLE, PLAY TAG, TUG-OF-WAR, FETCH, HIDE-AND-SEEK...

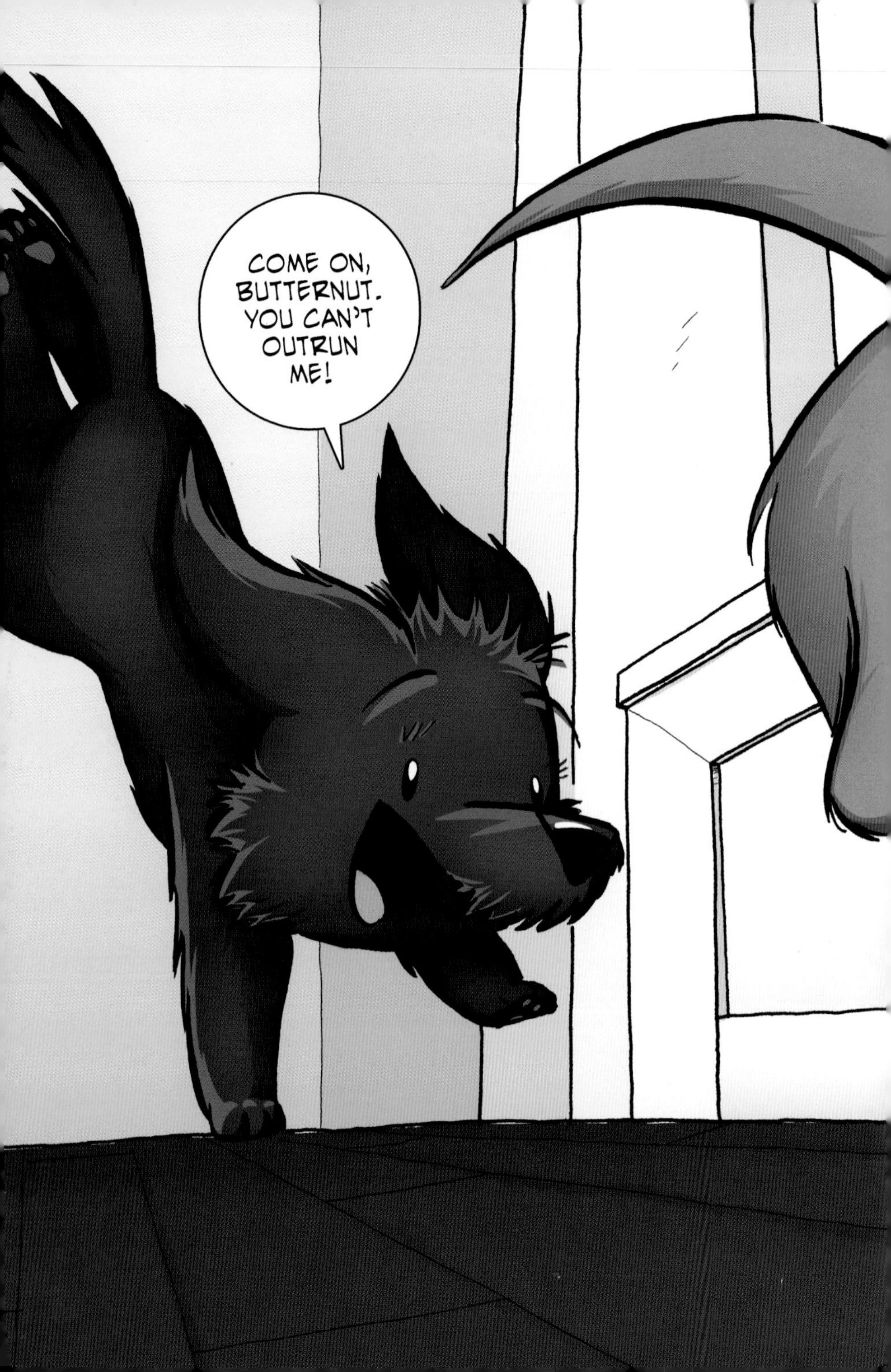
COME ON, BUTTERNUT. YOU CAN'T OUTRUN ME!

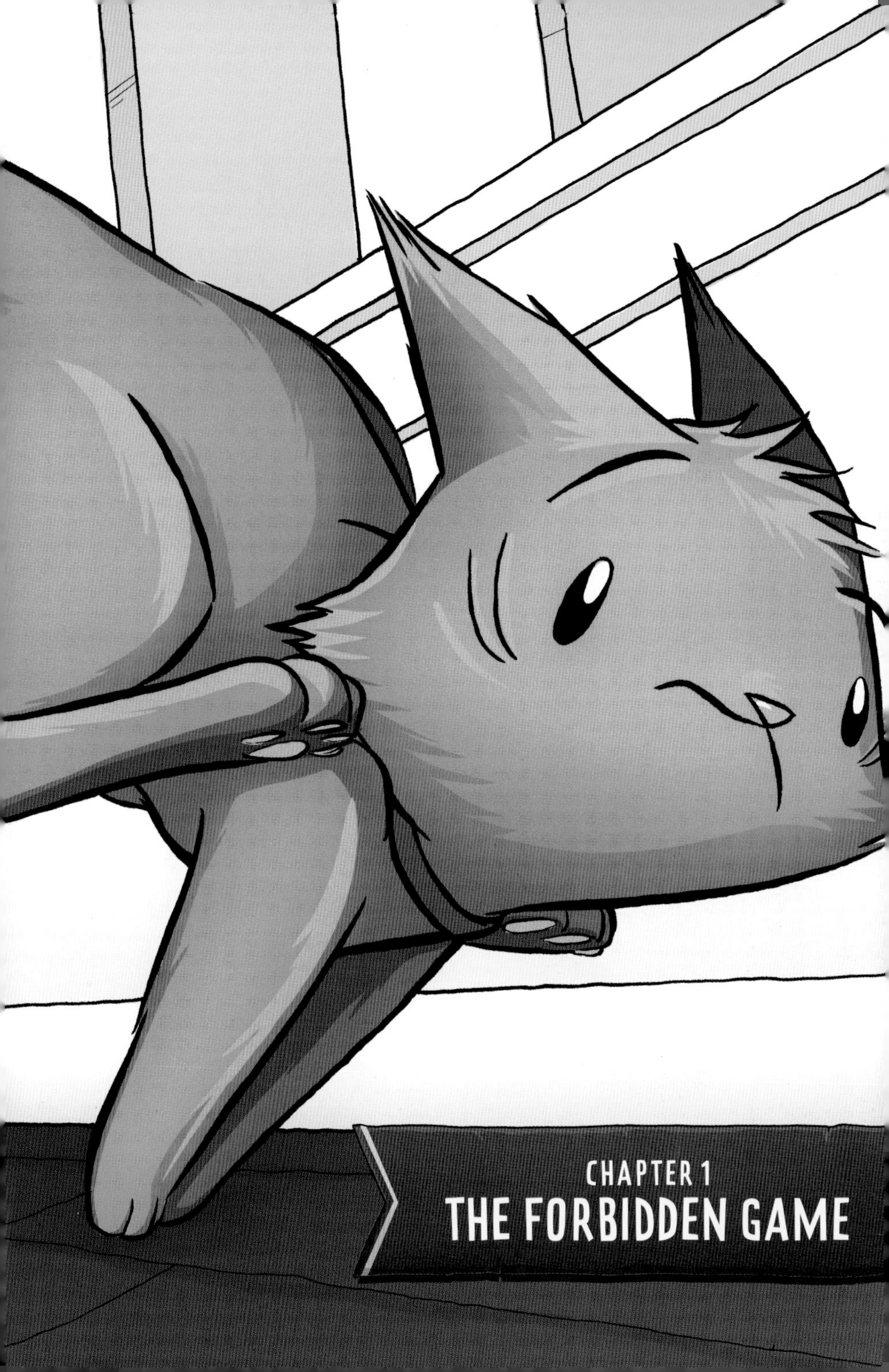

CHAPTER 1
THE FORBIDDEN GAME

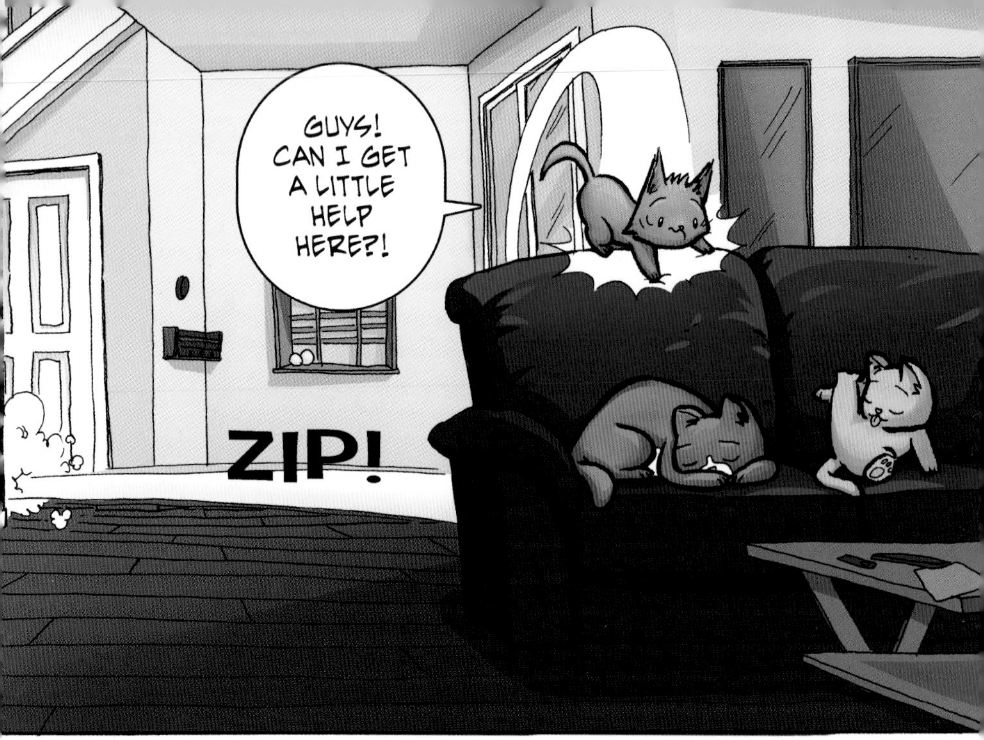
GUYS! CAN I GET A LITTLE HELP HERE?!
ZIP!

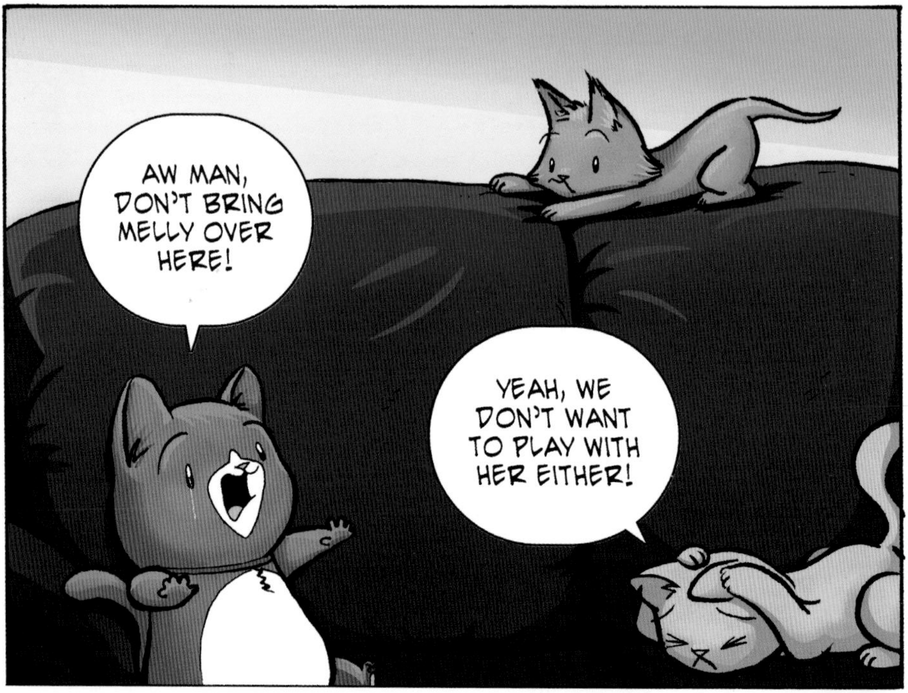
AW MAN, DON'T BRING MELLY OVER HERE!
YEAH, WE DON'T WANT TO PLAY WITH HER EITHER!

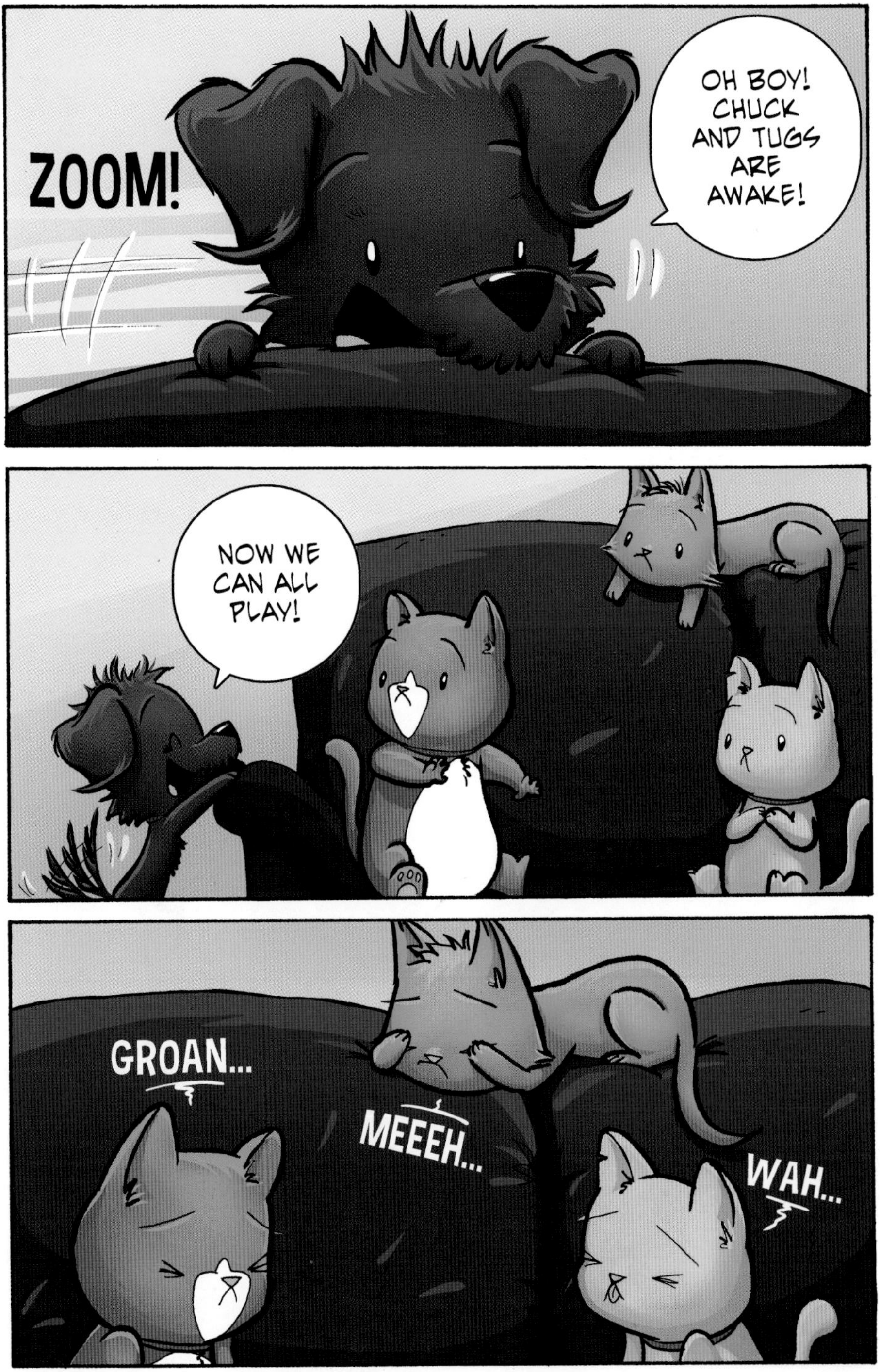
ZOOM!
OH BOY! CHUCK AND TUGS ARE AWAKE!
NOW WE CAN ALL PLAY!
GROAN...
MEEEH...
WAH...

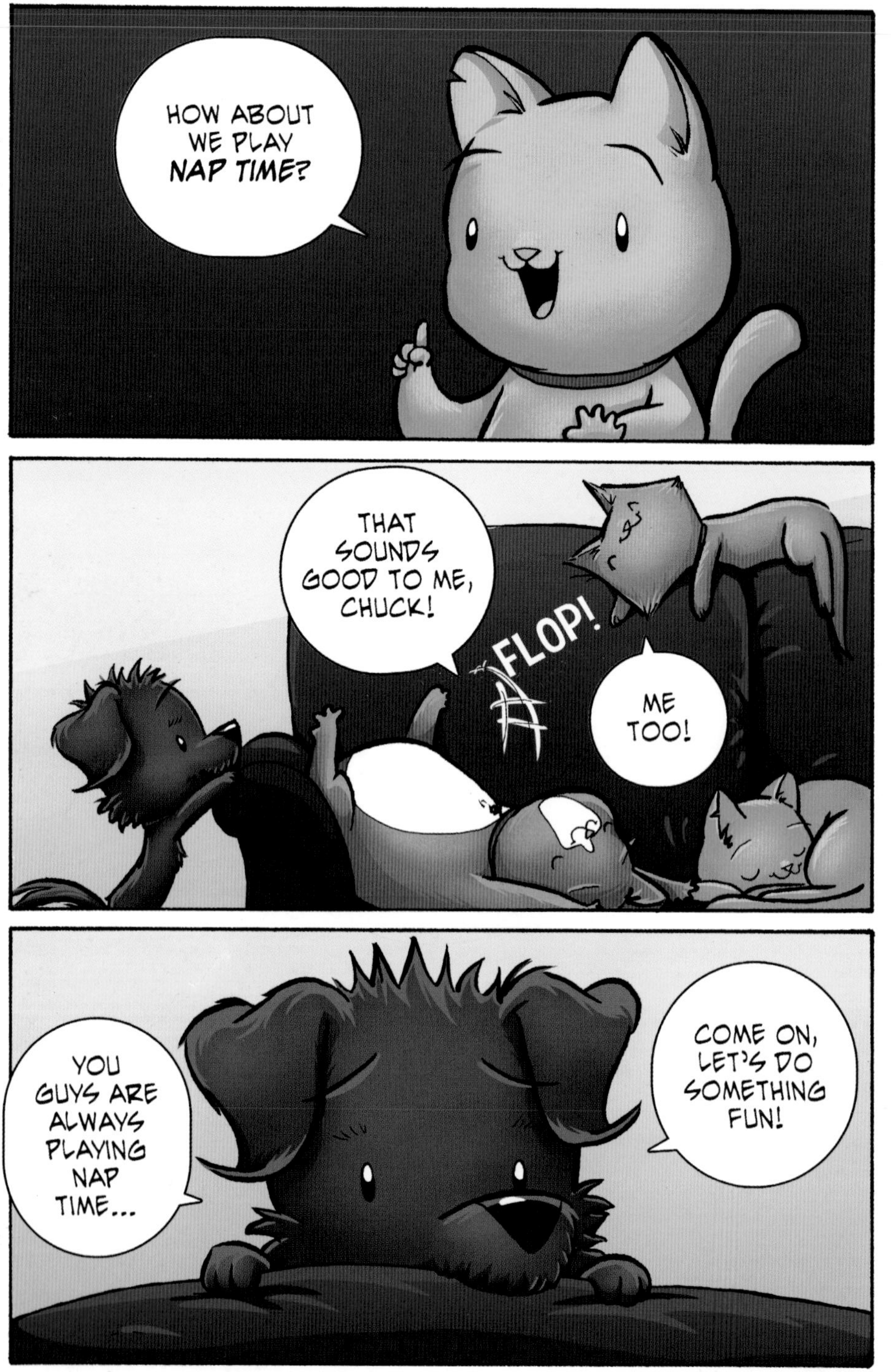
HOW ABOUT WE PLAY NAP TIME?
THAT SOUNDS GOOD TO ME, CHUCK!
FLOP!
ME TOO!
YOU GUYS ARE ALWAYS PLAYING NAP TIME...
COME ON, LET'S DO SOMETHING FUN!

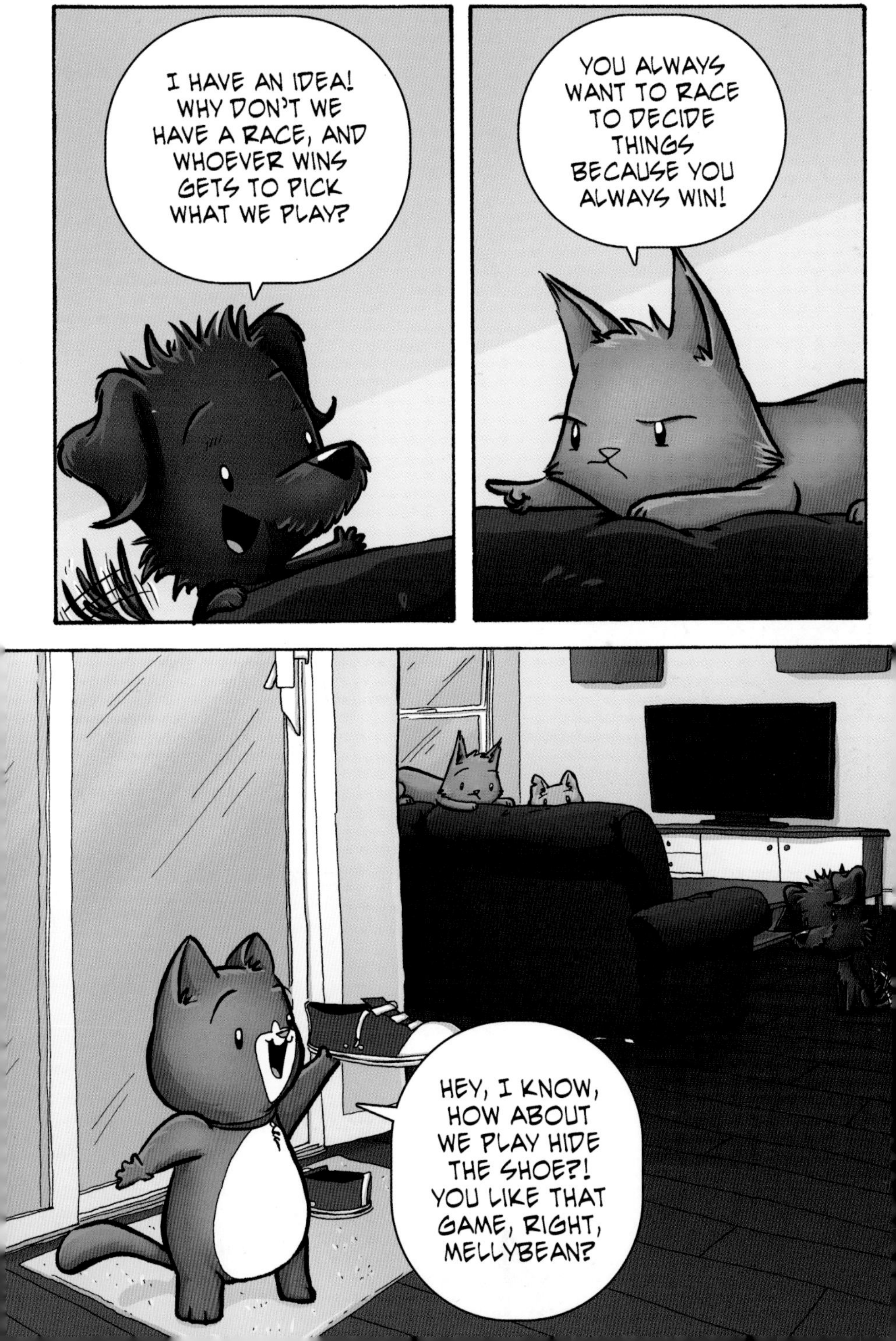
I HAVE AN IDEA! WHY DON'T WE HAVE A RACE, AND WHOEVER WINS GETS TO PICK WHAT WE PLAY?
YOU ALWAYS WANT TO RACE TO DECIDE THINGS BECAUSE YOU ALWAYS WIN!
HEY, I KNOW, HOW ABOUT WE PLAY HIDE THE SHOE?! YOU LIKE THAT GAME, RIGHT, MELLYBEAN?

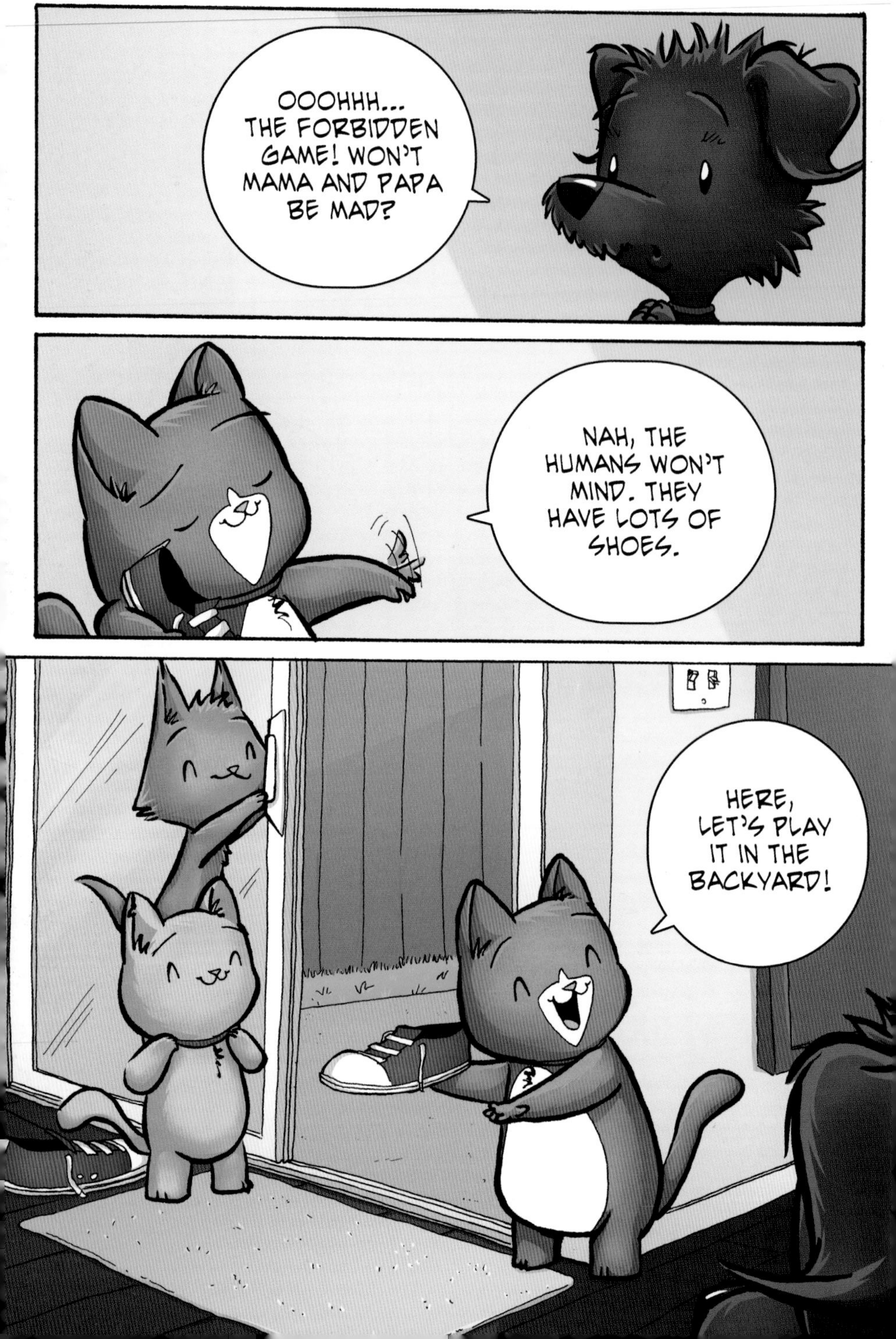
OOOHHH... THE FORBIDDEN GAME! WON'T MAMA AND PAPA BE MAD?
NAH, THE HUMANS WON'T MIND. THEY HAVE LOTS OF SHOES.
HERE, LET'S PLAY IT IN THE BACKYARD!

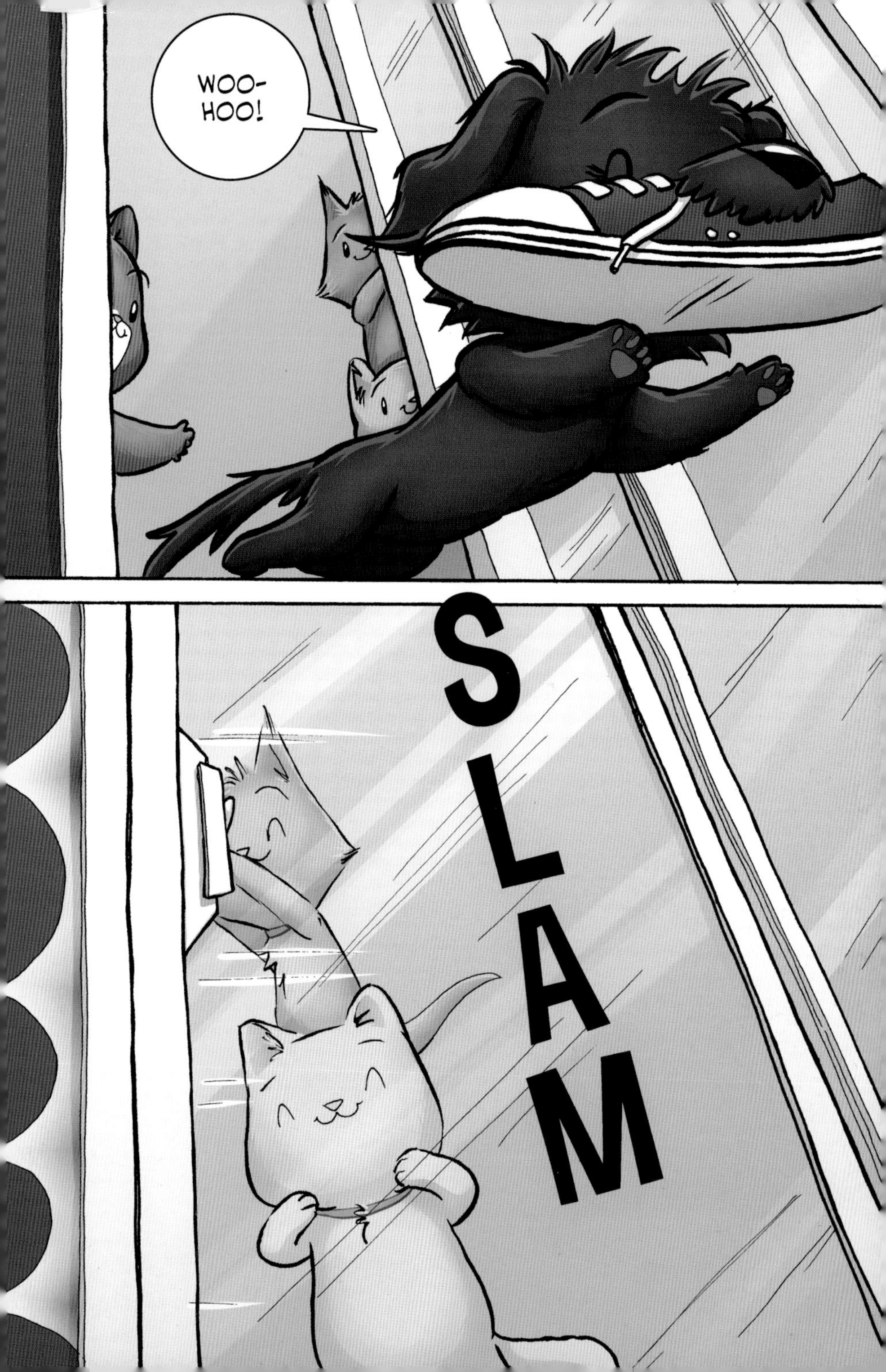
WOO-
HOO!
SLAM

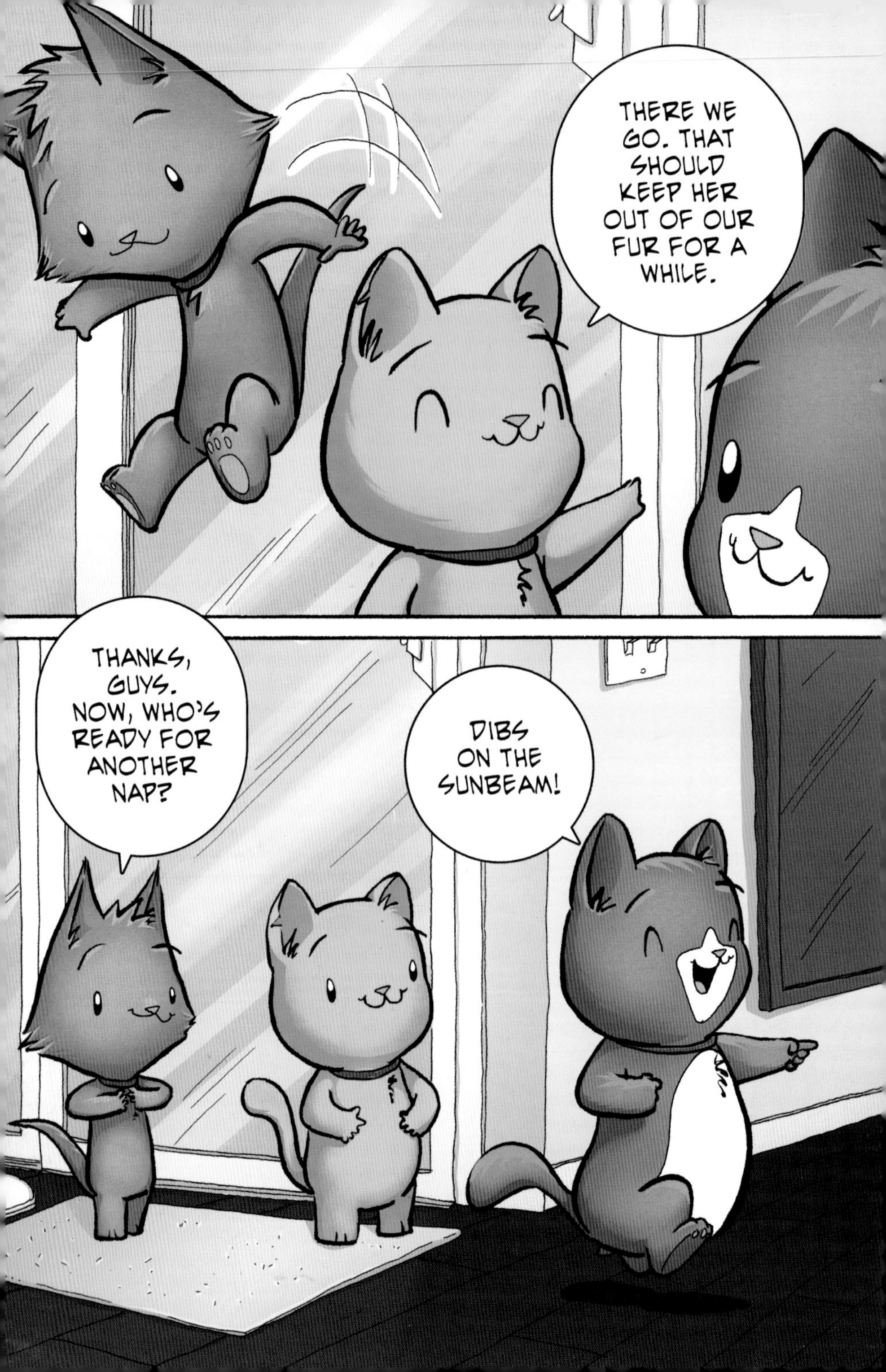
THERE WE GO. THAT SHOULD KEEP HER OUT OF OUR FUR FOR A WHILE.
THANKS, GUYS. NOW, WHO'S READY FOR ANOTHER NAP?
DIBS ON THE SUNBEAM!

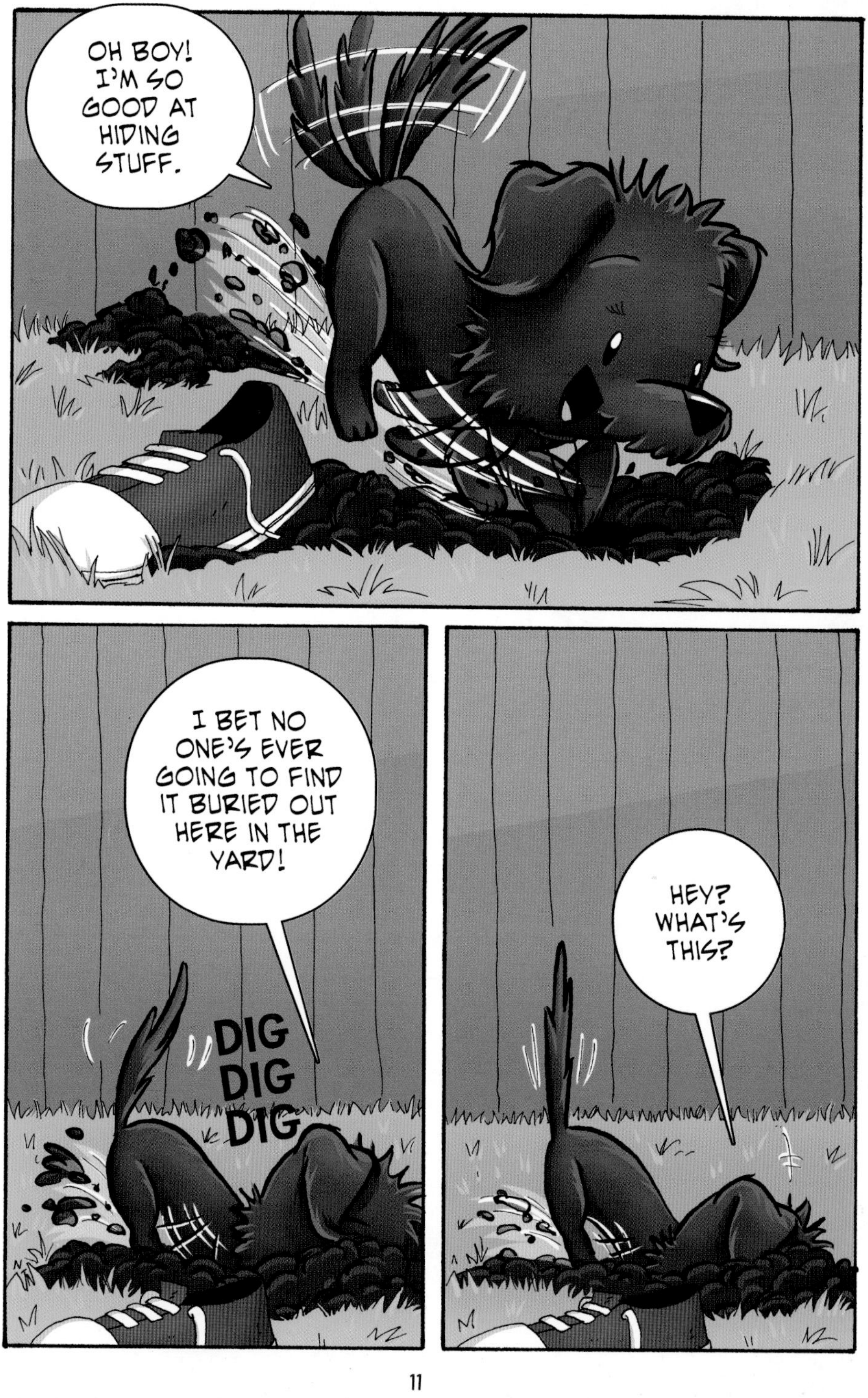
OH BOY! I'M SO GOOD AT HIDING STUFF.
I BET NO ONE'S EVER GOING TO FIND IT BURIED OUT HERE IN THE YARD!
DIG DIG DIG
HEY? WHAT'S THIS?

THERE'S ALREADY A GIANT HOLE DOWN HERE...

MUST BE THOSE PESKY SKUNKS AGAIN. THEY'RE ALWAYS DIGGING UNDER OUR HOUSE.

SNIFF SNIFF SNIFF

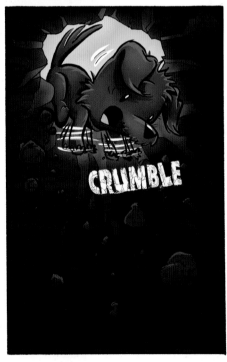

CRUMBLE

WHOA!

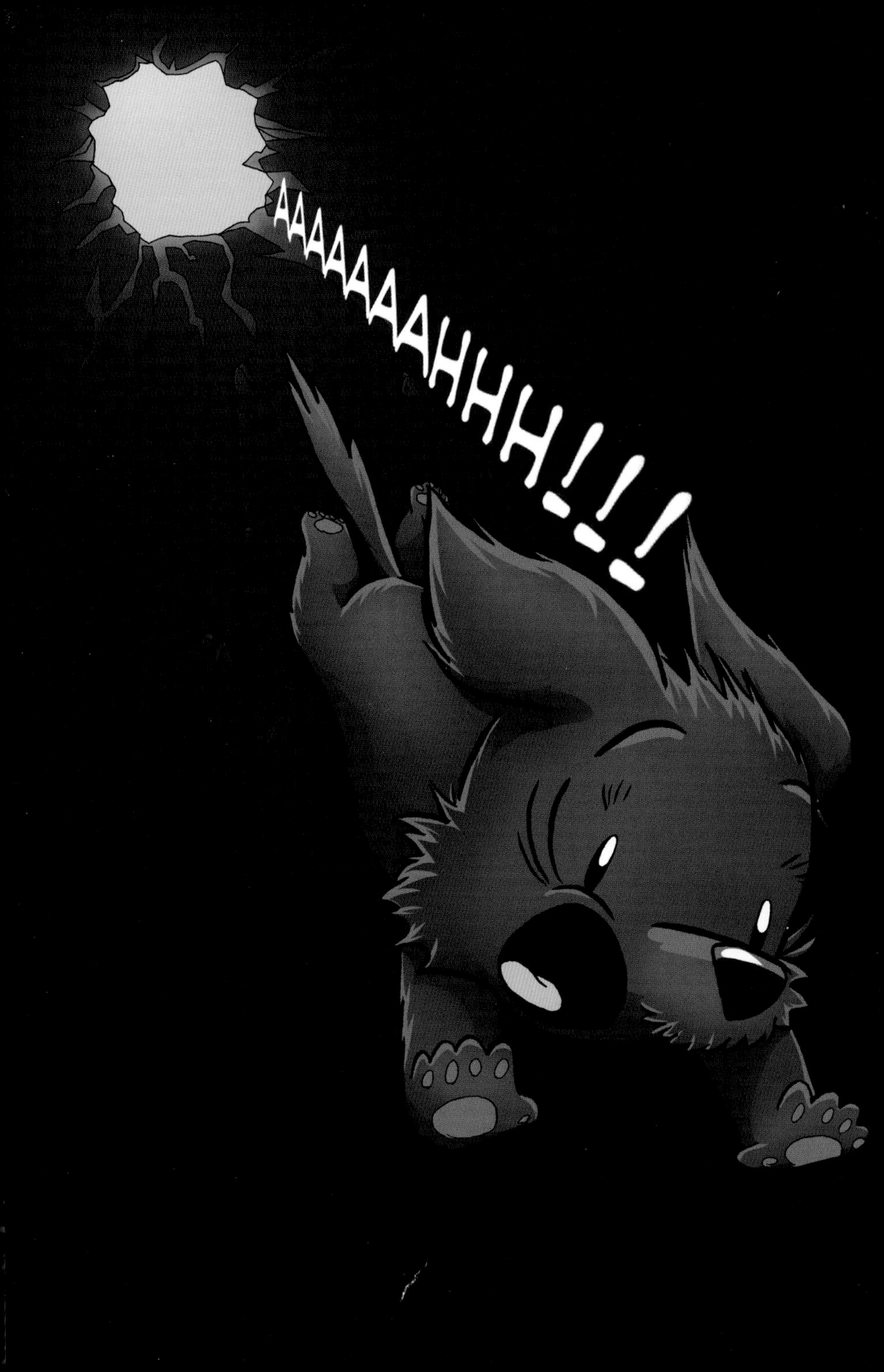
AAAAAAAAHHHH!!!!

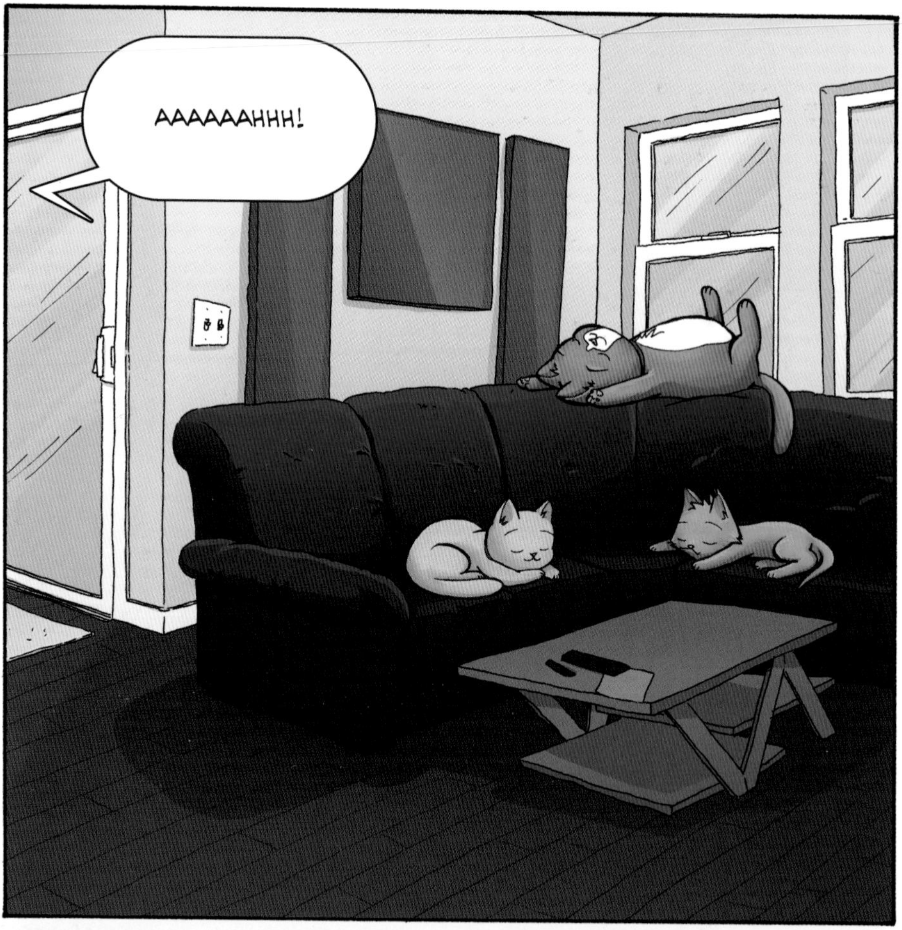
AAAAAAHHH!

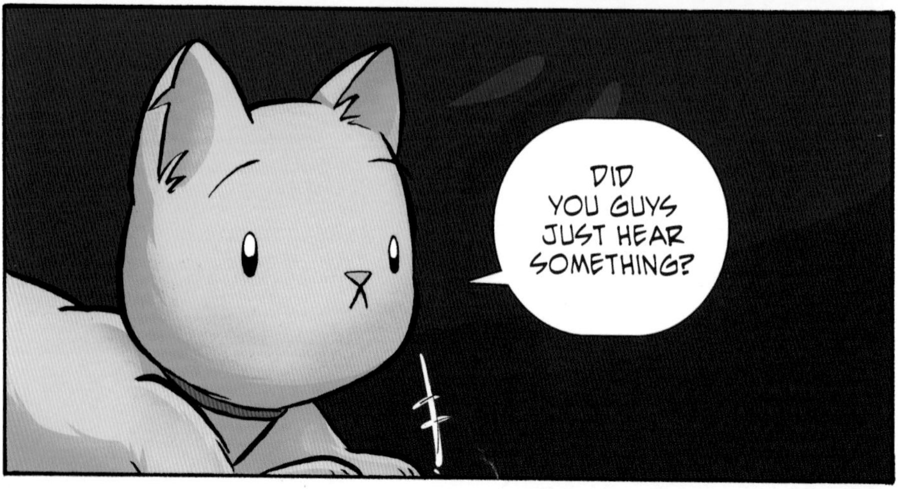
DID YOU GUYS JUST HEAR SOMETHING?

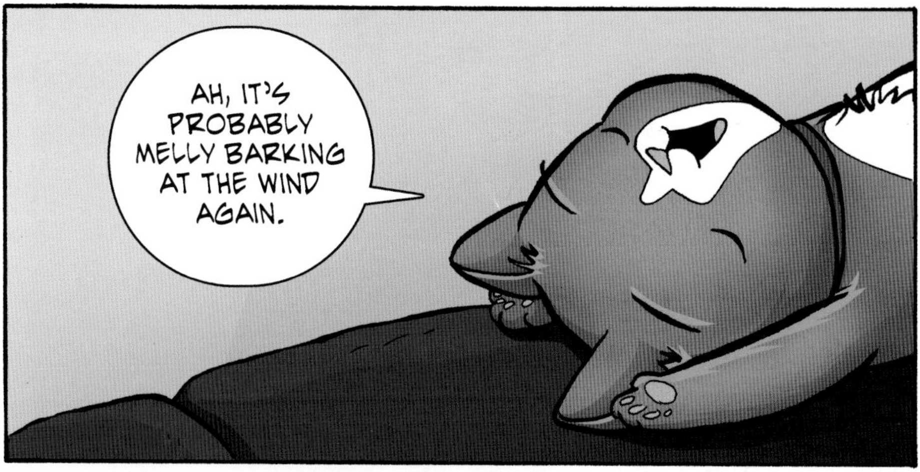
AH, IT'S PROBABLY MELLY BARKING AT THE WIND AGAIN.

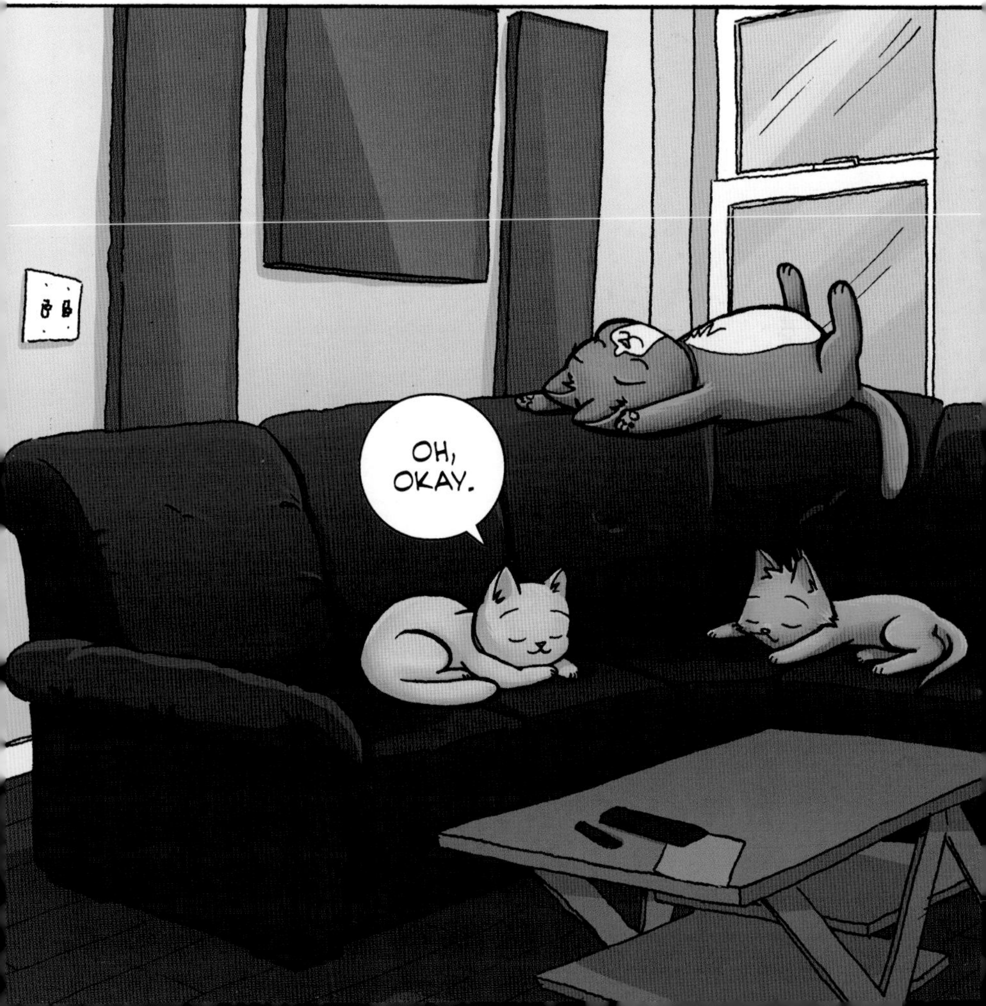
OH, OKAY.

CHAPTER 2
THE GIANT MONSTER

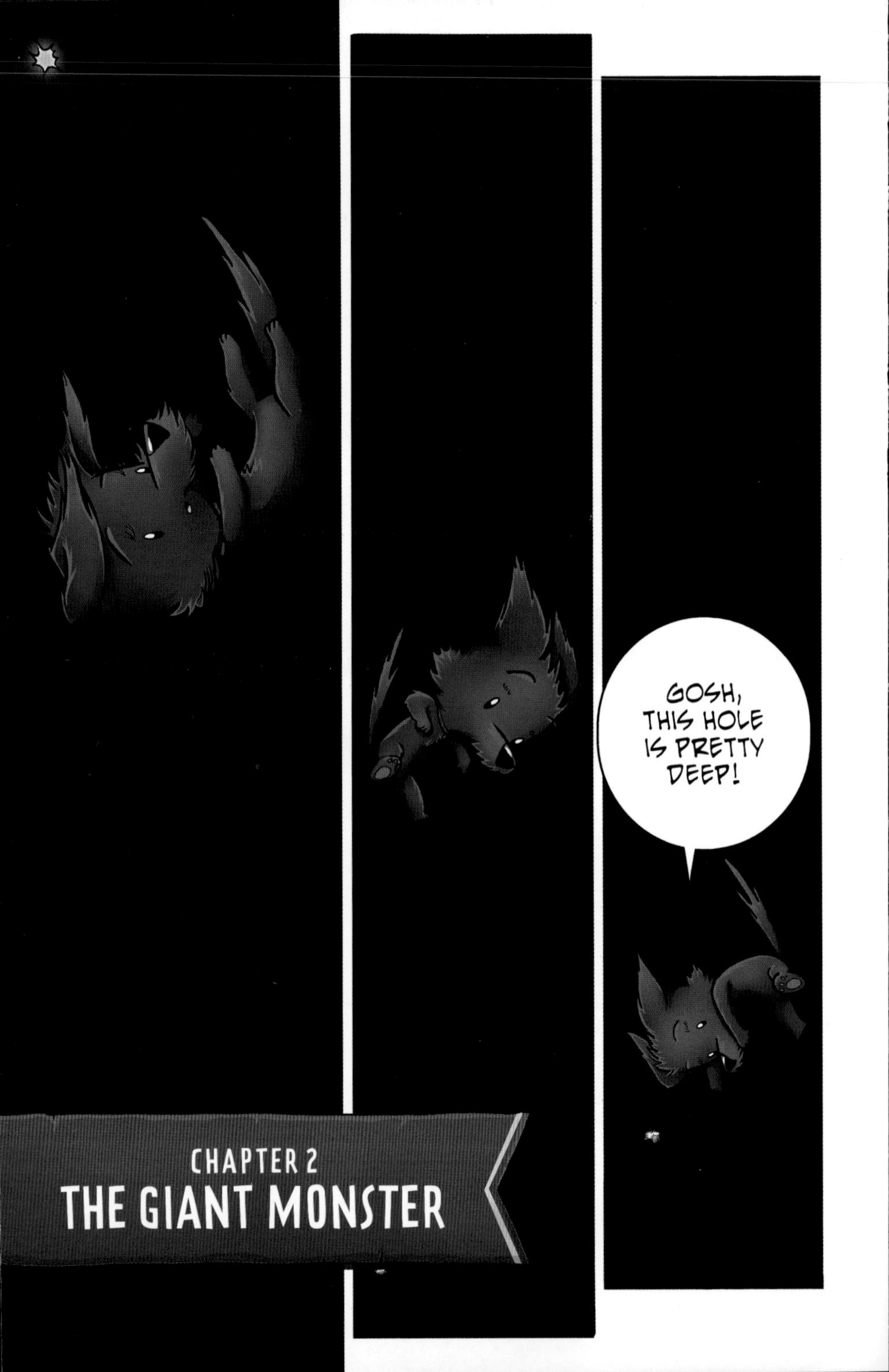
GOSH, THIS HOLE IS PRETTY DEEP!

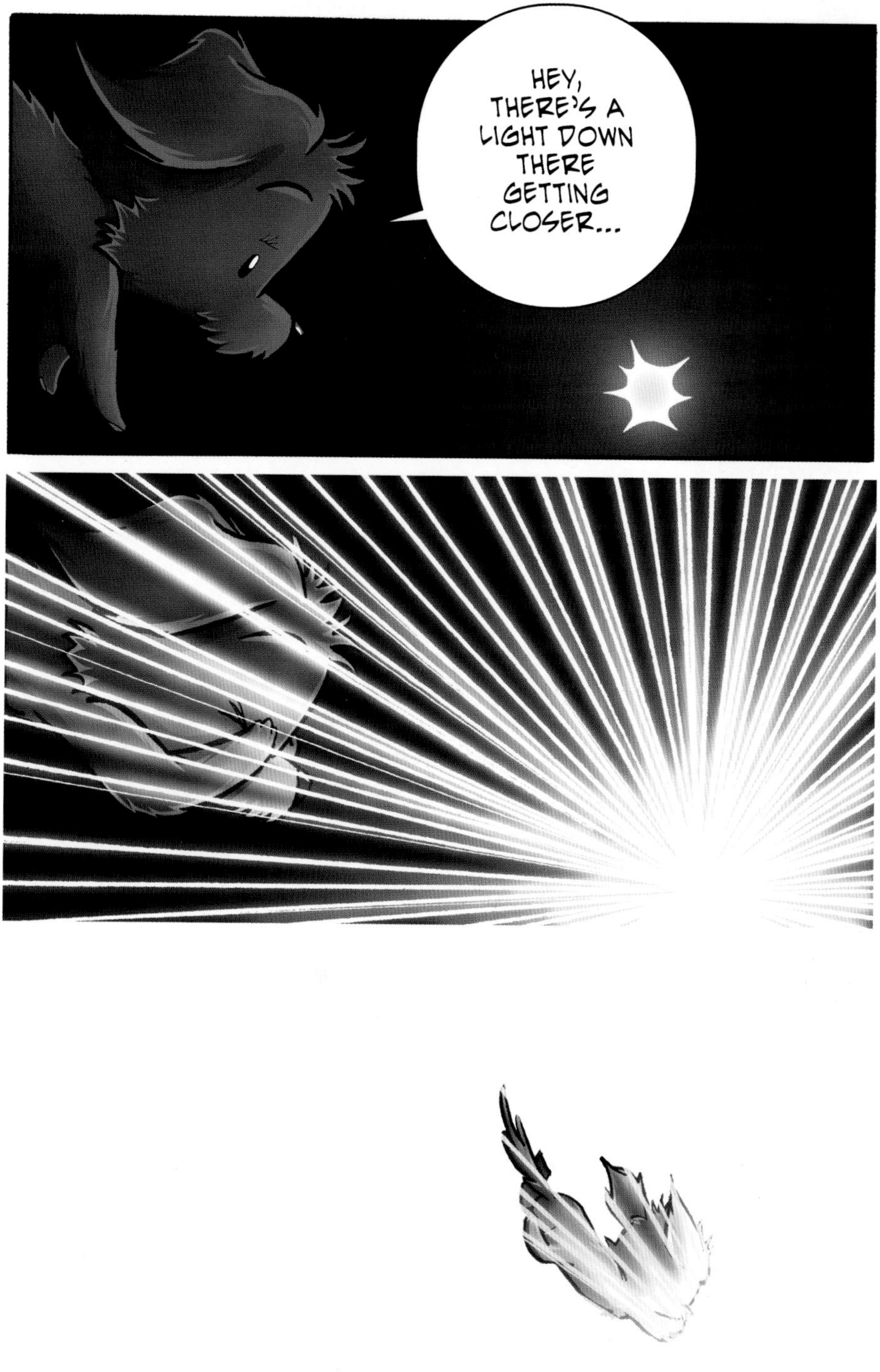
HEY, THERE'S A LIGHT DOWN THERE GETTING CLOSER...

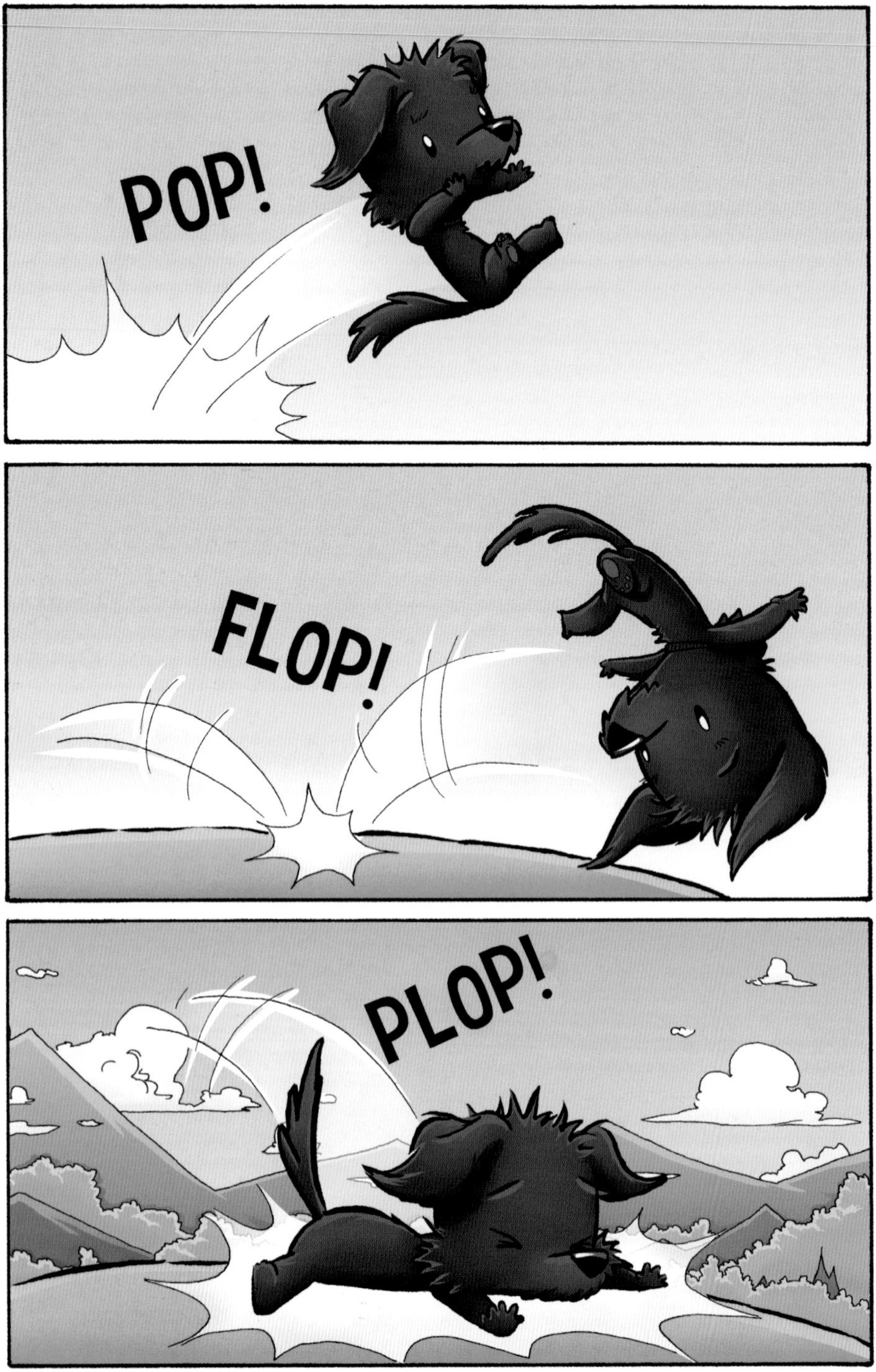
POP!
FLOP!
PLOP!

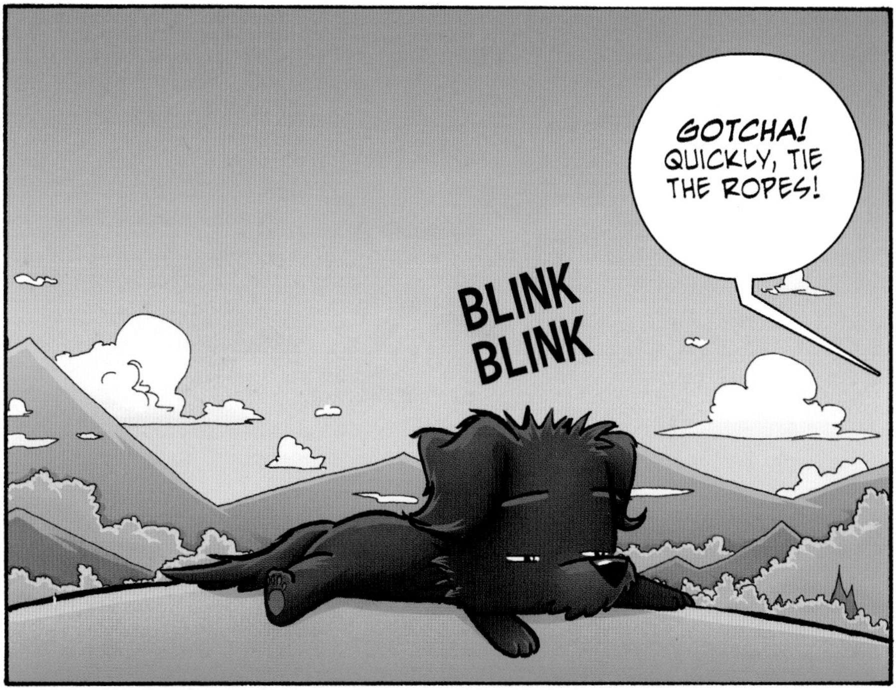
GOTCHA! QUICKLY, TIE THE ROPES!
BLINK BLINK

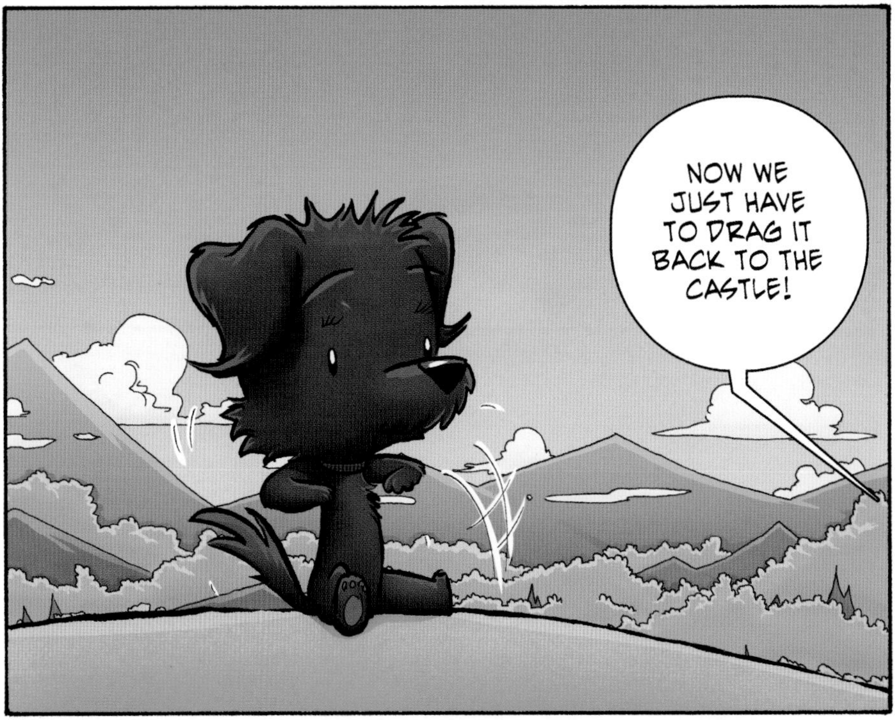
NOW WE JUST HAVE TO DRAG IT BACK TO THE CASTLE!

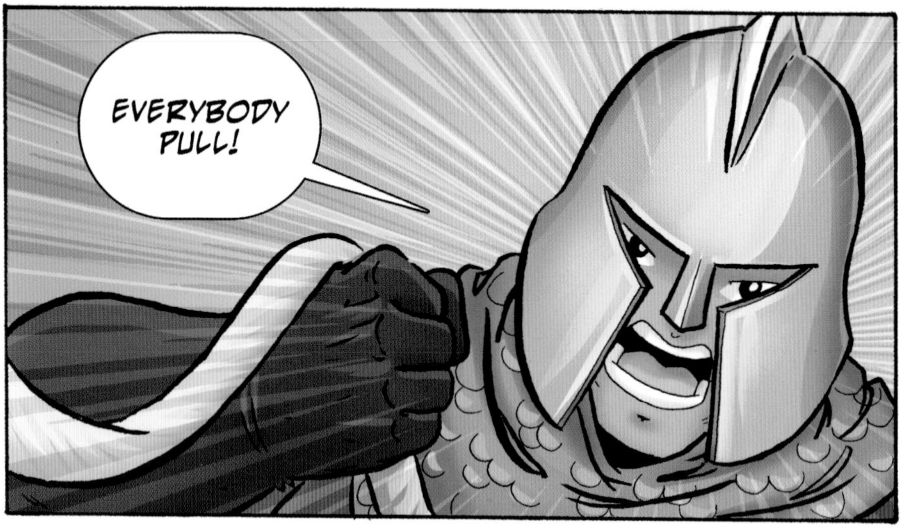
EVERYBODY PULL!

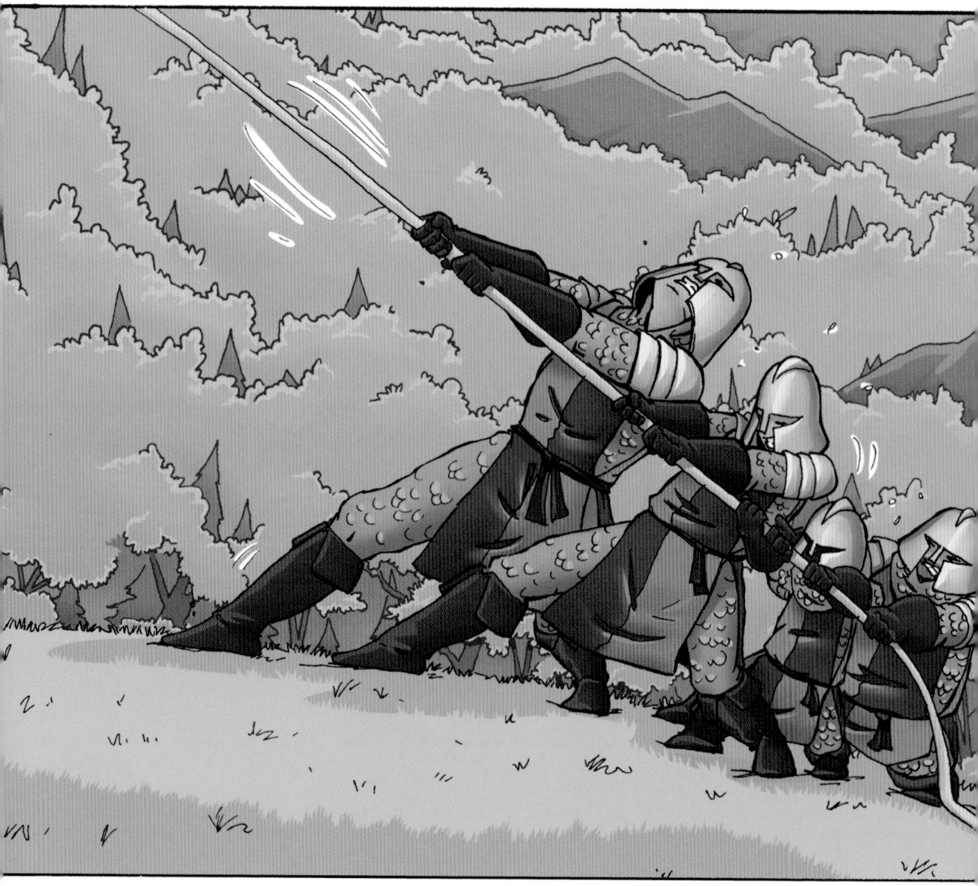

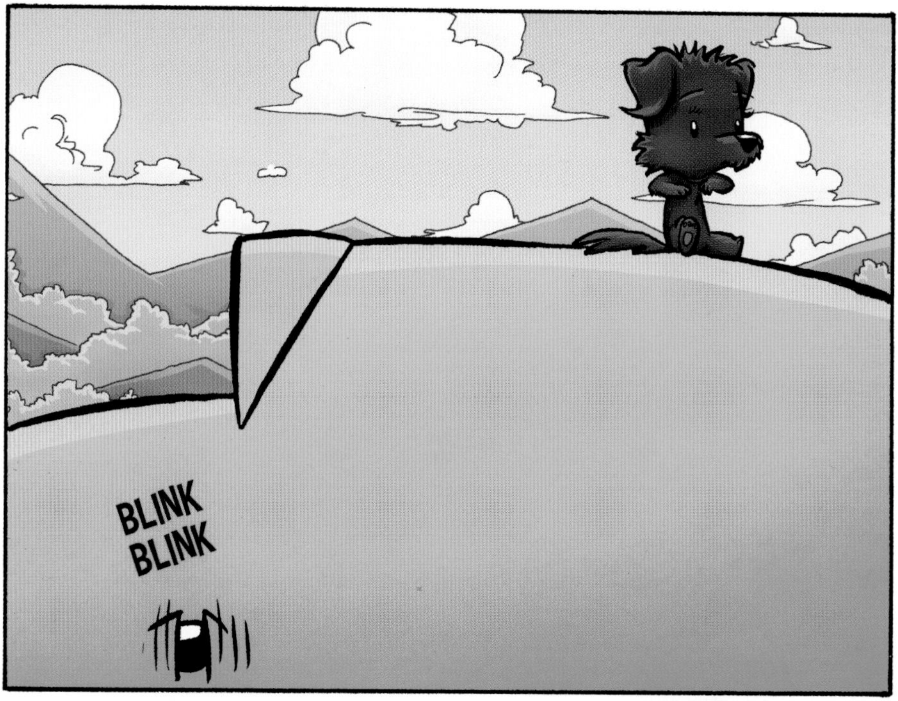
BLINK
BLINK

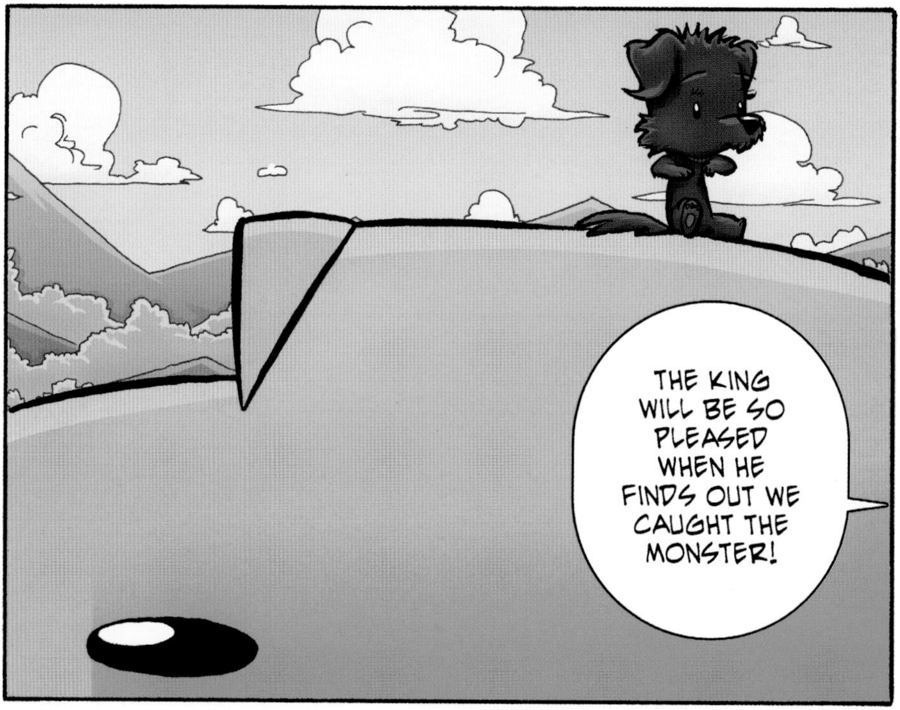
THE KING WILL BE SO PLEASED WHEN HE FINDS OUT WE CAUGHT THE MONSTER!

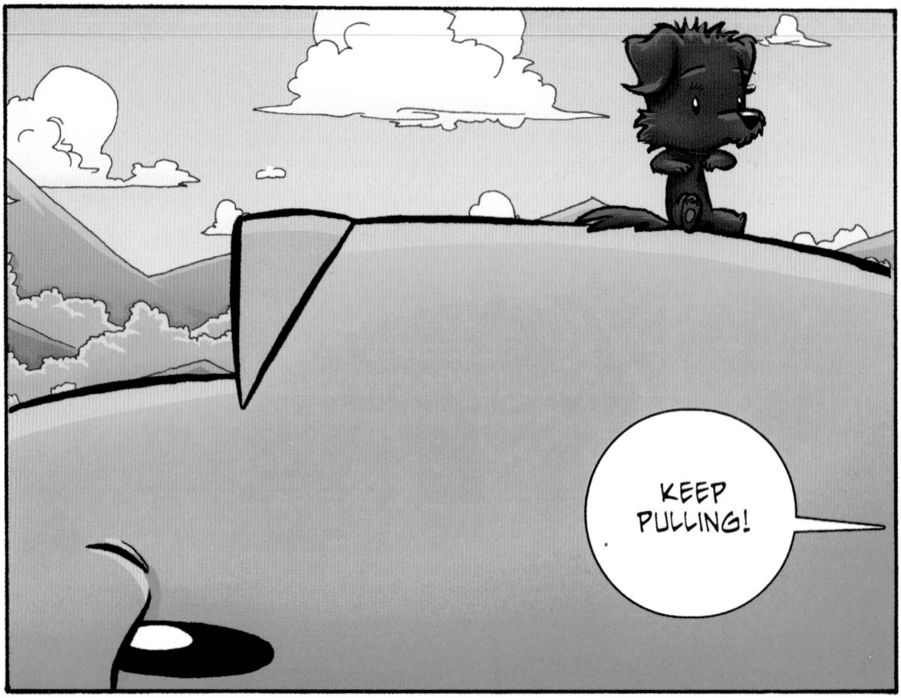
KEEP PULLING!

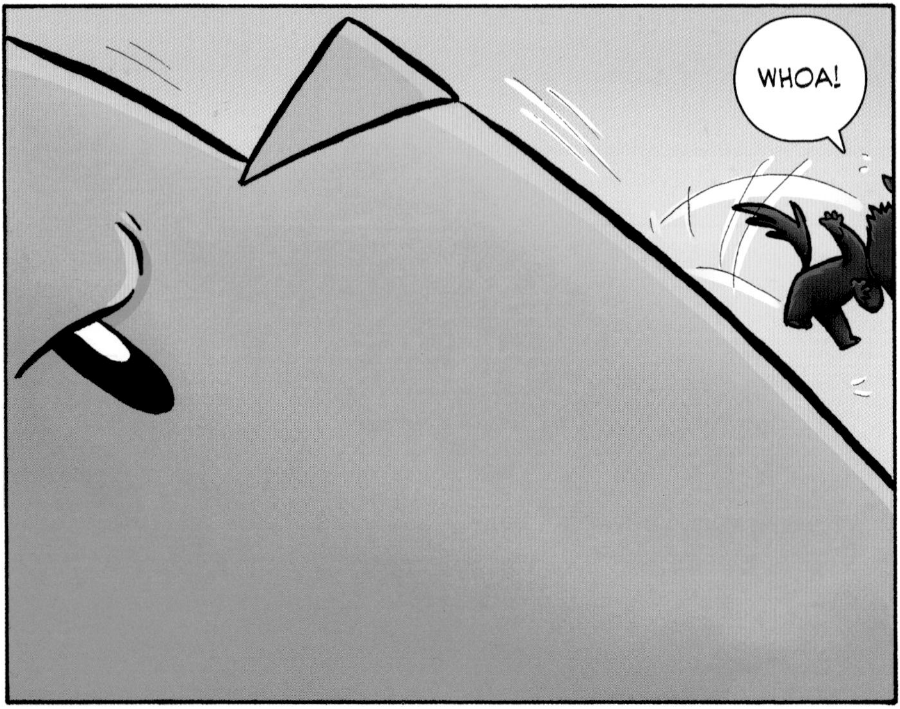
WHOA!

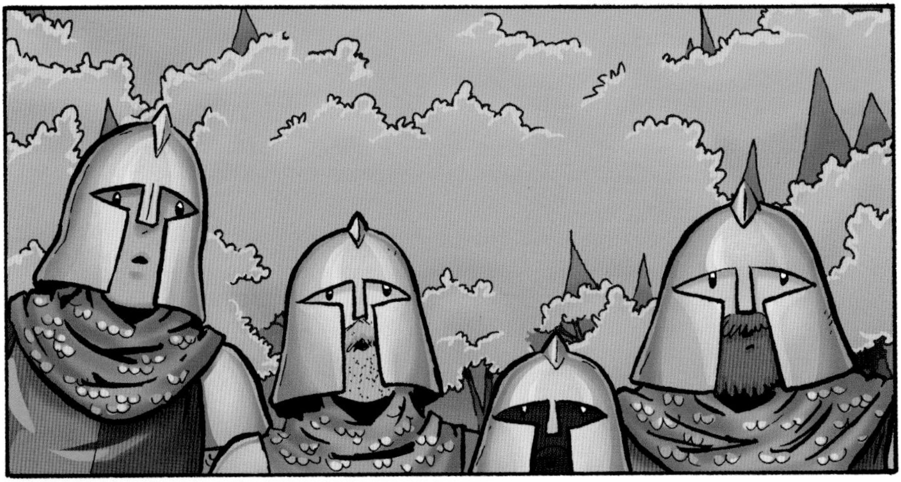

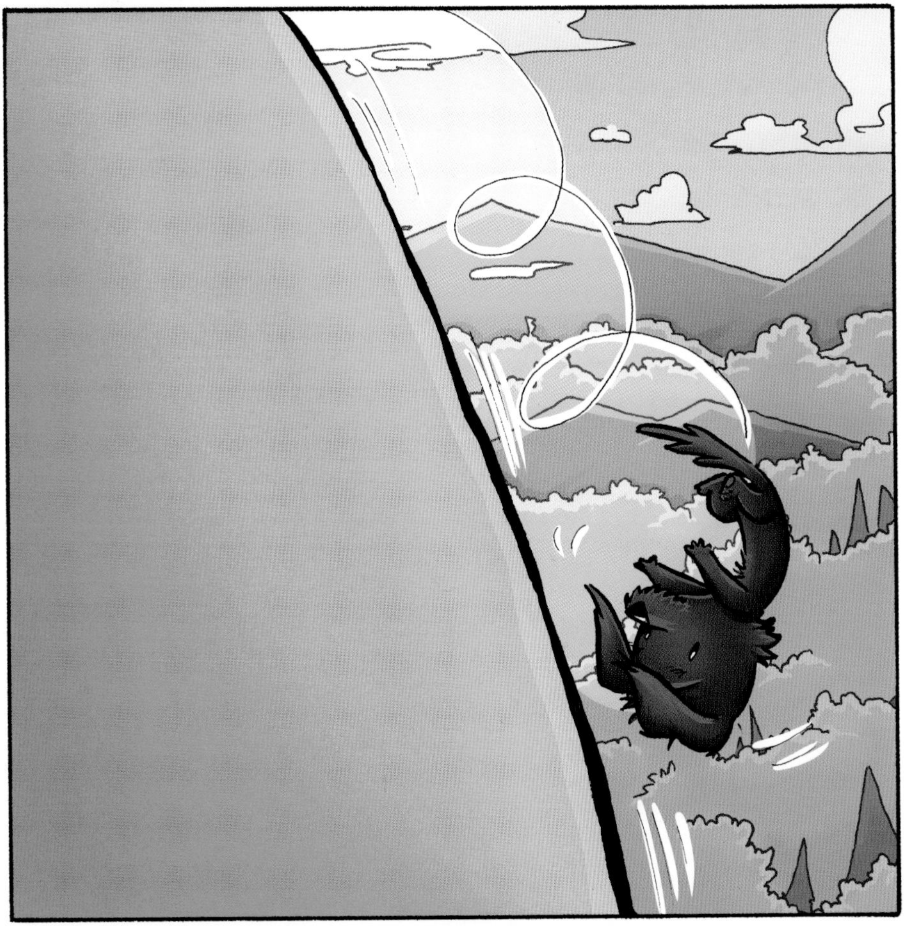

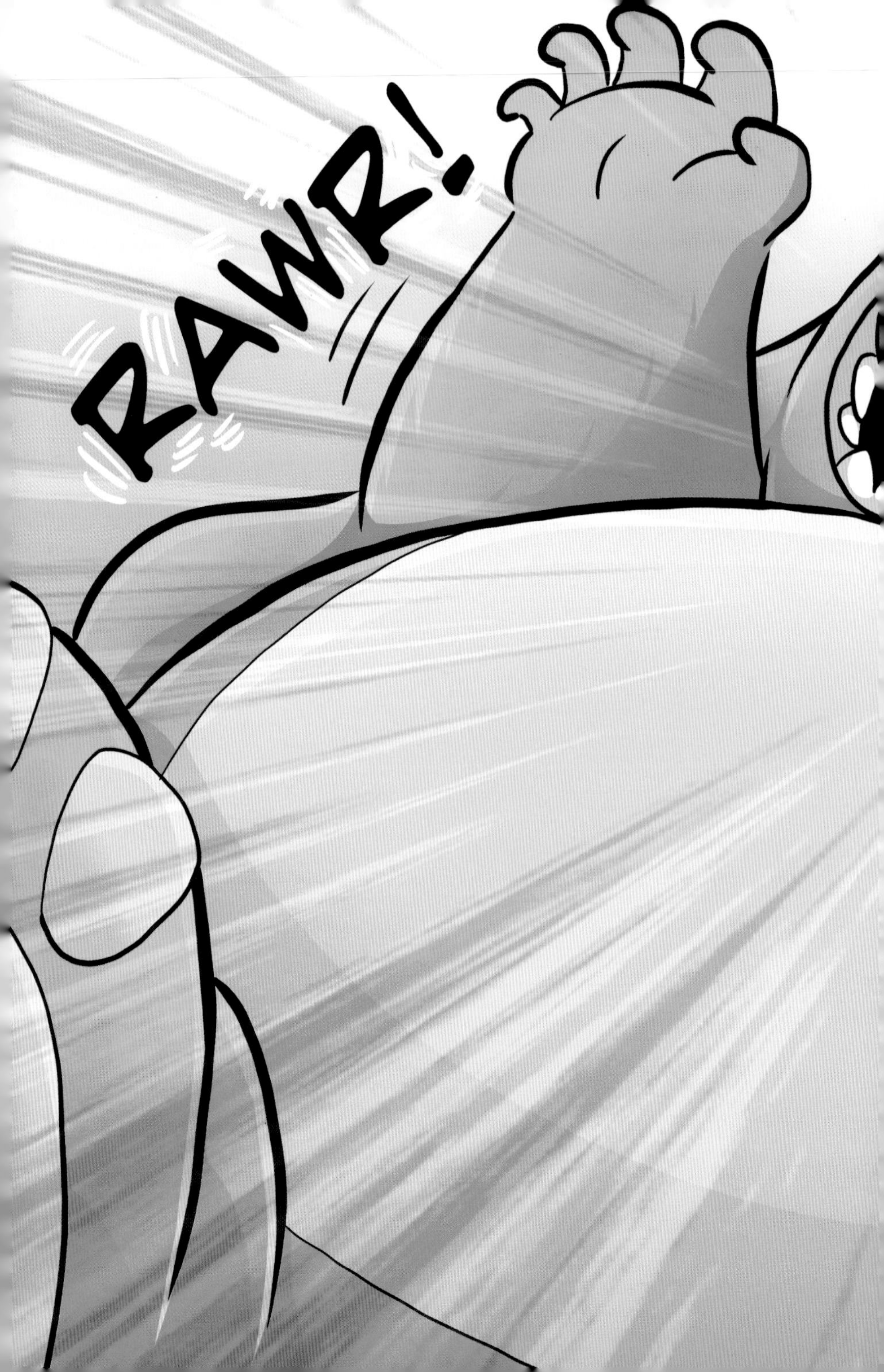
RAWR!

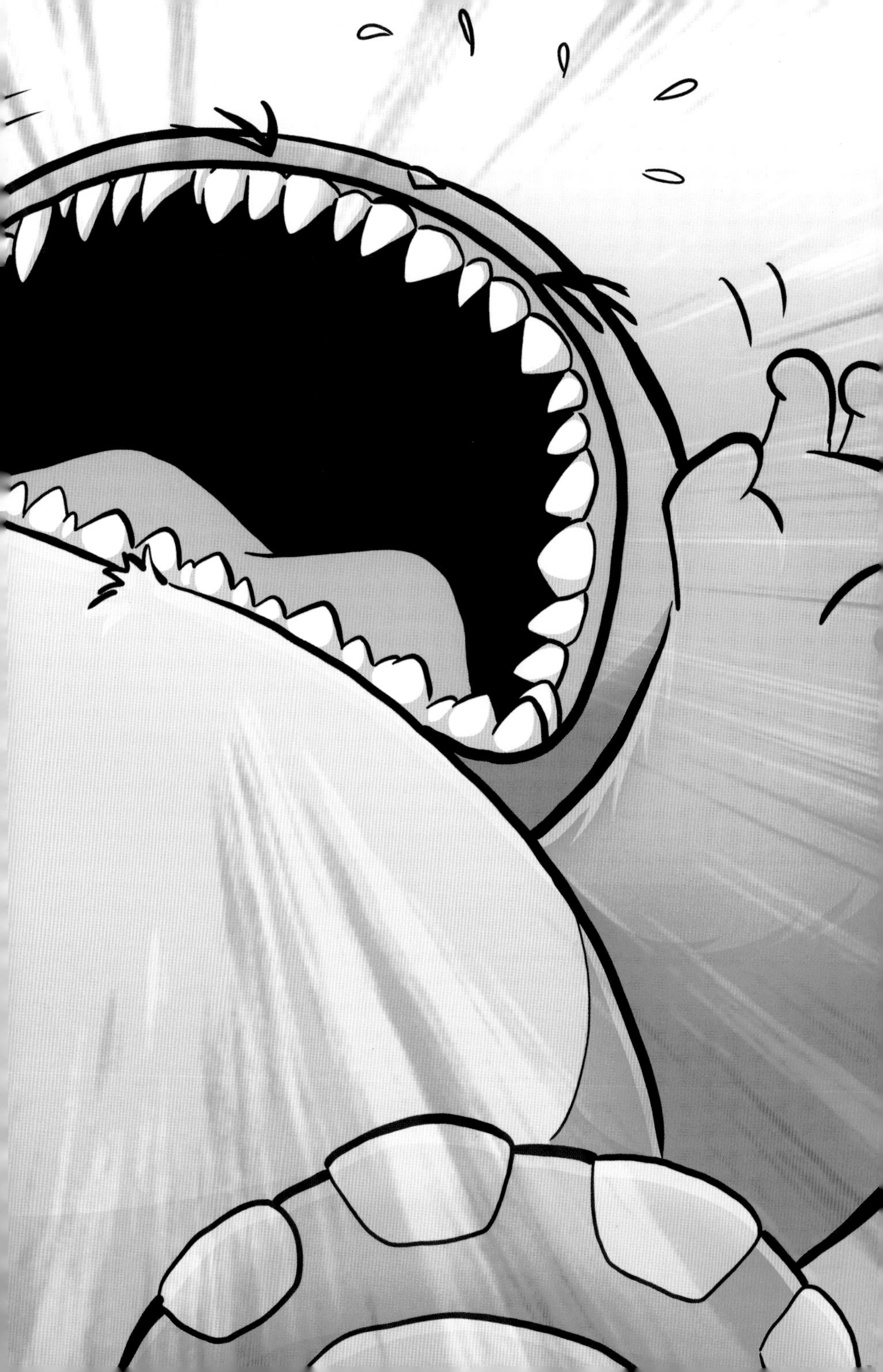

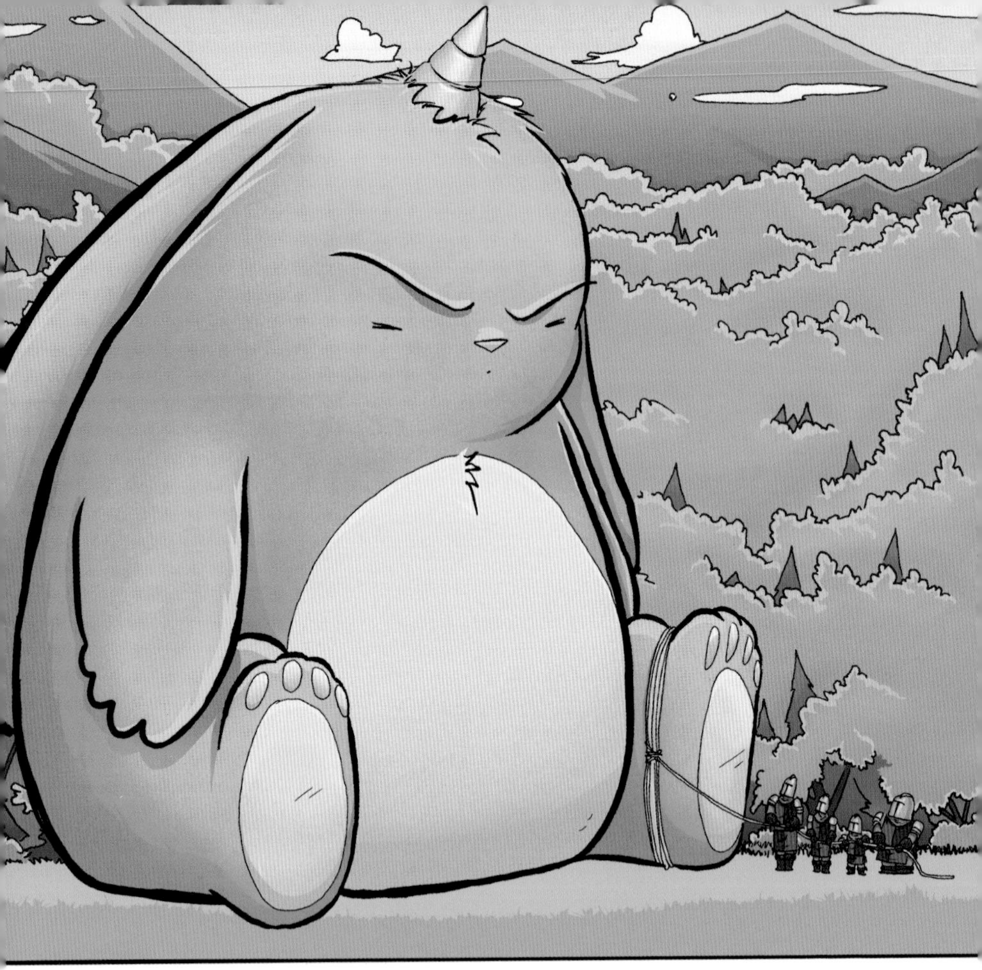

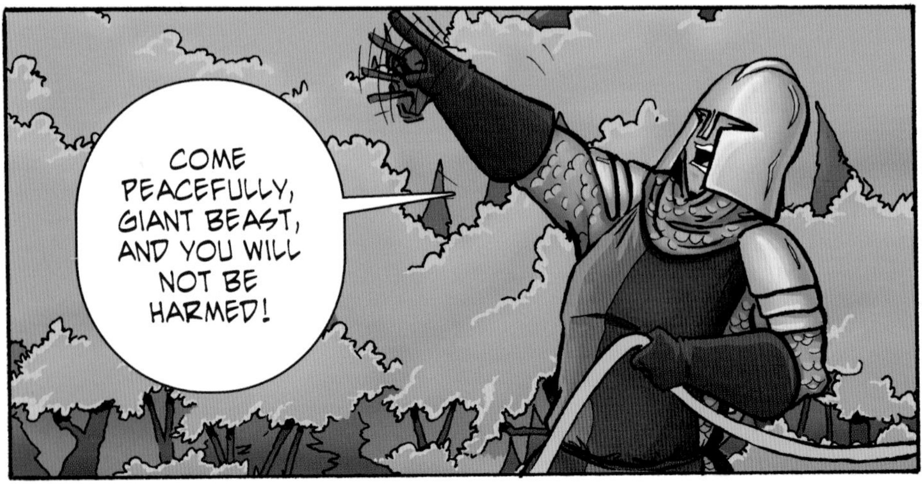
COME PEACEFULLY, GIANT BEAST, AND YOU WILL NOT BE HARMED!

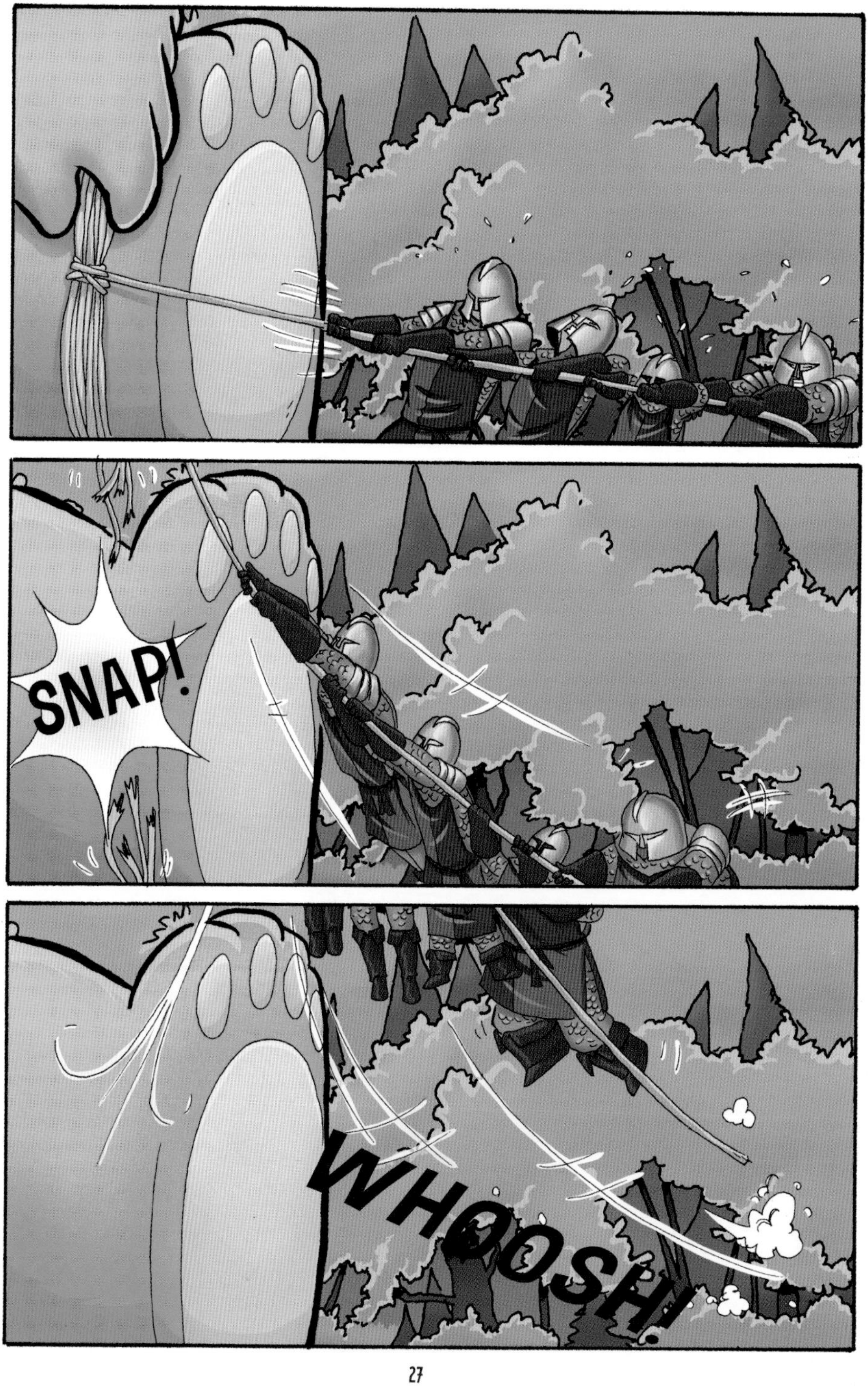
SNAP!
WHOOSH!

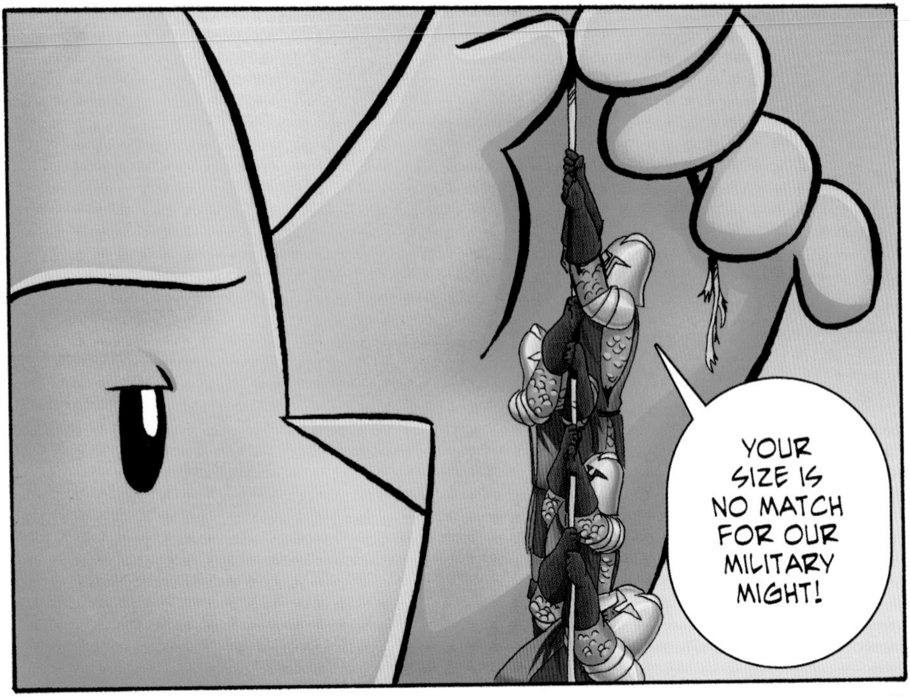
YOUR SIZE IS NO MATCH FOR OUR MILITARY MIGHT!

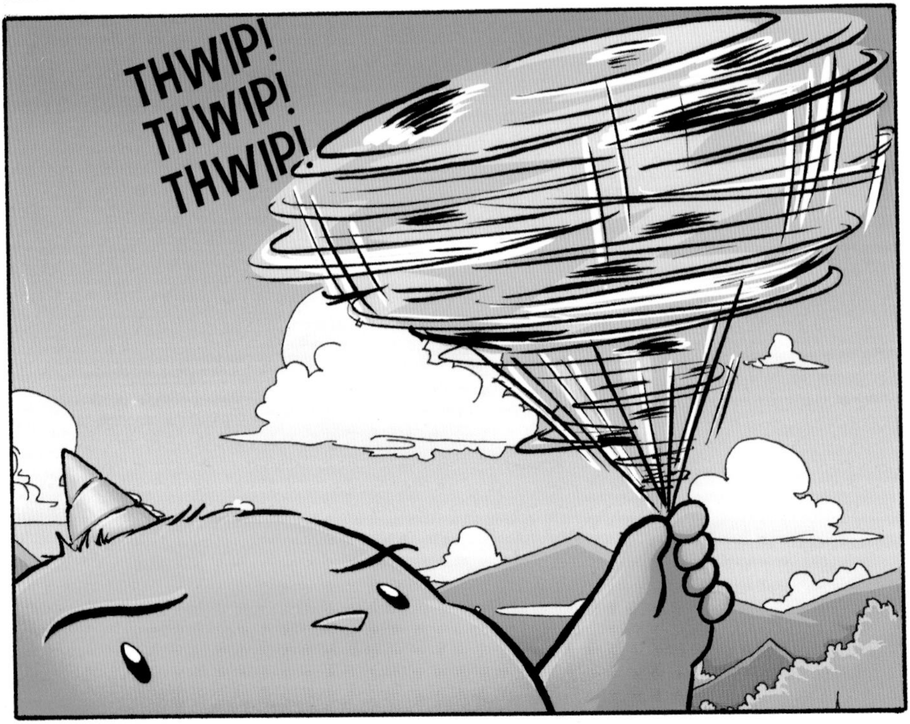
THWIP! THWIP! THWIP!

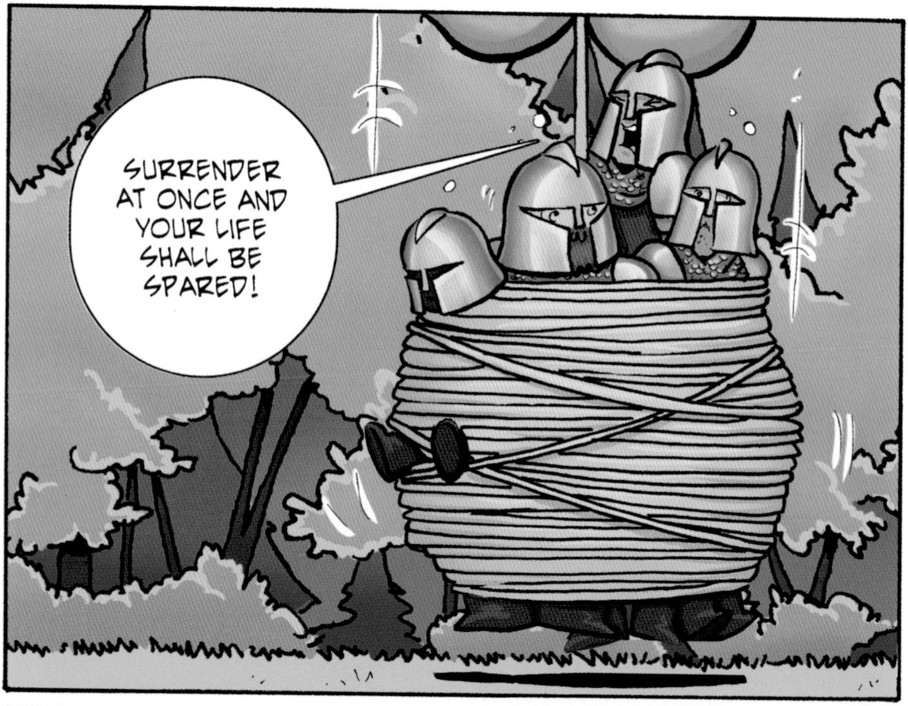
SURRENDER AT ONCE AND YOUR LIFE SHALL BE SPARED!

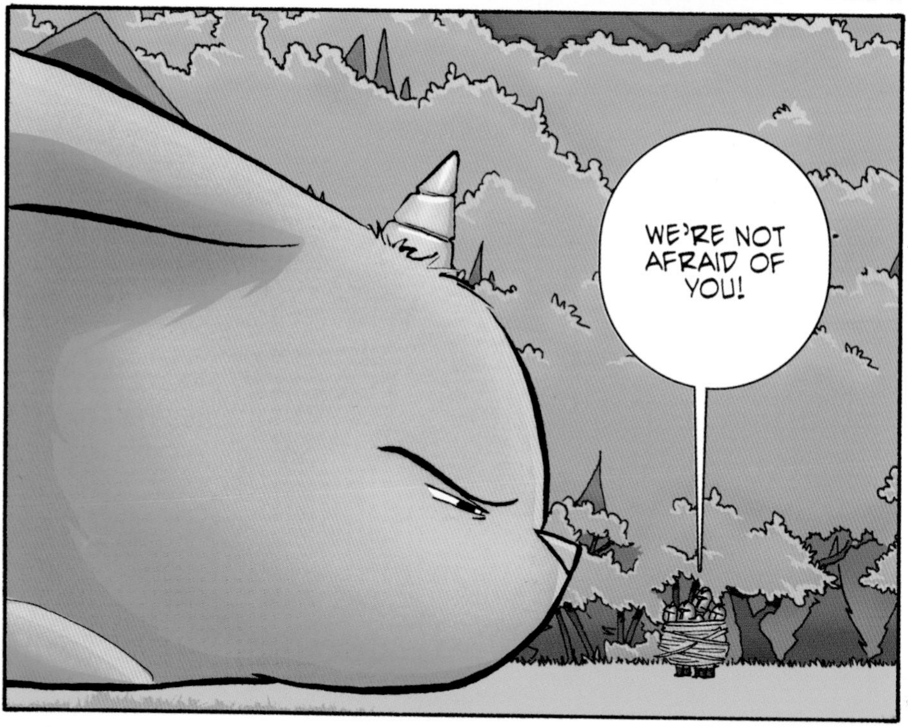
WE'RE NOT AFRAID OF YOU!

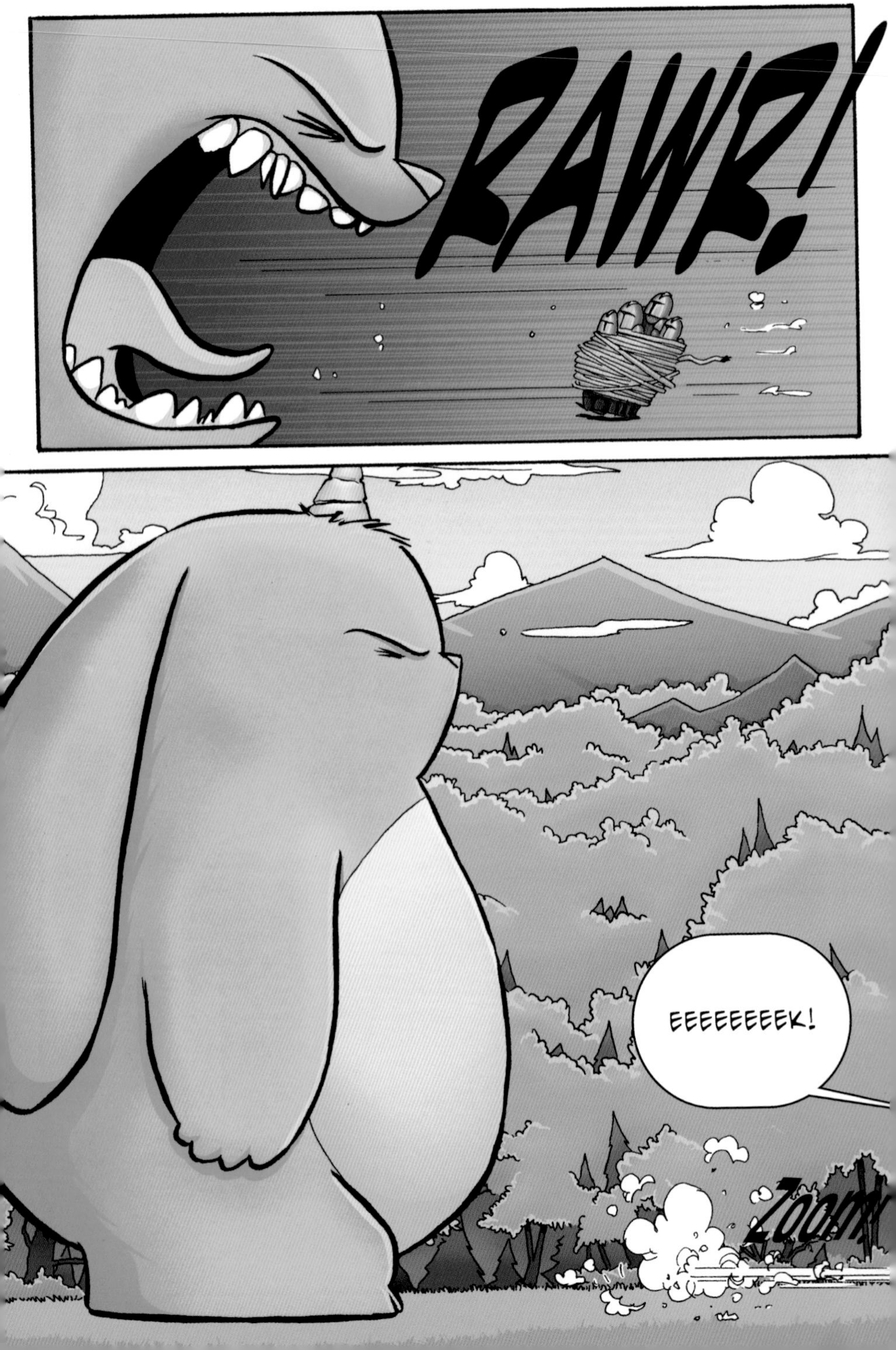
RAWR!
EEEEEEEEK!
ZOOM

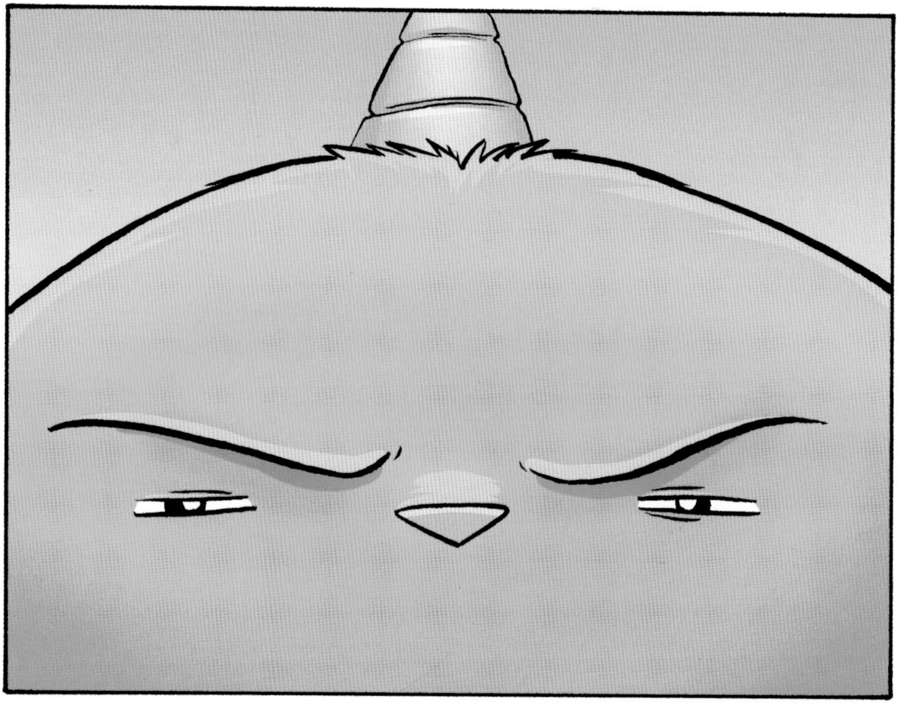

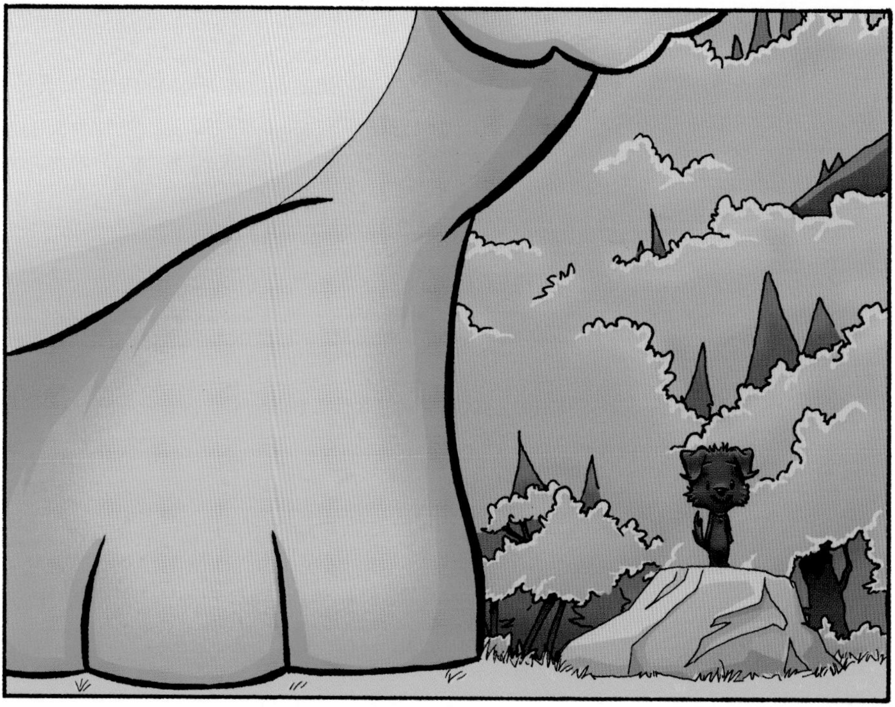

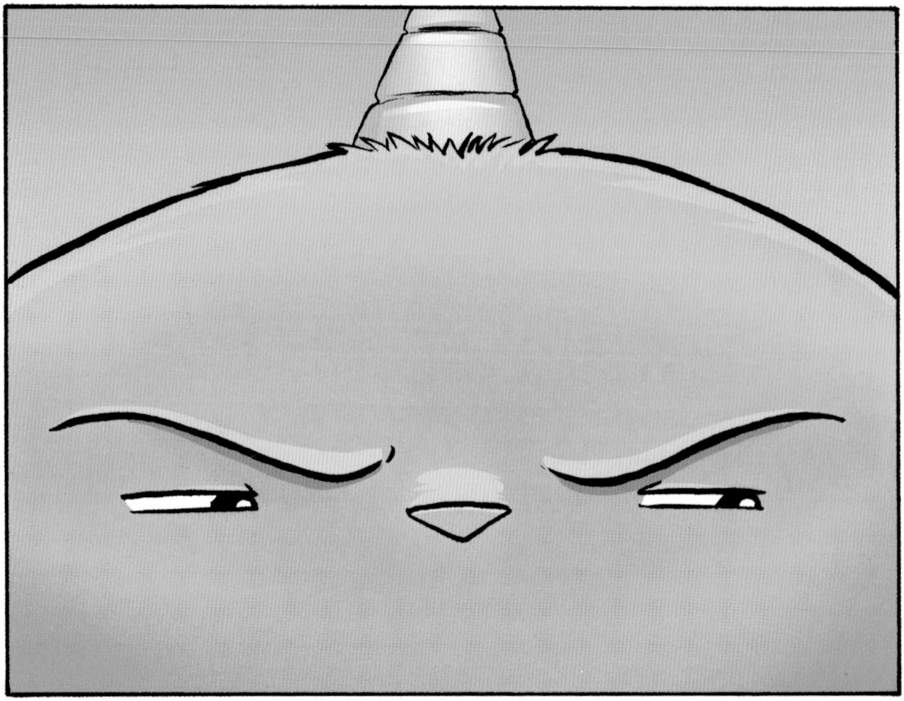

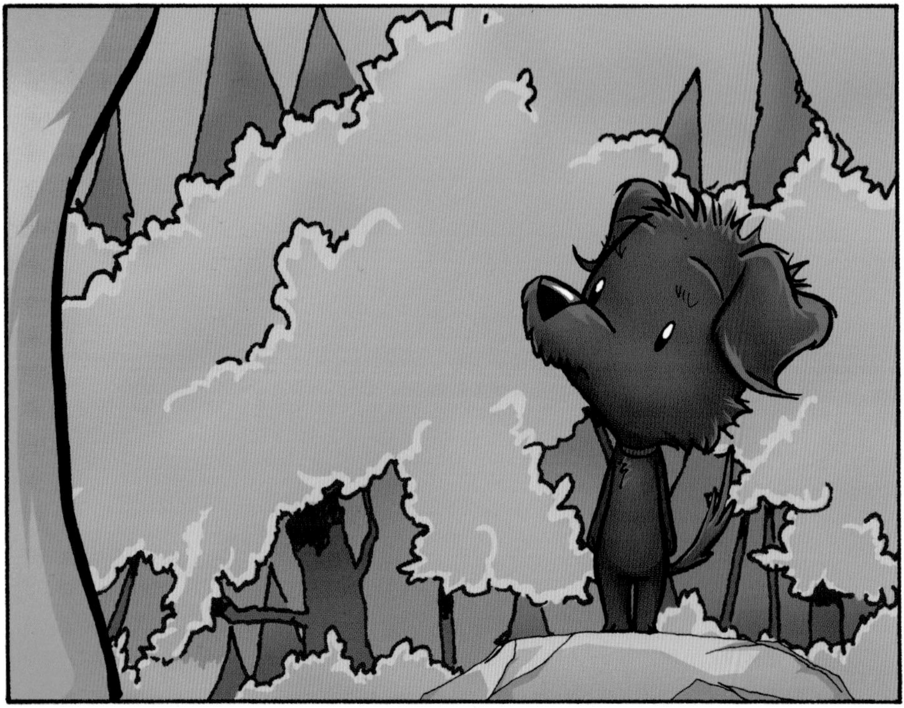

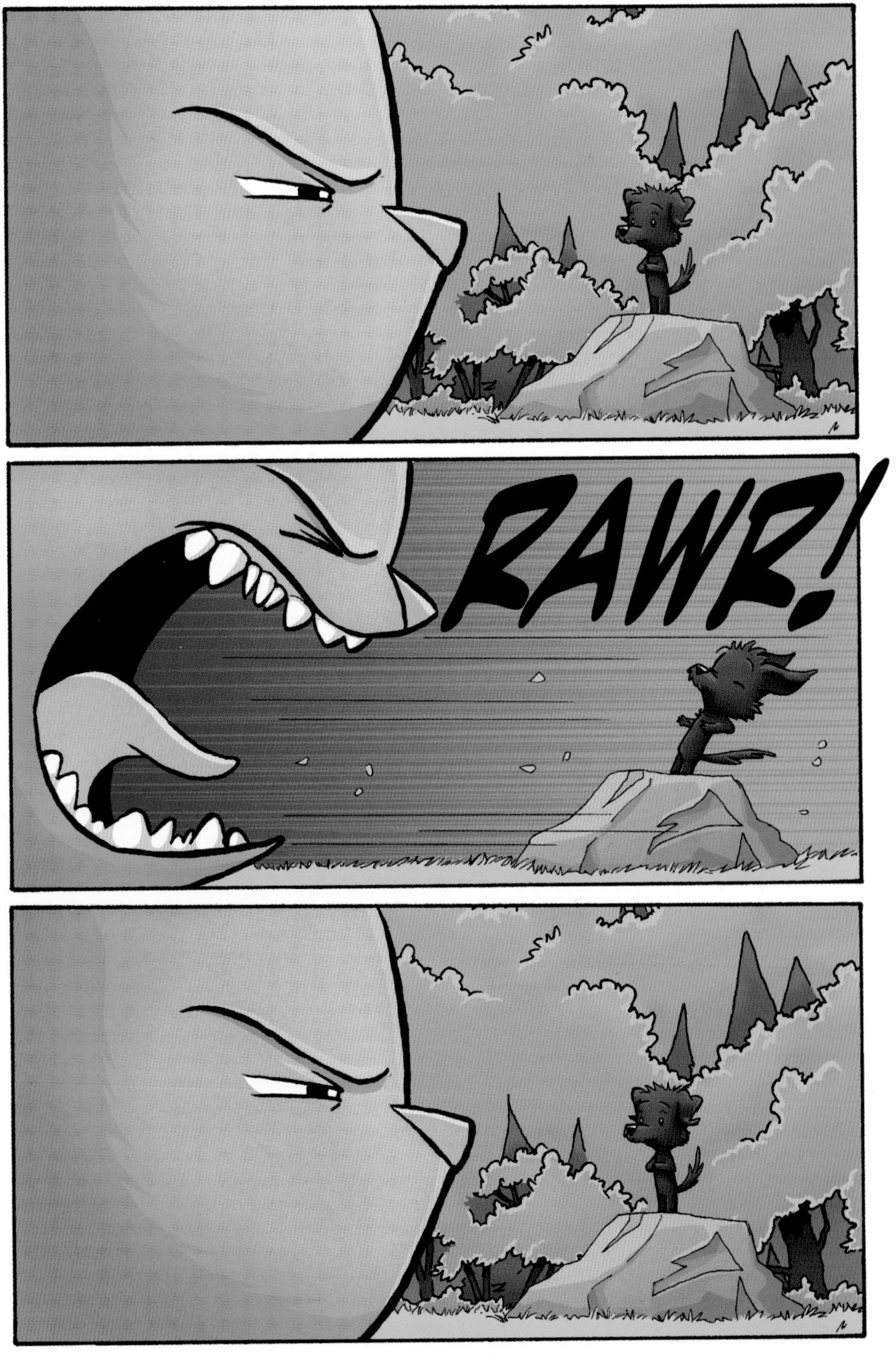
RAWR!

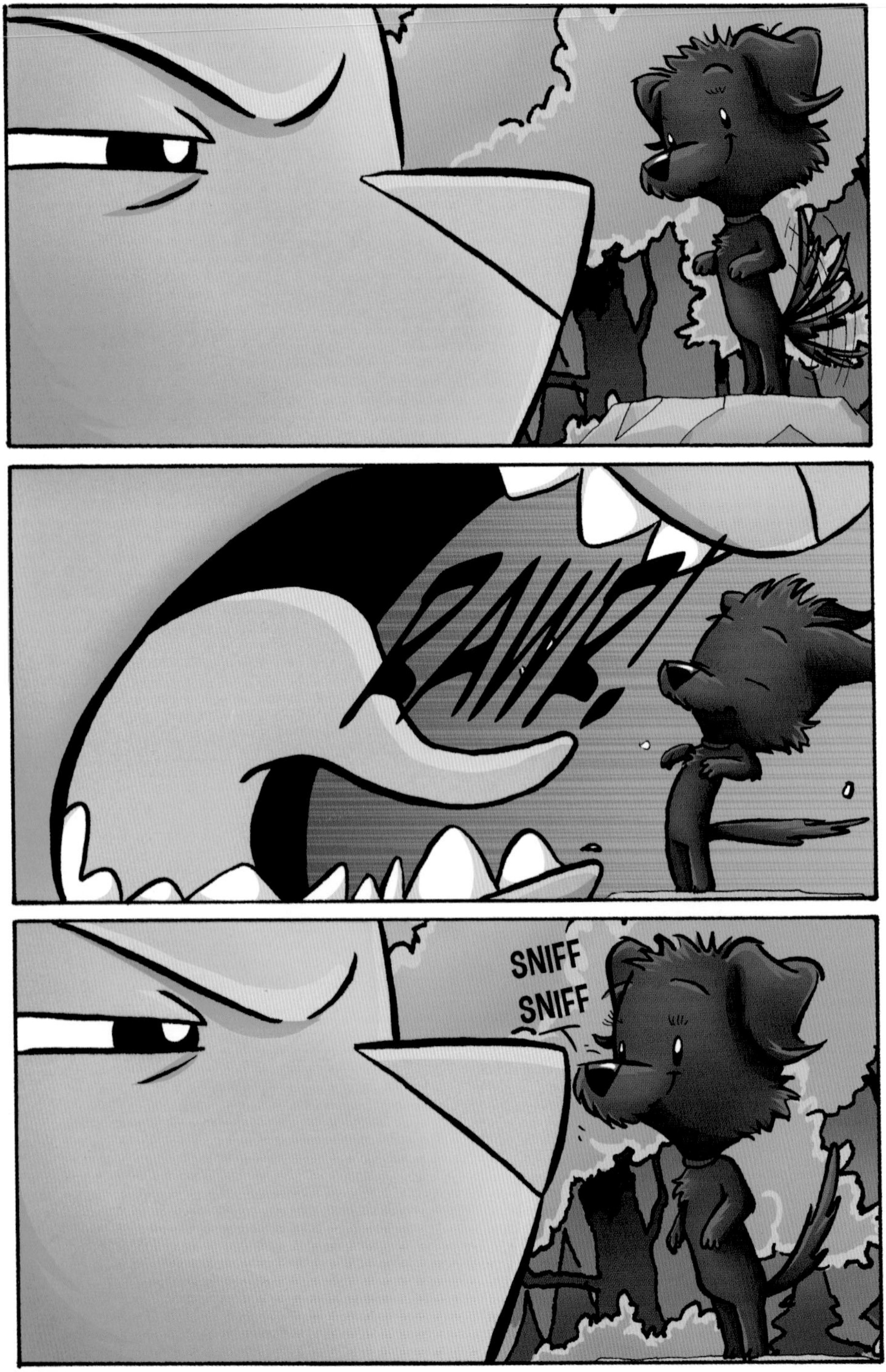
RAWR!
SNIFF
SNIFF

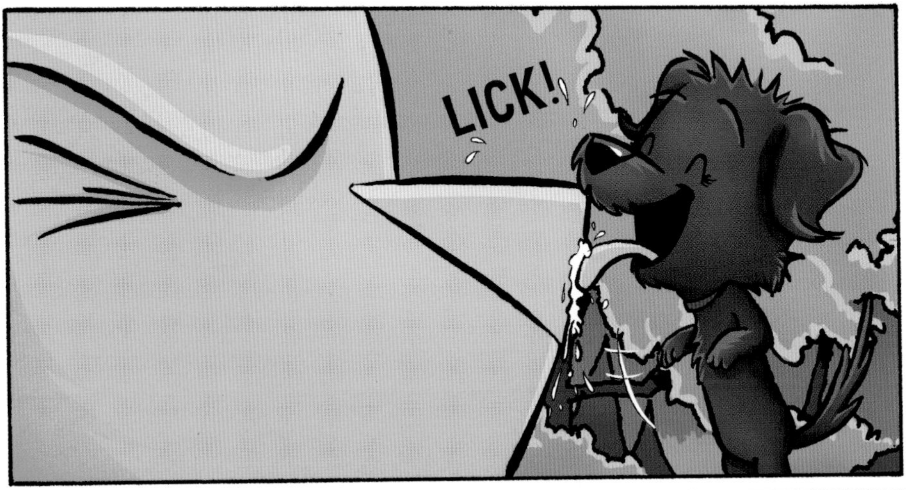
LICK!

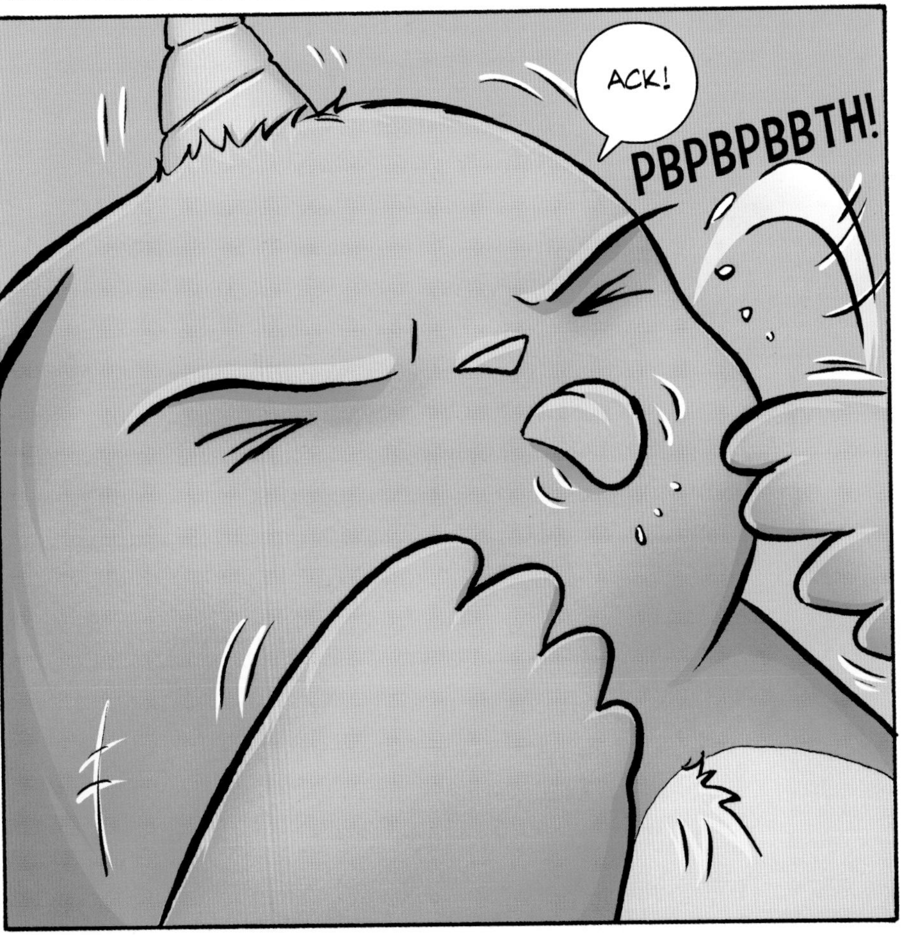
ACK!
PBPBPBBTH!

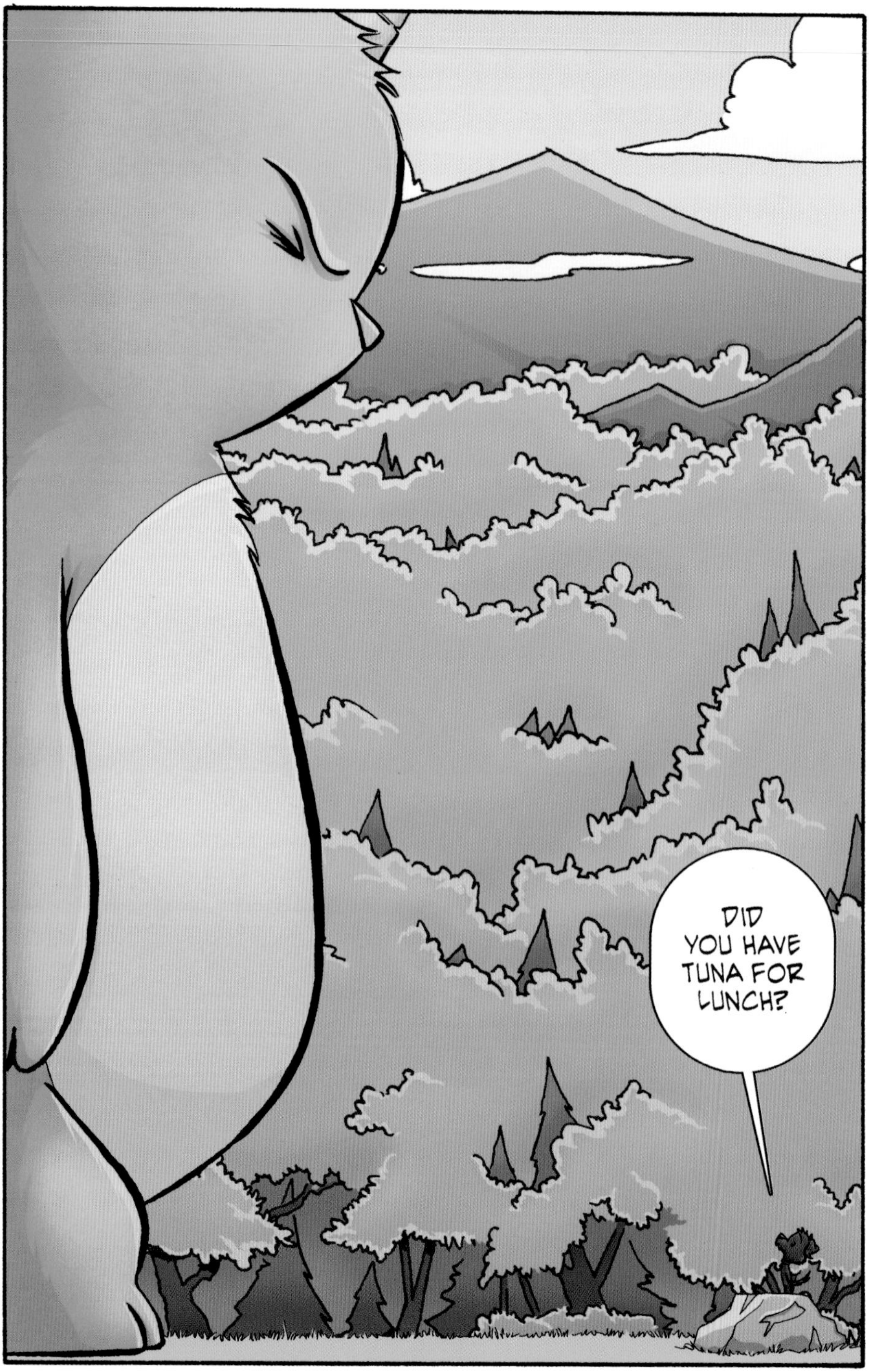
DID YOU HAVE TUNA FOR LUNCH?

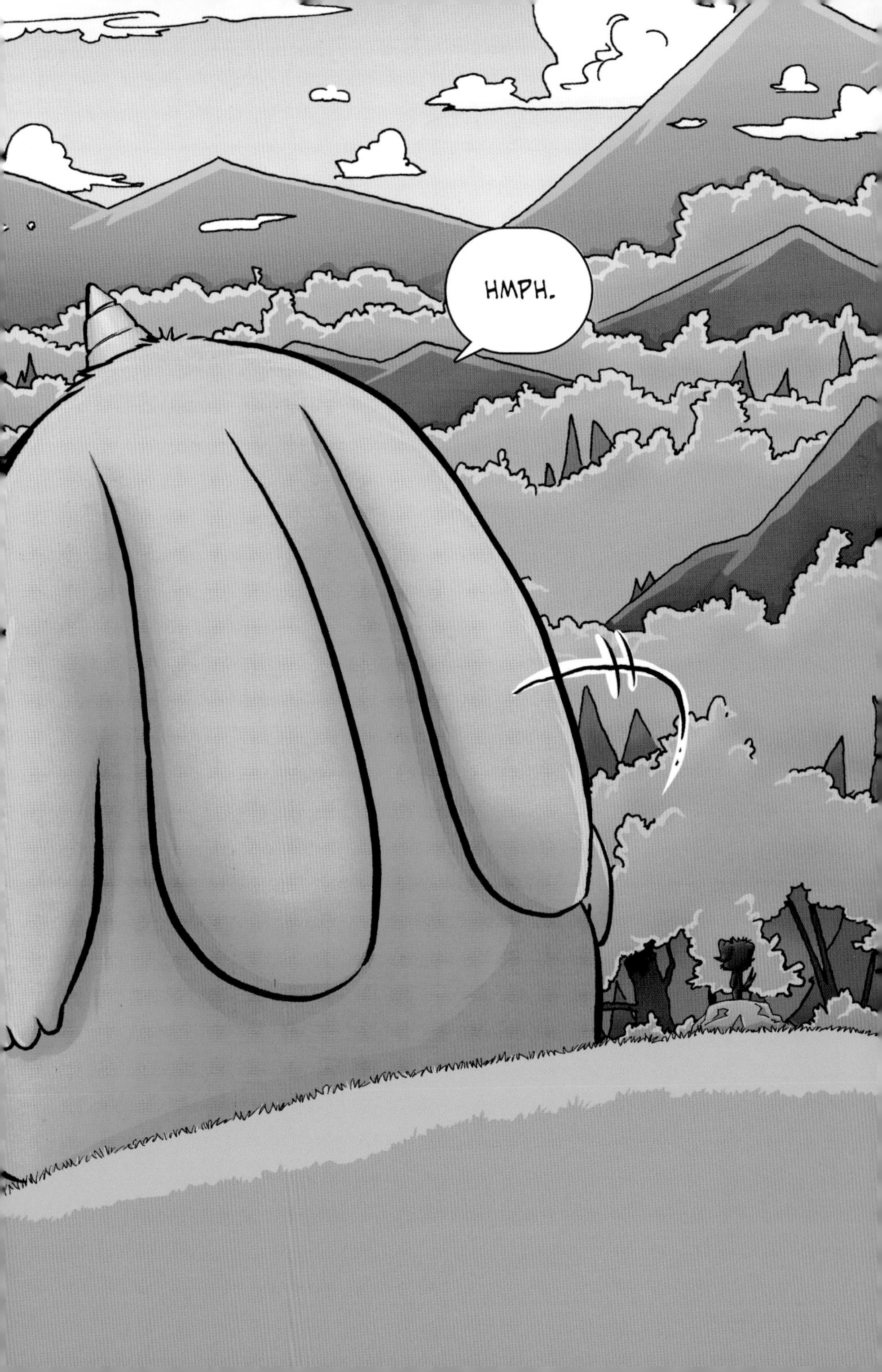
HMPH.

CHAPTER 3
A PERSISTENT PUP

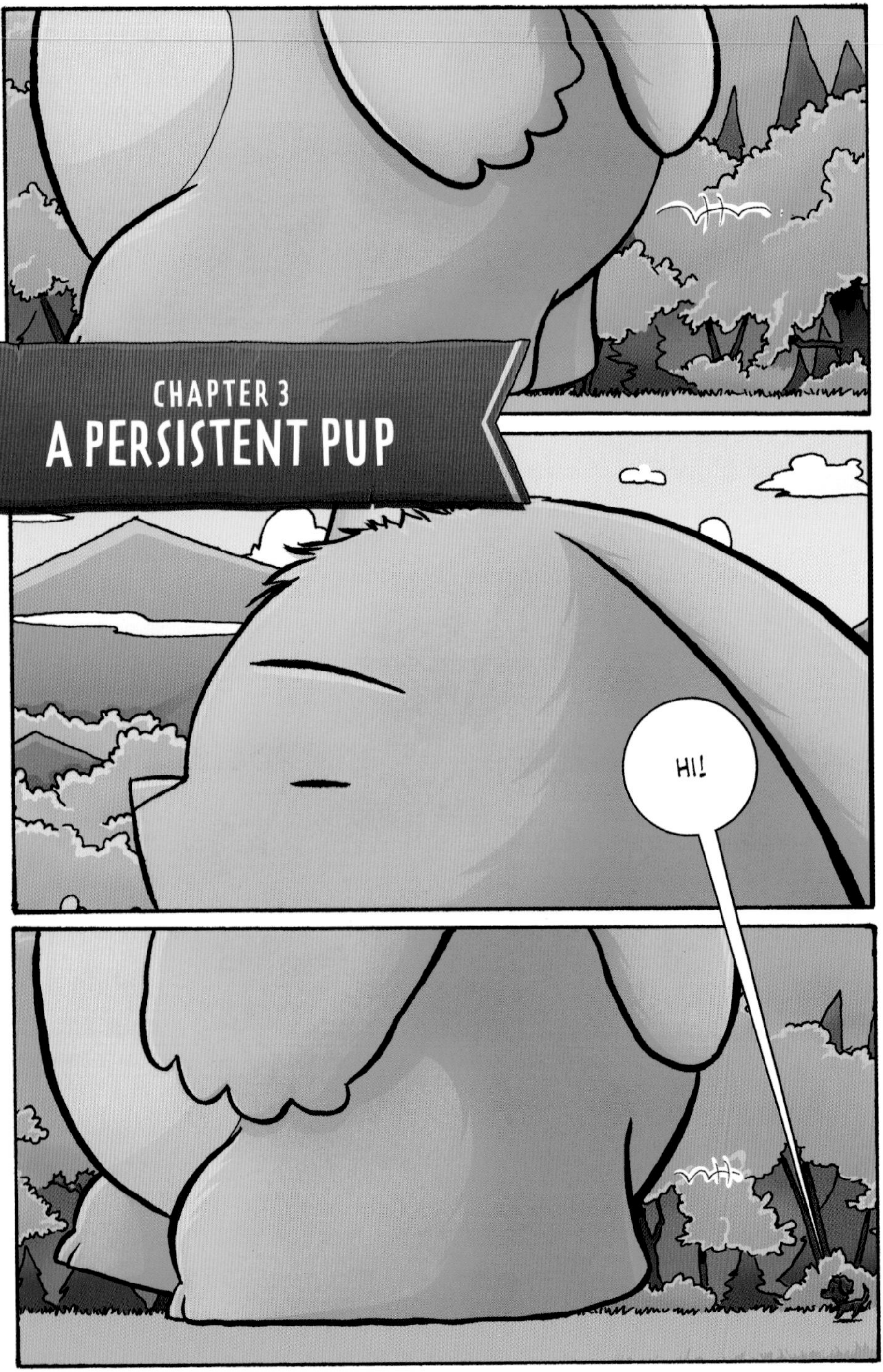
HI!

HELLO THERE!
UM, I THINK I MIGHT BE LOST...

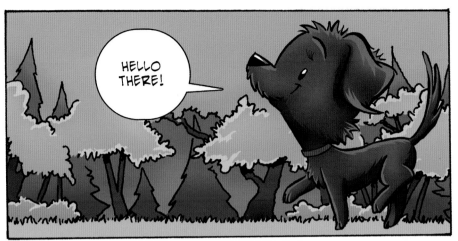

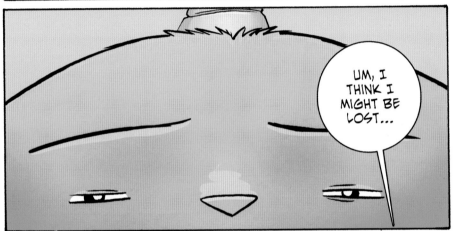

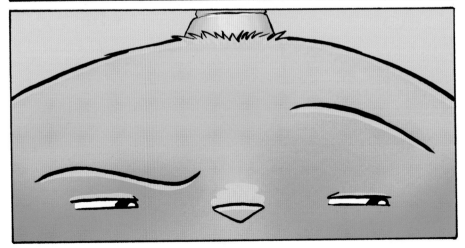

CAN YOU SEE MY HOUSE FROM UP THERE BY CHANCE? IT'S THE RED ONE THAT HAS CATS ON THE WINDOW-SILLS MOST OF THE TIME...

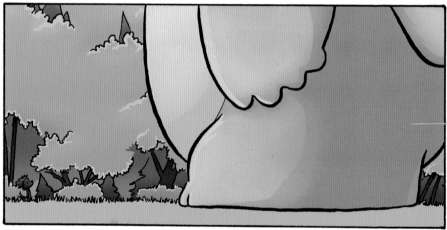

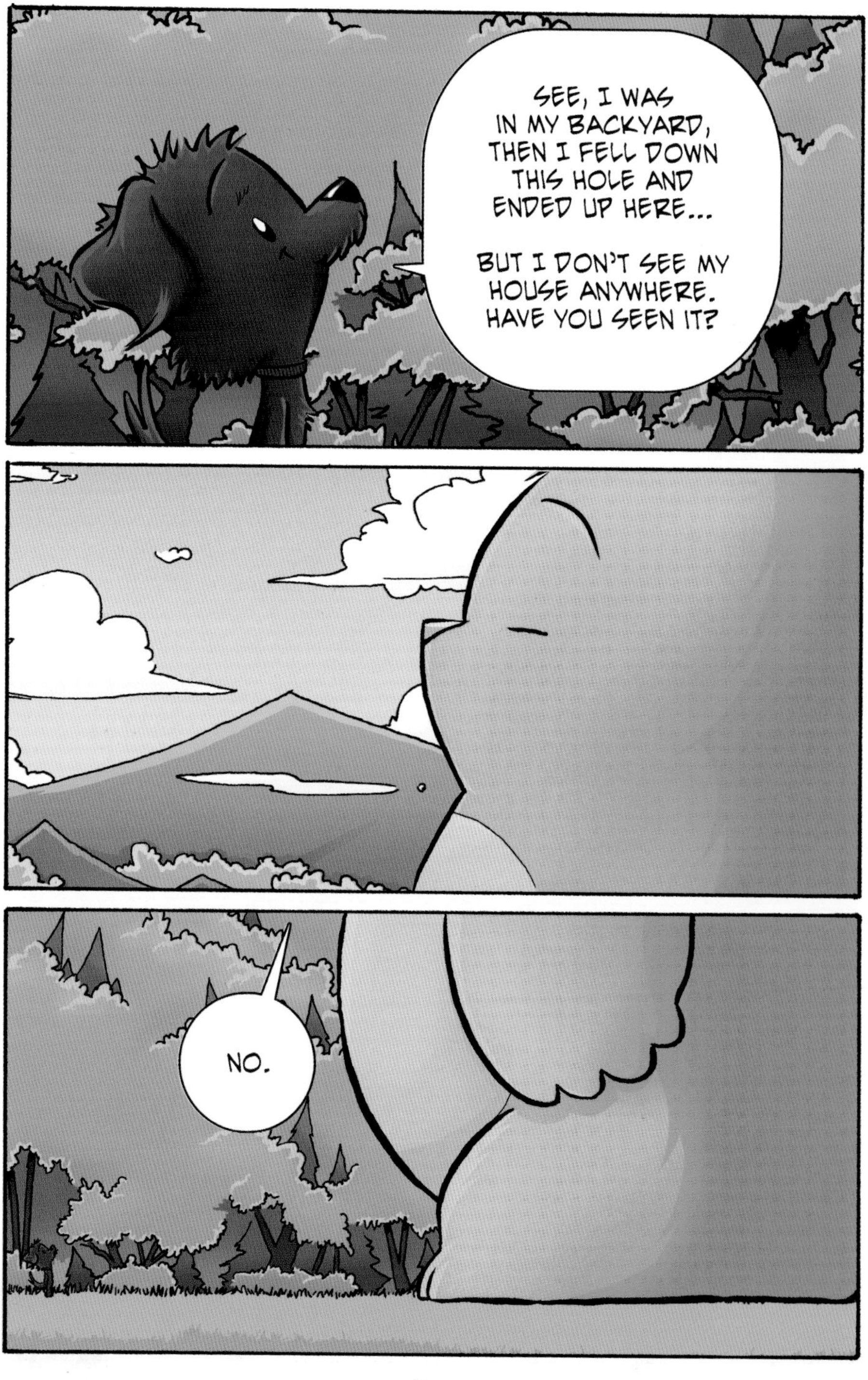
SEE, I WAS IN MY BACKYARD, THEN I FELL DOWN THIS HOLE AND ENDED UP HERE...
BUT I DON'T SEE MY HOUSE ANYWHERE. HAVE YOU SEEN IT?
NO.

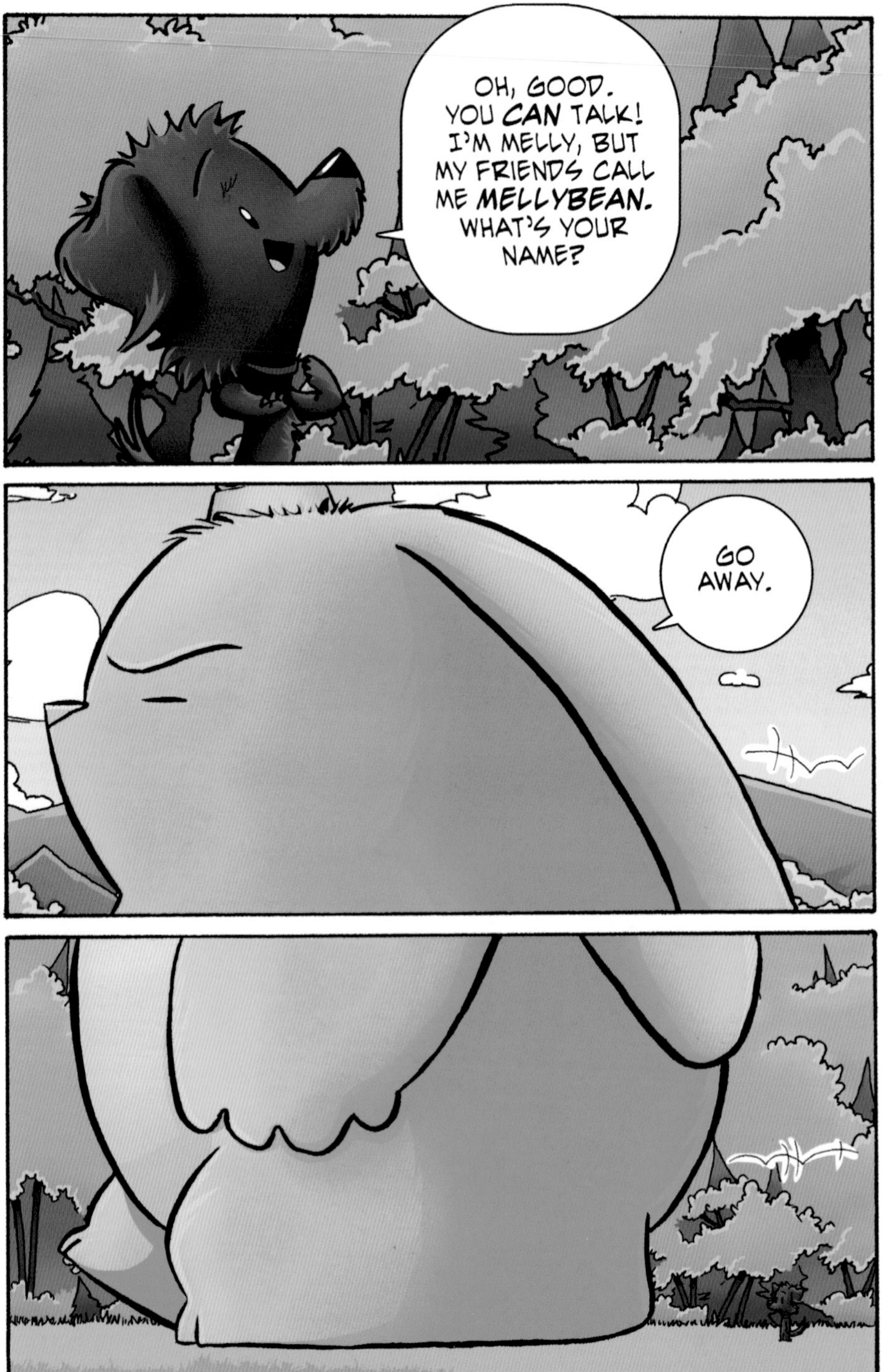
OH, GOOD. YOU CAN TALK! I'M MELLY, BUT MY FRIENDS CALL ME MELLYBEAN. WHAT'S YOUR NAME?
GO AWAY.

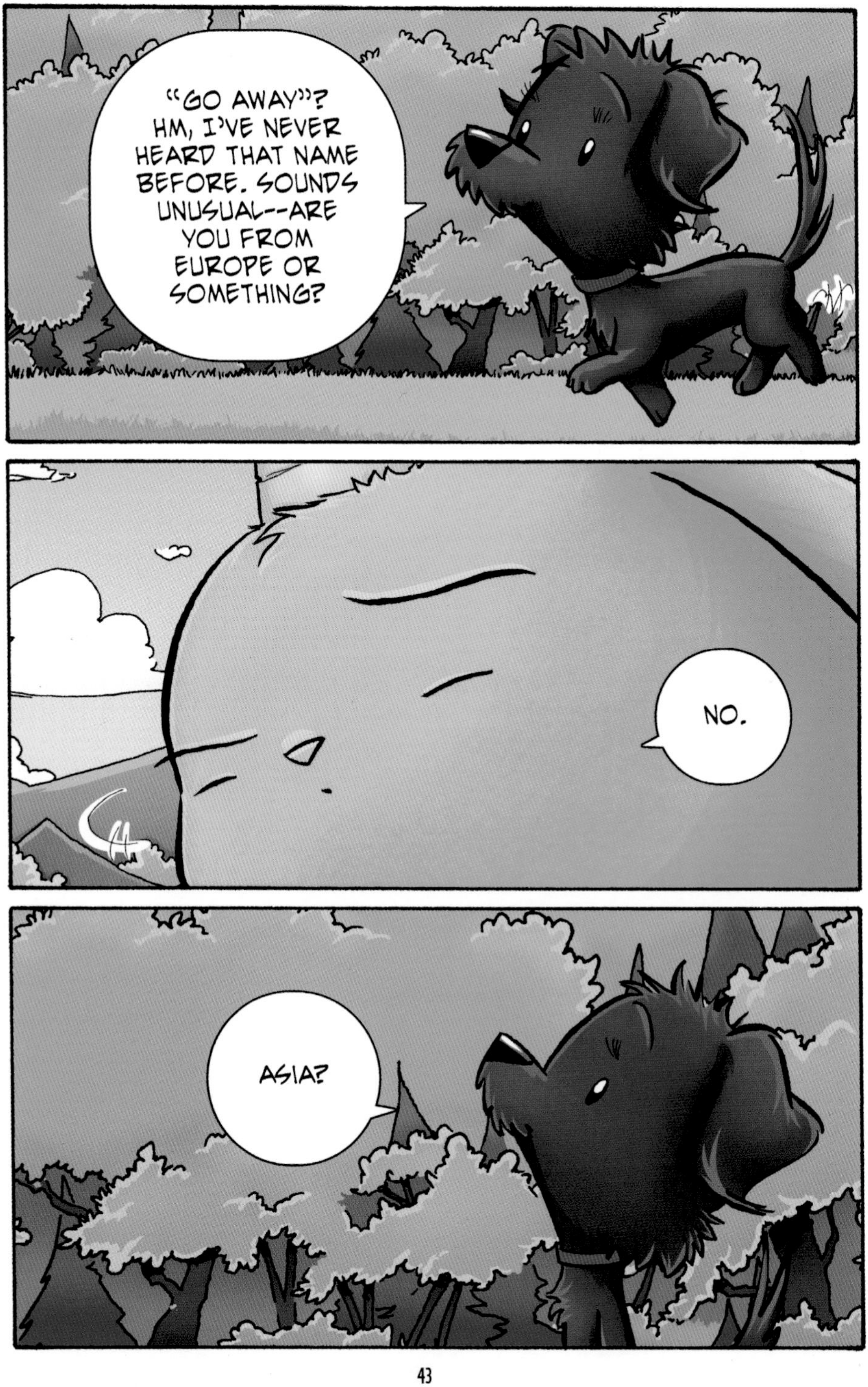
"GO AWAY"? HM, I'VE NEVER HEARD THAT NAME BEFORE. SOUNDS UNUSUAL--ARE YOU FROM EUROPE OR SOMETHING?
NO.
ASIA?

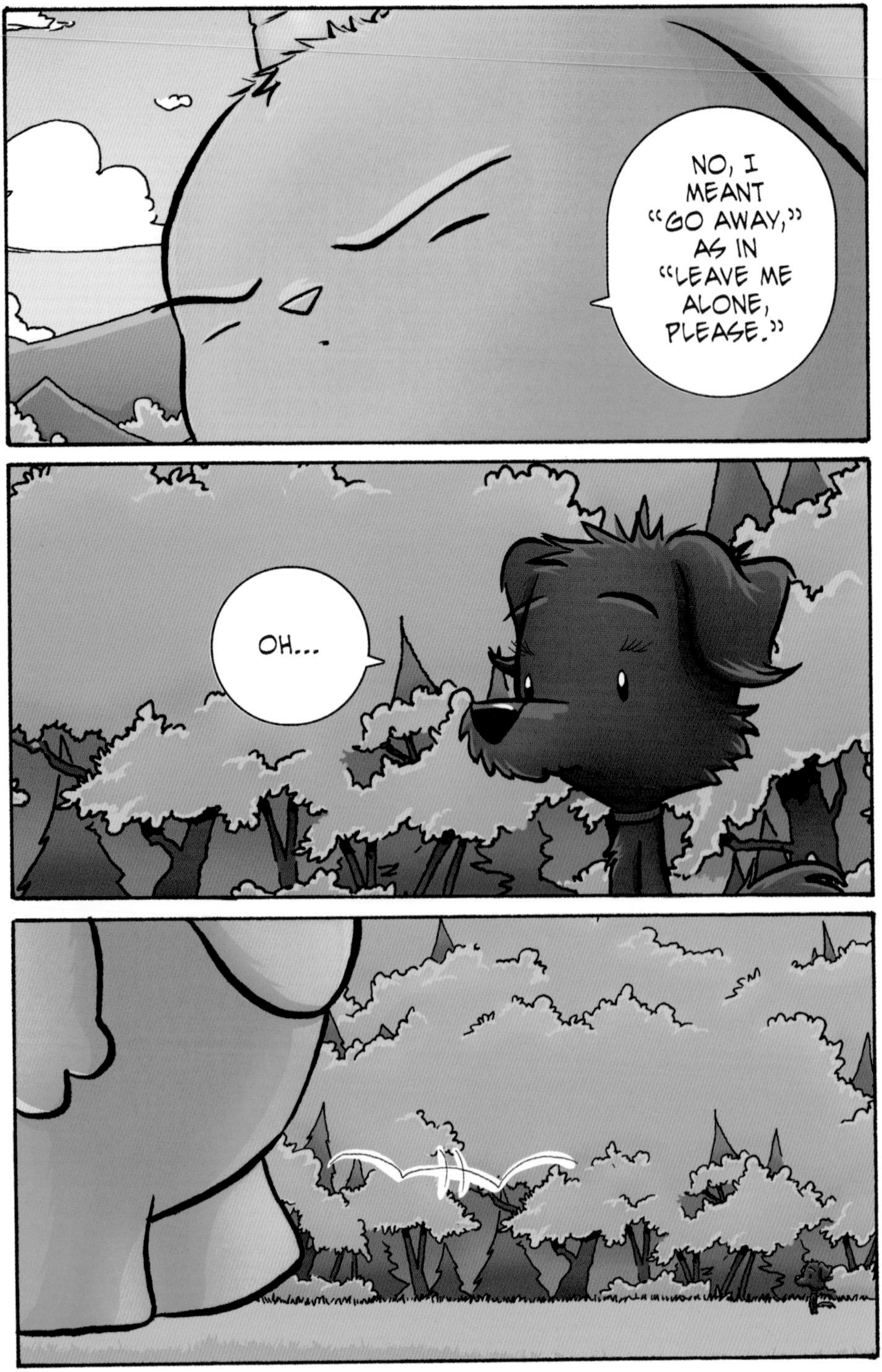
NO, I MEANT "GO AWAY," AS IN "LEAVE ME ALONE, PLEASE."
OH...

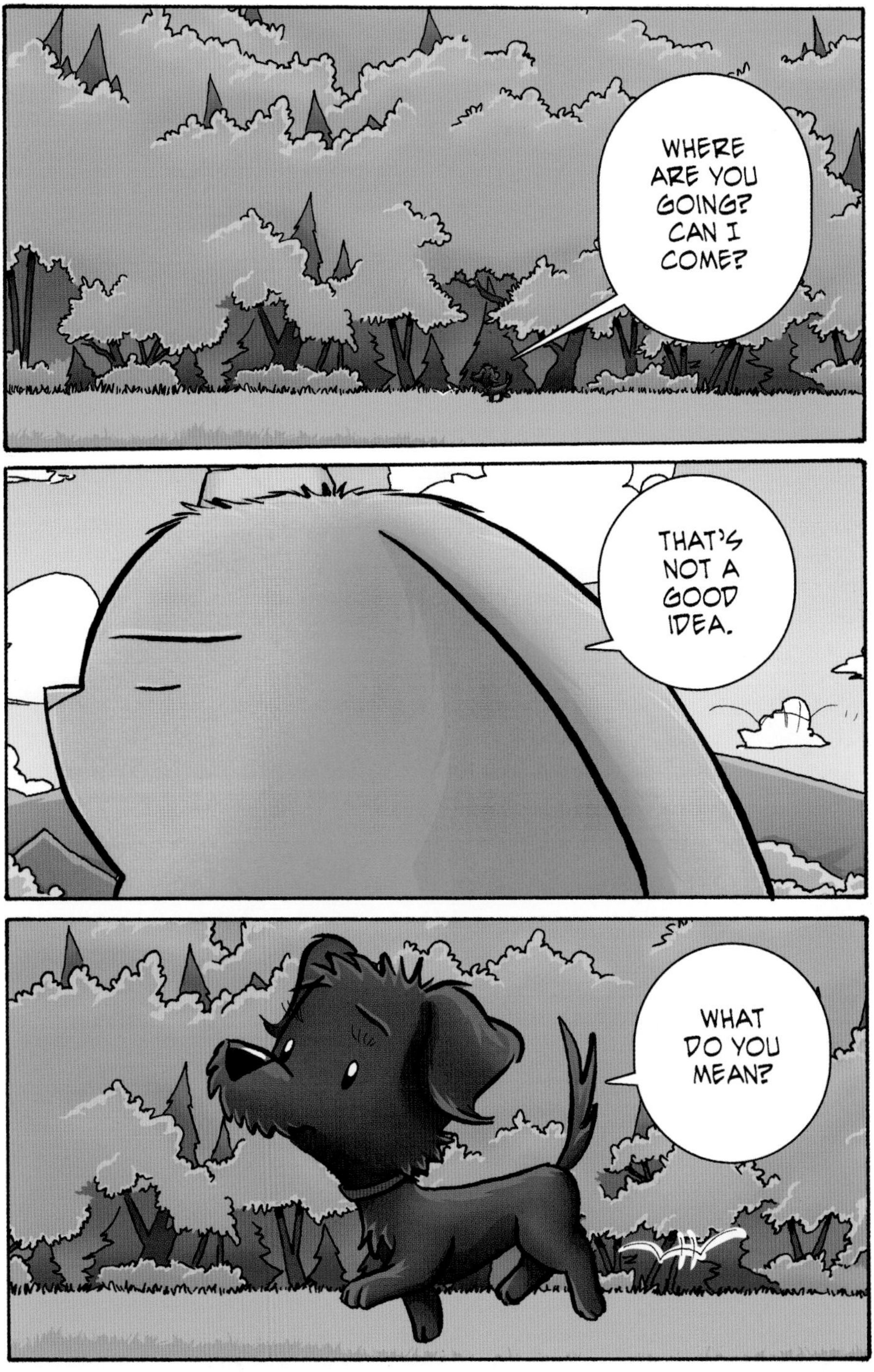
WHERE ARE YOU GOING? CAN I COME?
THAT'S NOT A GOOD IDEA.
WHAT DO YOU MEAN?

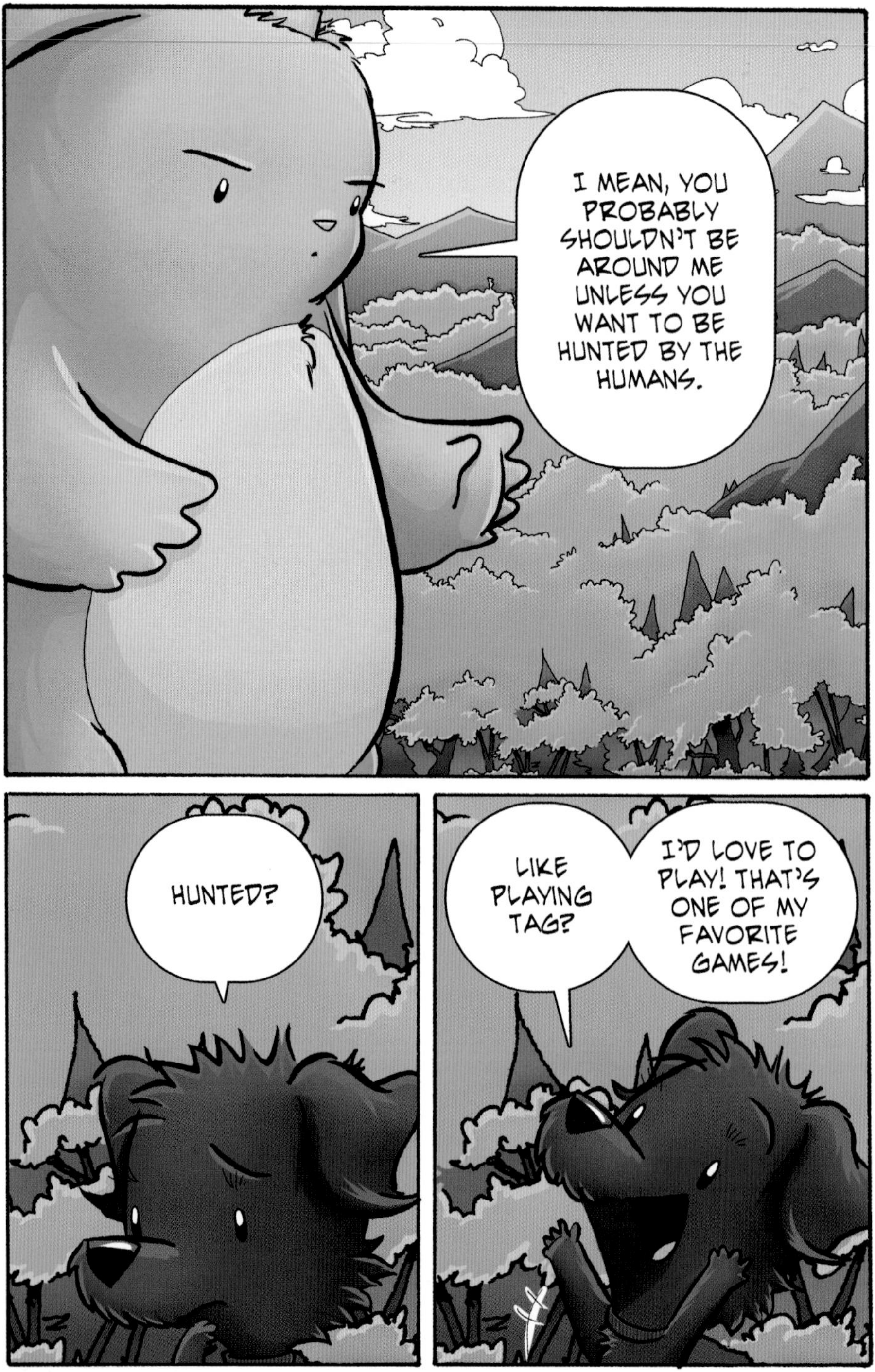
I MEAN, YOU PROBABLY SHOULDN'T BE AROUND ME UNLESS YOU WANT TO BE HUNTED BY THE HUMANS.
HUNTED?
LIKE PLAYING TAG?
I'D LOVE TO PLAY! THAT'S ONE OF MY FAVORITE GAMES!

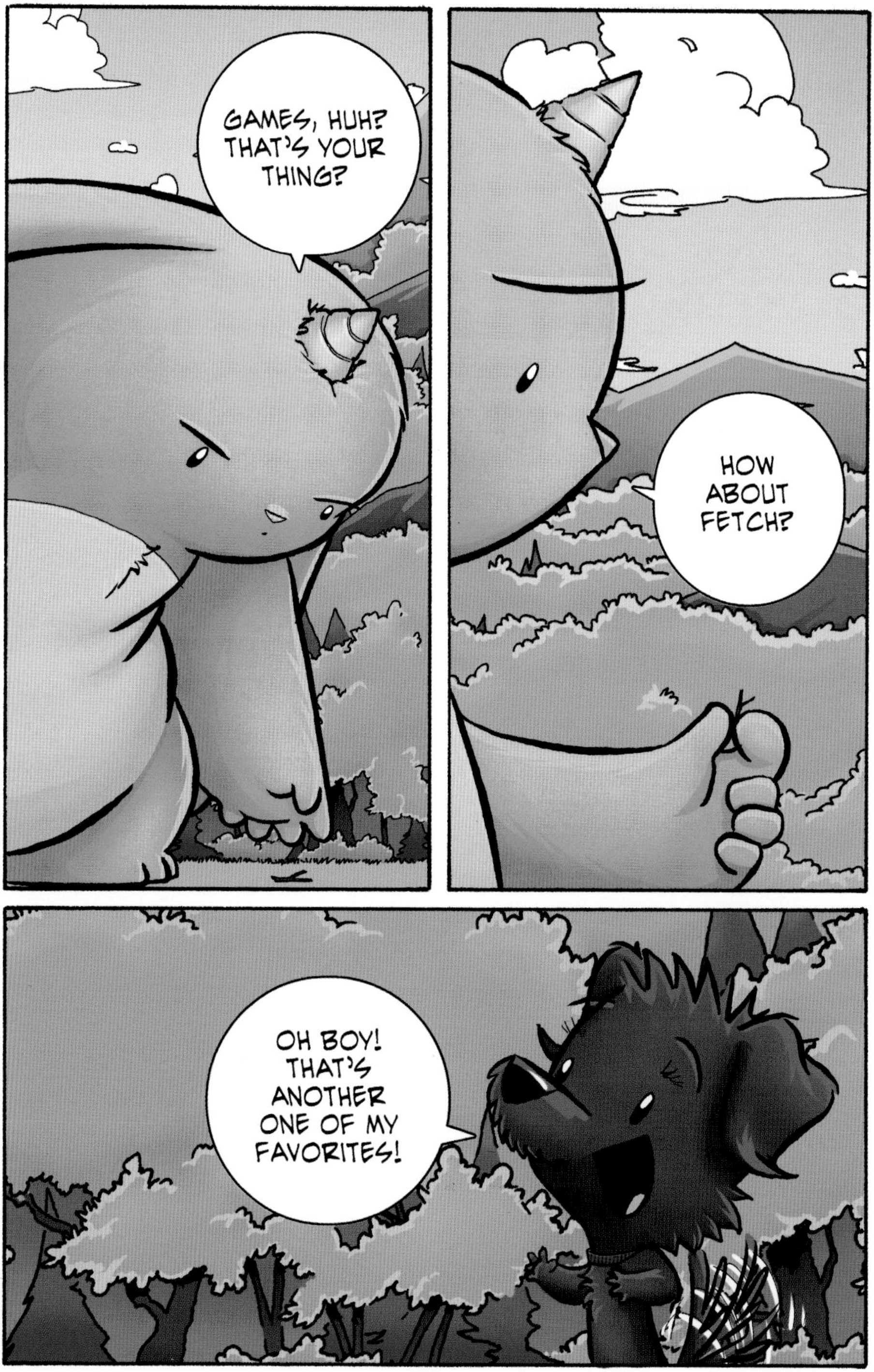
GAMES, HUH? THAT'S YOUR THING?
HOW ABOUT FETCH?
OH BOY! THAT'S ANOTHER ONE OF MY FAVORITES!

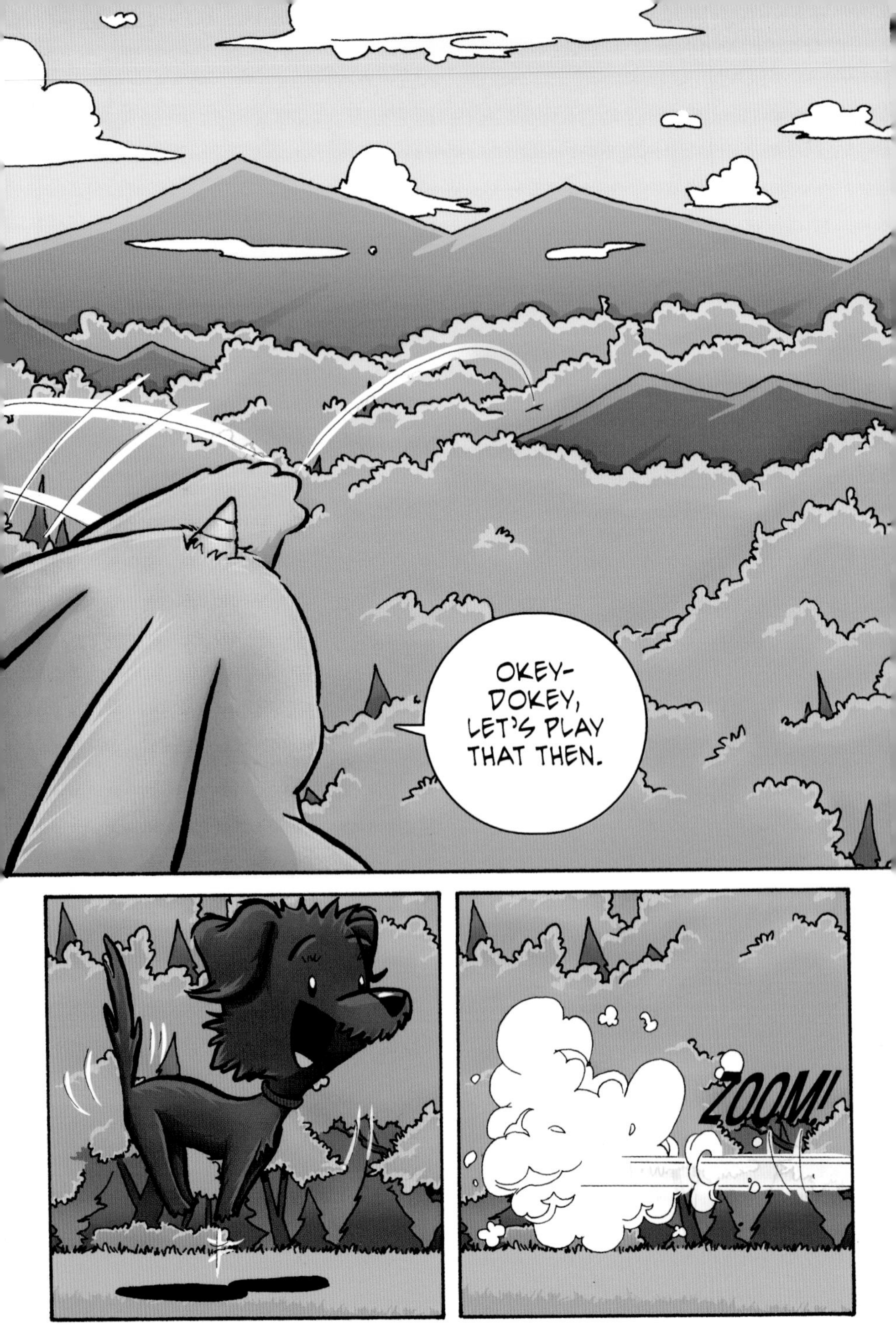
OKEY-
DOKEY,
LET'S PLAY
THAT THEN.
ZOOM!

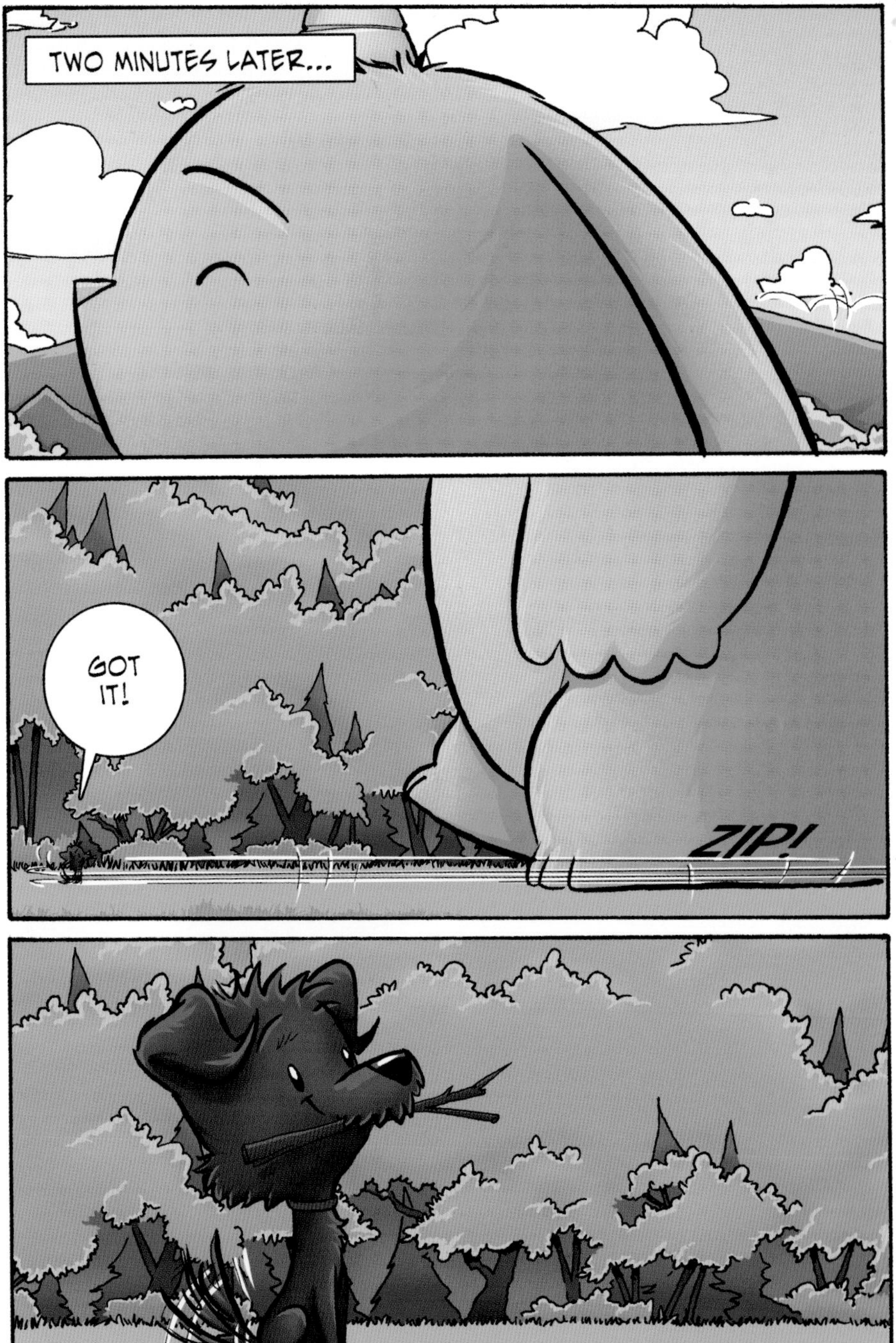
TWO MINUTES LATER...
GOT IT!
ZIP!

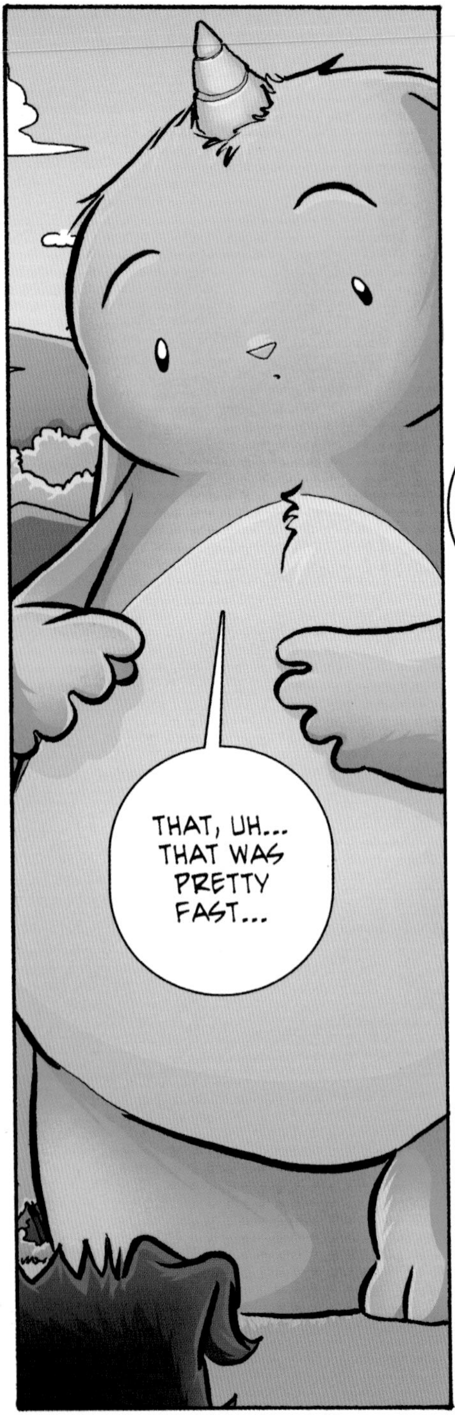
THAT, UH...
THAT WAS
PRETTY
FAST...

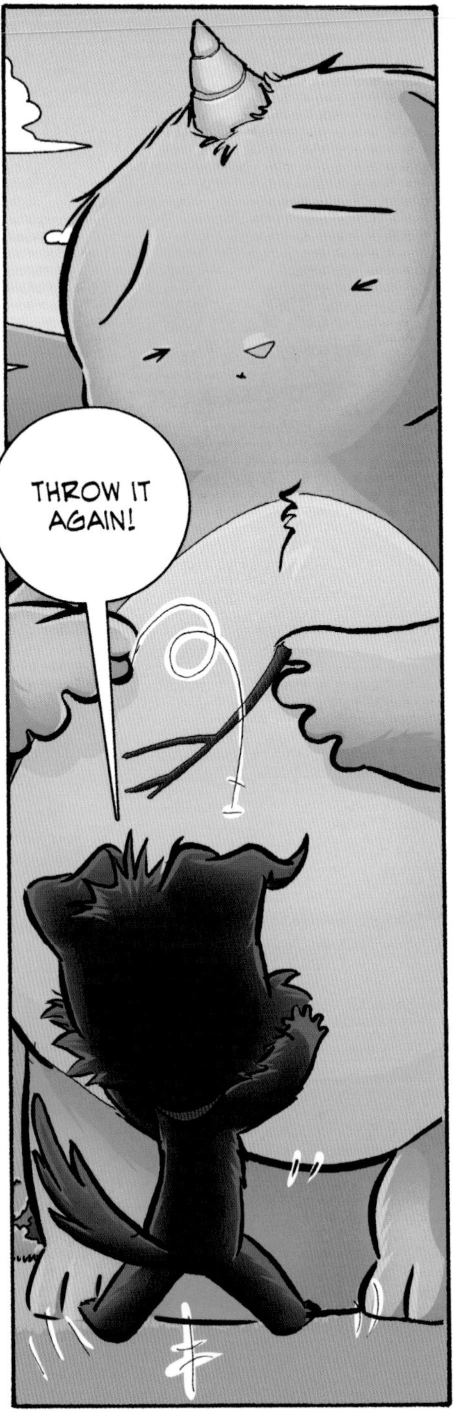
THROW IT
AGAIN!

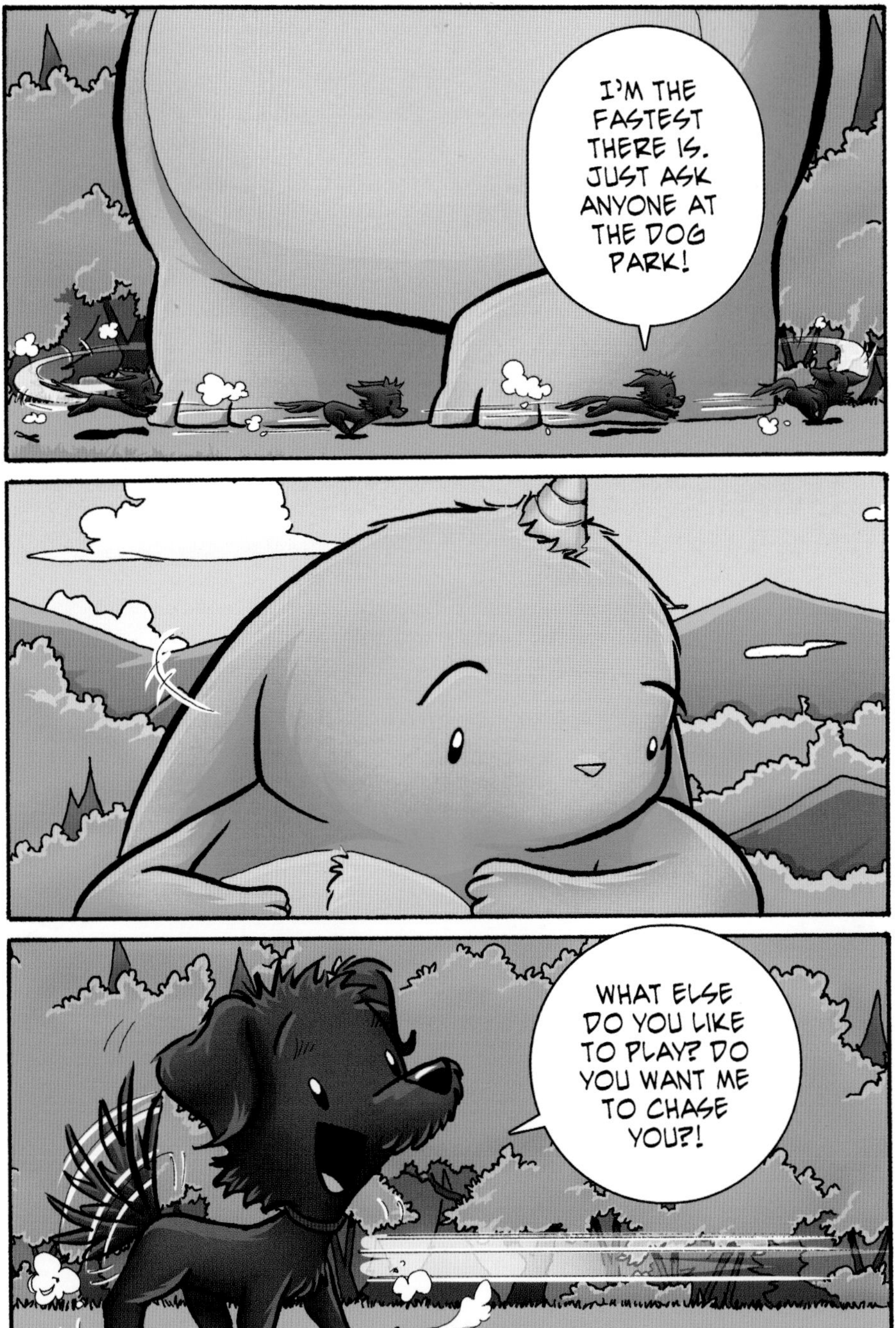
I'M THE FASTEST THERE IS. JUST ASK ANYONE AT THE DOG PARK!
WHAT ELSE DO YOU LIKE TO PLAY? DO YOU WANT ME TO CHASE YOU?!

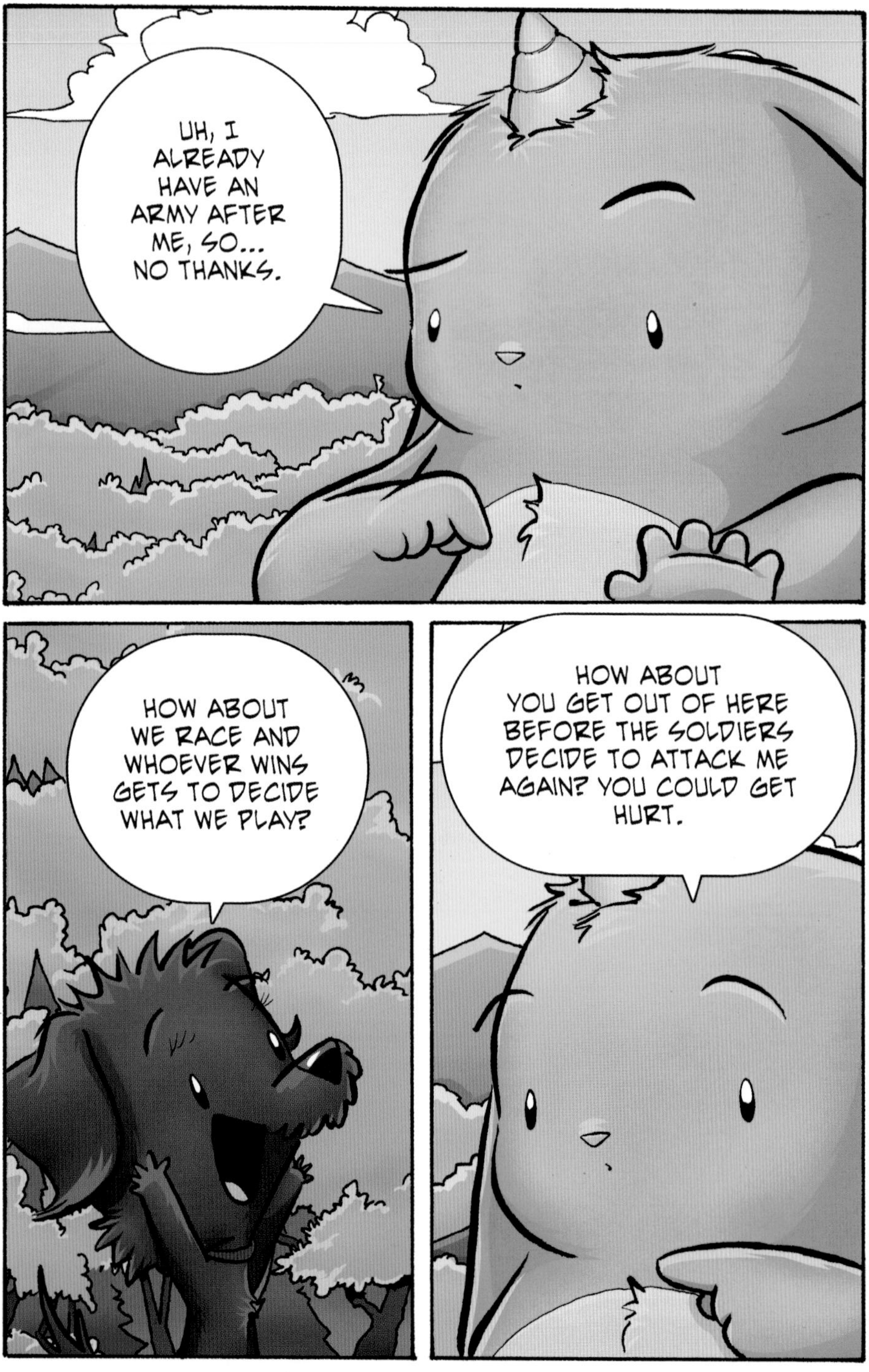
UH, I ALREADY HAVE AN ARMY AFTER ME, SO... NO THANKS.
HOW ABOUT WE RACE AND WHOEVER WINS GETS TO DECIDE WHAT WE PLAY?
HOW ABOUT YOU GET OUT OF HERE BEFORE THE SOLDIERS DECIDE TO ATTACK ME AGAIN? YOU COULD GET HURT.

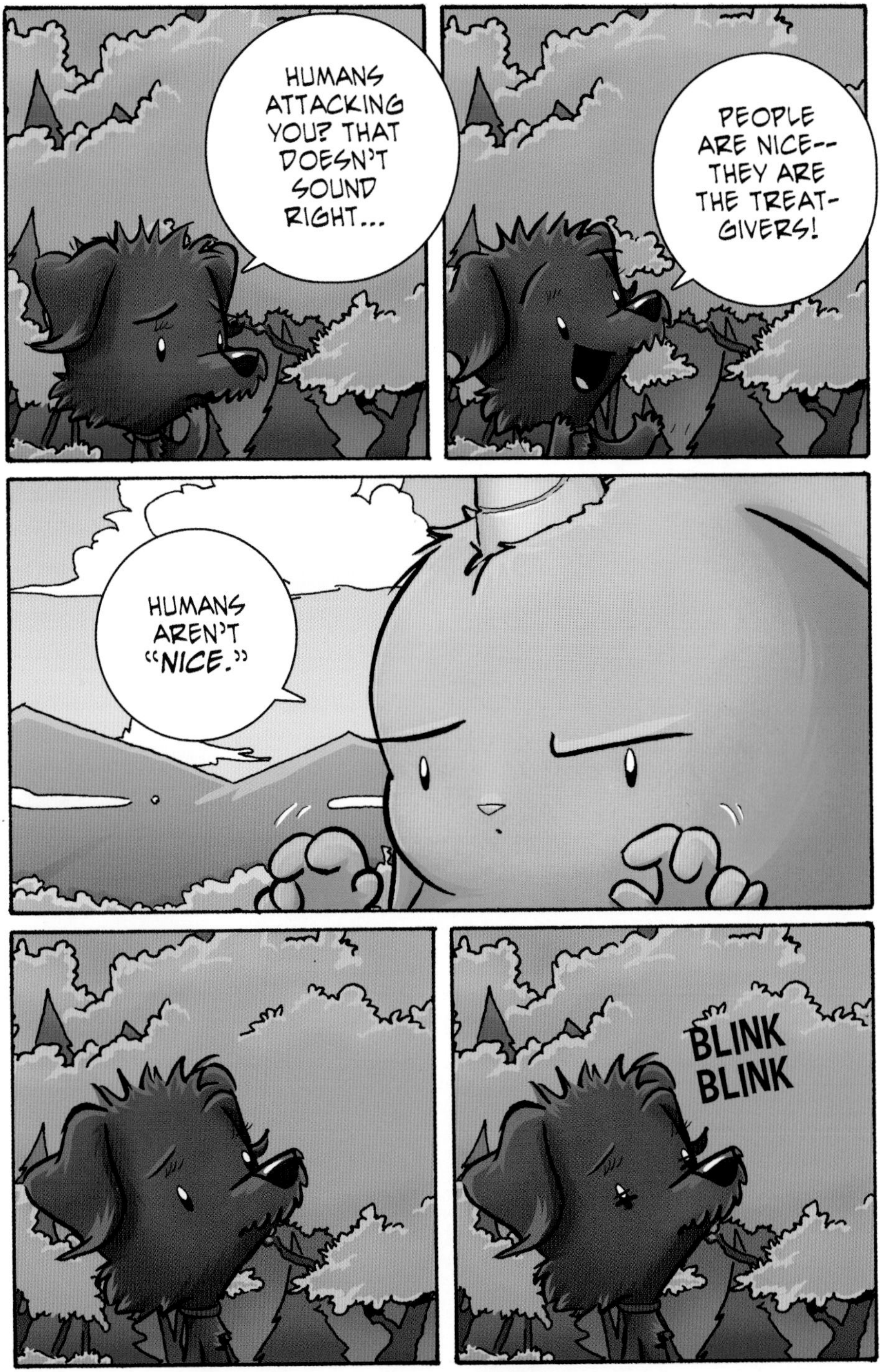
HUMANS ATTACKING YOU? THAT DOESN'T SOUND RIGHT...
PEOPLE ARE NICE--THEY ARE THE TREAT-GIVERS!
HUMANS AREN'T "NICE."
BLINK
BLINK

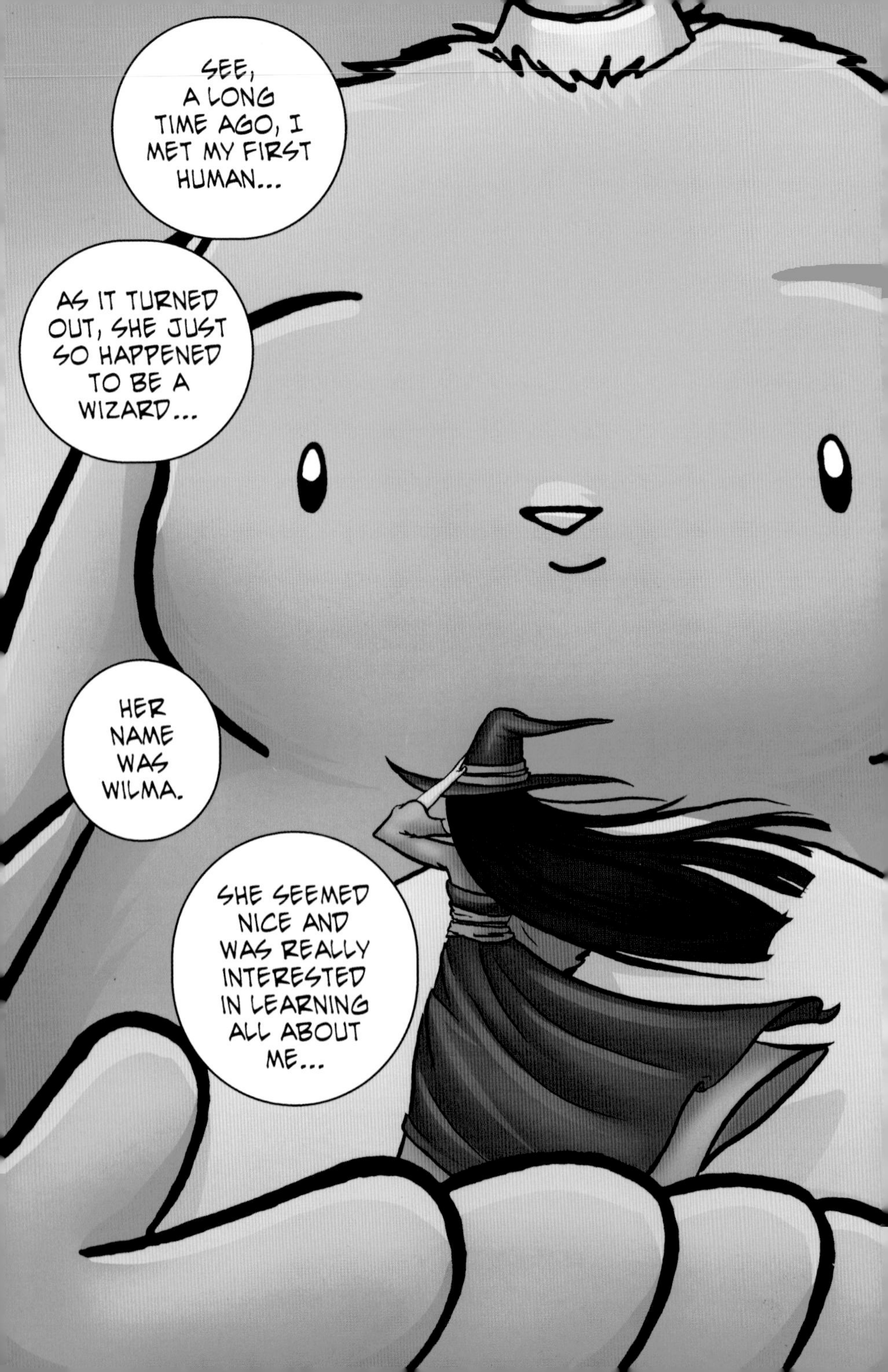
SEE, A LONG TIME AGO, I MET MY FIRST HUMAN...
AS IT TURNED OUT, SHE JUST SO HAPPENED TO BE A WIZARD...
HER NAME WAS WILMA.
SHE SEEMED NICE AND WAS REALLY INTERESTED IN LEARNING ALL ABOUT ME...

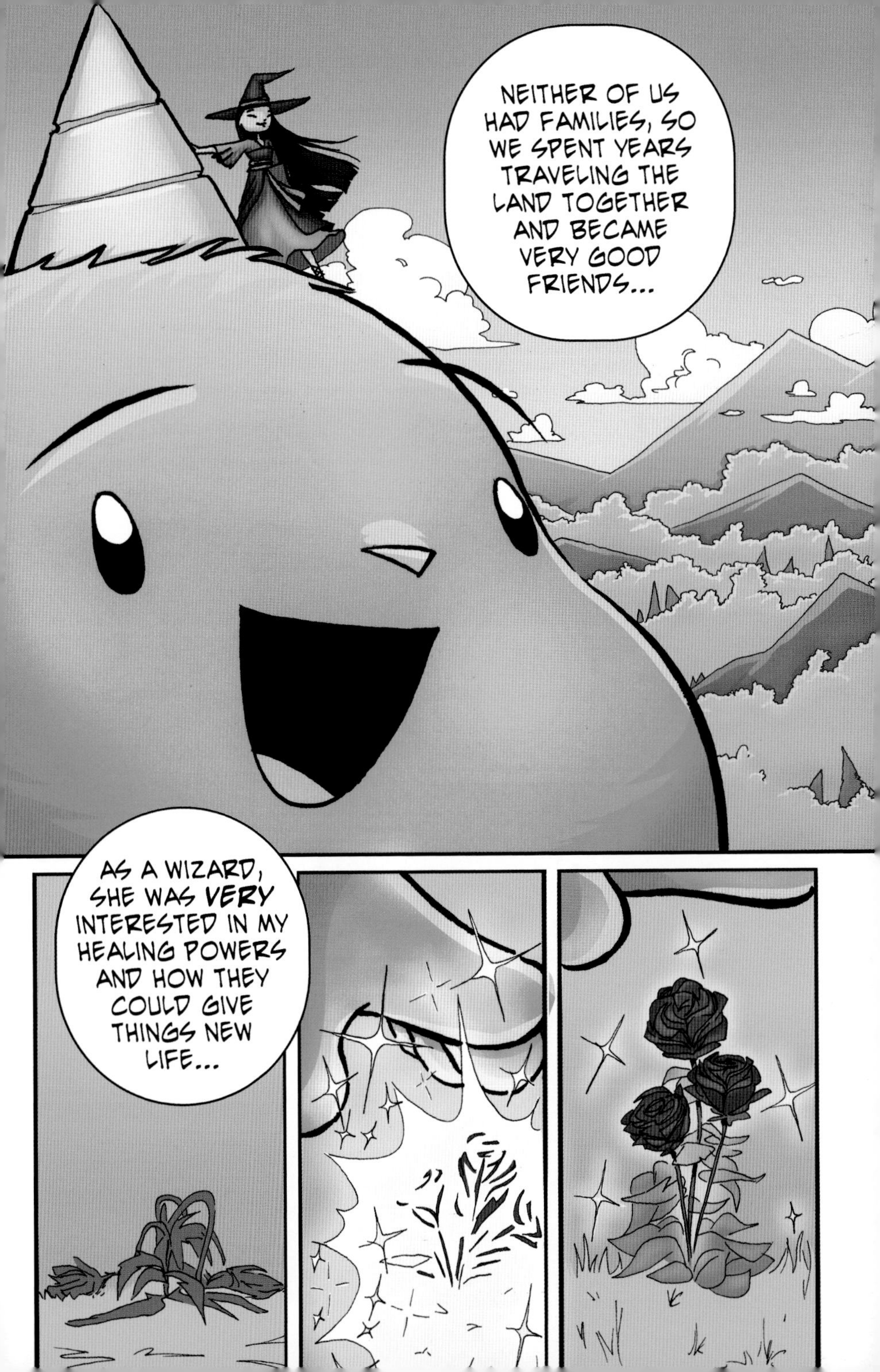
NEITHER OF US HAD FAMILIES, SO WE SPENT YEARS TRAVELING THE LAND TOGETHER AND BECAME VERY GOOD FRIENDS...
AS A WIZARD, SHE WAS **VERY** INTERESTED IN MY HEALING POWERS AND HOW THEY COULD GIVE THINGS NEW LIFE...

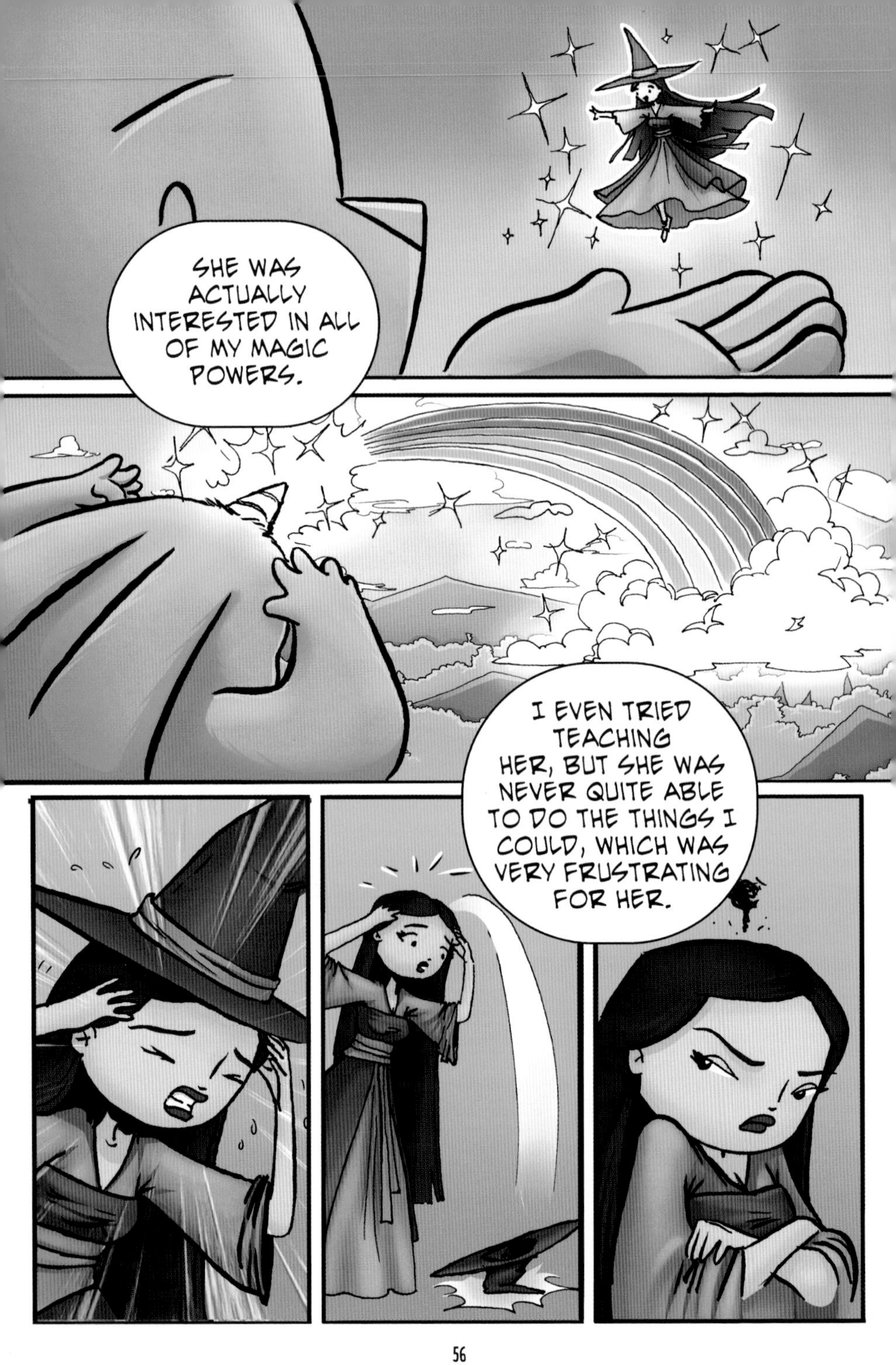
SHE WAS ACTUALLY INTERESTED IN ALL OF MY MAGIC POWERS.
I EVEN TRIED TEACHING HER, BUT SHE WAS NEVER QUITE ABLE TO DO THE THINGS I COULD, WHICH WAS VERY FRUSTRATING FOR HER.

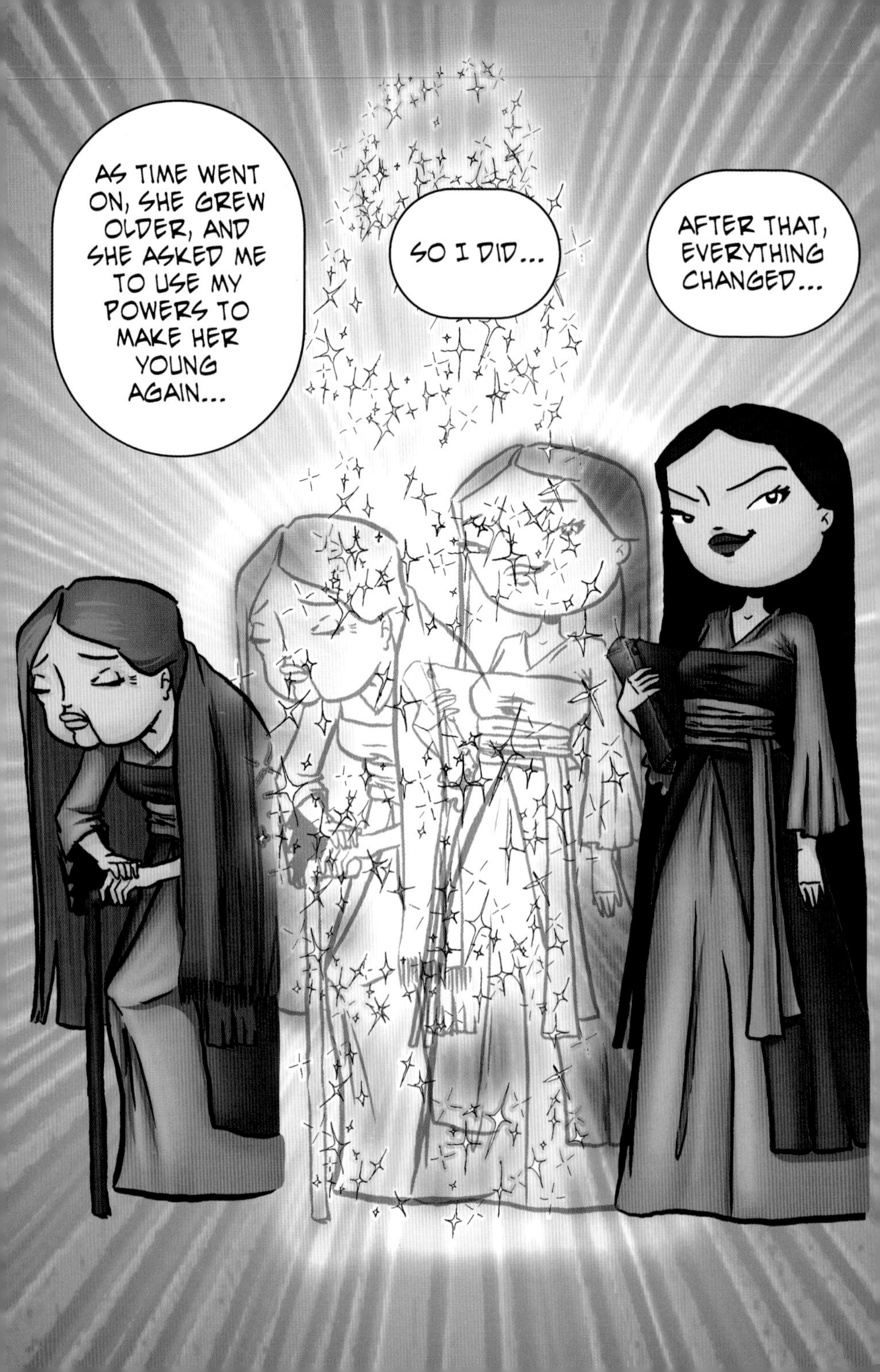
AS TIME WENT ON, SHE GREW OLDER, AND SHE ASKED ME TO USE MY POWERS TO MAKE HER YOUNG AGAIN...
SO I DID...
AFTER THAT, EVERYTHING CHANGED...

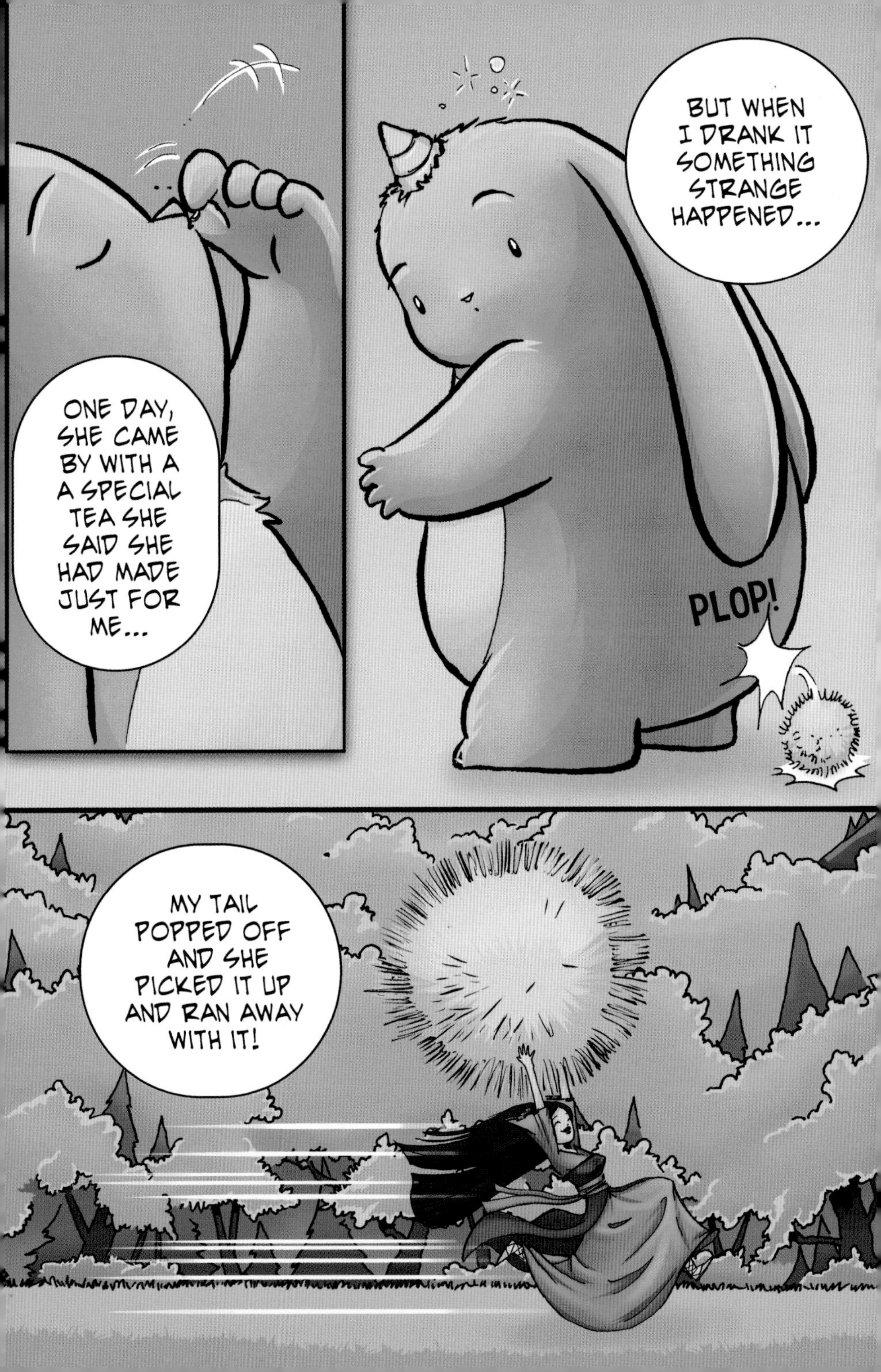
ONE DAY, SHE CAME BY WITH A A SPECIAL TEA SHE SAID SHE HAD MADE JUST FOR ME...
BUT WHEN I DRANK IT SOMETHING STRANGE HAPPENED...
PLOP!
MY TAIL POPPED OFF AND SHE PICKED IT UP AND RAN AWAY WITH IT!

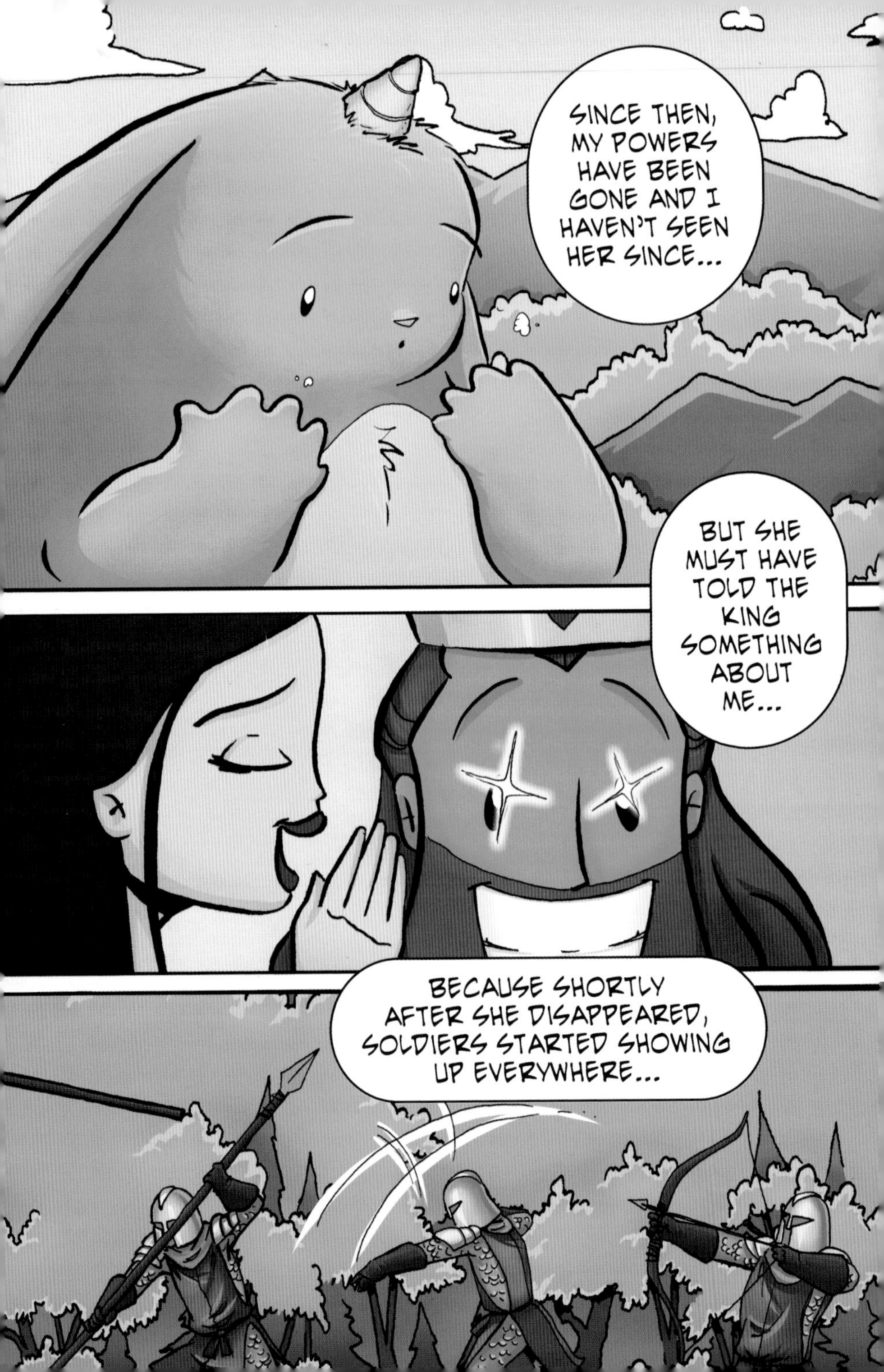
SINCE THEN, MY POWERS HAVE BEEN GONE AND I HAVEN'T SEEN HER SINCE...
BUT SHE MUST HAVE TOLD THE KING SOMETHING ABOUT ME...
BECAUSE SHORTLY AFTER SHE DISAPPEARED, SOLDIERS STARTED SHOWING UP EVERYWHERE...

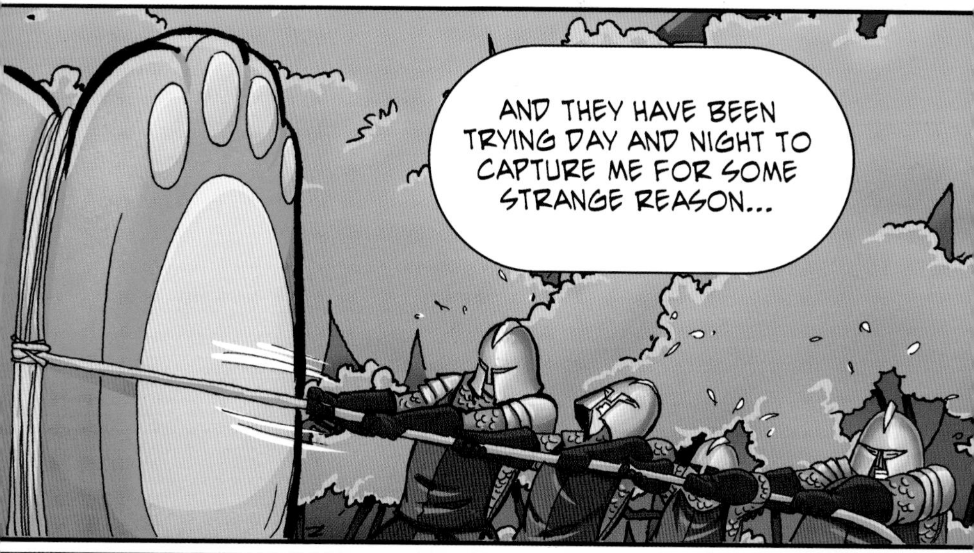
AND THEY HAVE BEEN TRYING DAY AND NIGHT TO CAPTURE ME FOR SOME STRANGE REASON...

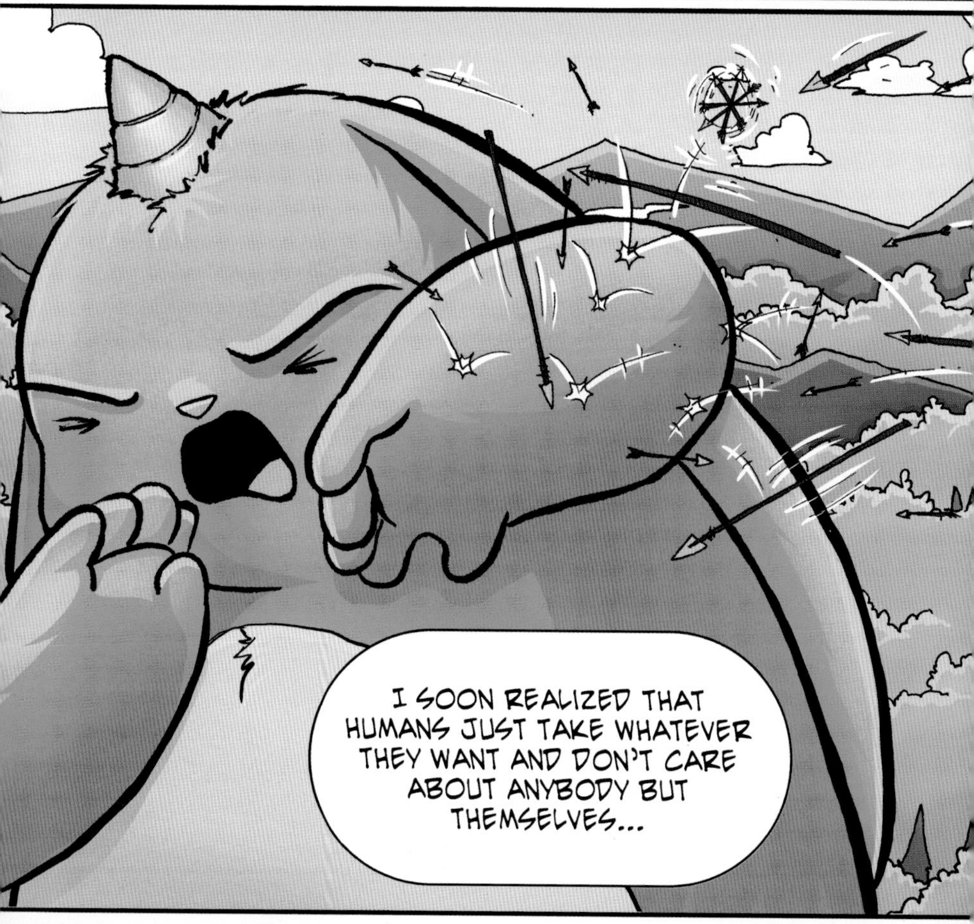
I SOON REALIZED THAT HUMANS JUST TAKE WHATEVER THEY WANT AND DON'T CARE ABOUT ANYBODY BUT THEMSELVES...

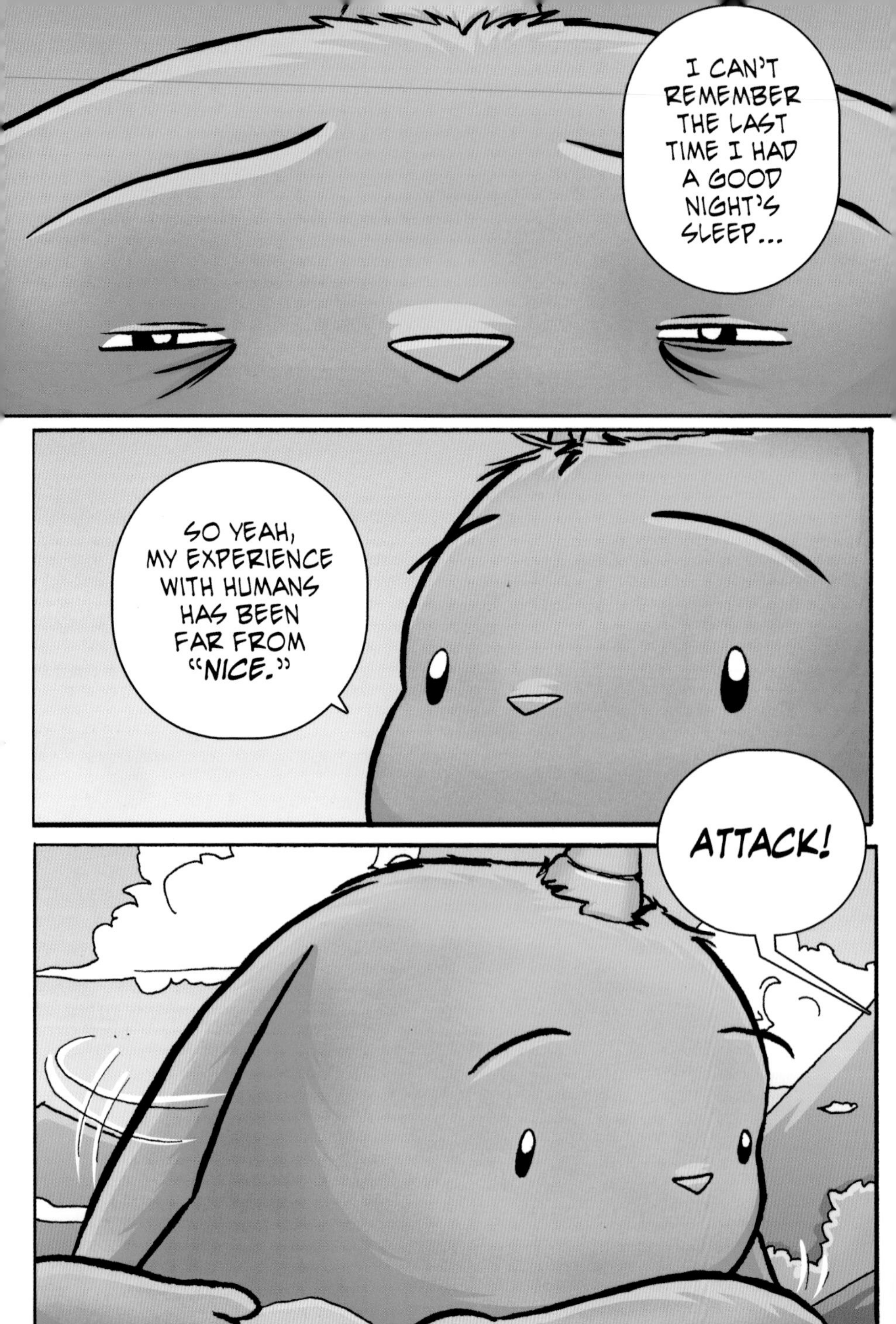
I CAN'T REMEMBER THE LAST TIME I HAD A GOOD NIGHT'S SLEEP...
SO YEAH, MY EXPERIENCE WITH HUMANS HAS BEEN FAR FROM "NICE."
ATTACK!

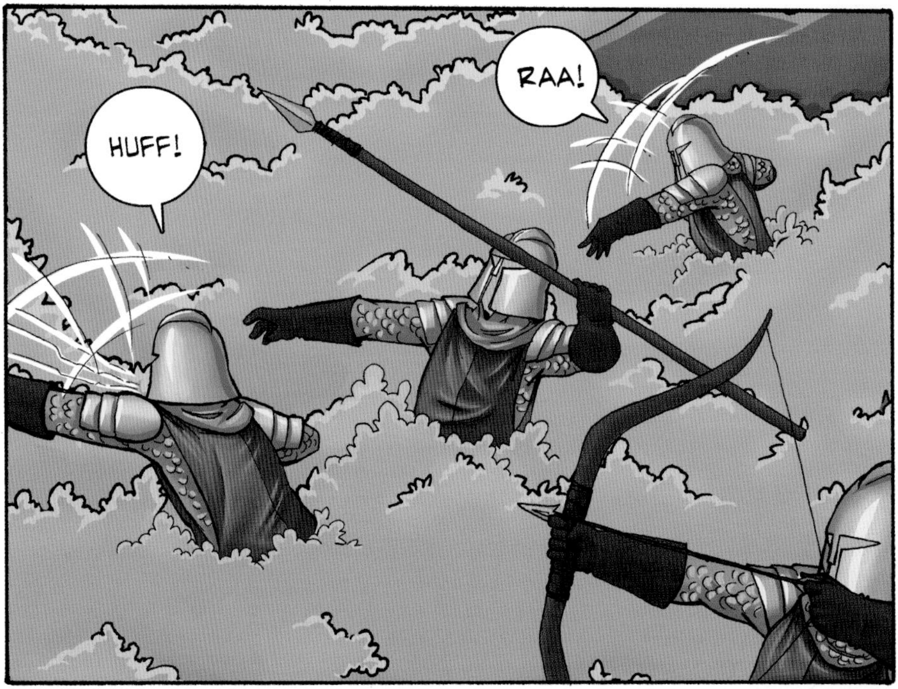
HUFF!
RAA!

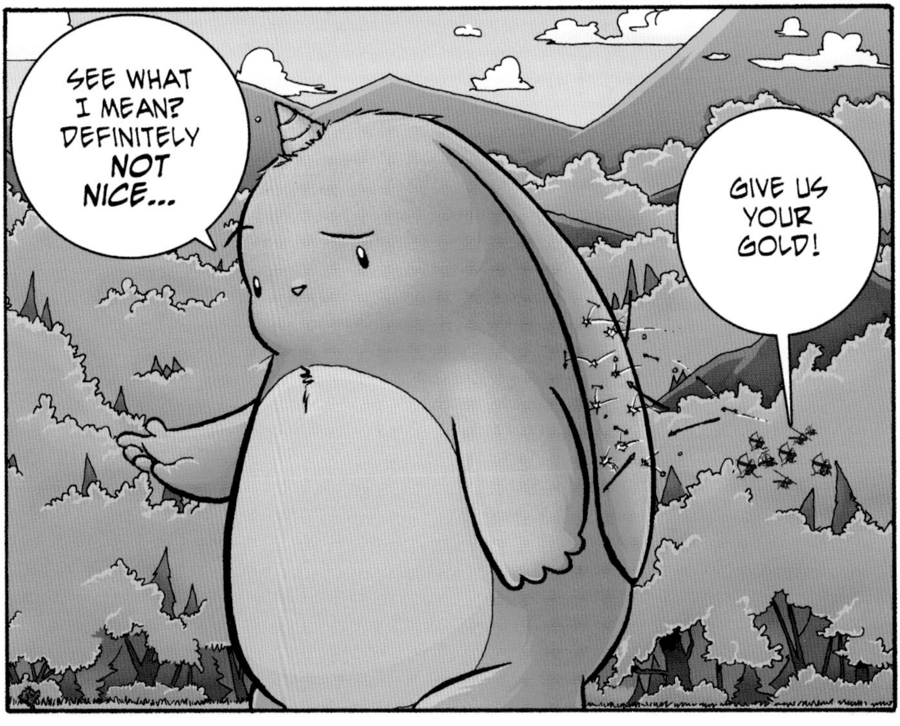
SEE WHAT I MEAN? DEFINITELY NOT NICE...
GIVE US YOUR GOLD!

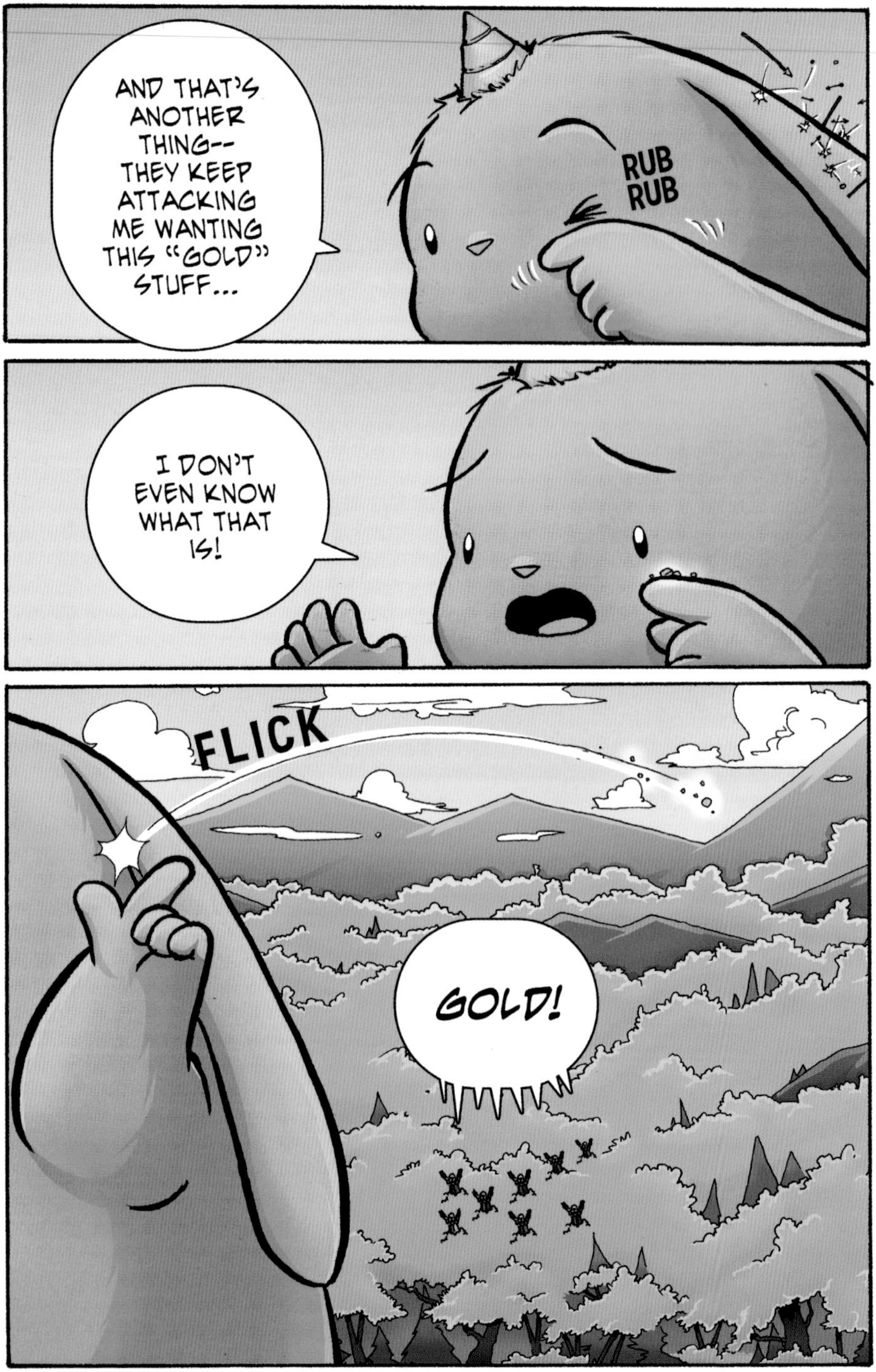
AND THAT'S ANOTHER THING-- THEY KEEP ATTACKING ME WANTING THIS "GOLD" STUFF...
RUB RUB
I DON'T EVEN KNOW WHAT THAT IS!
FLICK
GOLD!

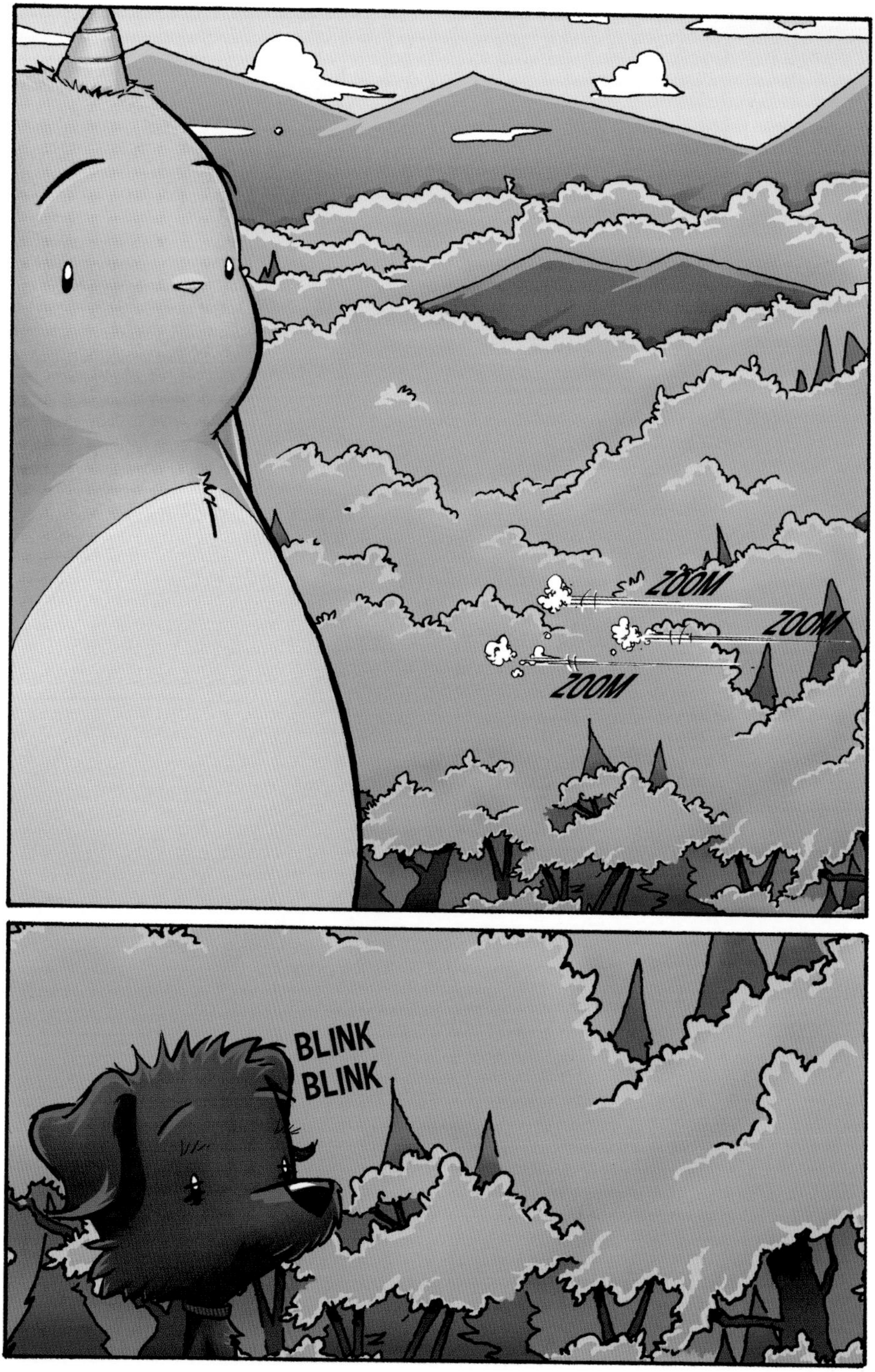
ZOOM
ZOOM
ZOOM
BLINK
BLINK

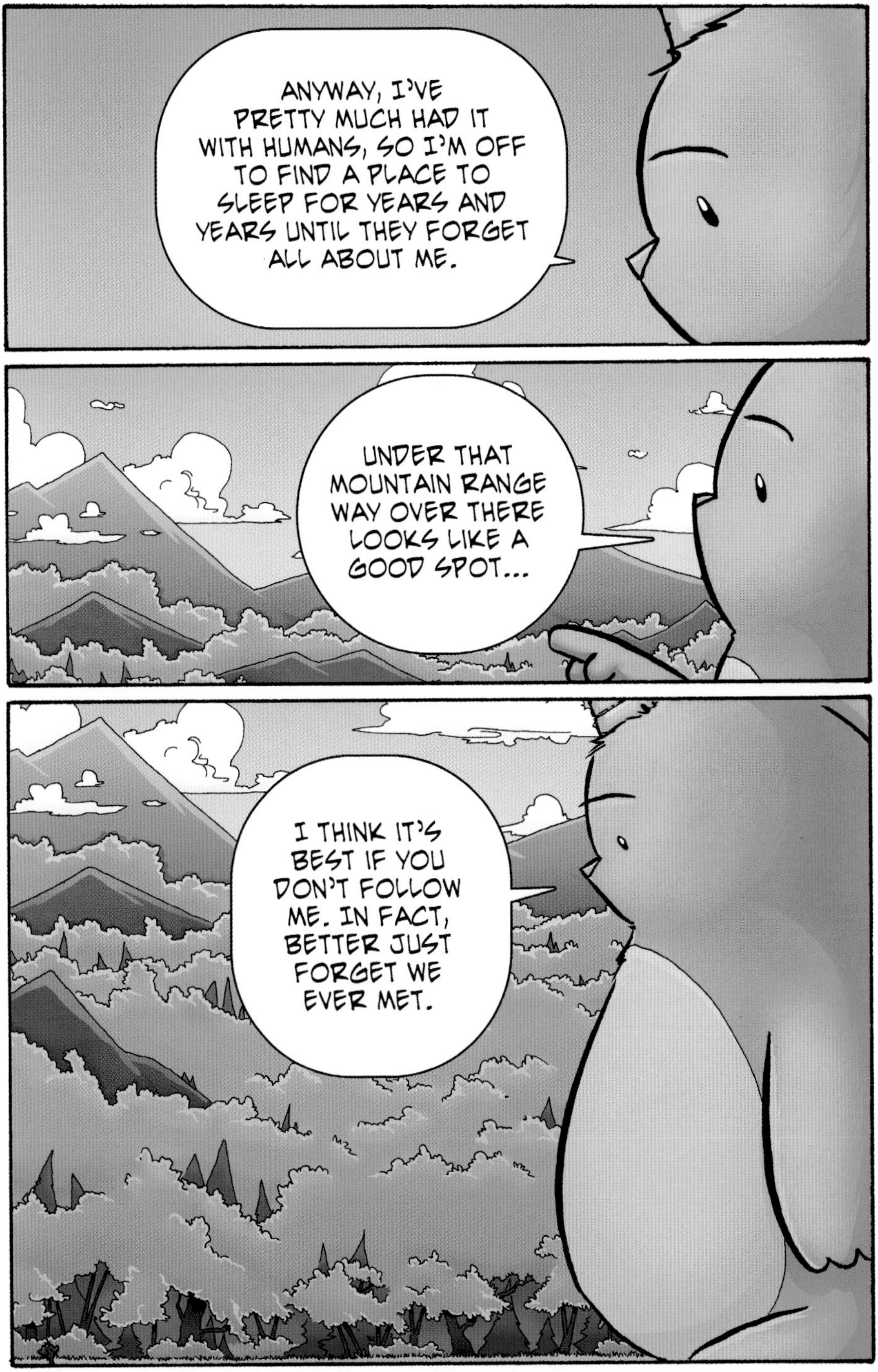
ANYWAY, I'VE PRETTY MUCH HAD IT WITH HUMANS, SO I'M OFF TO FIND A PLACE TO SLEEP FOR YEARS AND YEARS UNTIL THEY FORGET ALL ABOUT ME.
UNDER THAT MOUNTAIN RANGE WAY OVER THERE LOOKS LIKE A GOOD SPOT...
I THINK IT'S BEST IF YOU DON'T FOLLOW ME. IN FACT, BETTER JUST FORGET WE EVER MET.

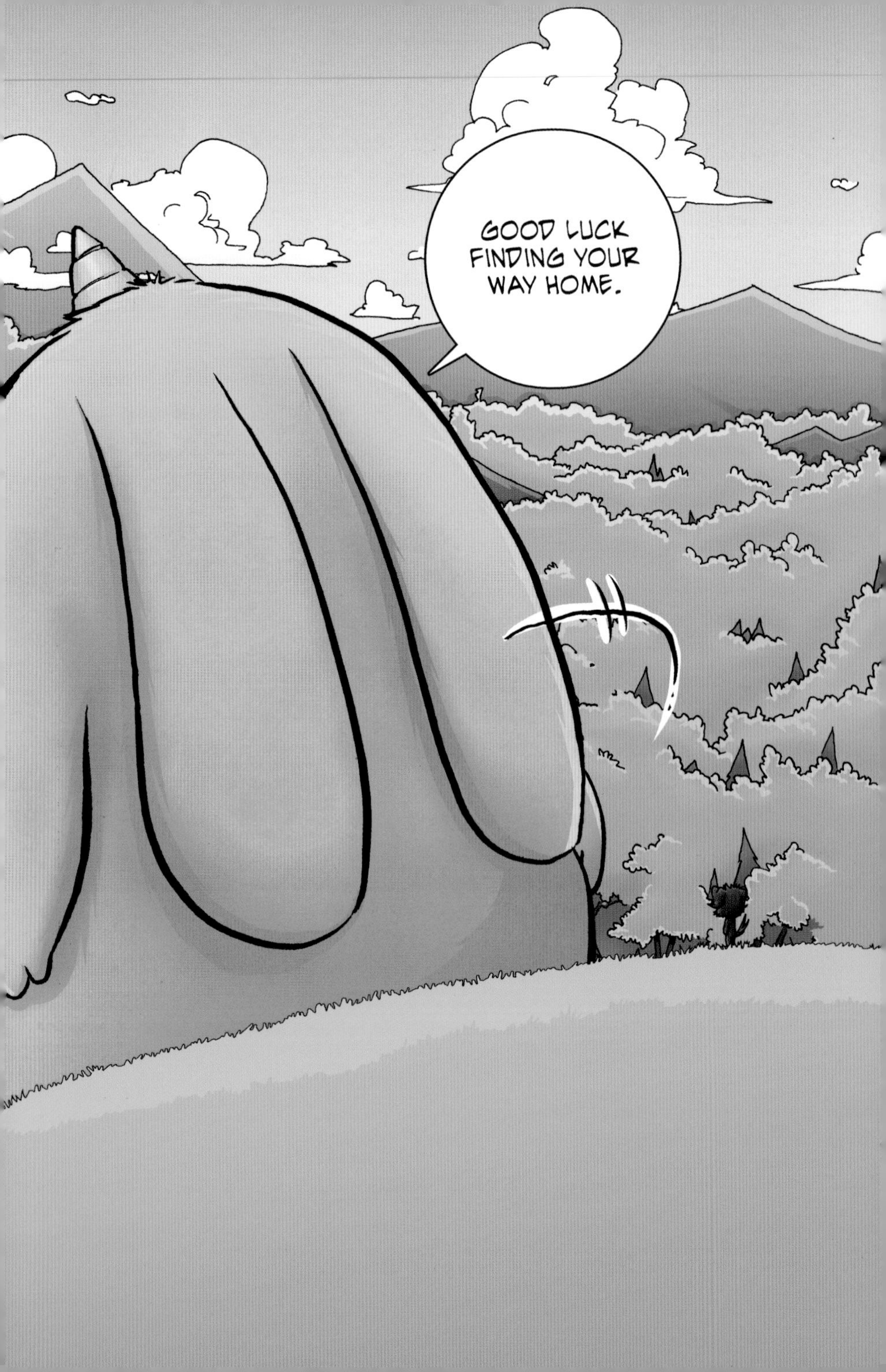
GOOD LUCK FINDING YOUR WAY HOME.

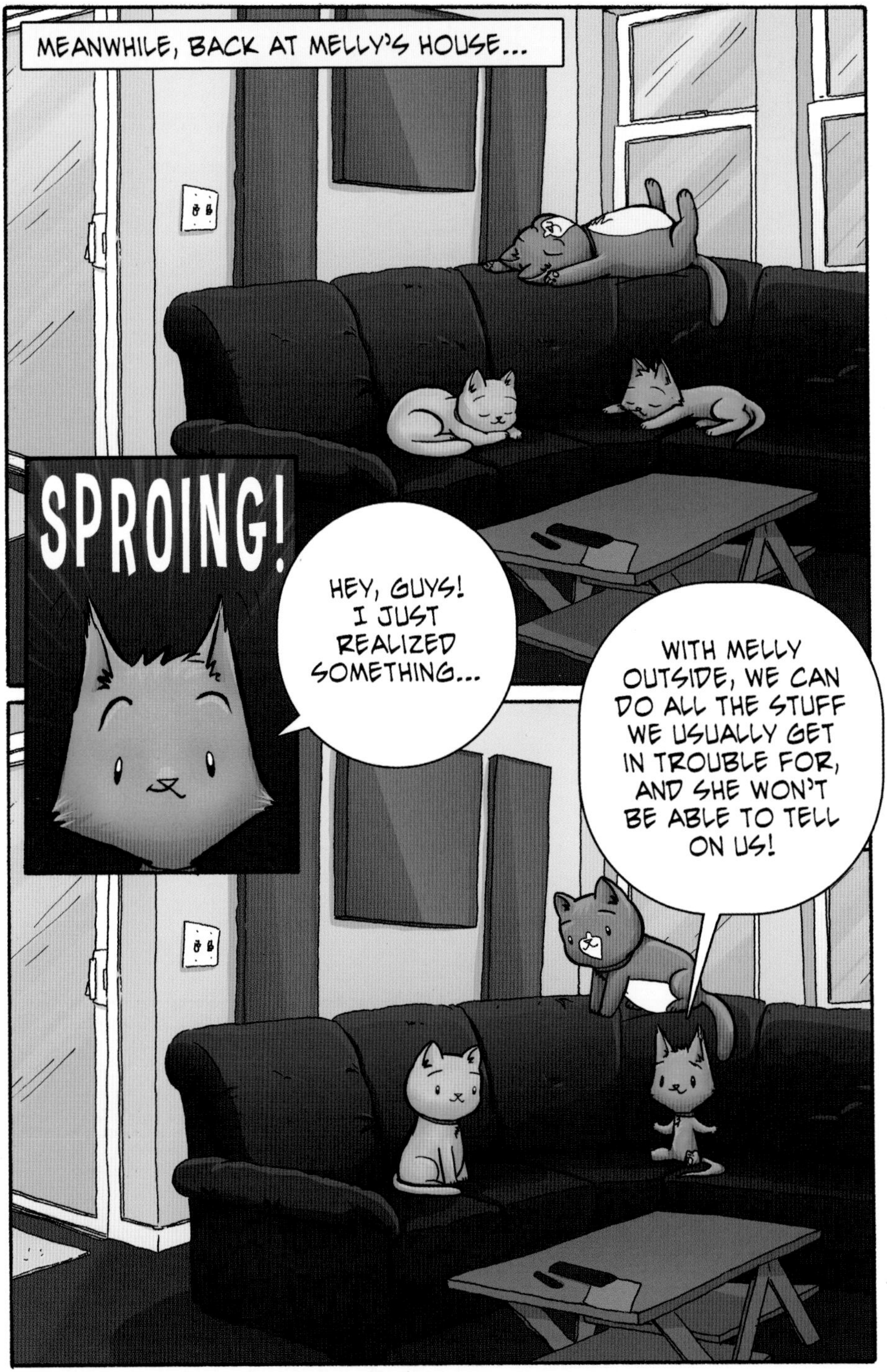
MEANWHILE, BACK AT MELLY'S HOUSE...
SPROING!
HEY, GUYS! I JUST REALIZED SOMETHING...
WITH MELLY OUTSIDE, WE CAN DO ALL THE STUFF WE USUALLY GET IN TROUBLE FOR, AND SHE WON'T BE ABLE TO TELL ON US!

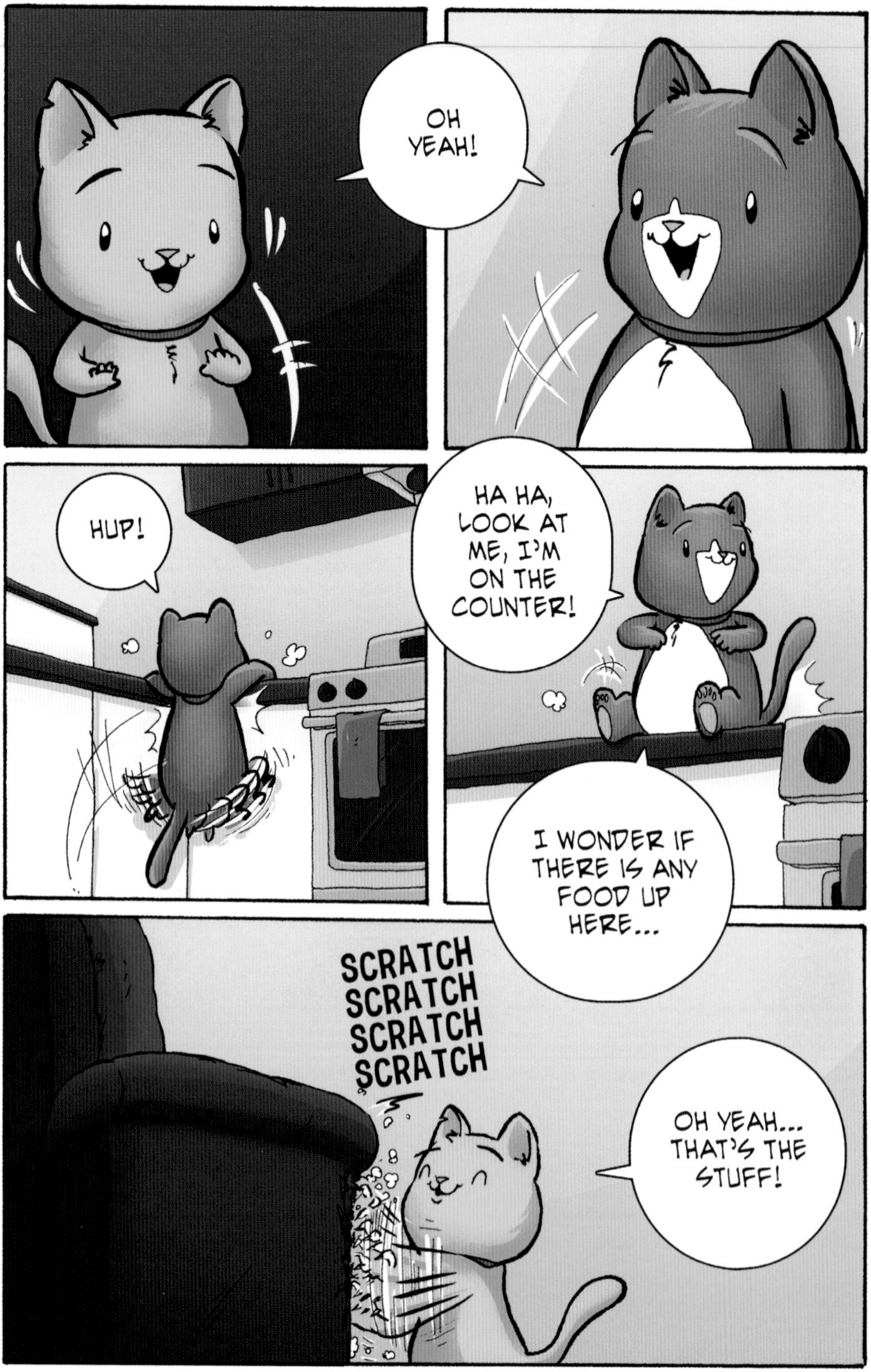
OH YEAH!
HUP!
HA HA, LOOK AT ME, I'M ON THE COUNTER!
I WONDER IF THERE IS ANY FOOD UP HERE...
SCRATCH SCRATCH SCRATCH SCRATCH
OH YEAH... THAT'S THE STUFF!

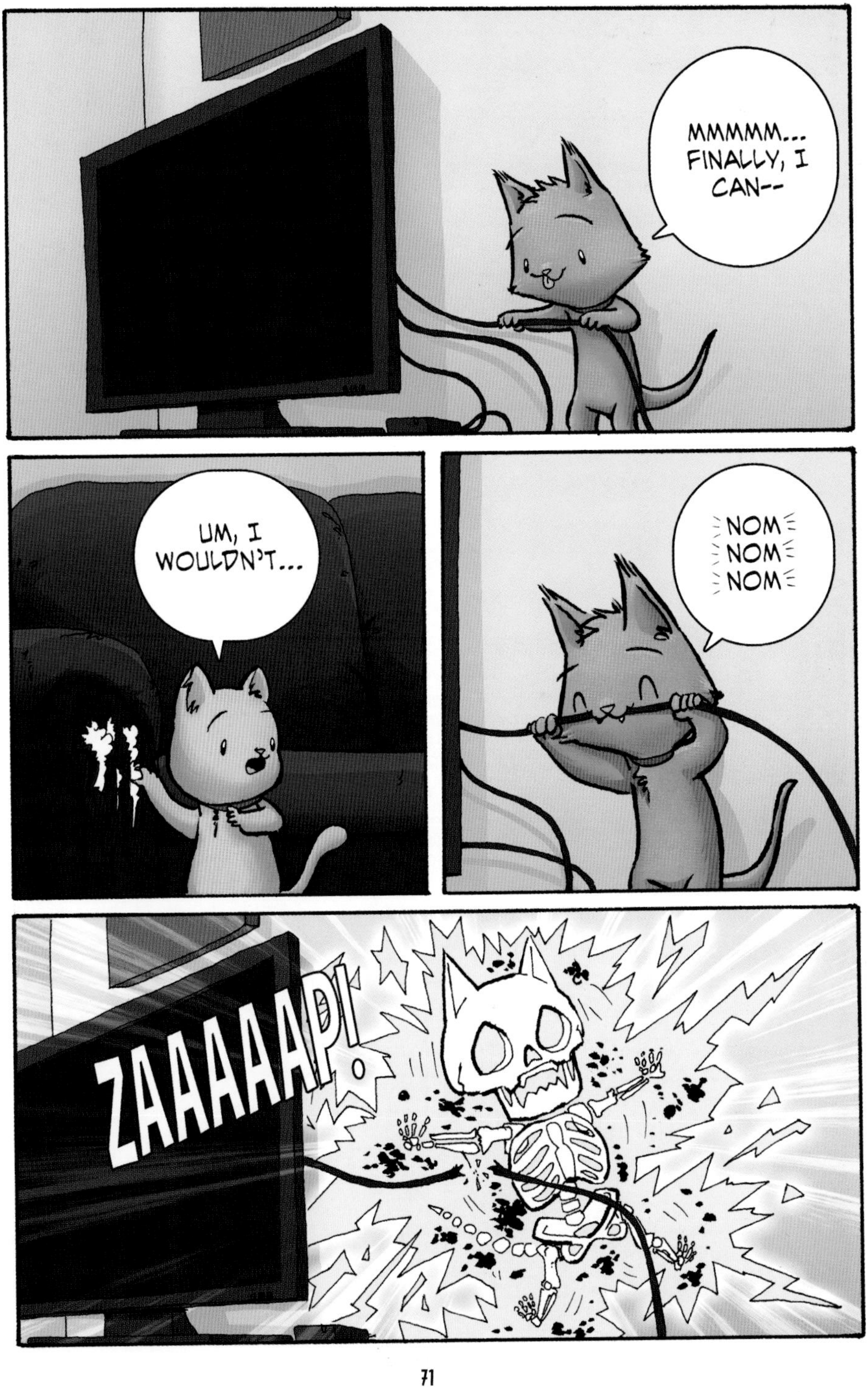
MMMMM... FINALLY, I CAN--
UM, I WOULDN'T...
NOM NOM NOM
ZAAAAAP!

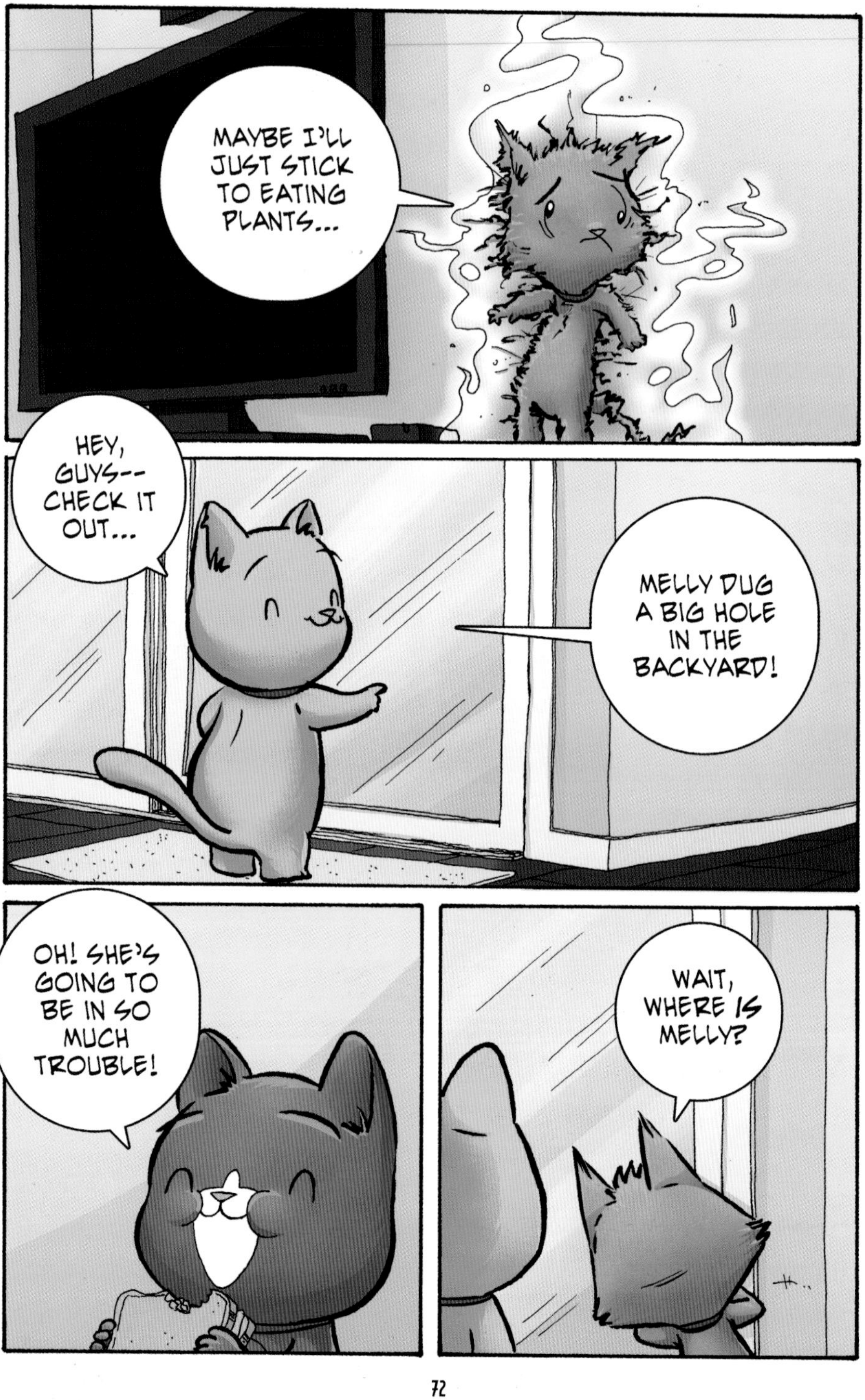
MAYBE I'LL JUST STICK TO EATING PLANTS...
HEY, GUYS--CHECK IT OUT...
MELLY DUG A BIG HOLE IN THE BACKYARD!
OH! SHE'S GOING TO BE IN SO MUCH TROUBLE!
WAIT, WHERE *IS* MELLY?

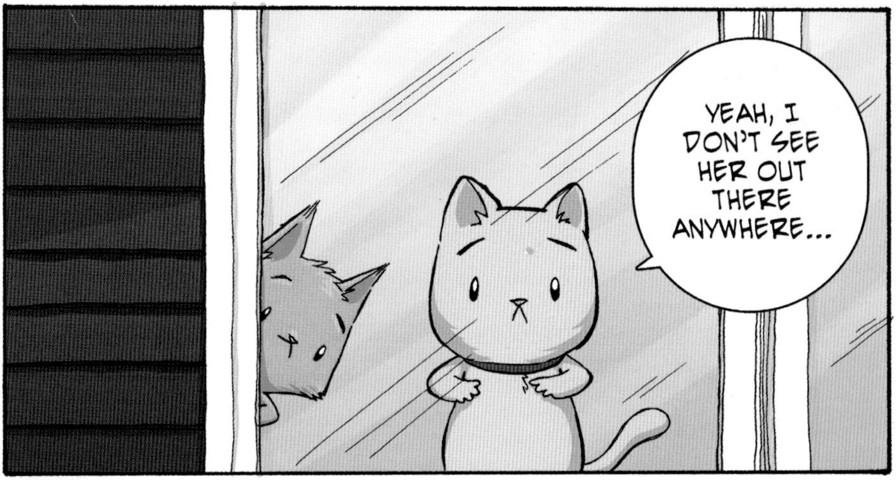
YEAH, I DON'T SEE HER OUT THERE ANYWHERE...

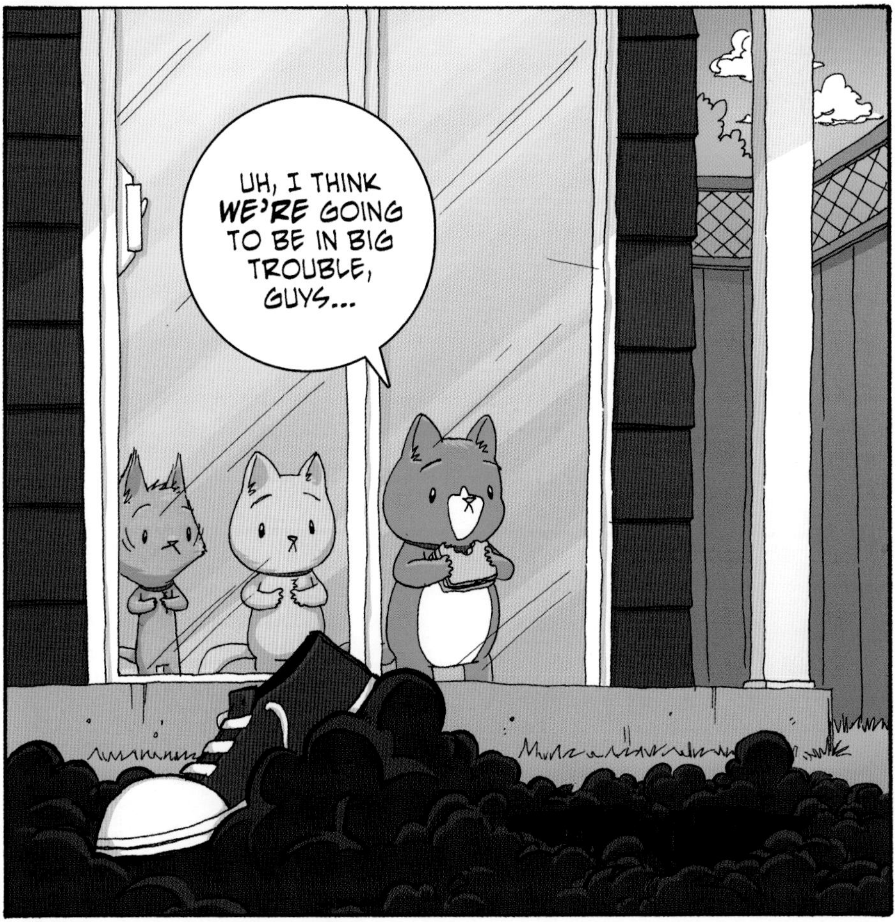
UH, I THINK **WE'RE** GOING TO BE IN BIG TROUBLE, GUYS...

CHAPTER 4
THE BAD KING

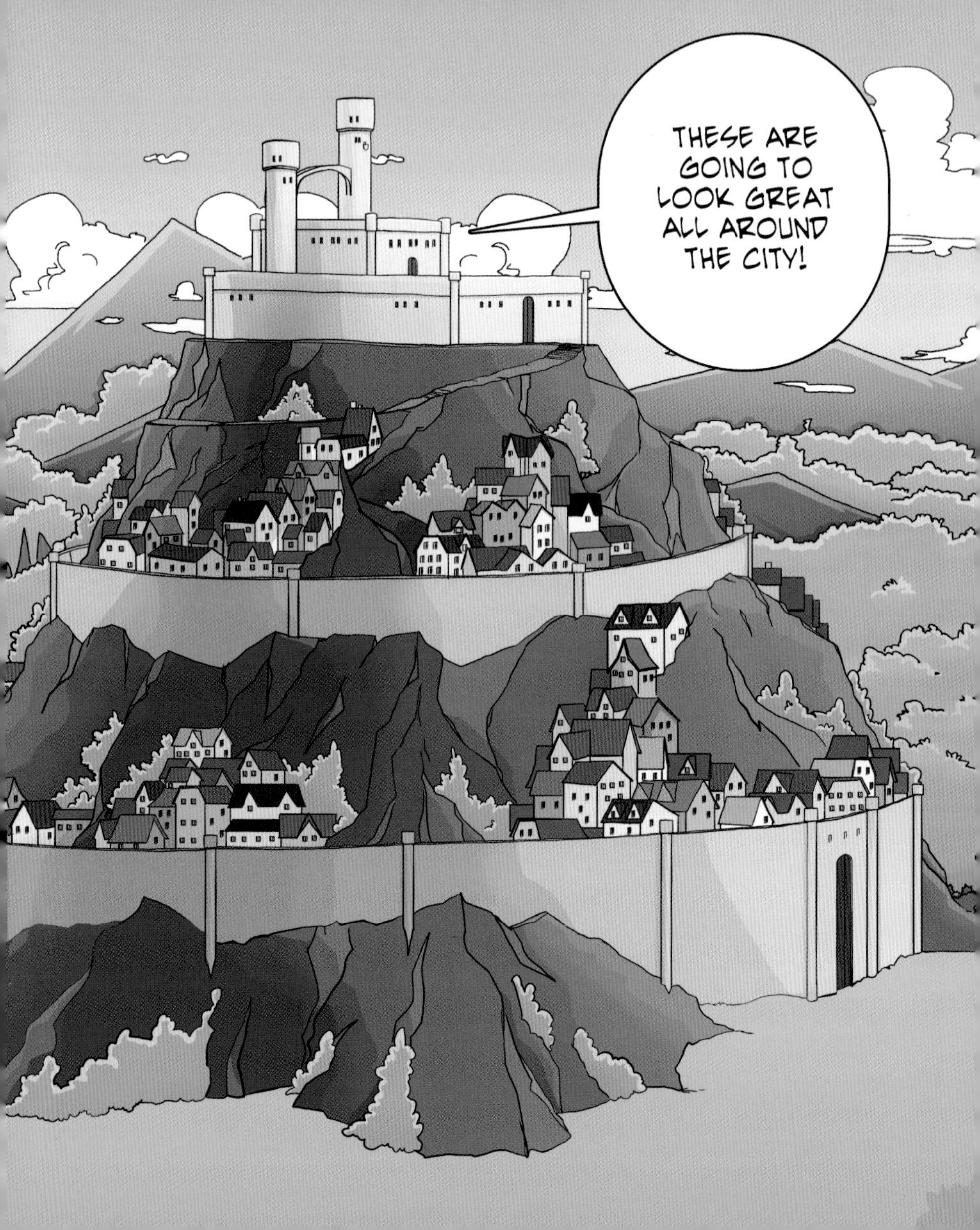
THESE ARE GOING TO LOOK GREAT ALL AROUND THE CITY!

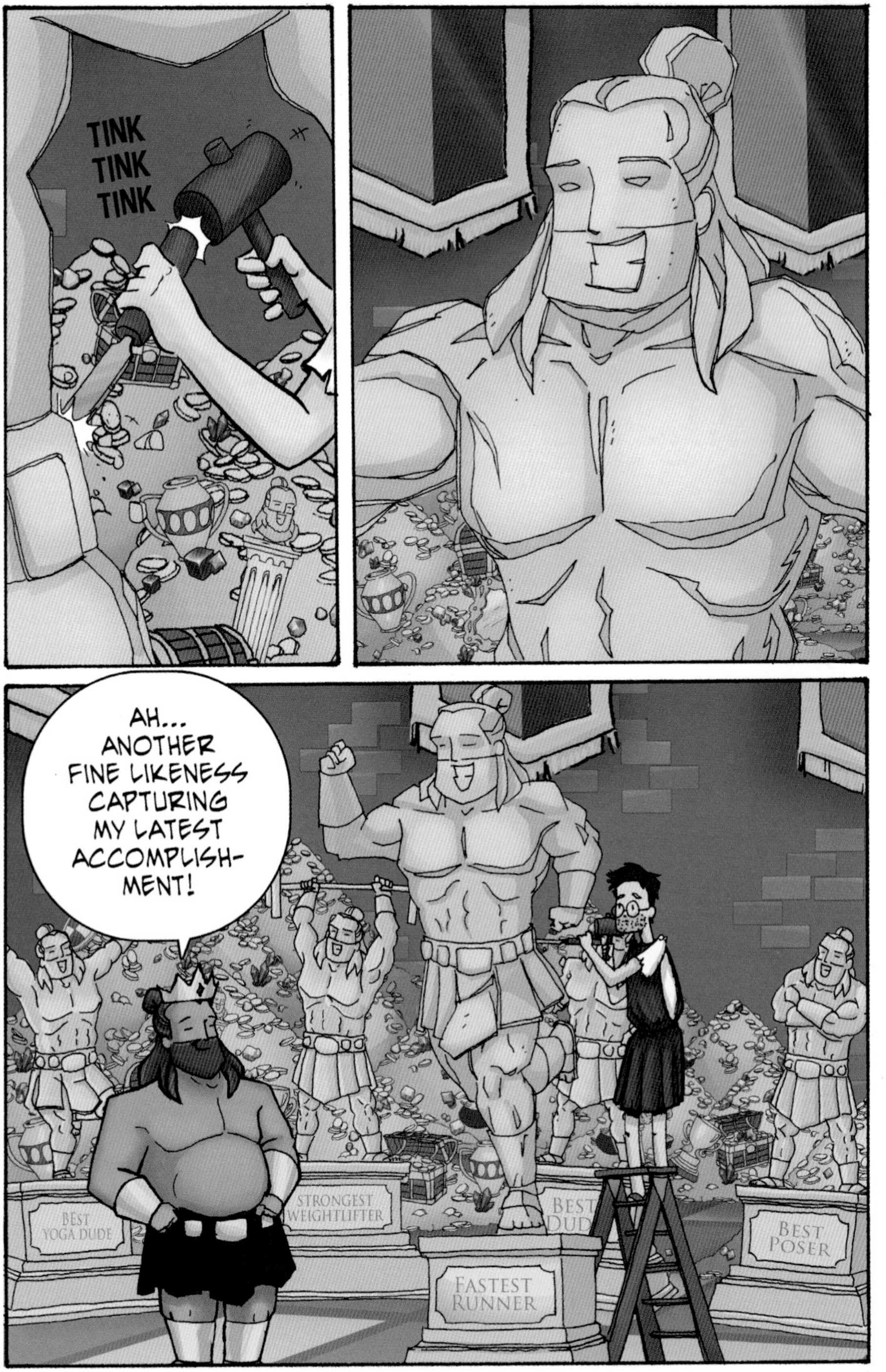
TINK
TINK
TINK
AH... ANOTHER FINE LIKENESS CAPTURING MY LATEST ACCOMPLISH-MENT!
BEST YOGA DUDE
STRONGEST WEIGHTLIFTER
BEST DUD
FASTEST RUNNER
BEST POSER

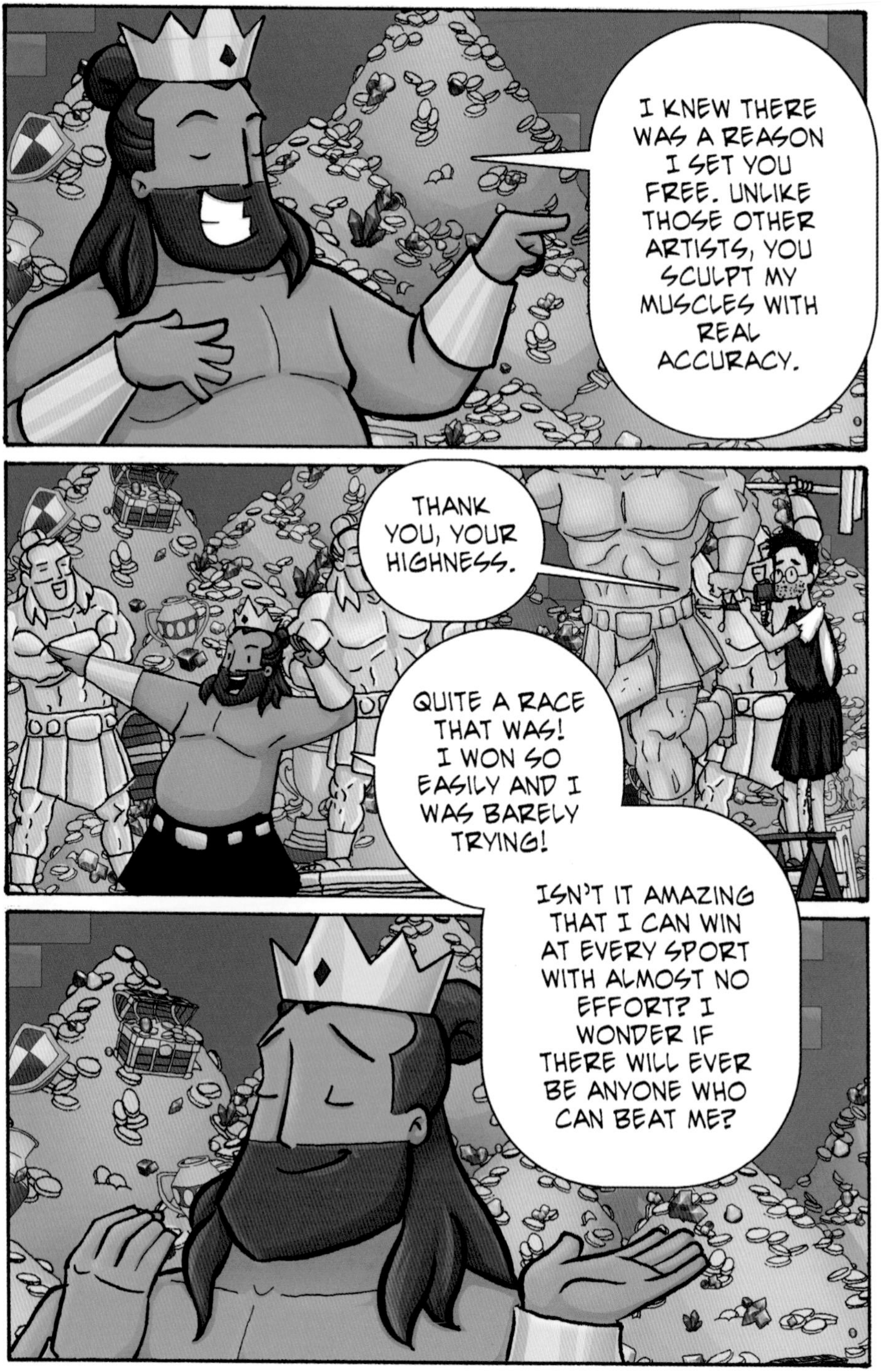
I KNEW THERE WAS A REASON I SET YOU FREE. UNLIKE THOSE OTHER ARTISTS, YOU SCULPT MY MUSCLES WITH REAL ACCURACY.
THANK YOU, YOUR HIGHNESS.
QUITE A RACE THAT WAS! I WON SO EASILY AND I WAS BARELY TRYING!
ISN'T IT AMAZING THAT I CAN WIN AT EVERY SPORT WITH ALMOST NO EFFORT? I WONDER IF THERE WILL EVER BE ANYONE WHO CAN BEAT ME?

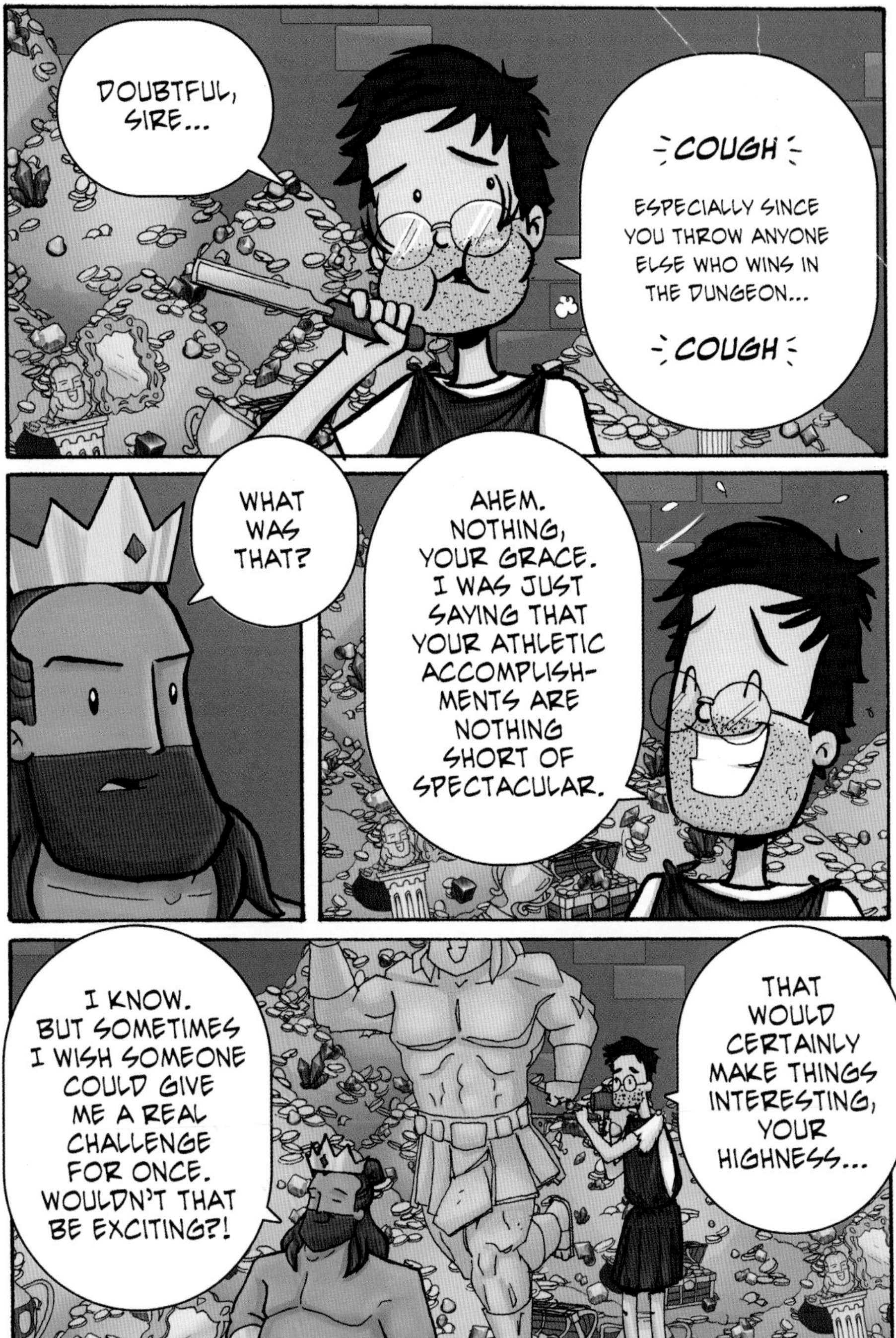
DOUBTFUL, SIRE...
COUGH
ESPECIALLY SINCE YOU THROW ANYONE ELSE WHO WINS IN THE DUNGEON...
COUGH
WHAT WAS THAT?
AHEM. NOTHING, YOUR GRACE. I WAS JUST SAYING THAT YOUR ATHLETIC ACCOMPLISH-MENTS ARE NOTHING SHORT OF SPECTACULAR.
I KNOW. BUT SOMETIMES I WISH SOMEONE COULD GIVE ME A REAL CHALLENGE FOR ONCE. WOULDN'T THAT BE EXCITING?!
THAT WOULD CERTAINLY MAKE THINGS INTERESTING, YOUR HIGHNESS...

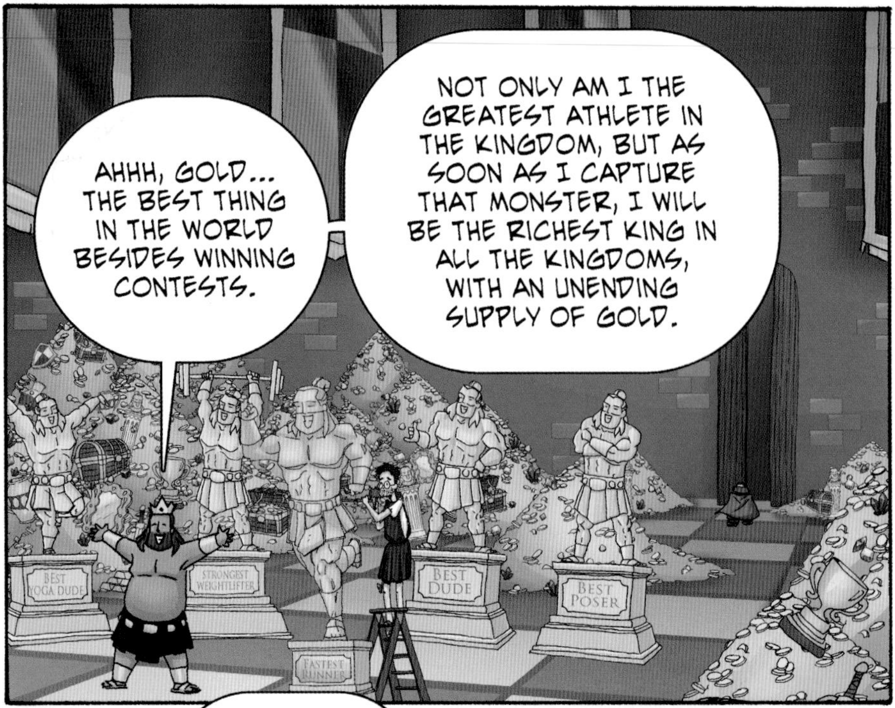
AHHH, GOLD... THE BEST THING IN THE WORLD BESIDES WINNING CONTESTS.
NOT ONLY AM I THE GREATEST ATHLETE IN THE KINGDOM, BUT AS SOON AS I CAPTURE THAT MONSTER, I WILL BE THE RICHEST KING IN ALL THE KINGDOMS, WITH AN UNENDING SUPPLY OF GOLD.
BEST YOGA DUDE
STRONGEST WEIGHTLIFTER
BEST DUDE
BEST POSER
FASTEST RUNNER

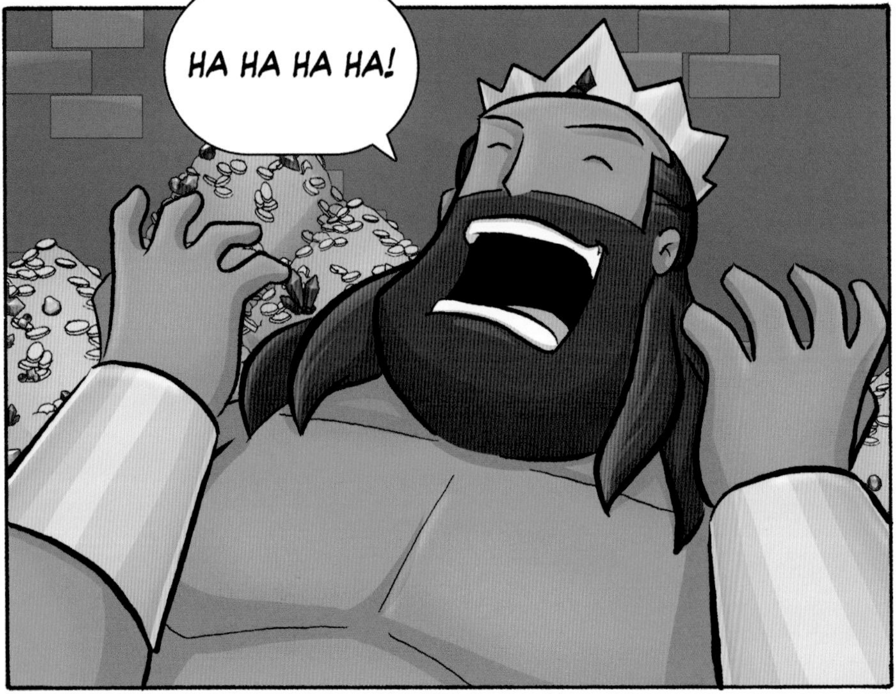
HA HA HA HA!

82

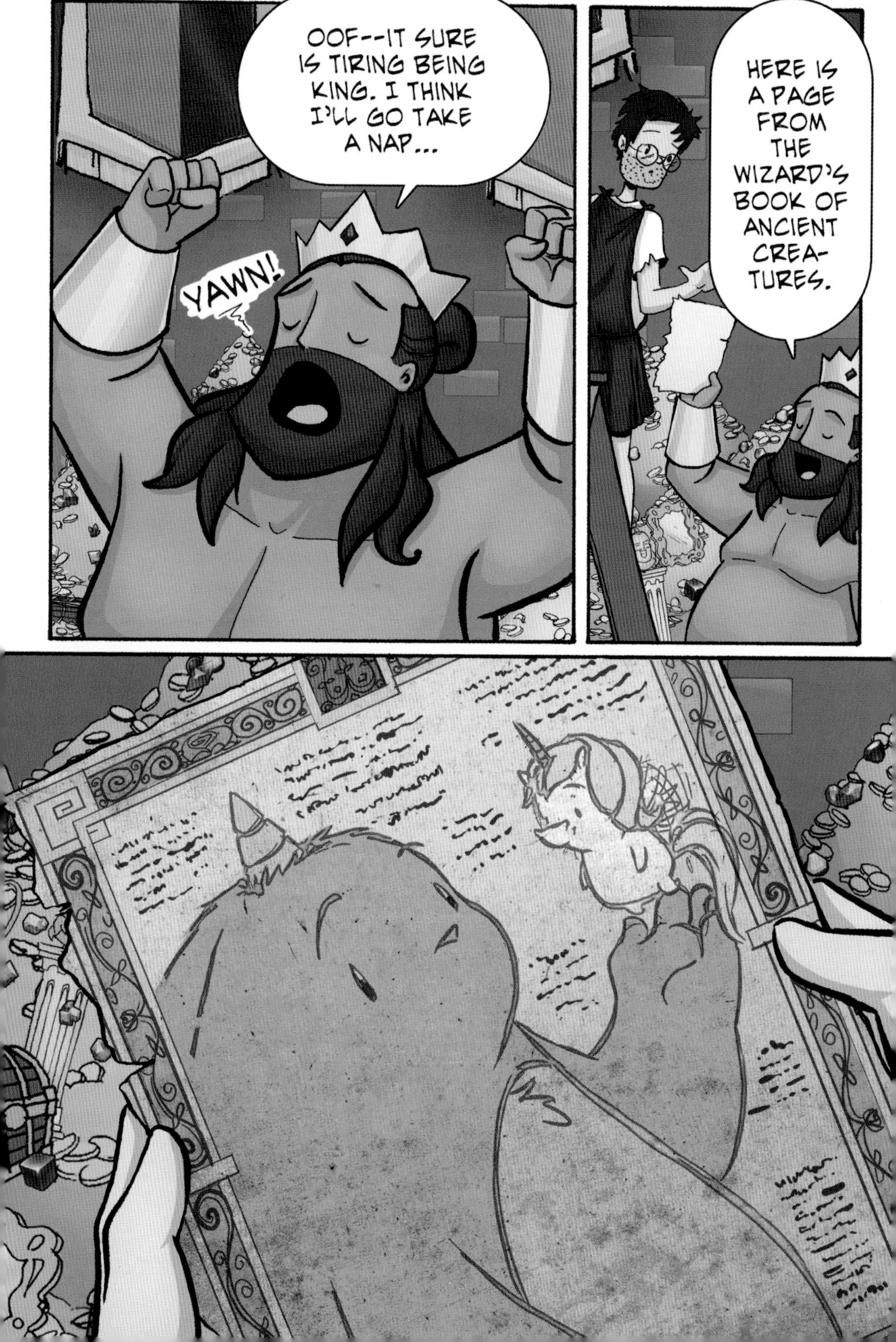
OOF--IT SURE IS TIRING BEING KING. I THINK I'LL GO TAKE A NAP...
YAWN!
HERE IS A PAGE FROM THE WIZARD'S BOOK OF ANCIENT CREA-TURES.

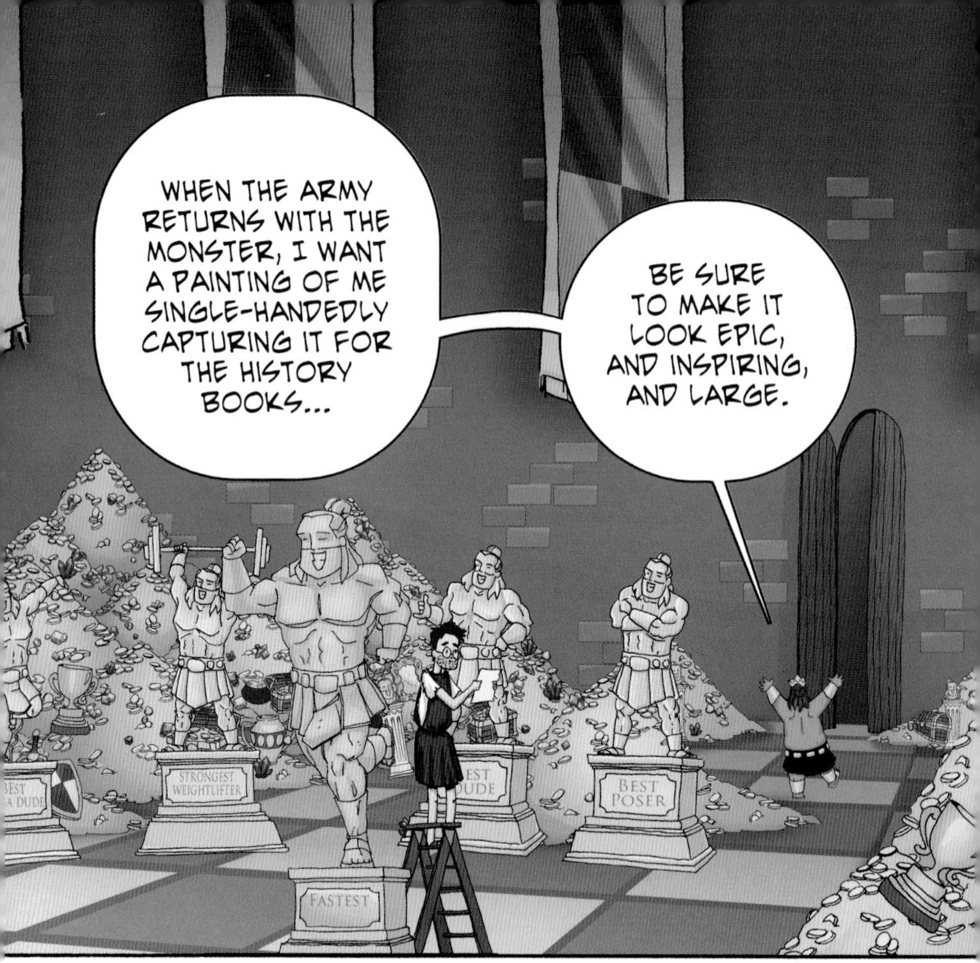
WHEN THE ARMY RETURNS WITH THE MONSTER, I WANT A PAINTING OF ME SINGLE-HANDEDLY CAPTURING IT FOR THE HISTORY BOOKS...
BE SURE TO MAKE IT LOOK EPIC, AND INSPIRING, AND LARGE.
STRONGEST WEIGHTLIFTER
BEST POSER
FASTEST

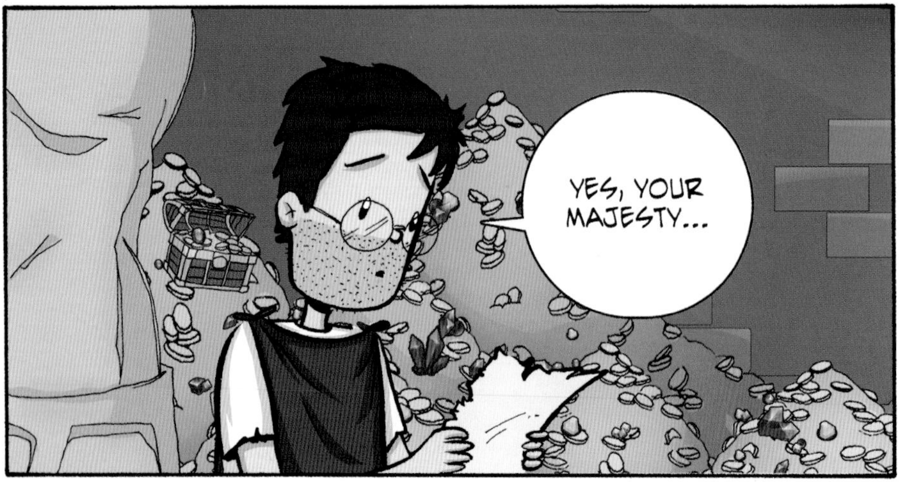
YES, YOUR MAJESTY...

CHAPTER 5
THE GOOD PEOPLE

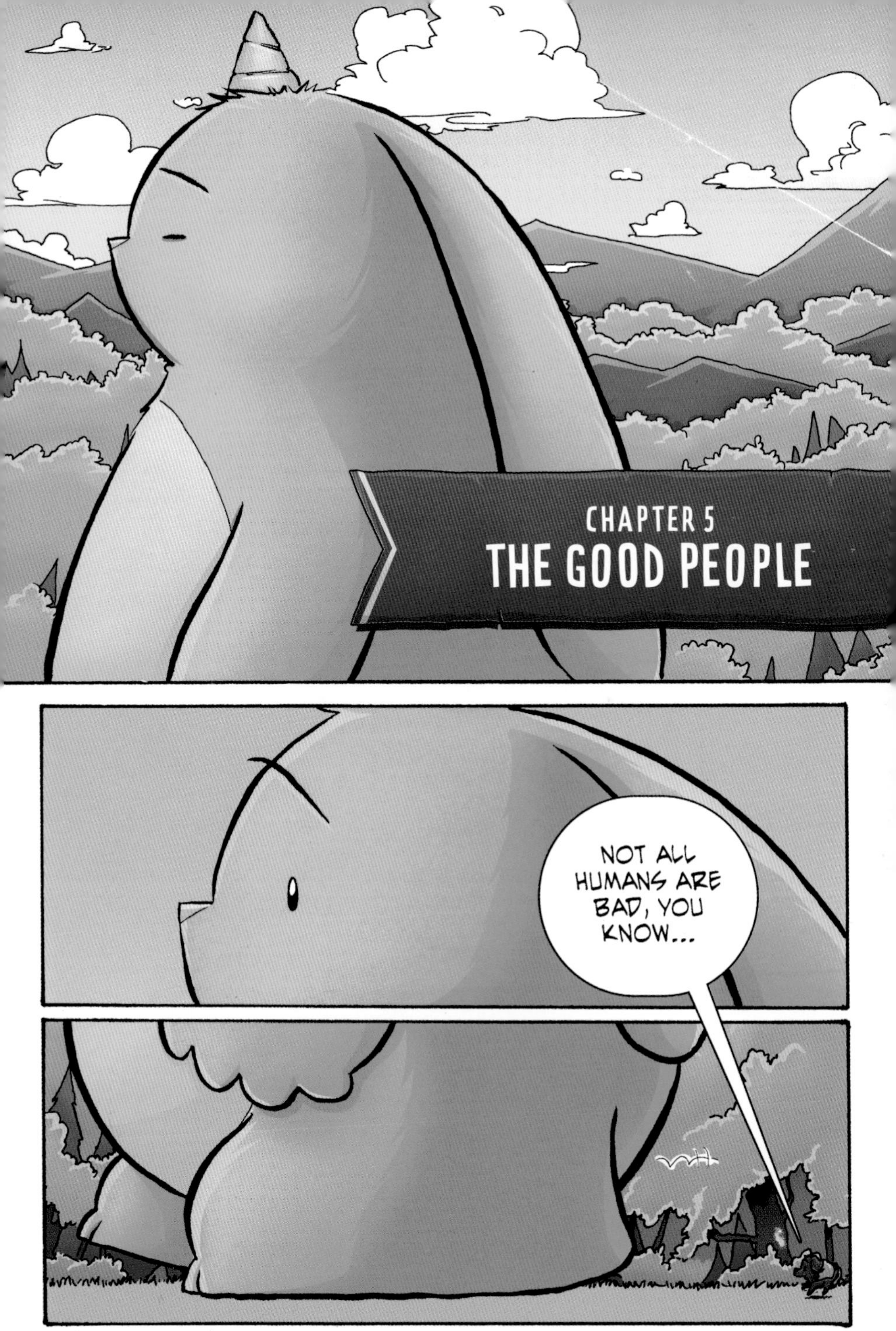
NOT ALL HUMANS ARE BAD, YOU KNOW...

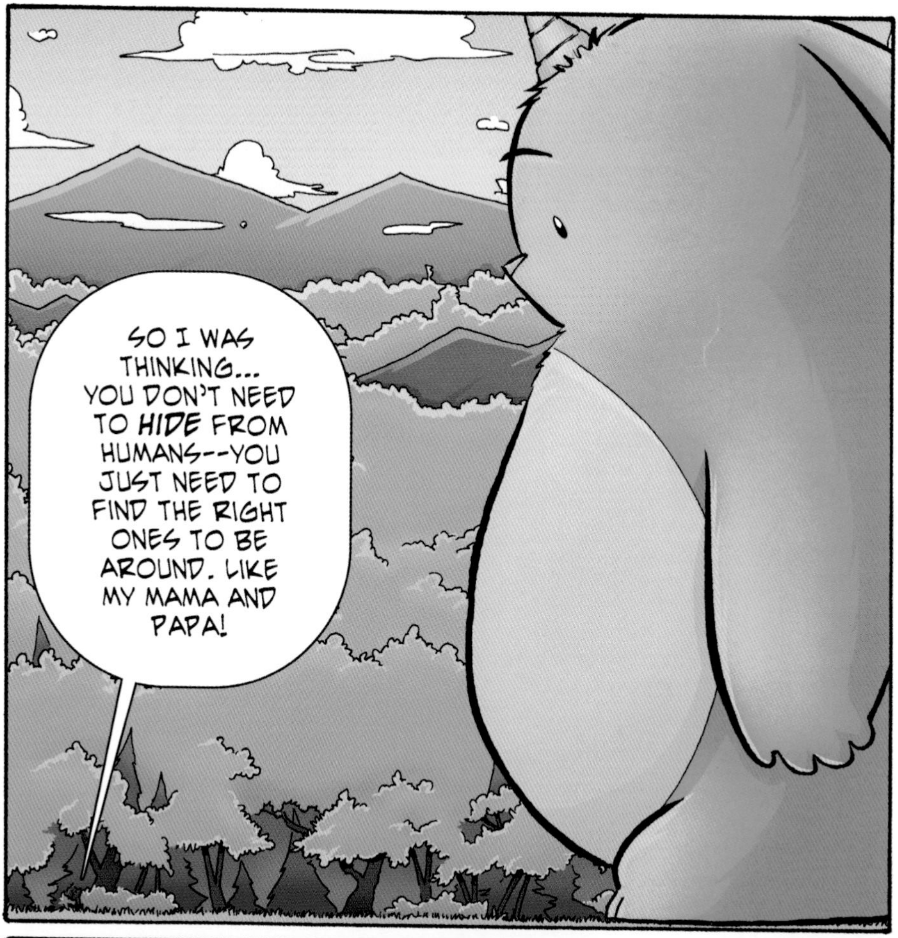
SO I WAS THINKING... YOU DON'T NEED TO *HIDE* FROM HUMANS--YOU JUST NEED TO FIND THE RIGHT ONES TO BE AROUND. LIKE MY MAMA AND PAPA!

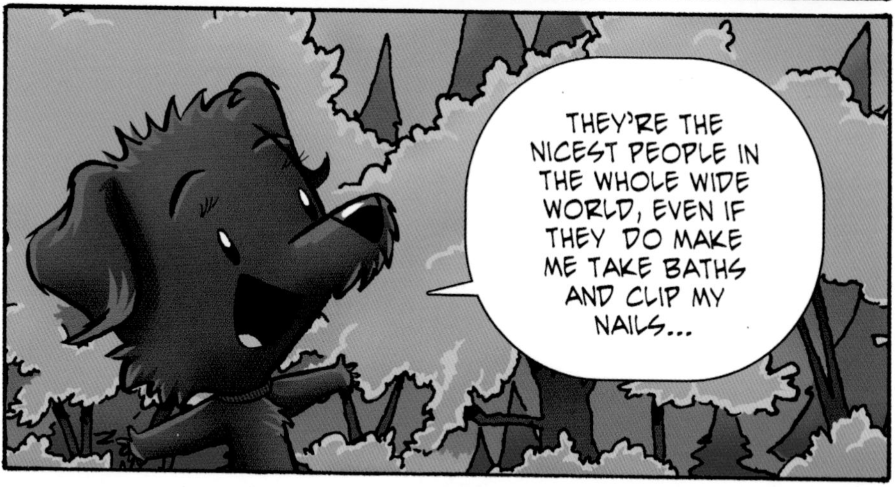
THEY'RE THE NICEST PEOPLE IN THE WHOLE WIDE WORLD, EVEN IF THEY DO MAKE ME TAKE BATHS AND CLIP MY NAILS...

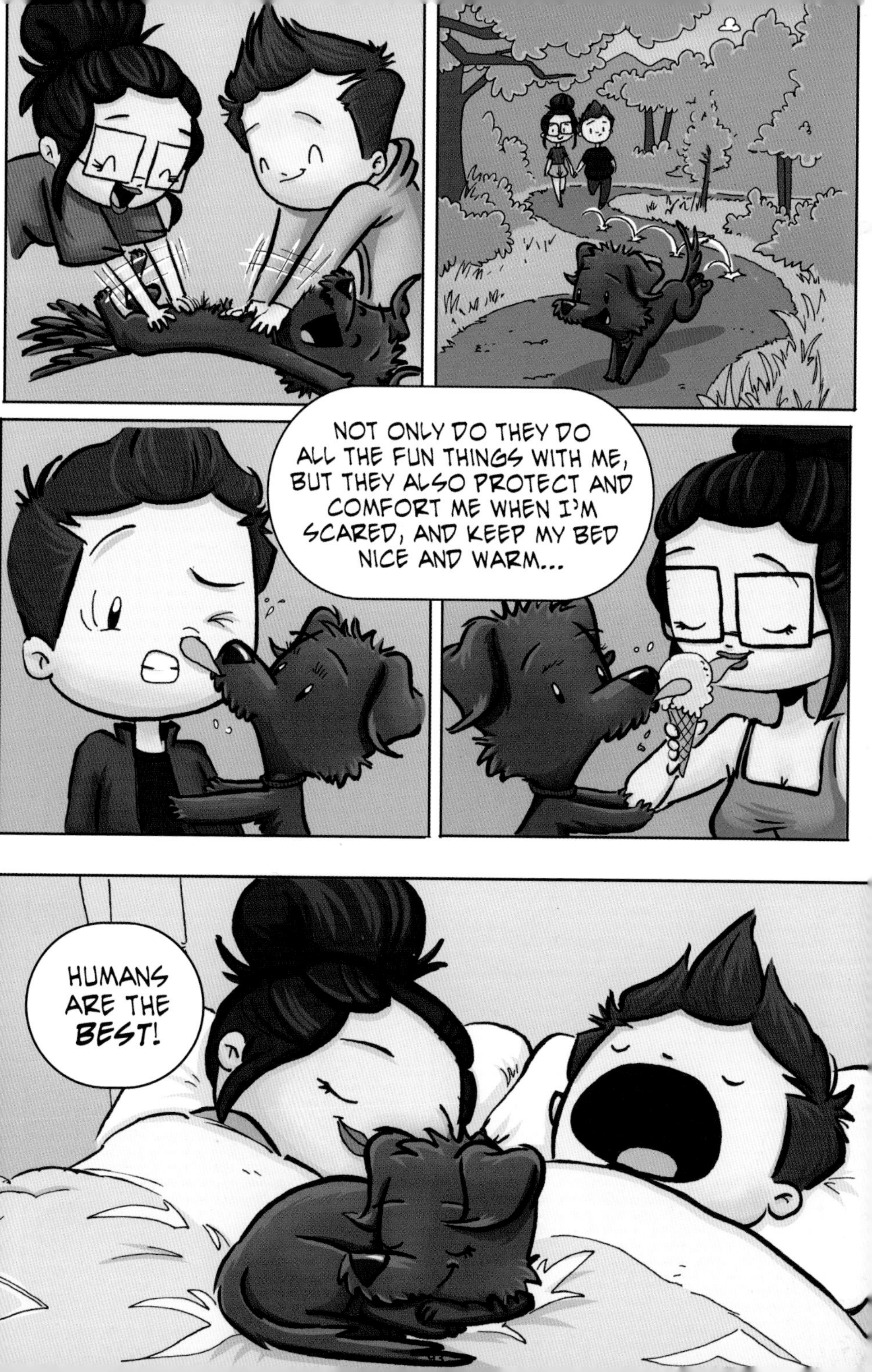
NOT ONLY DO THEY DO ALL THE FUN THINGS WITH ME, BUT THEY ALSO PROTECT AND COMFORT ME WHEN I'M SCARED, AND KEEP MY BED NICE AND WARM...
HUMANS ARE THE BEST!

EVEN STRANGERS ON THE STREET ARE NICE AND STOP TO GIVE ME PETS AND BELLY RUBS!

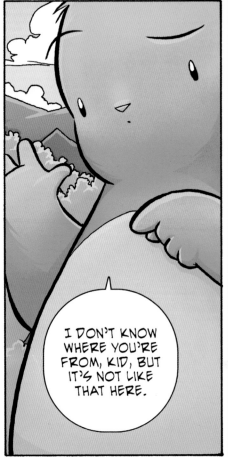

I DON'T KNOW WHERE YOU'RE FROM, KID, BUT IT'S NOT LIKE THAT HERE.

HEY, WHY DON'T YOU COME TO MY HOUSE? IF YOU HELP ME FIND IT, WE CAN HAVE A SLEEPOVER! WE DON'T HAVE ANY SOLDIERS OR WIZARDS, SO YOU WON'T BE BOTHERED ANYMORE. YOU CAN SLEEP ALL YOU WANT, JUST LIKE THE CATS!

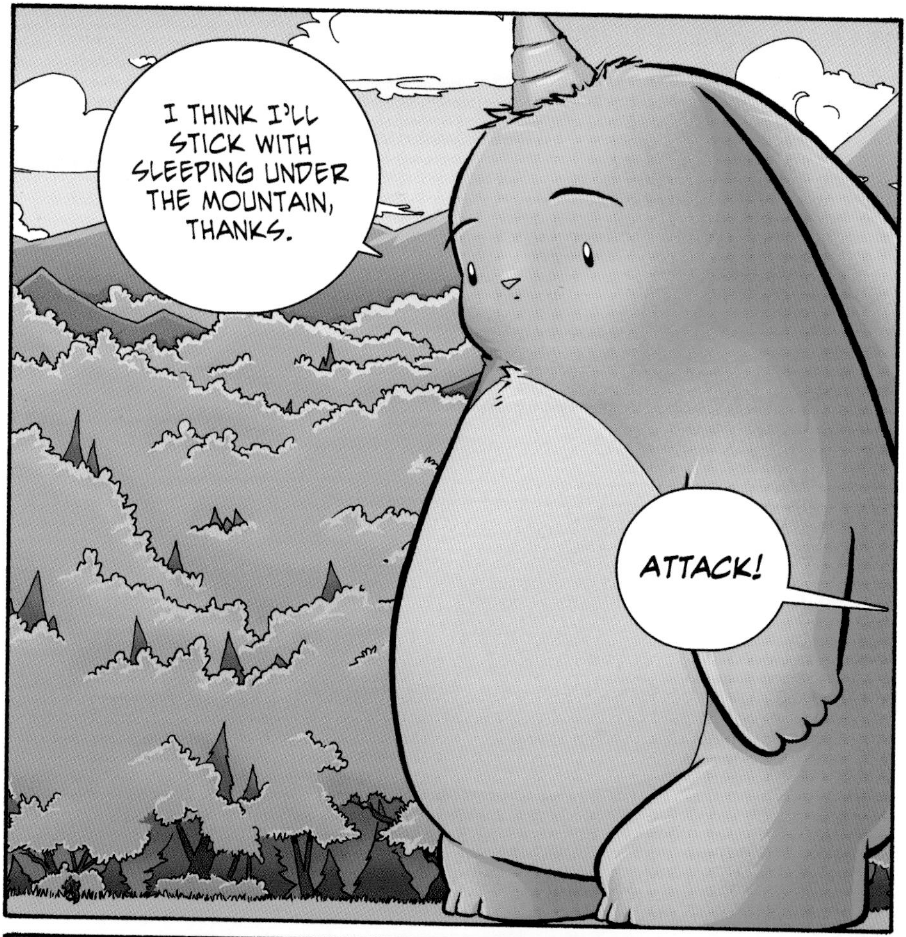
I THINK I'LL STICK WITH SLEEPING UNDER THE MOUNTAIN, THANKS.
ATTACK!

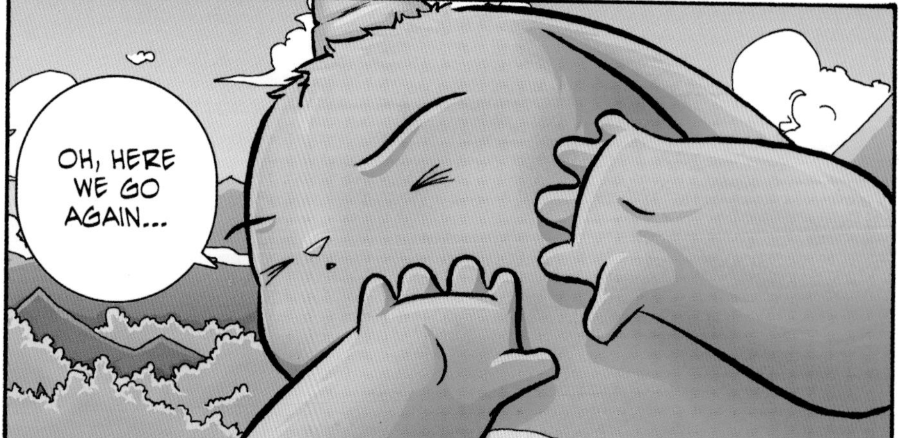
OH, HERE WE GO AGAIN...

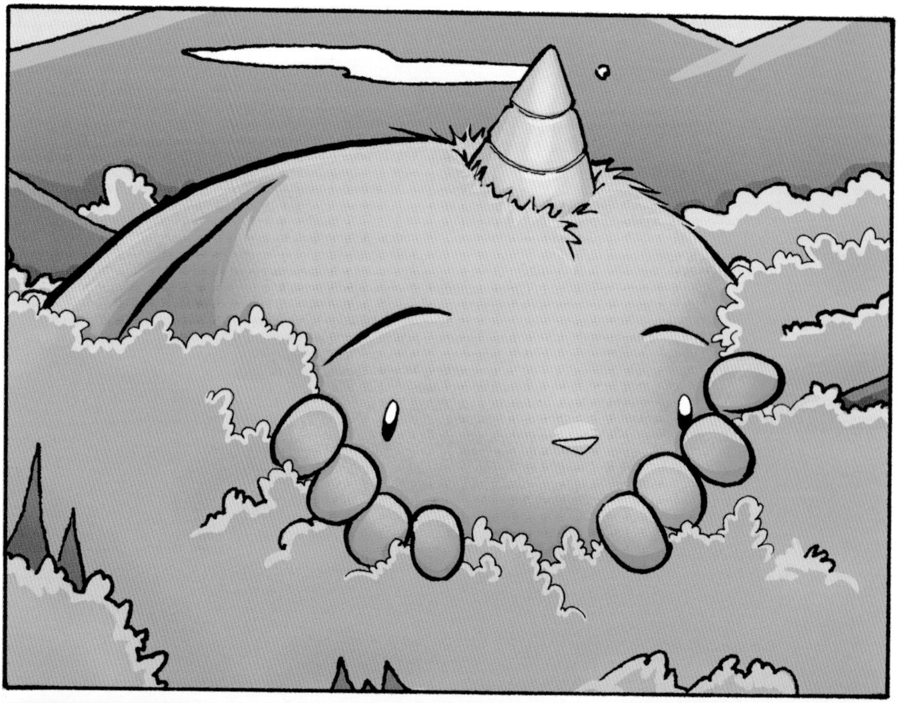

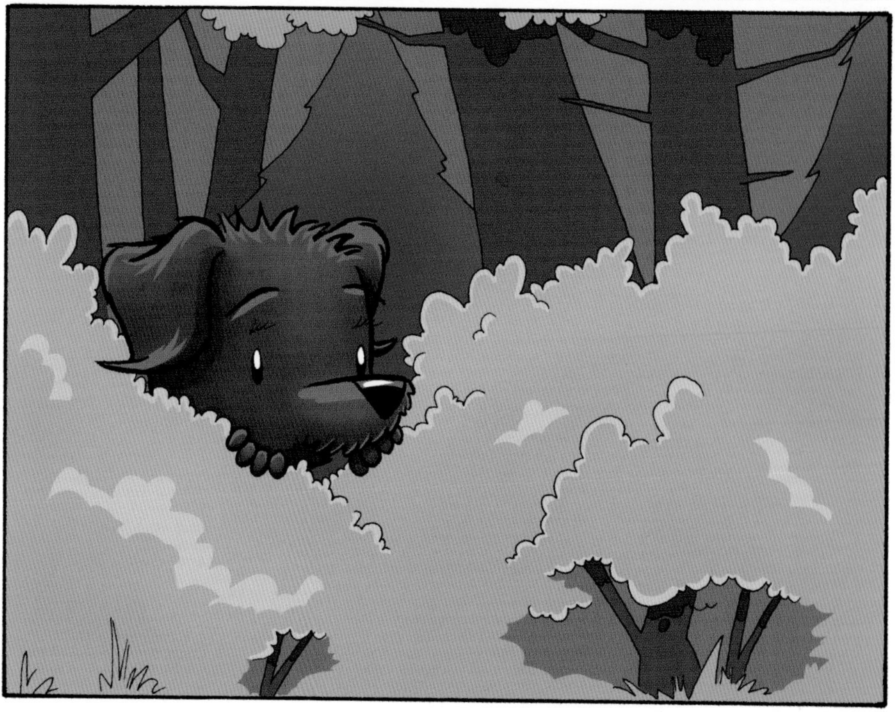

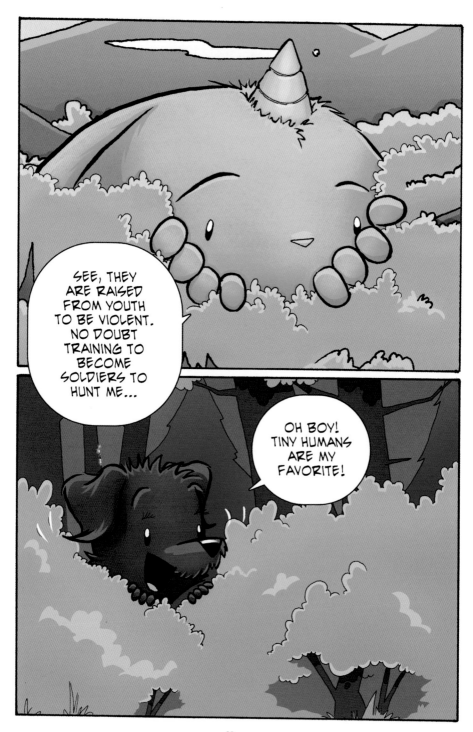

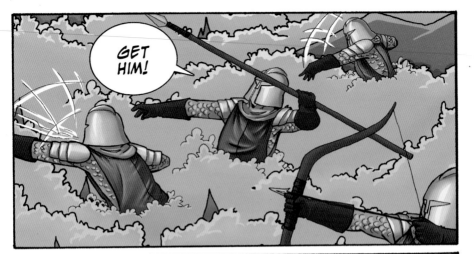

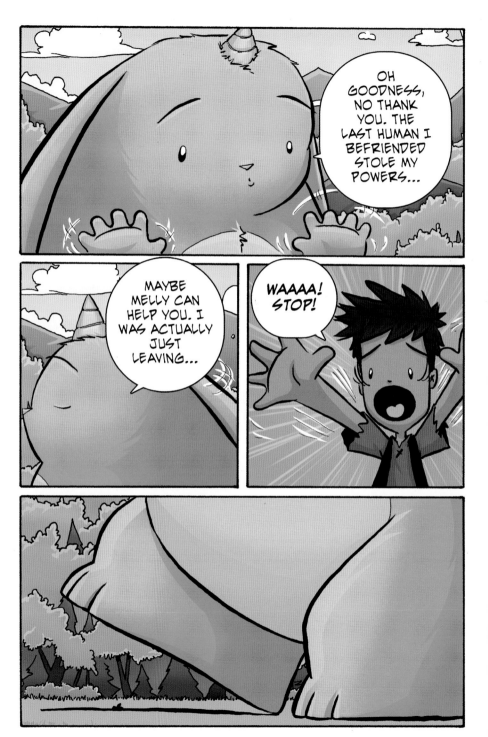

105

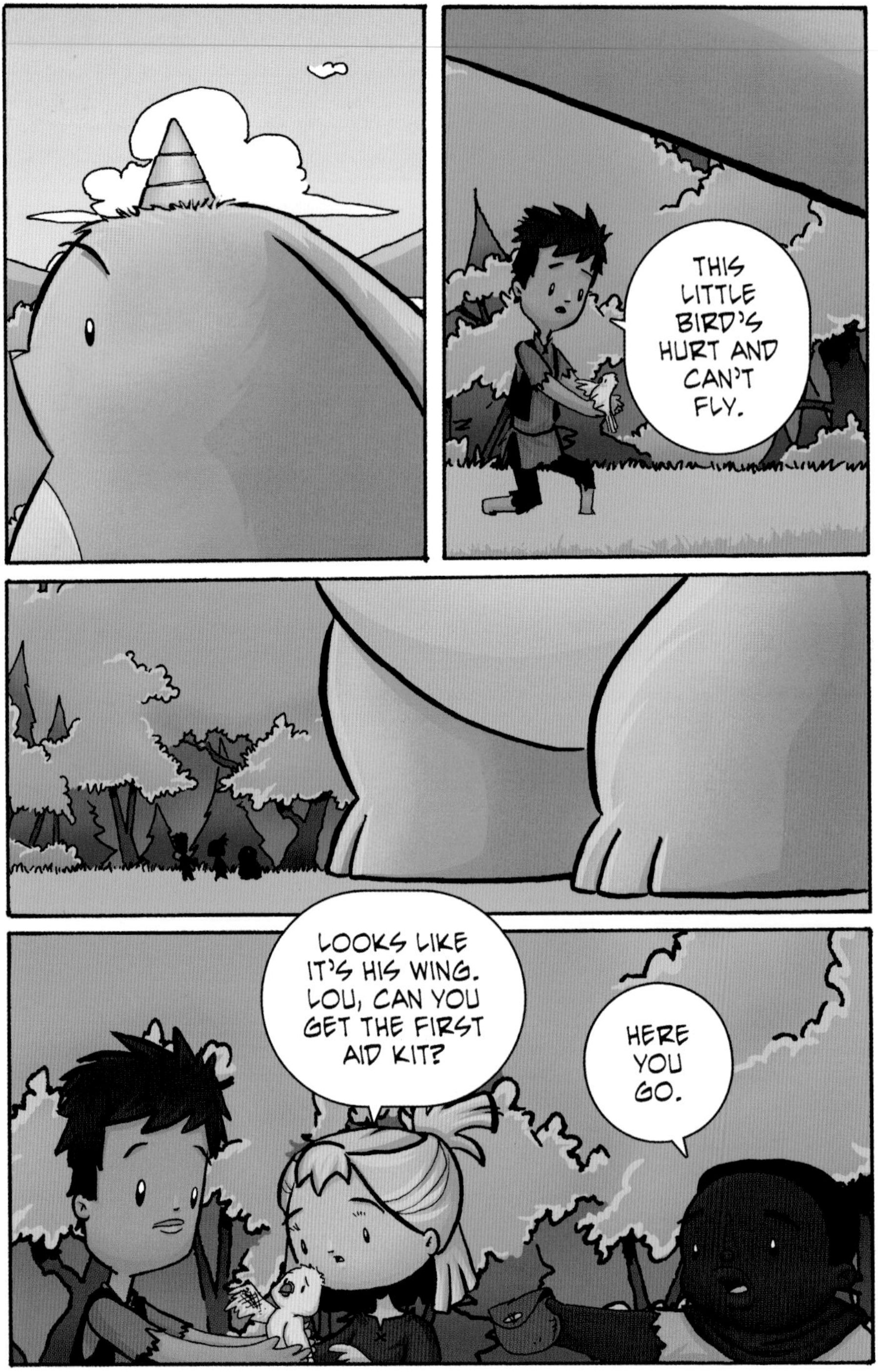
THIS LITTLE BIRD'S HURT AND CAN'T FLY.
LOOKS LIKE IT'S HIS WING. LOU, CAN YOU GET THE FIRST AID KIT?
HERE YOU GO.

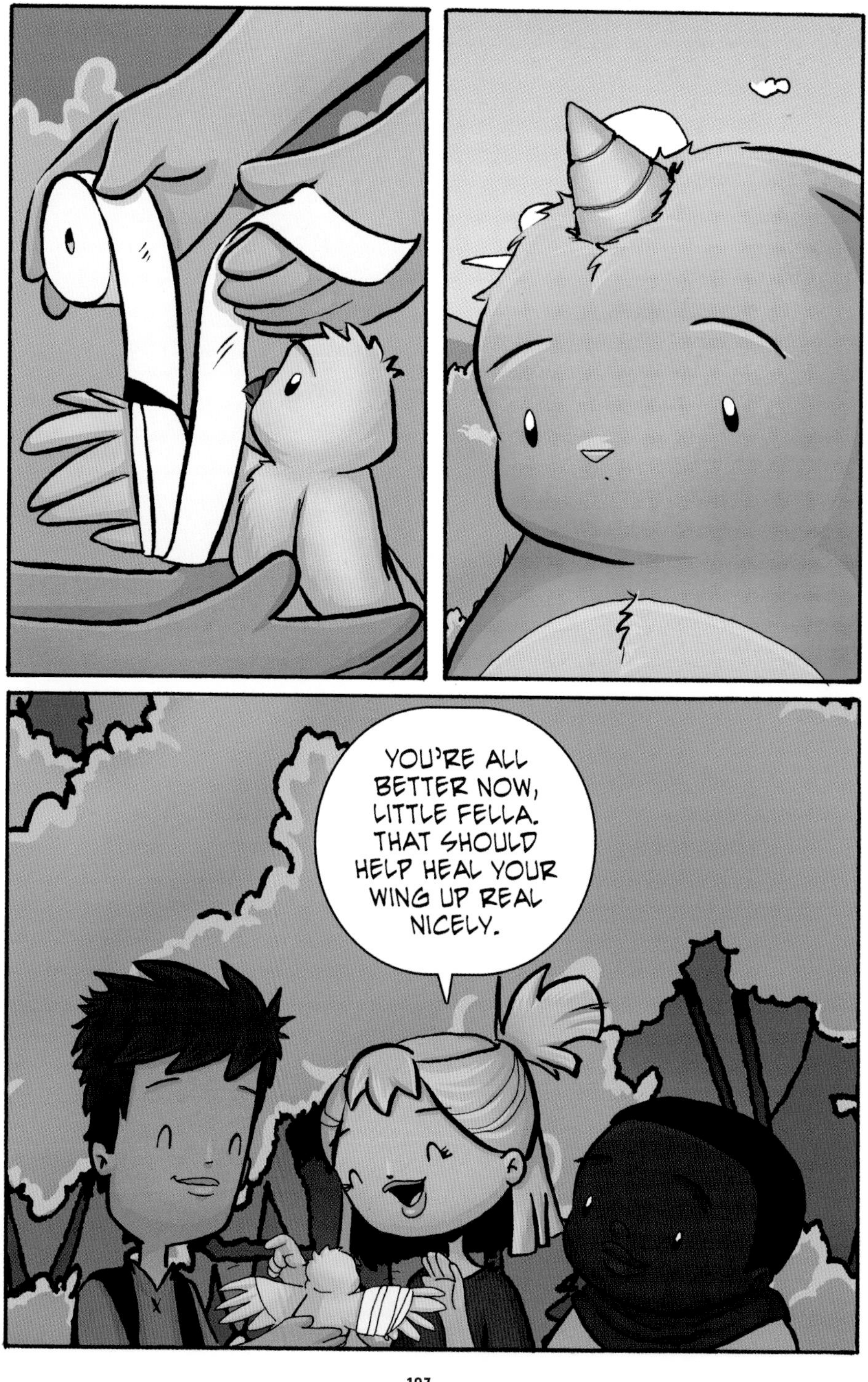
YOU'RE ALL BETTER NOW, LITTLE FELLA. THAT SHOULD HELP HEAL YOUR WING UP REAL NICELY.

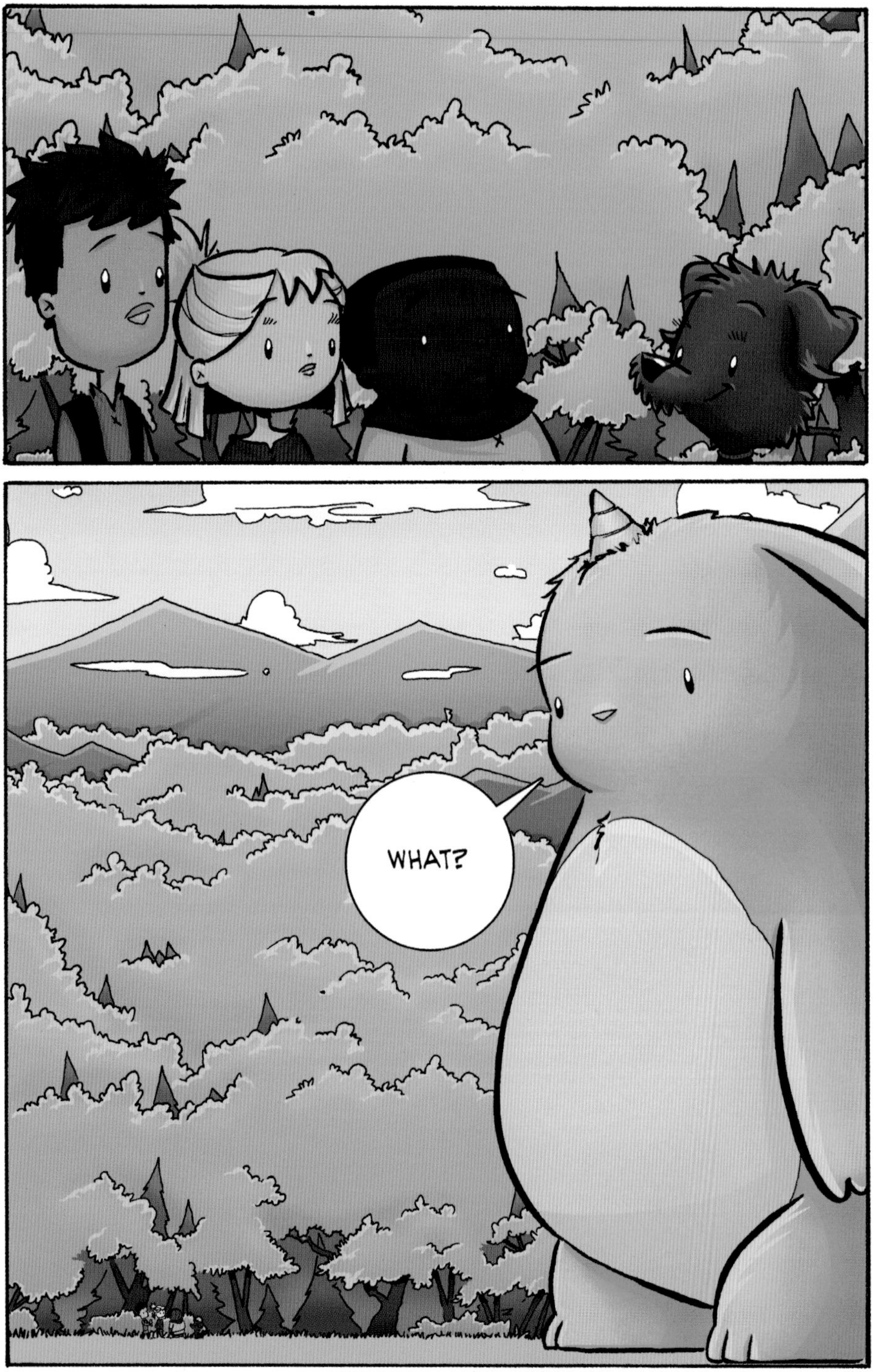
WHAT?

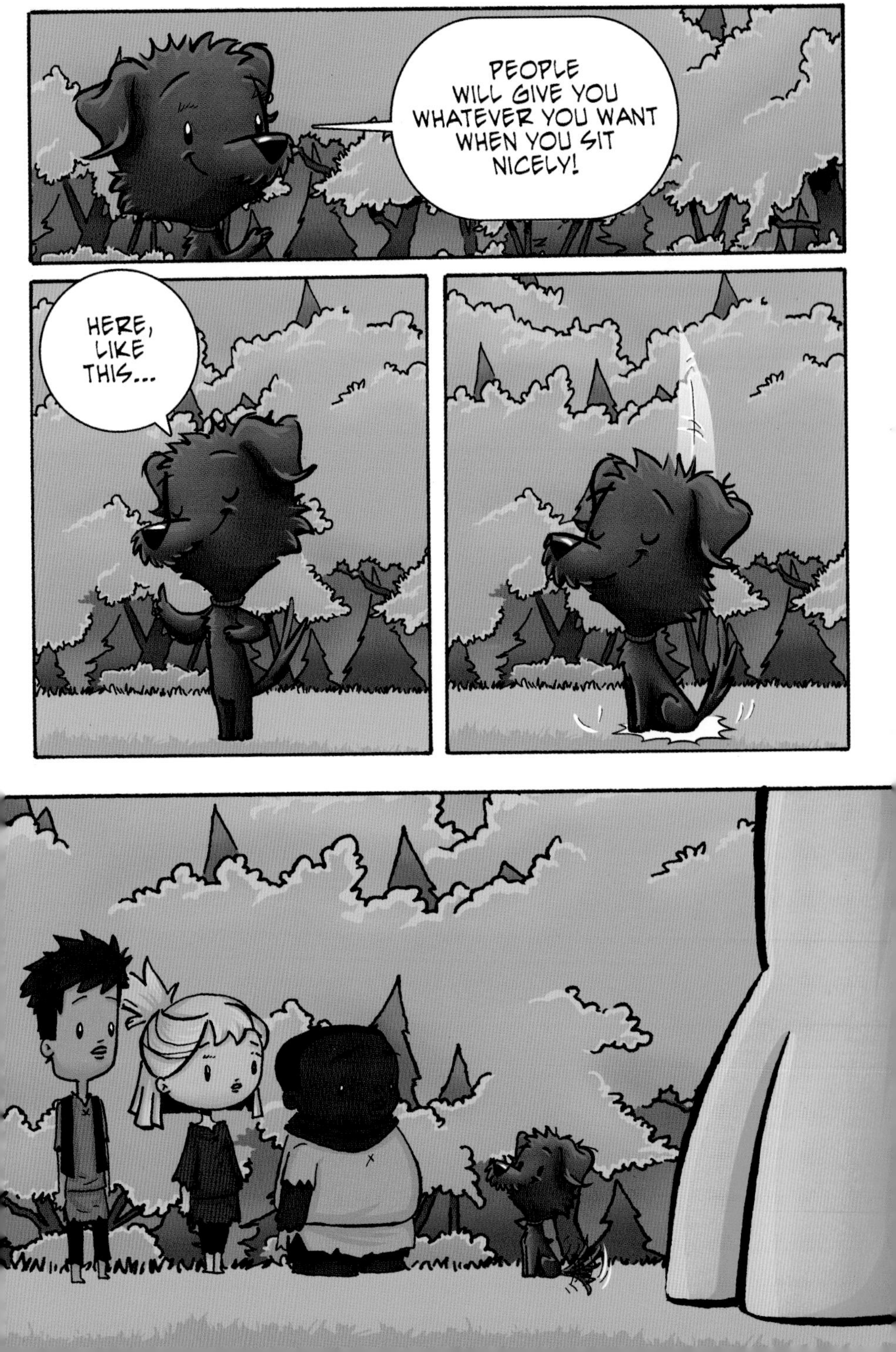
PEOPLE WILL GIVE YOU WHATEVER YOU WANT WHEN YOU SIT NICELY!
HERE, LIKE THIS...

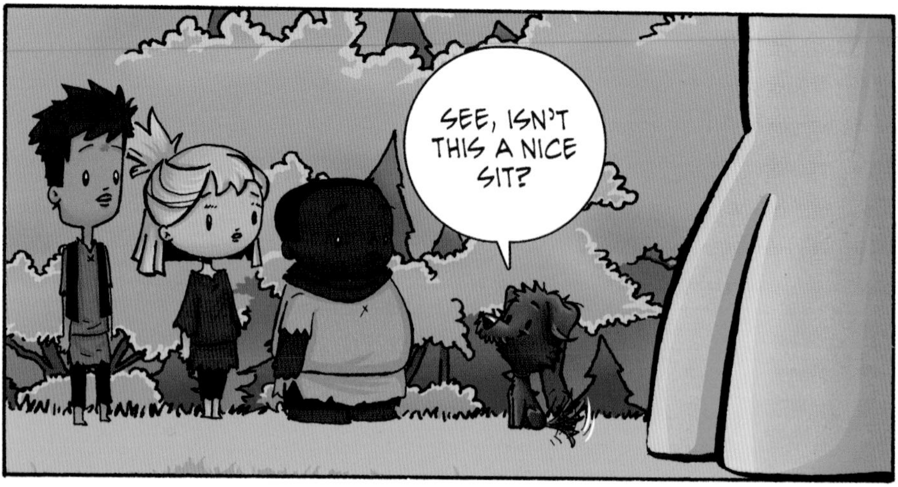
SEE, ISN'T THIS A NICE SIT?

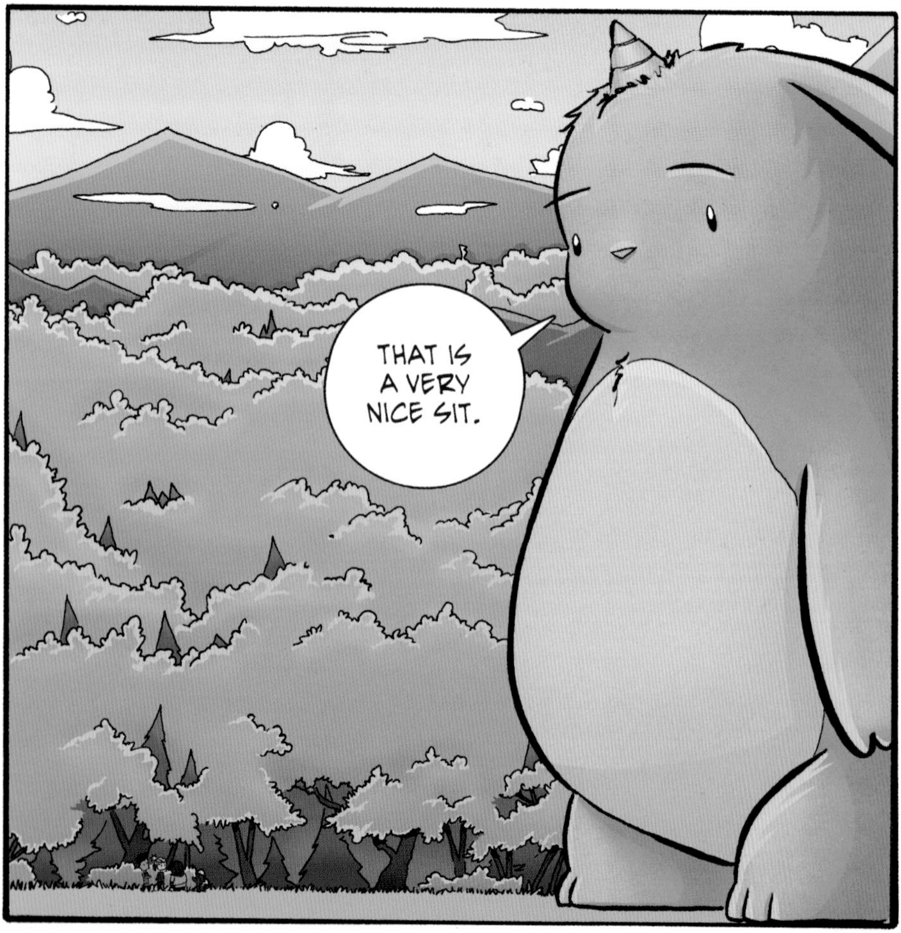
THAT IS A VERY NICE SIT.

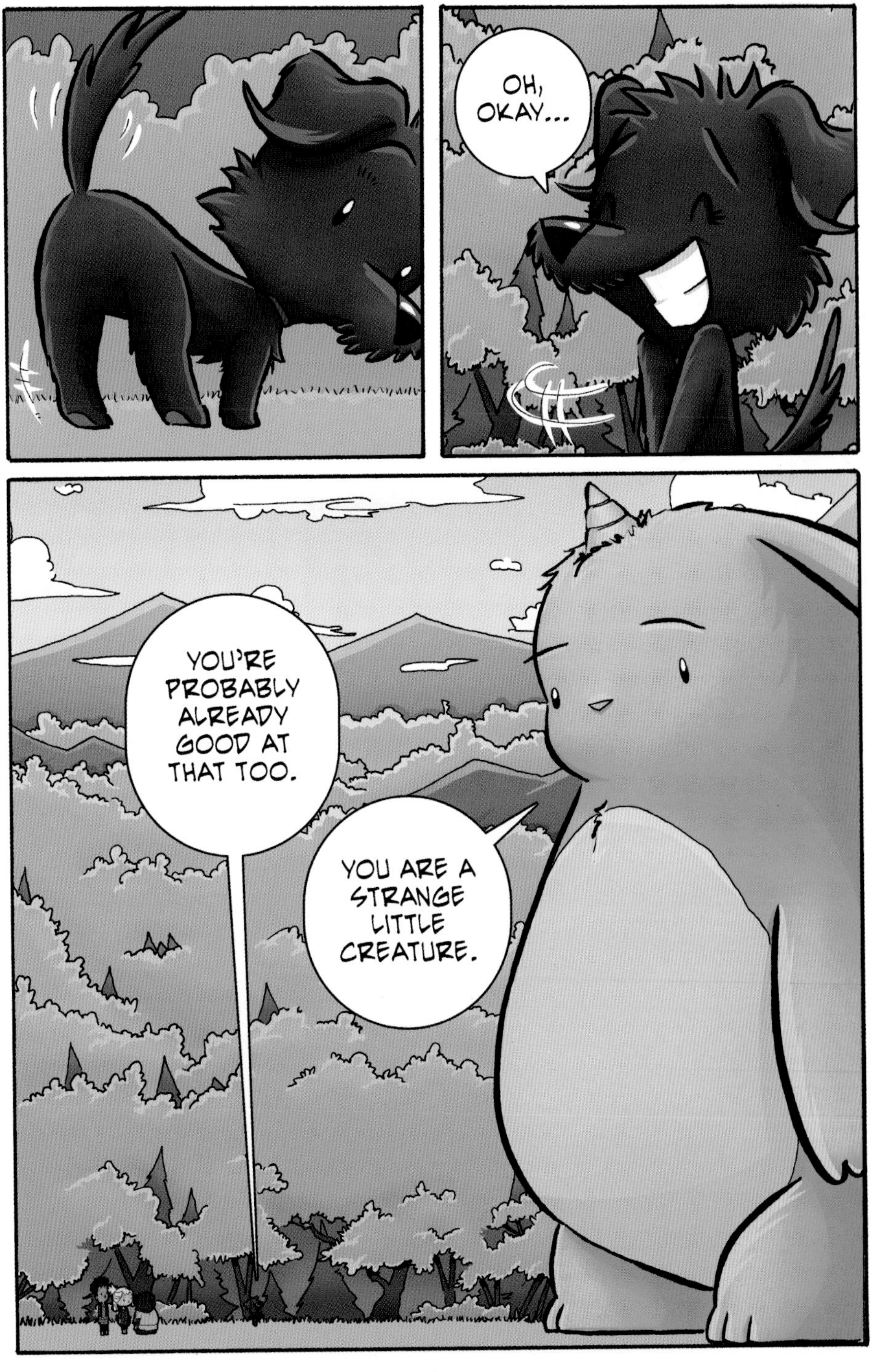
OH, OKAY...
YOU'RE PROBABLY ALREADY GOOD AT THAT TOO.
YOU ARE A STRANGE LITTLE CREATURE.

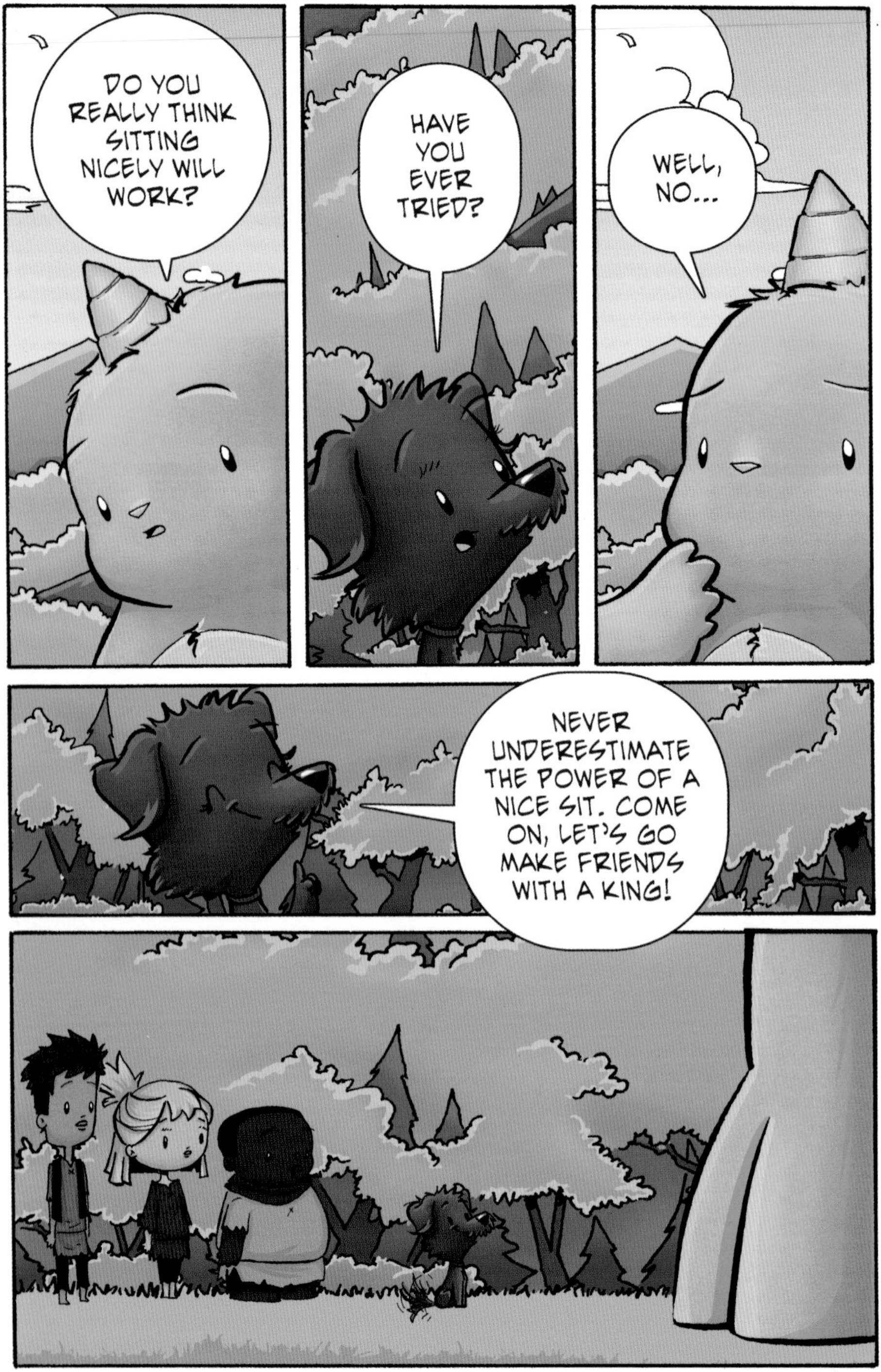
DO YOU REALLY THINK SITTING NICELY WILL WORK?
HAVE YOU EVER TRIED?
WELL, NO...
NEVER UNDERESTIMATE THE POWER OF A NICE SIT. COME ON, LET'S GO MAKE FRIENDS WITH A KING!

MELLY MUST HAVE DUG HER WAY OUT OF THE YARD!

THIS HOLE IS PRETTY DEEP... I CAN'T EVEN SEE THE BOTTOM.

HEY, GUYS, I'VE GOT AN IDEA...

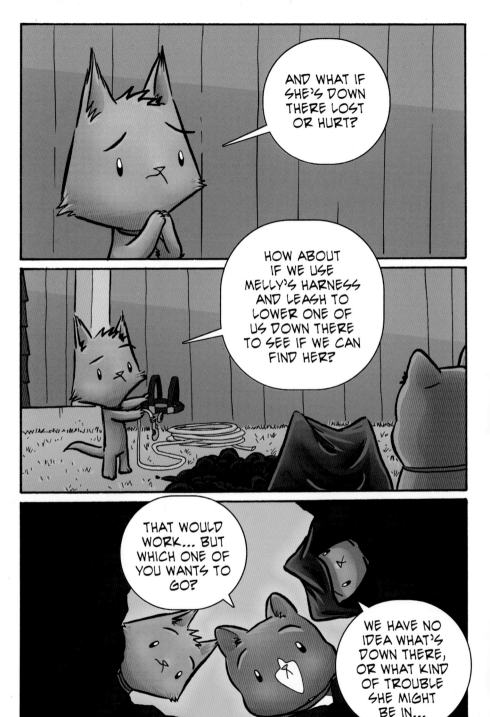

125

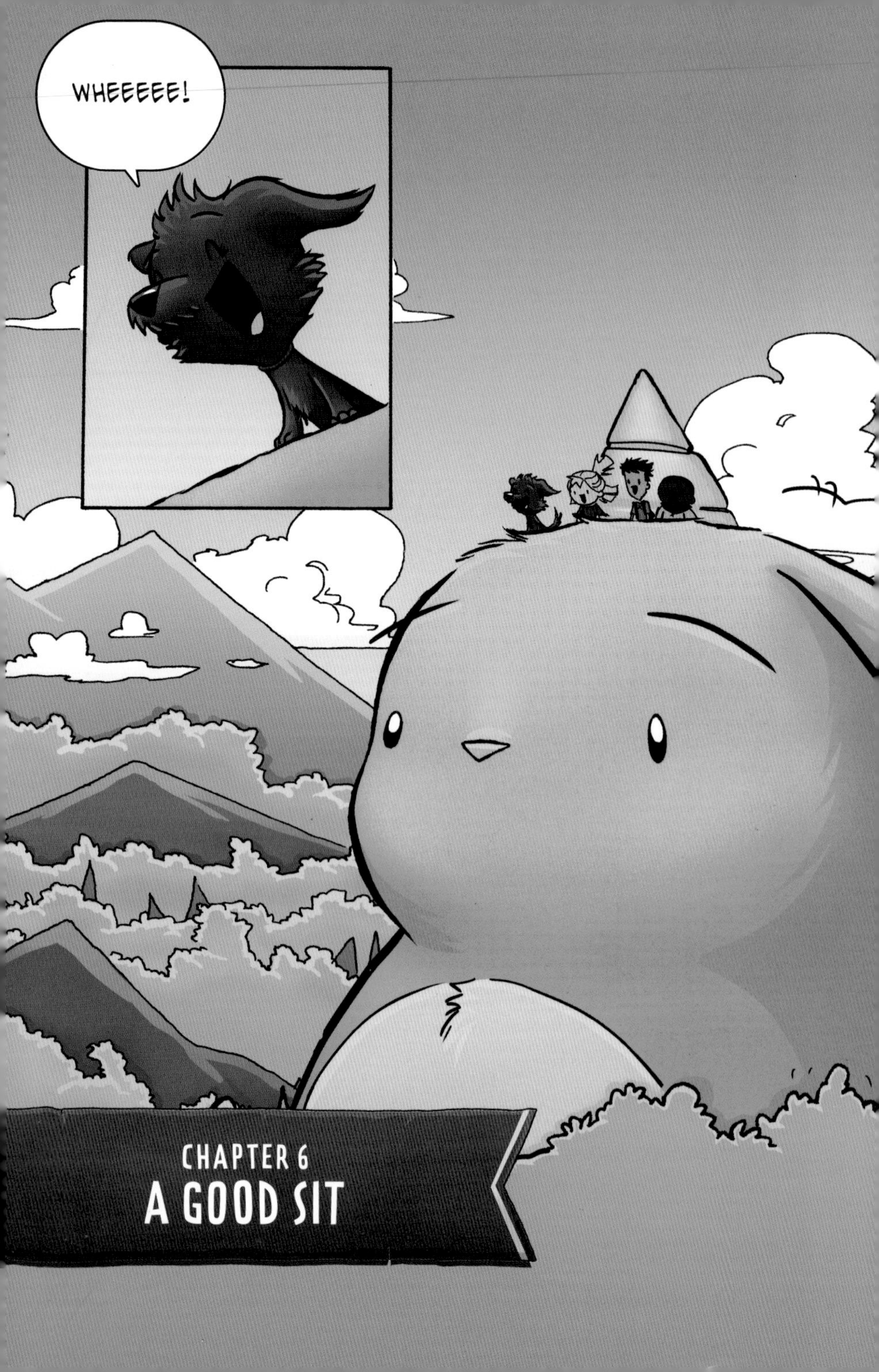
WHEEEEEE!
CHAPTER 6
A GOOD SIT

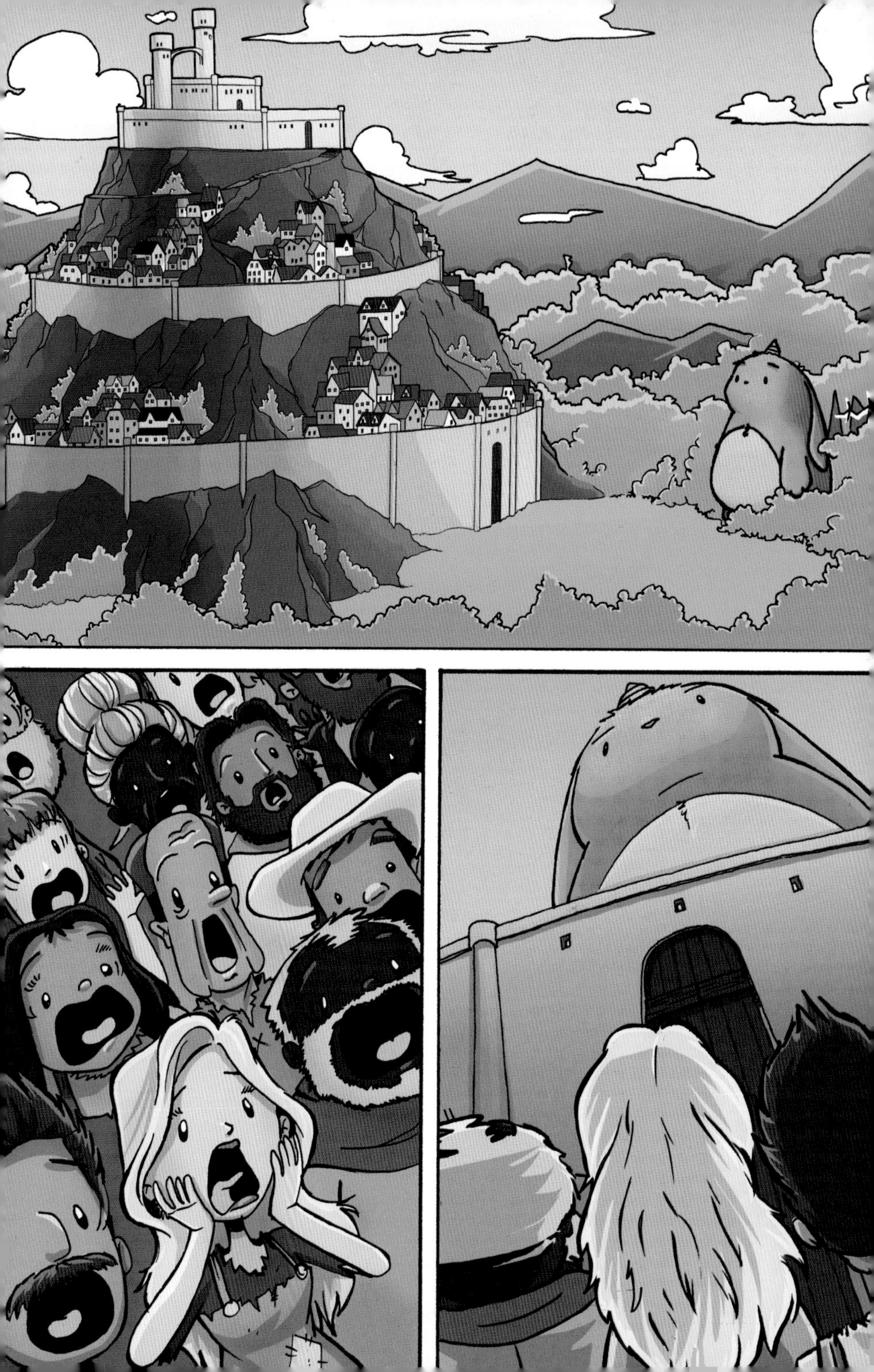

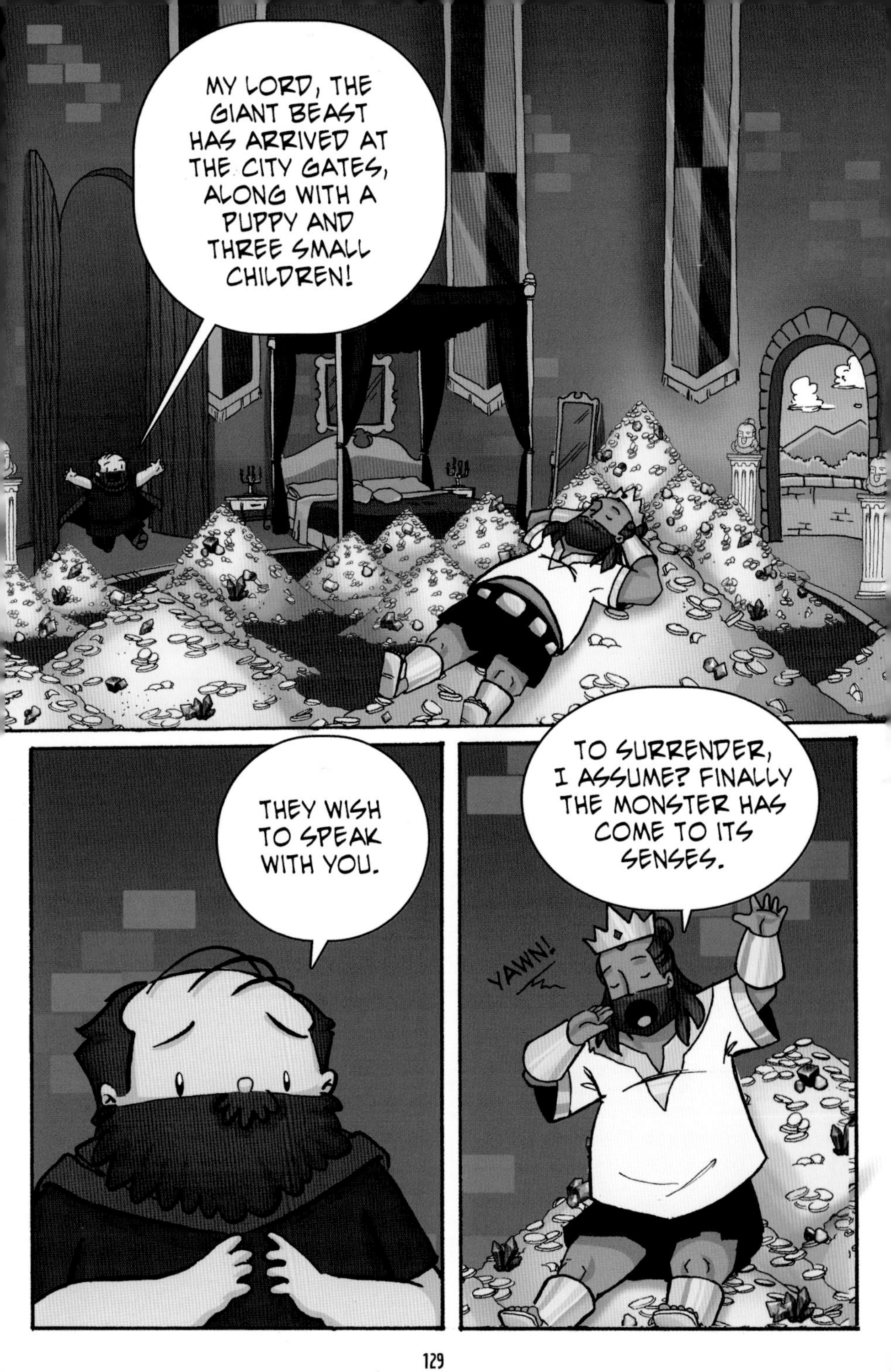
MY LORD, THE GIANT BEAST HAS ARRIVED AT THE CITY GATES, ALONG WITH A PUPPY AND THREE SMALL CHILDREN!
THEY WISH TO SPEAK WITH YOU.
TO SURRENDER, I ASSUME? FINALLY THE MONSTER HAS COME TO ITS SENSES.
YAWN!

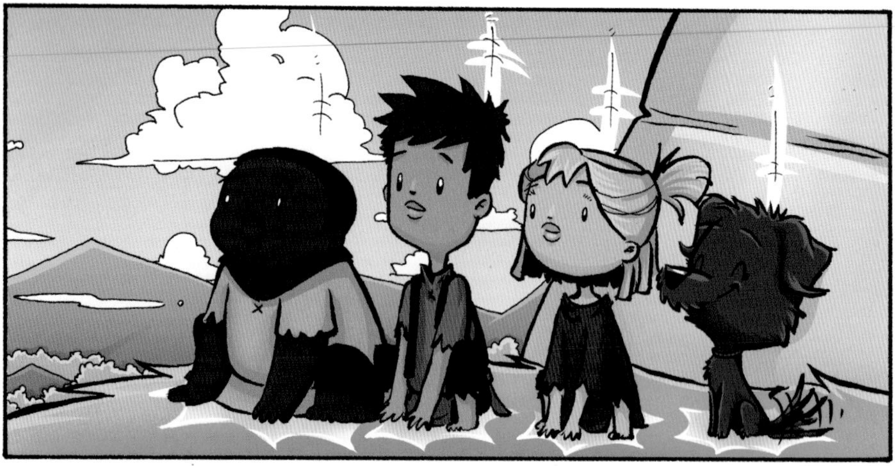

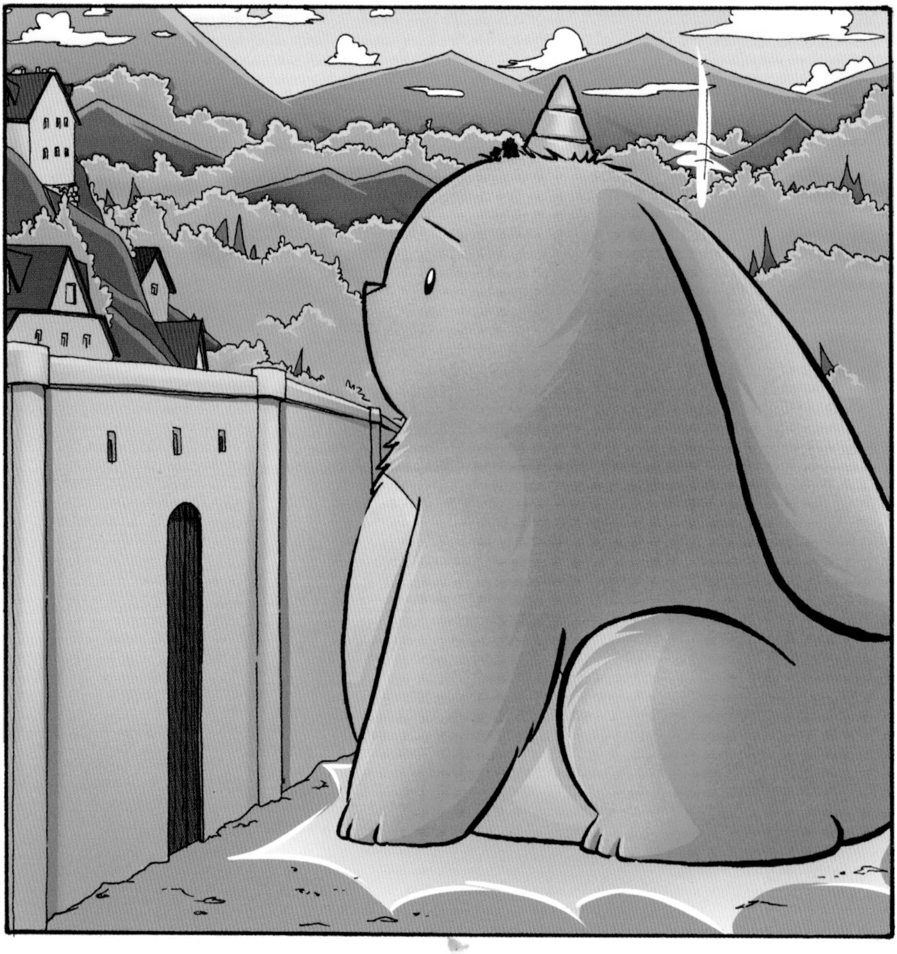

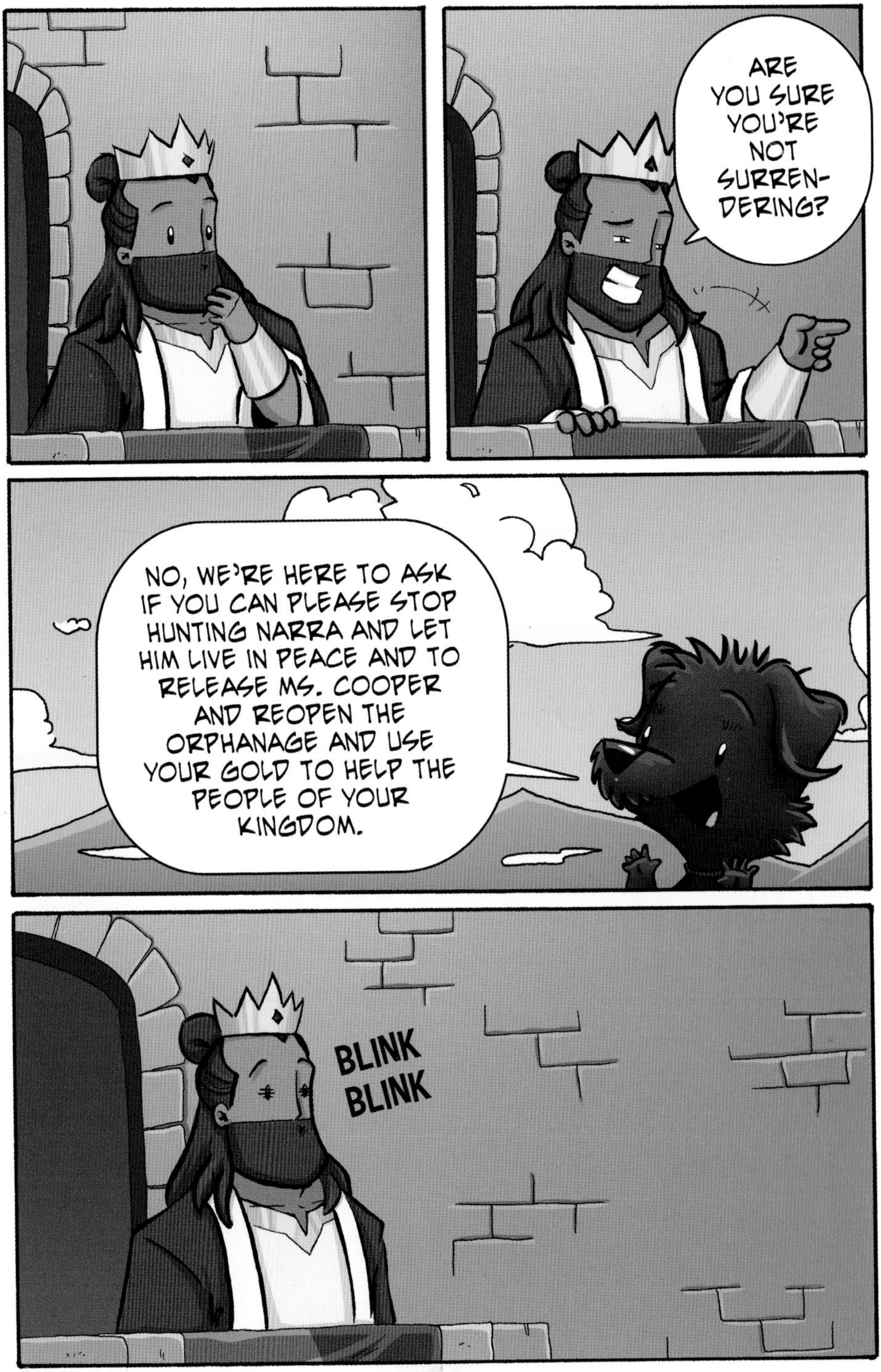
ARE YOU SURE YOU'RE NOT SURREN-DERING?
NO, WE'RE HERE TO ASK IF YOU CAN PLEASE STOP HUNTING NARRA AND LET HIM LIVE IN PEACE AND TO RELEASE MS. COOPER AND REOPEN THE ORPHANAGE AND USE YOUR GOLD TO HELP THE PEOPLE OF YOUR KINGDOM.
BLINK BLINK

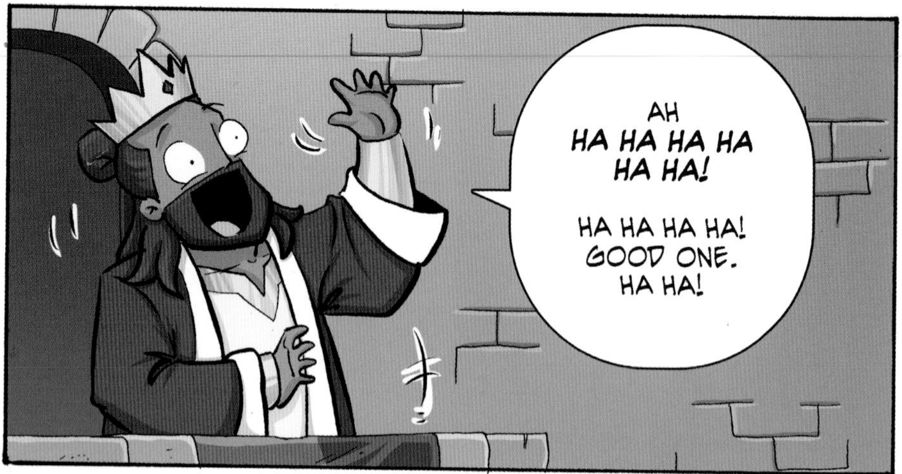
AH
HA HA HA HA
HA HA!
HA HA HA HA!
GOOD ONE.
HA HA!

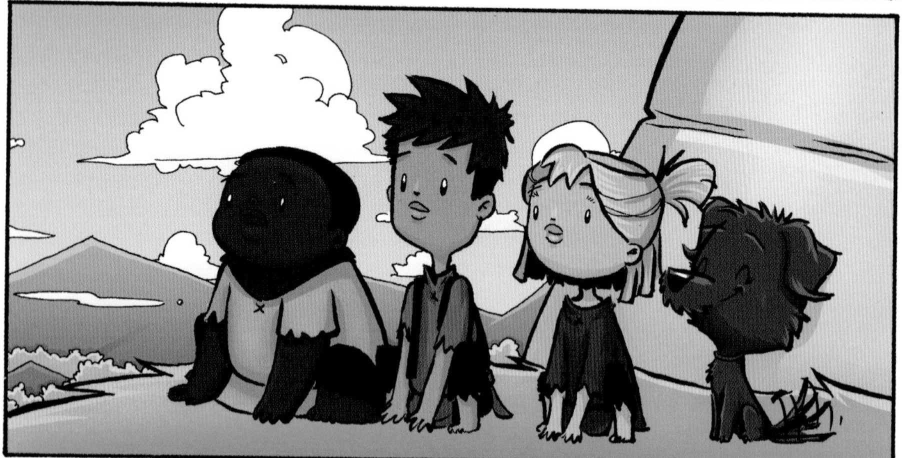

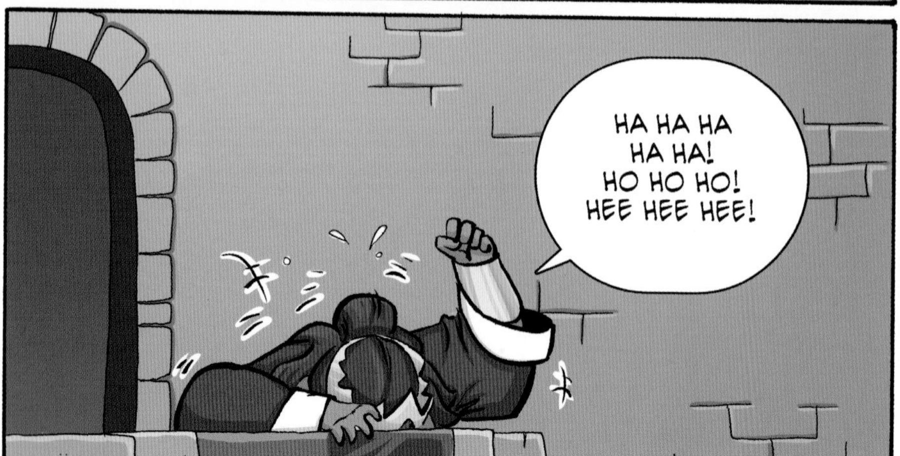
HA HA HA
HA HA!
HO HO HO!
HEE HEE HEE!

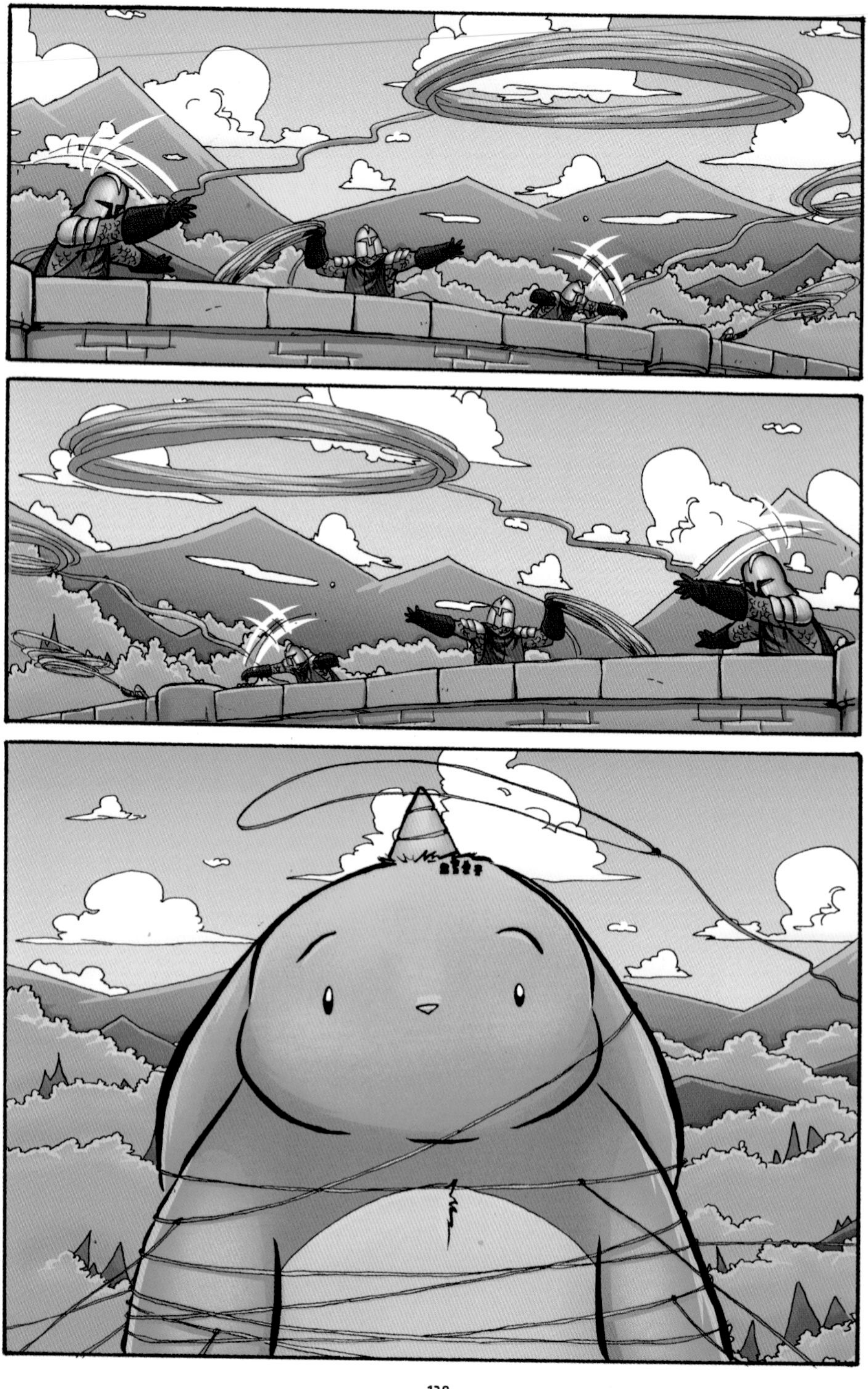

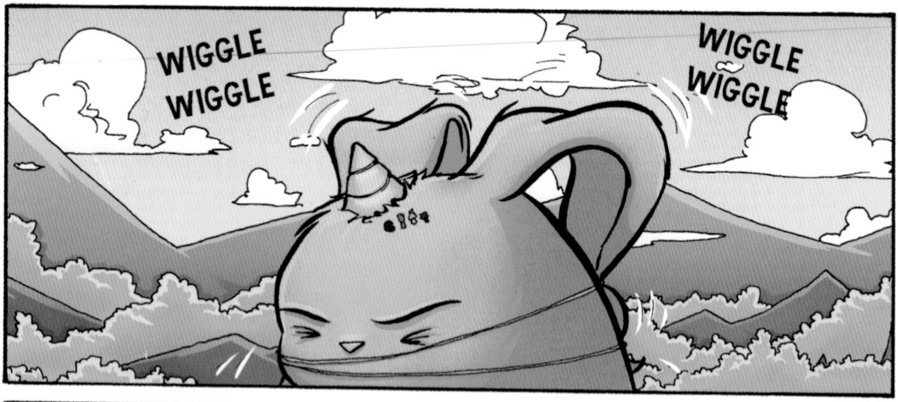
WIGGLE
WIGGLE
WIGGLE
WIGGLE

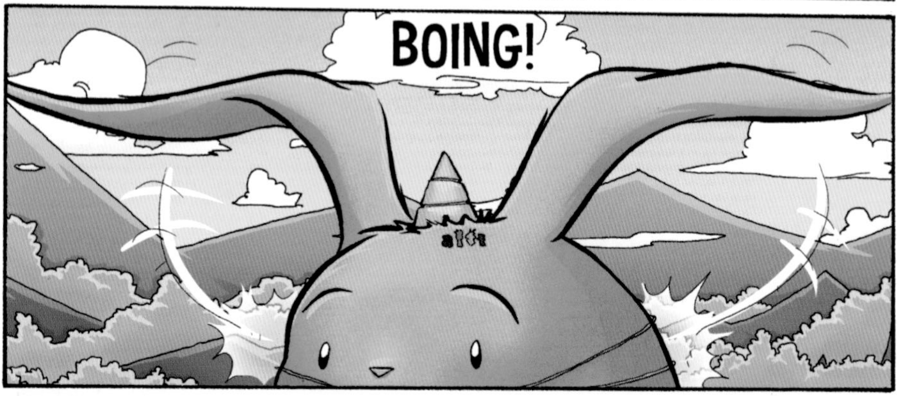
BOING!

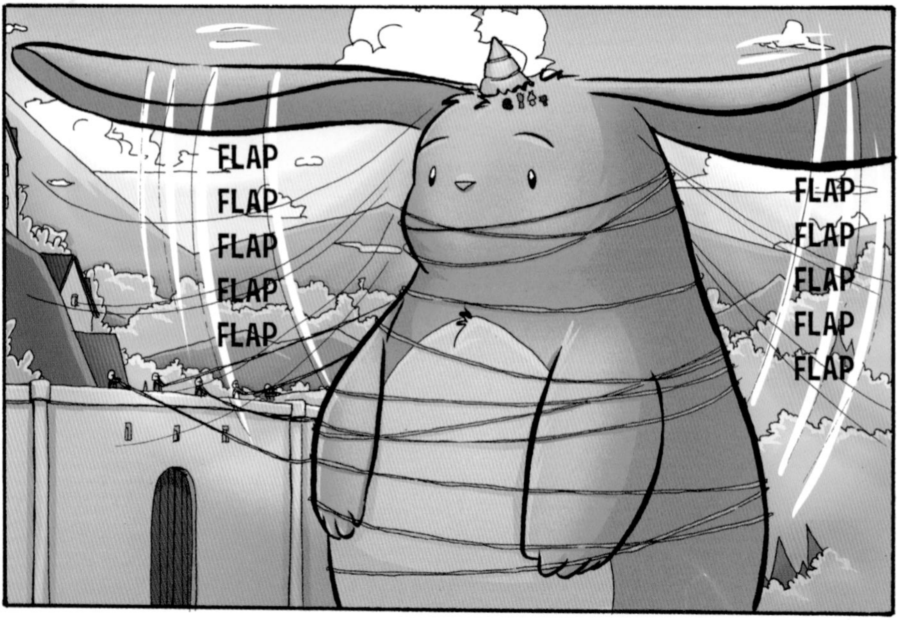
FLAP
FLAP
FLAP
FLAP
FLAP
FLAP
FLAP
FLAP
FLAP
FLAP

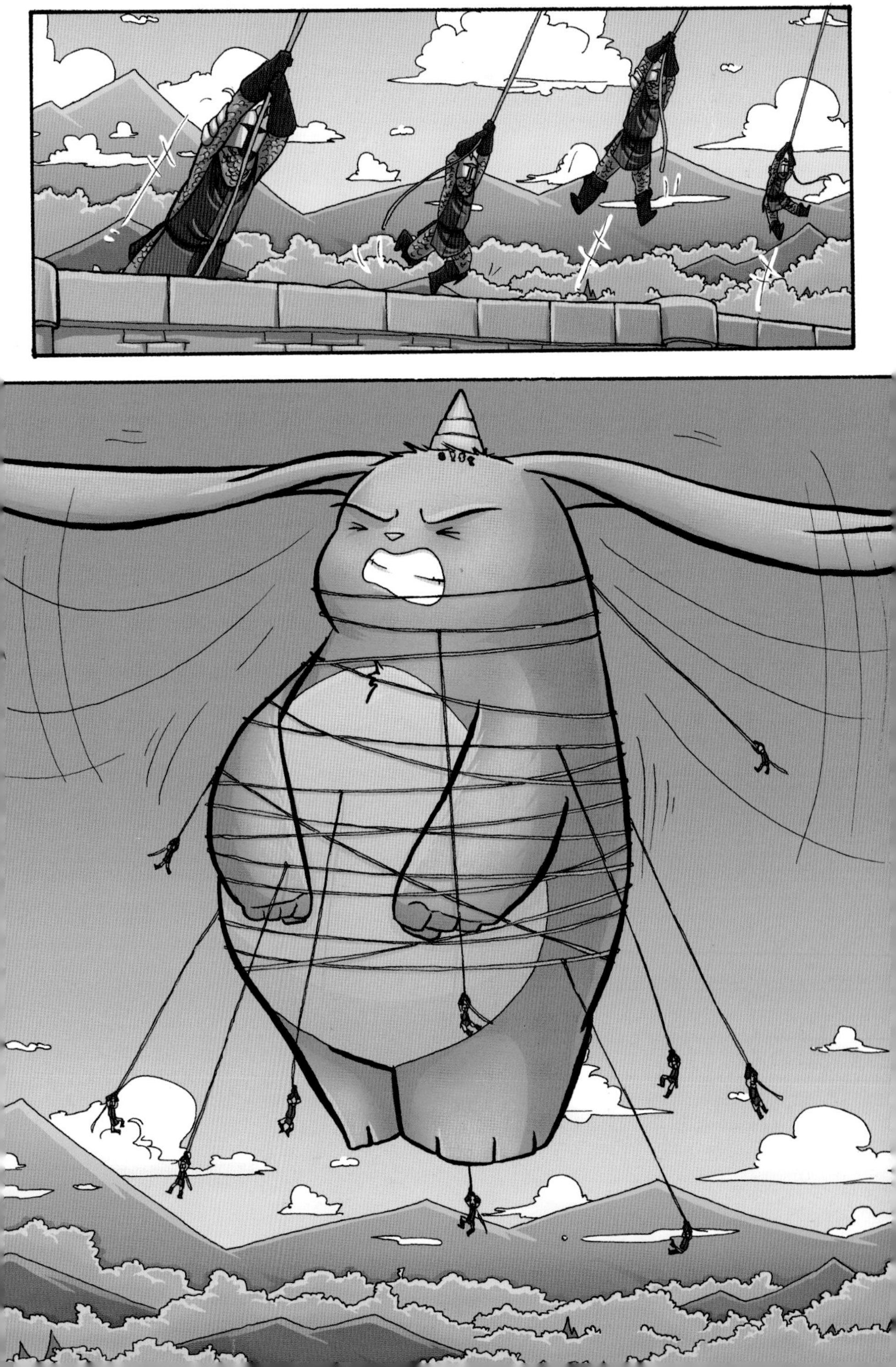

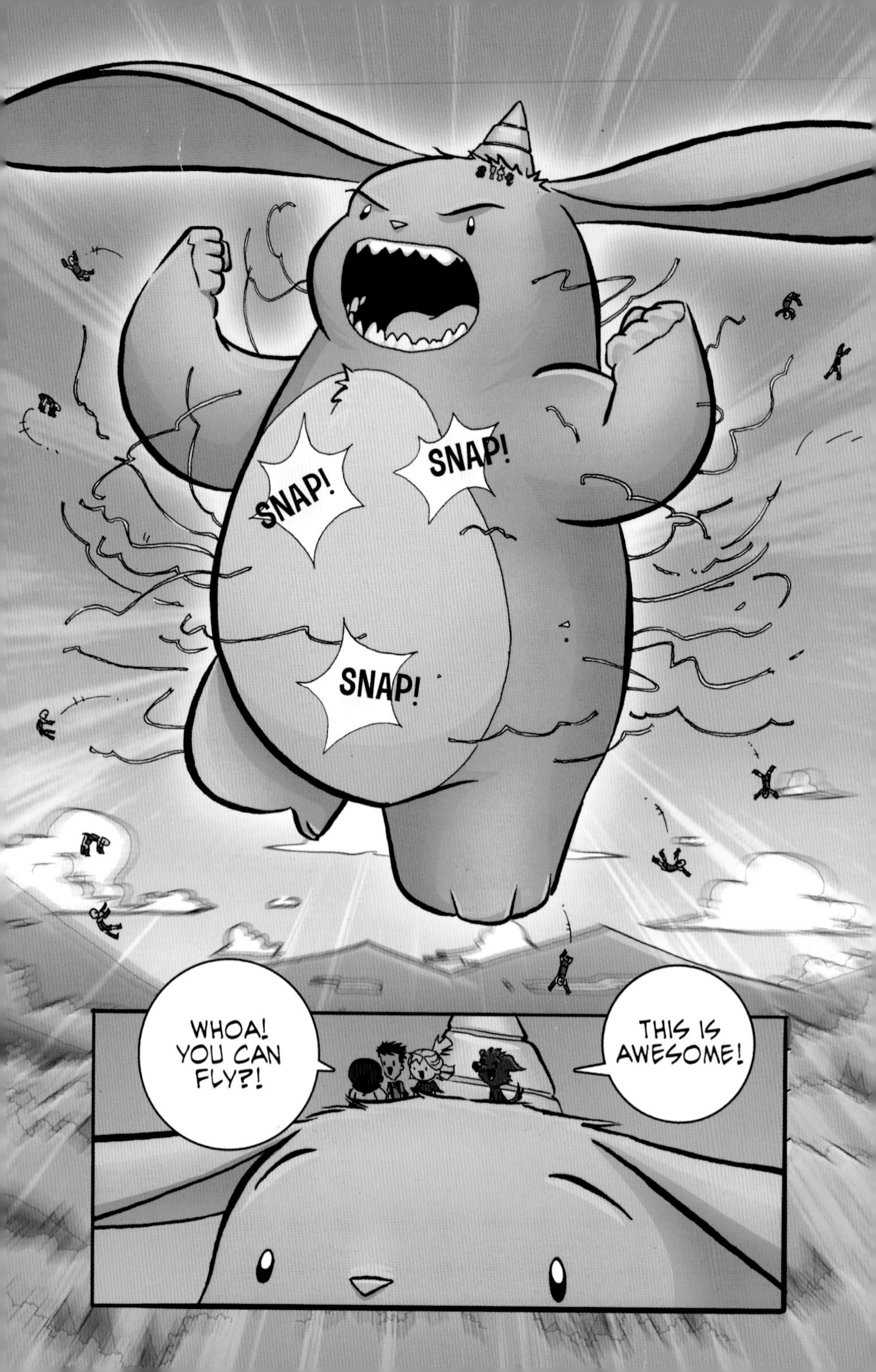
SNAP!
SNAP!
SNAP!
WHOA! YOU CAN FLY?!
THIS IS AWESOME!

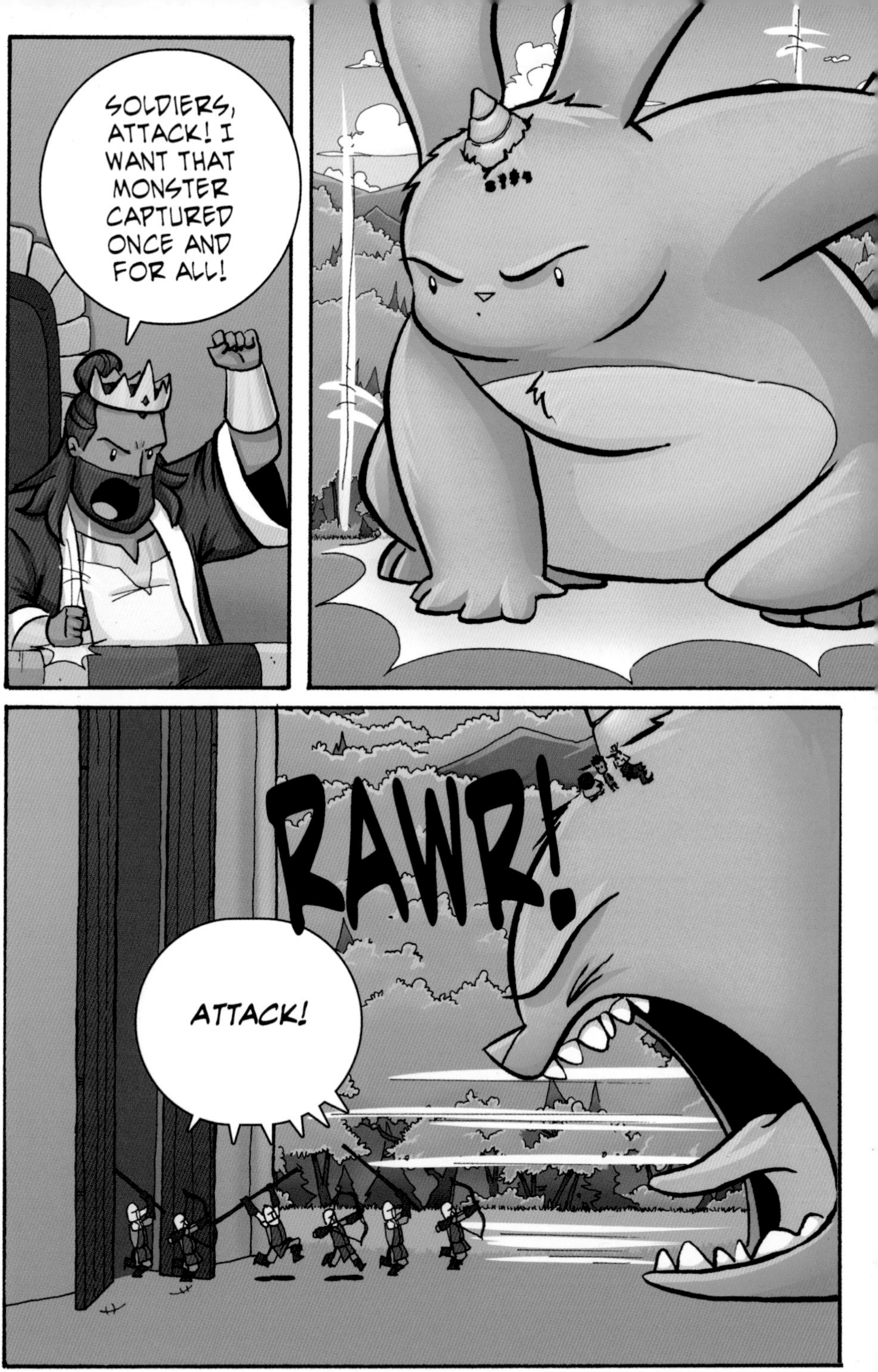
SOLDIERS, ATTACK! I WANT THAT MONSTER CAPTURED ONCE AND FOR ALL!
RAWR!
ATTACK!

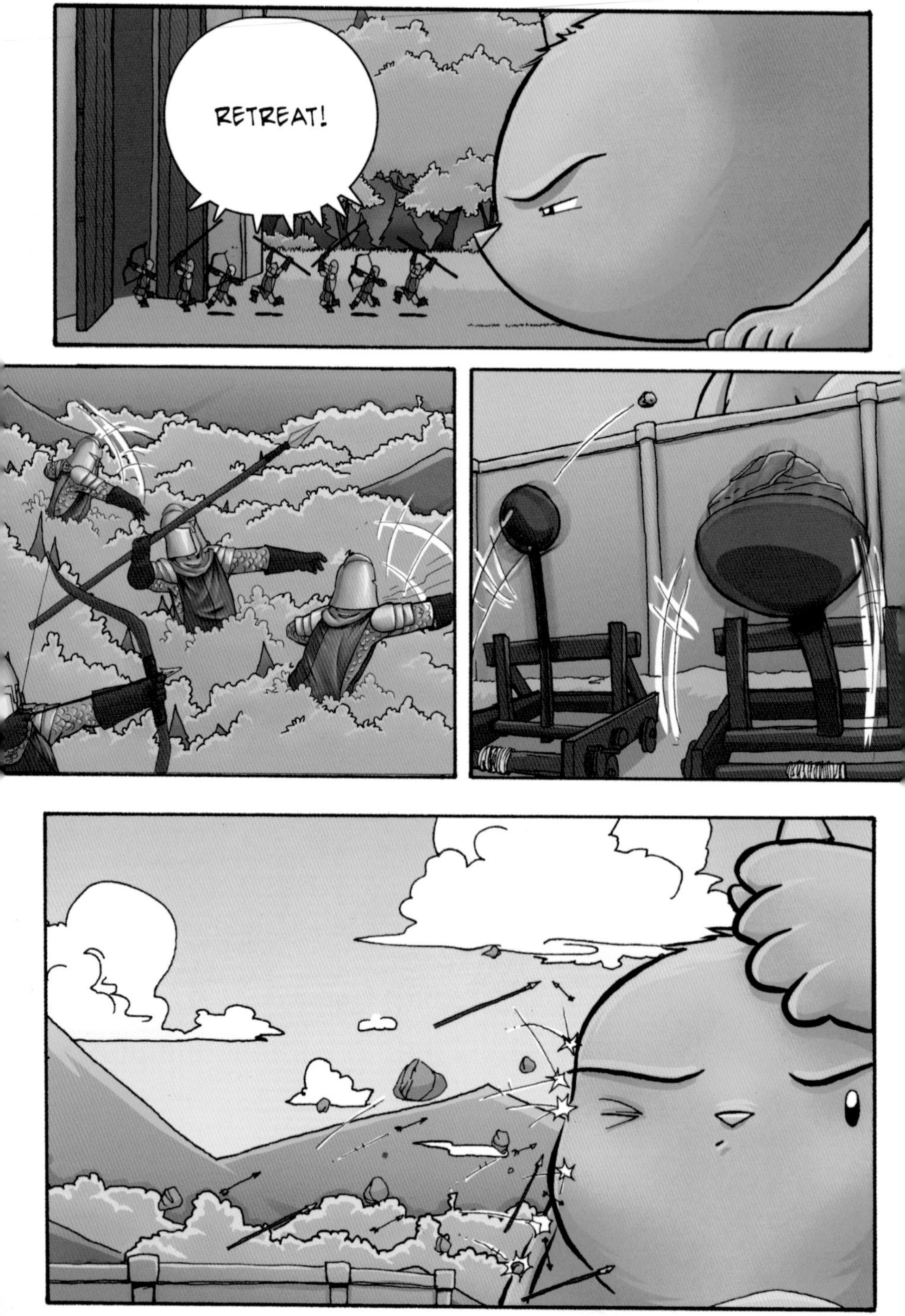
RETREAT!

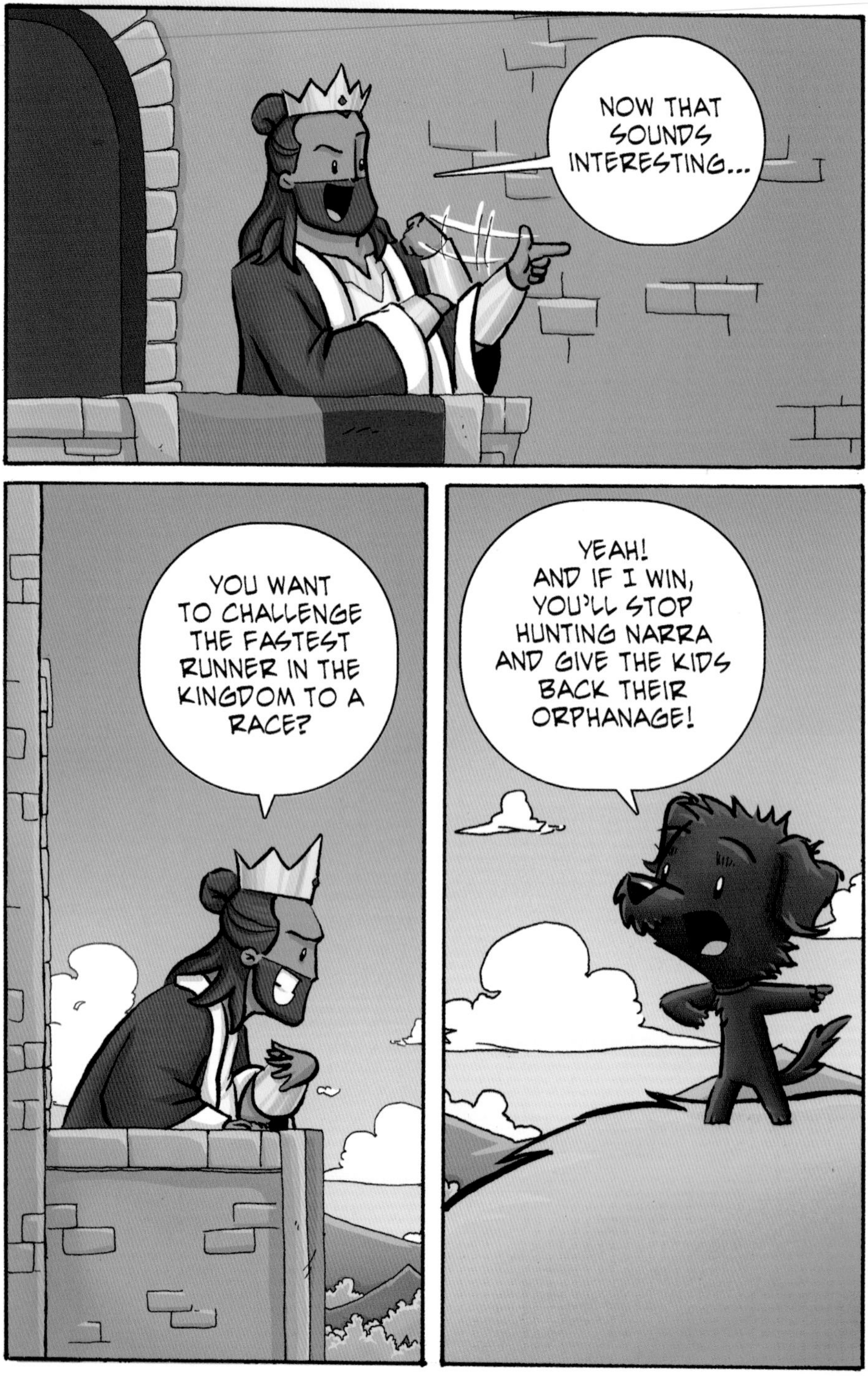
NOW THAT SOUNDS INTERESTING...
YOU WANT TO CHALLENGE THE FASTEST RUNNER IN THE KINGDOM TO A RACE?
YEAH! AND IF I WIN, YOU'LL STOP HUNTING NARRA AND GIVE THE KIDS BACK THEIR ORPHANAGE!

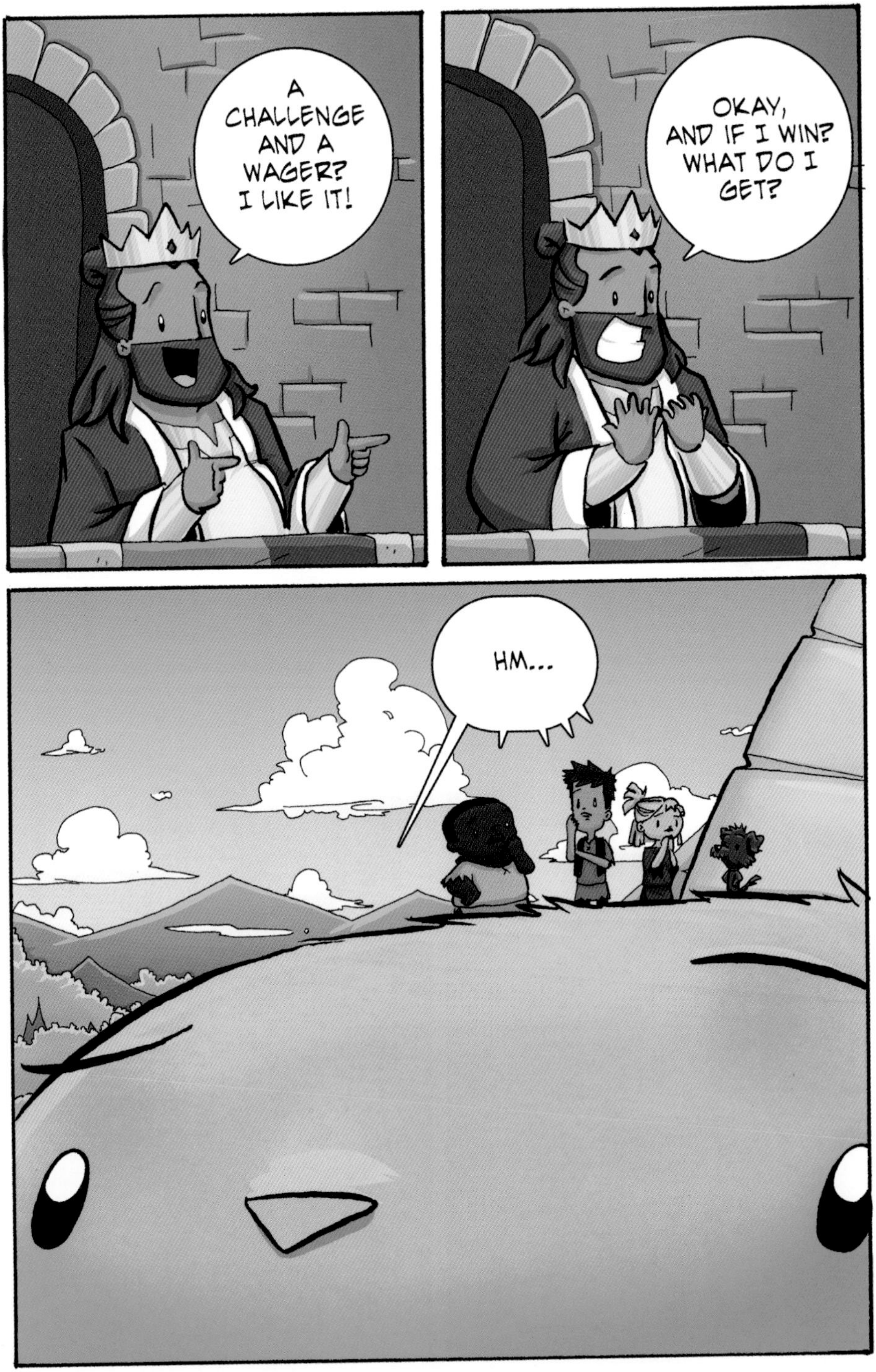
A CHALLENGE AND A WAGER? I LIKE IT!
OKAY, AND IF I WIN? WHAT DO I GET?
HM...

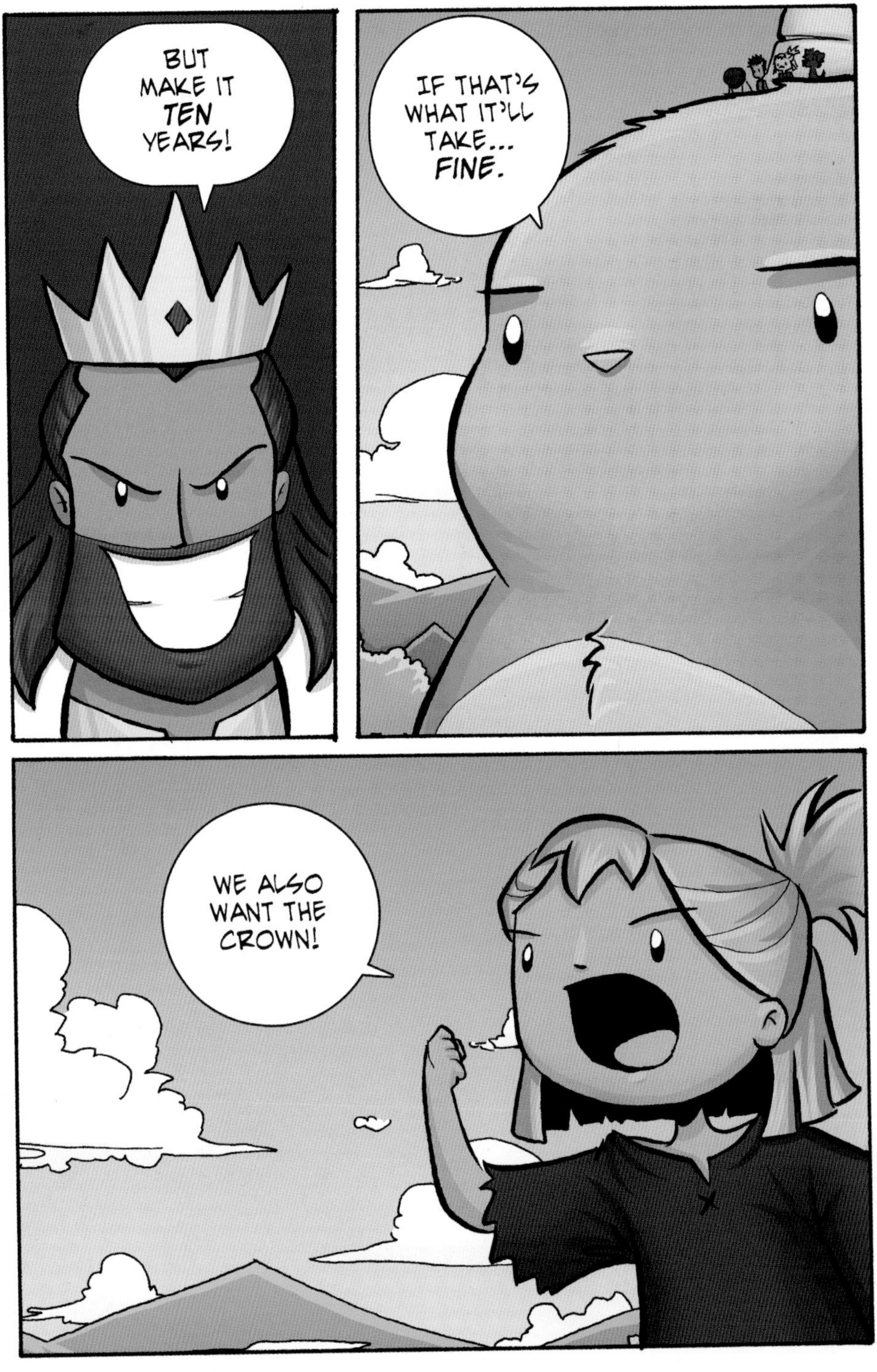
BUT MAKE IT TEN YEARS!
IF THAT'S WHAT IT'LL TAKE... FINE.
WE ALSO WANT THE CROWN!

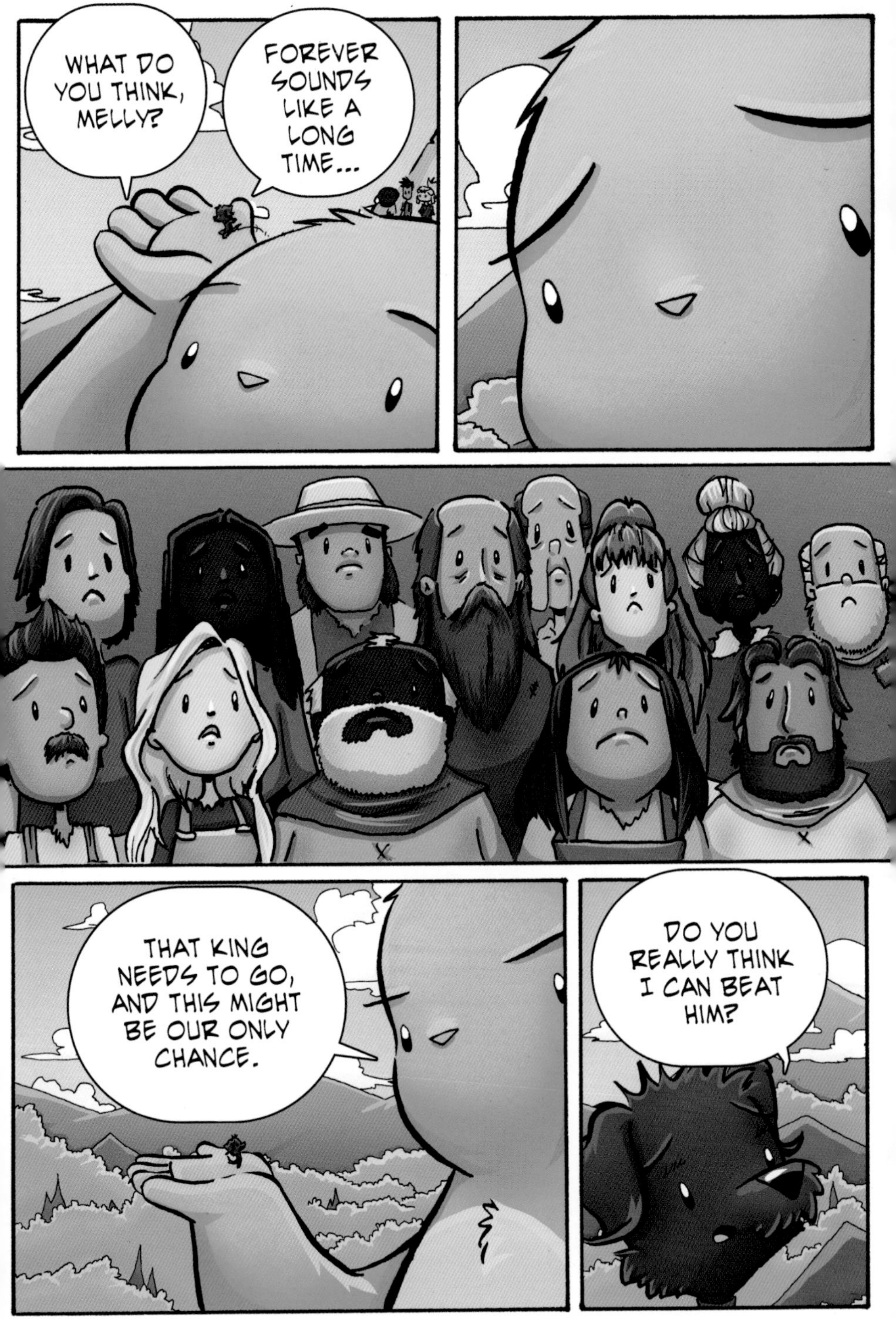
WHAT DO YOU THINK, MELLY?
FOREVER SOUNDS LIKE A LONG TIME...
THAT KING NEEDS TO GO, AND THIS MIGHT BE OUR ONLY CHANCE.
DO YOU REALLY THINK I CAN BEAT HIM?

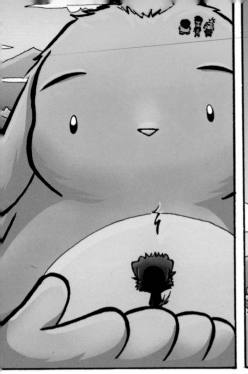

I DO...

I BELIEVE IN YOU, MELLY.

YOU HAVE YOURSELF A DEAL!

HA HA HA HA HA!

EXCELLENT...

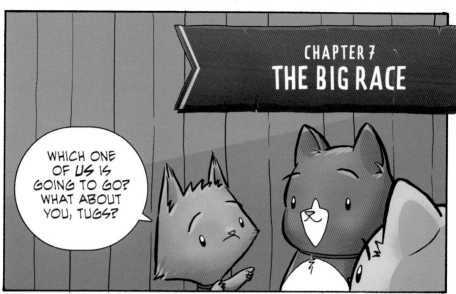

CHAPTER 7
THE BIG RACE

WHICH ONE OF *US* IS GOING TO GO? WHAT ABOUT YOU, TUGS?

WELL, I'M THE BIGGEST, SO YOU GUYS WON'T BE ABLE TO HOLD ME...

BESIDES, YOU'LL NEED MY STRENGTH TO PULL YOU BACK UP WHEN YOU FIND HER.

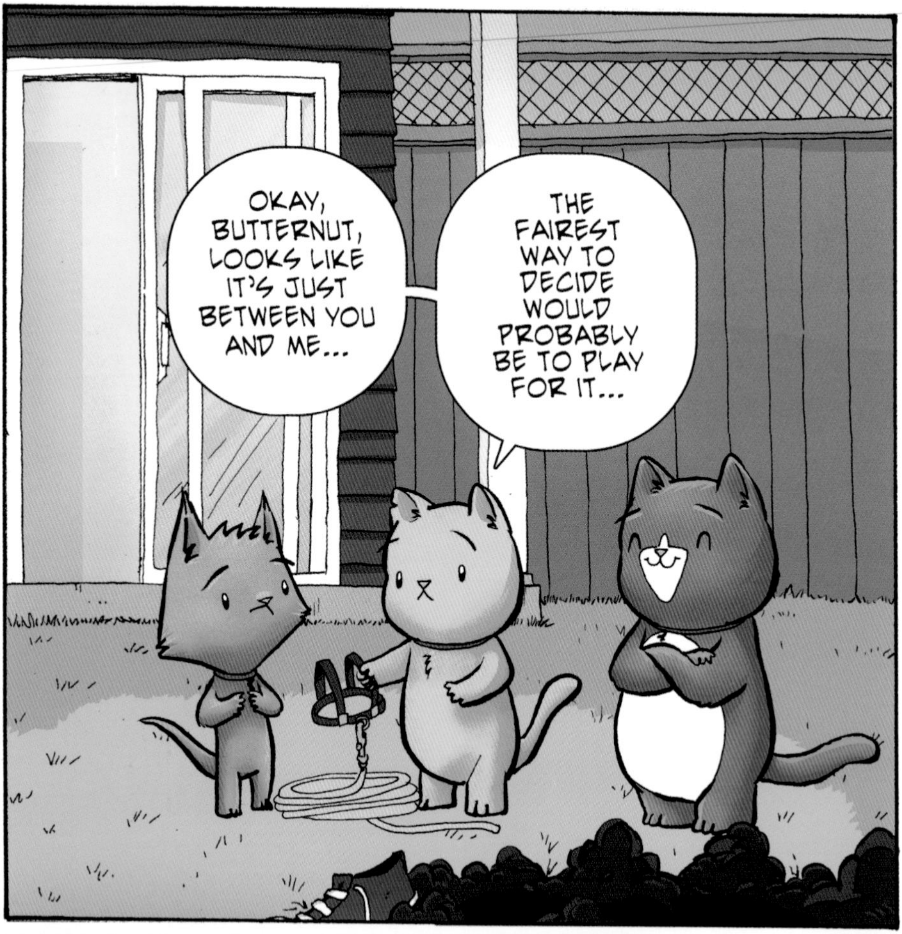
OKAY, BUTTERNUT, LOOKS LIKE IT'S JUST BETWEEN YOU AND ME...
THE FAIREST WAY TO DECIDE WOULD PROBABLY BE TO PLAY FOR IT...

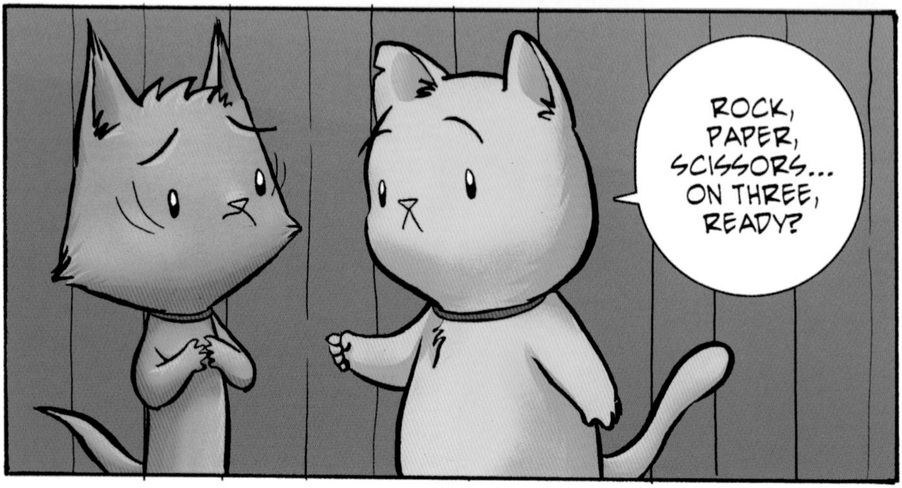
ROCK, PAPER, SCISSORS... ON THREE, READY?

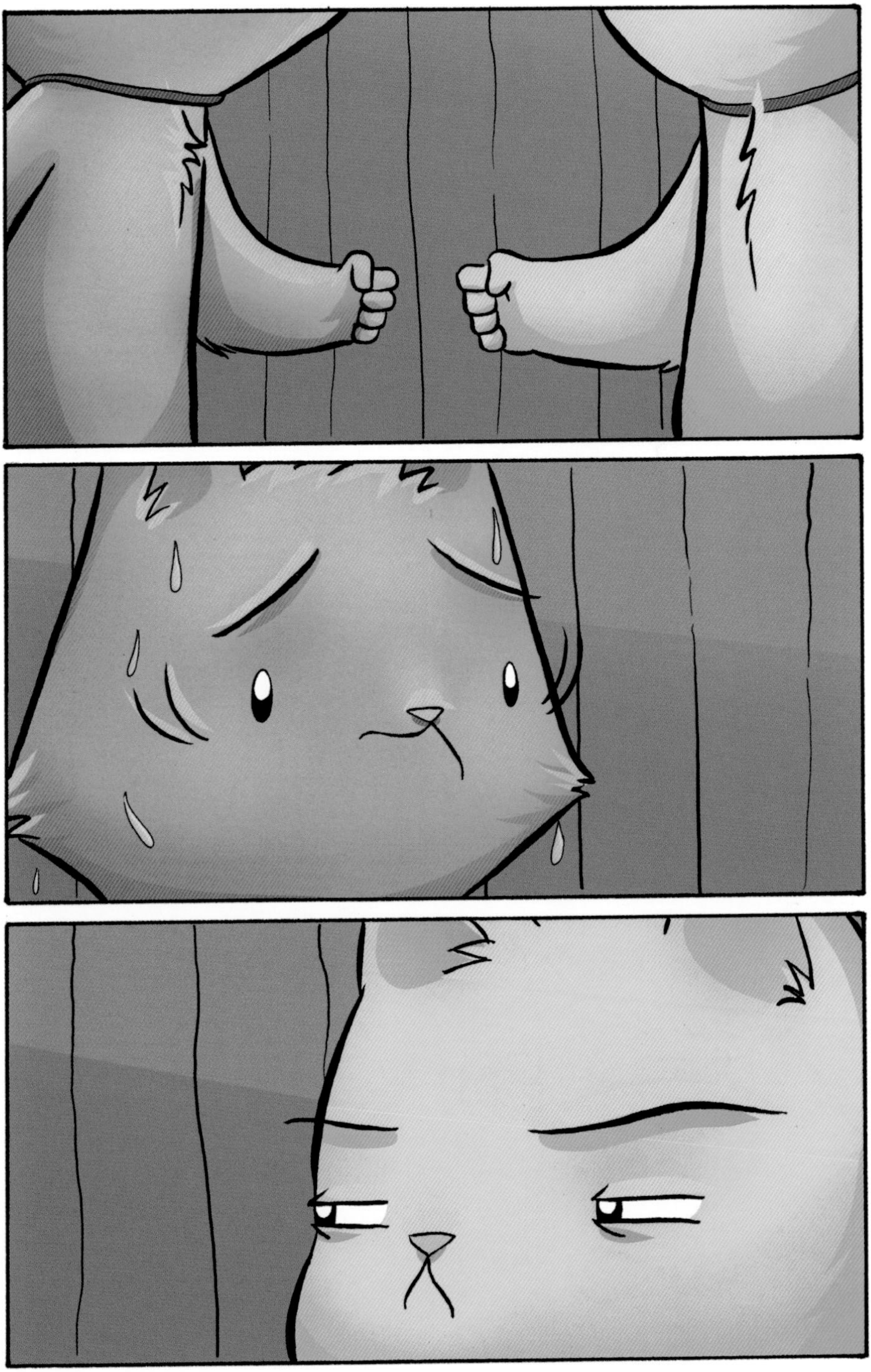

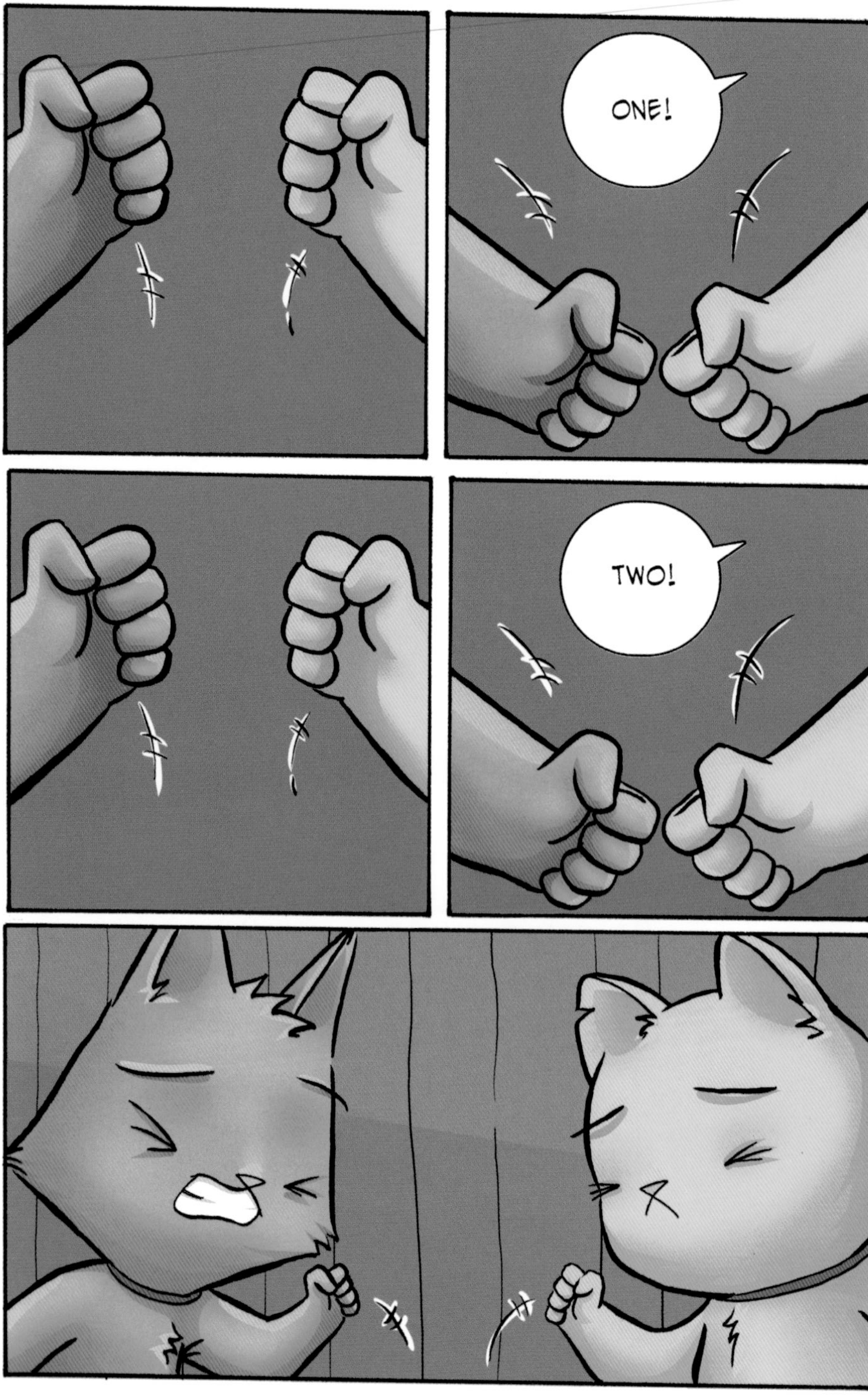
ONE!
TWO!

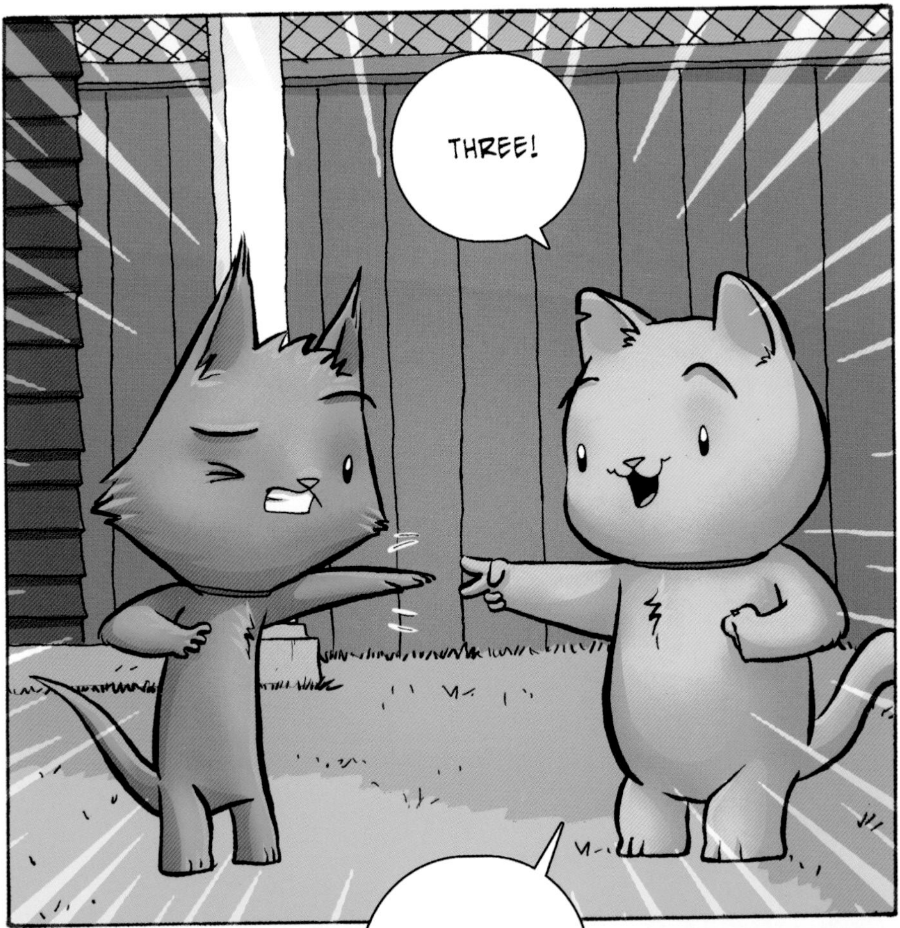
THREE!
SCISSORS CUTS PAPER!

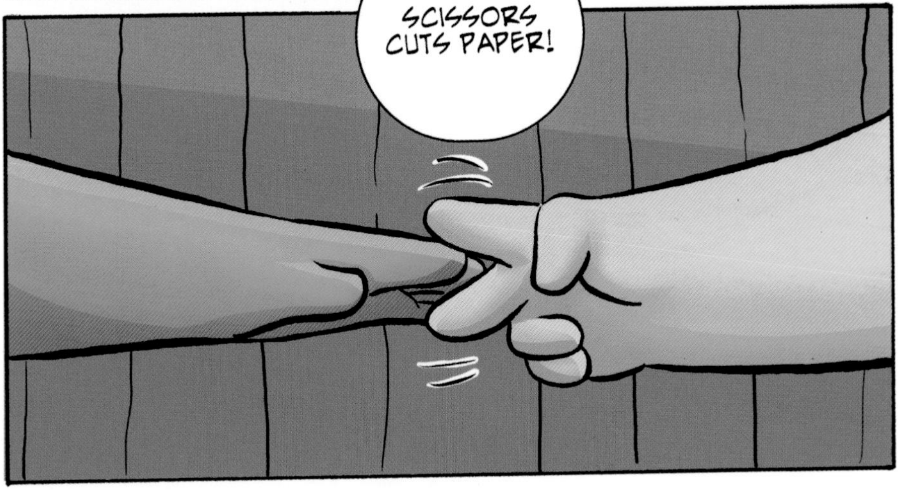

PREPARE TO EAT MY DUST, LITTLE SCRUFFY ONE!

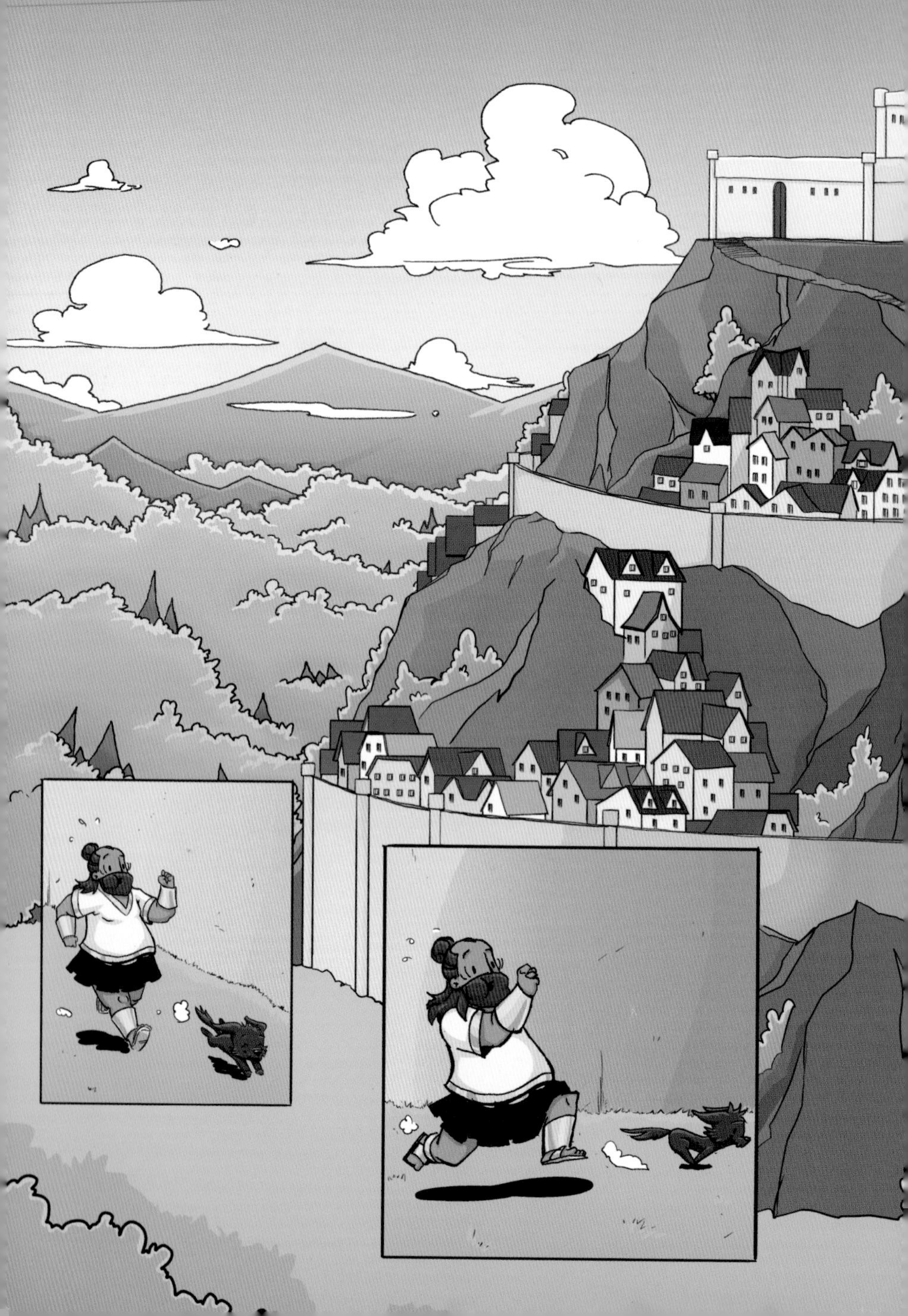

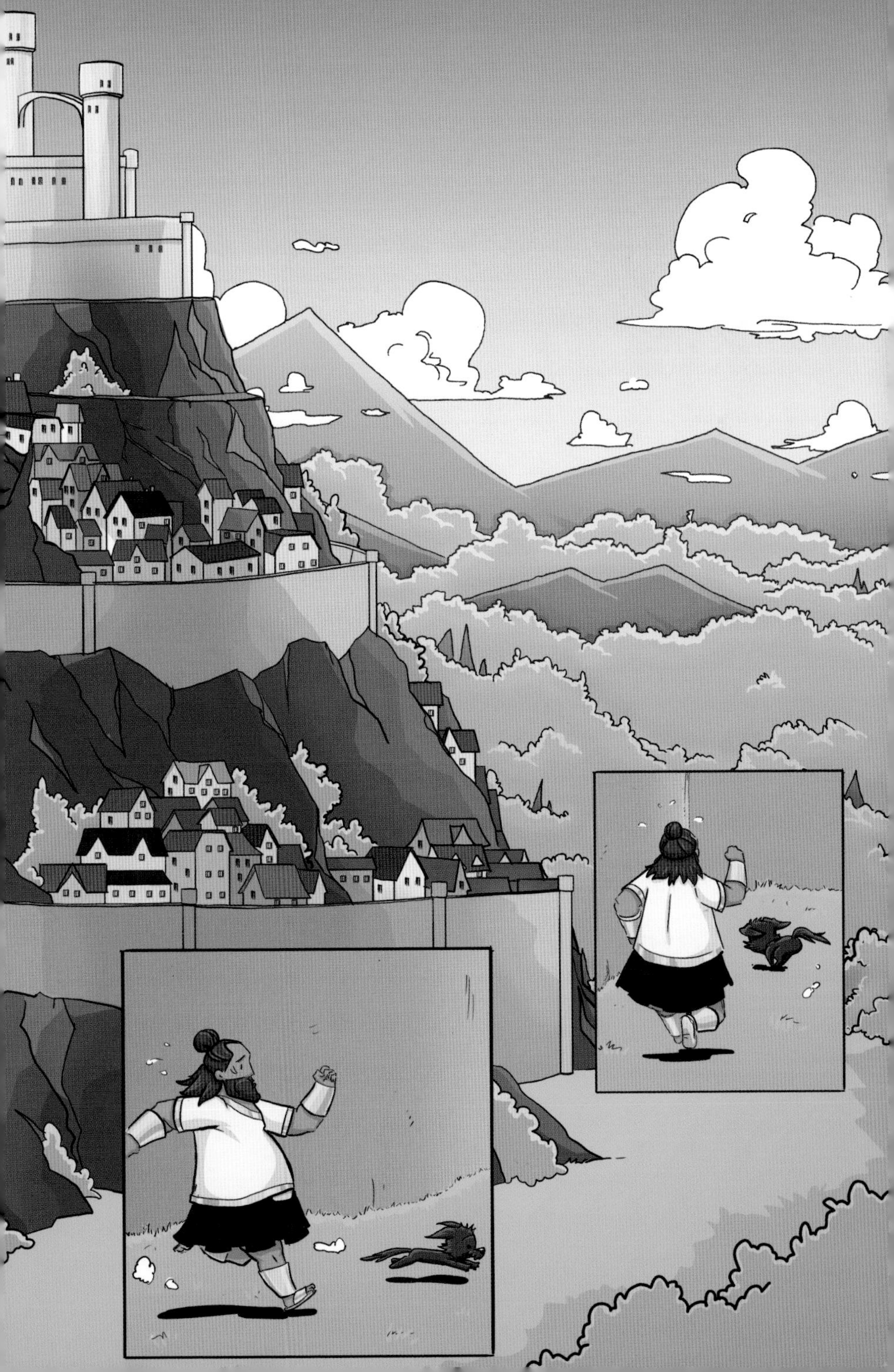

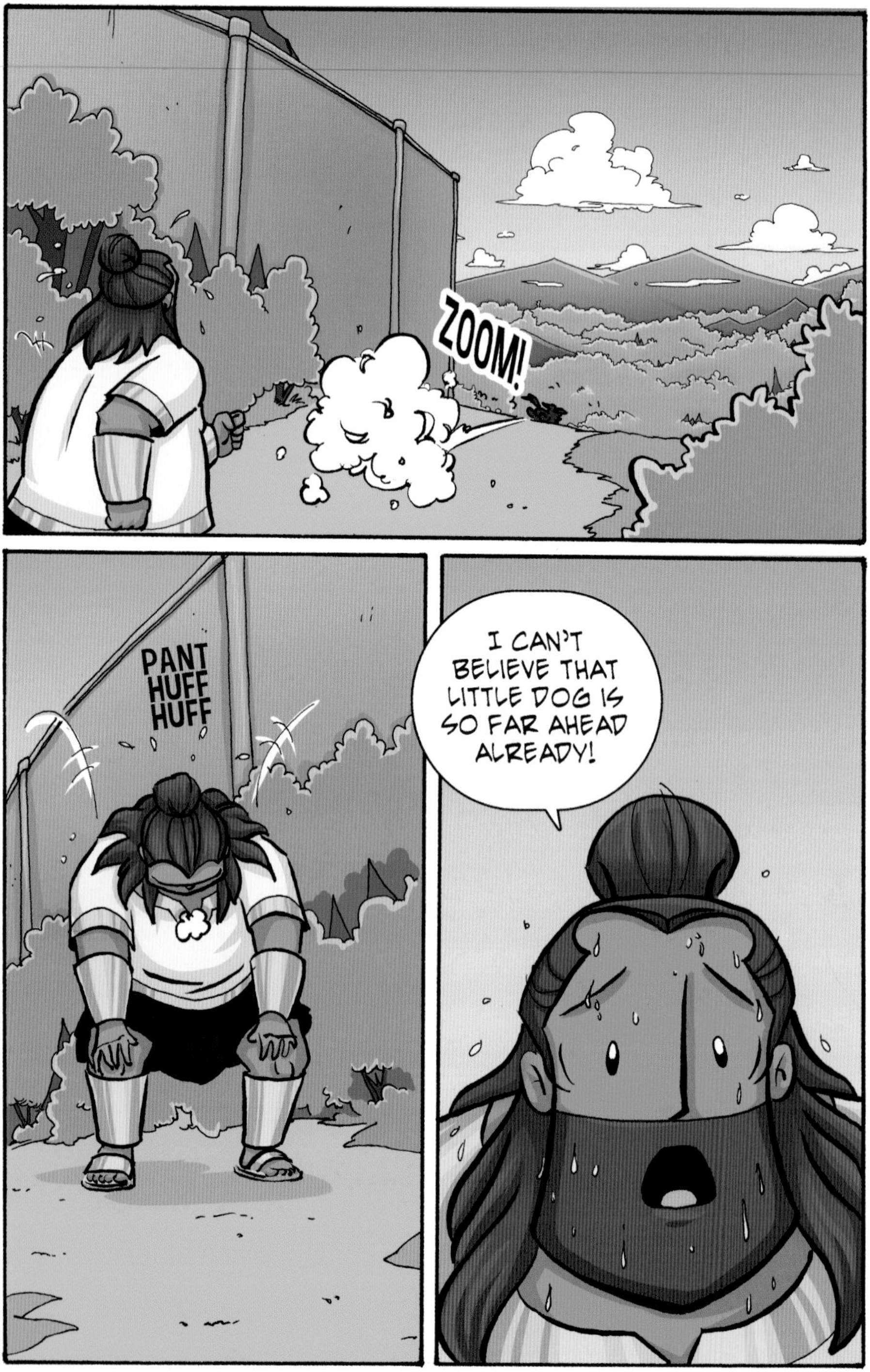
ZOOM!
PANT
HUFF
HUFF
I CAN'T BELIEVE THAT LITTLE DOG IS SO FAR AHEAD ALREADY!

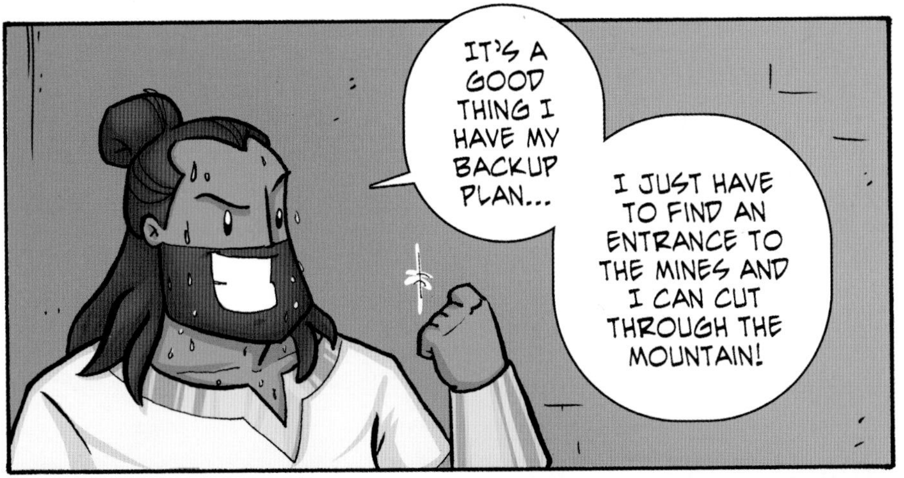
IT'S A GOOD THING I HAVE MY BACKUP PLAN...
I JUST HAVE TO FIND AN ENTRANCE TO THE MINES AND I CAN CUT THROUGH THE MOUNTAIN!
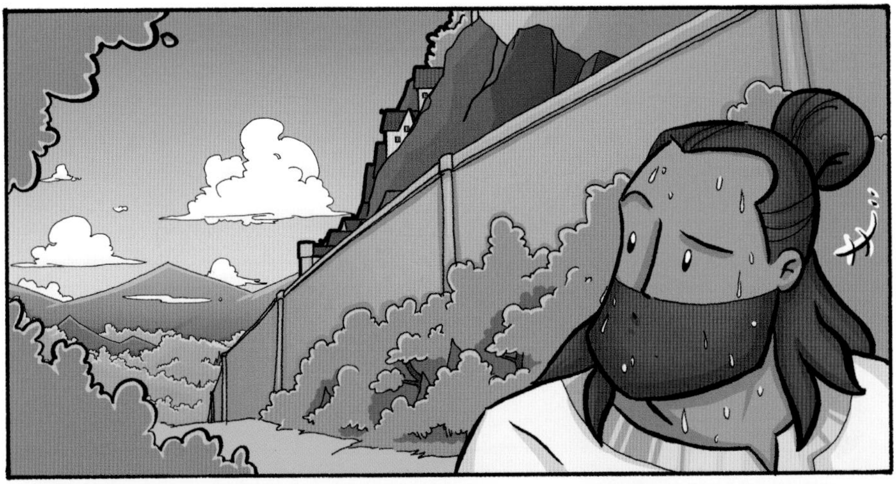
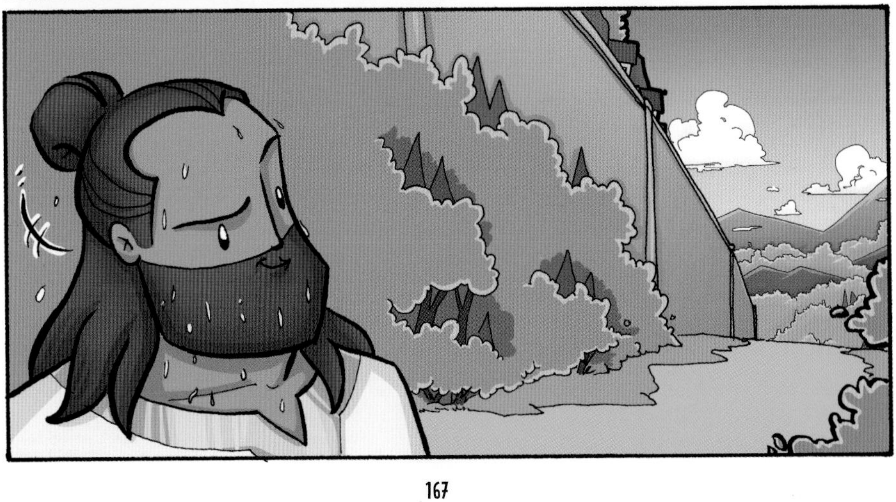

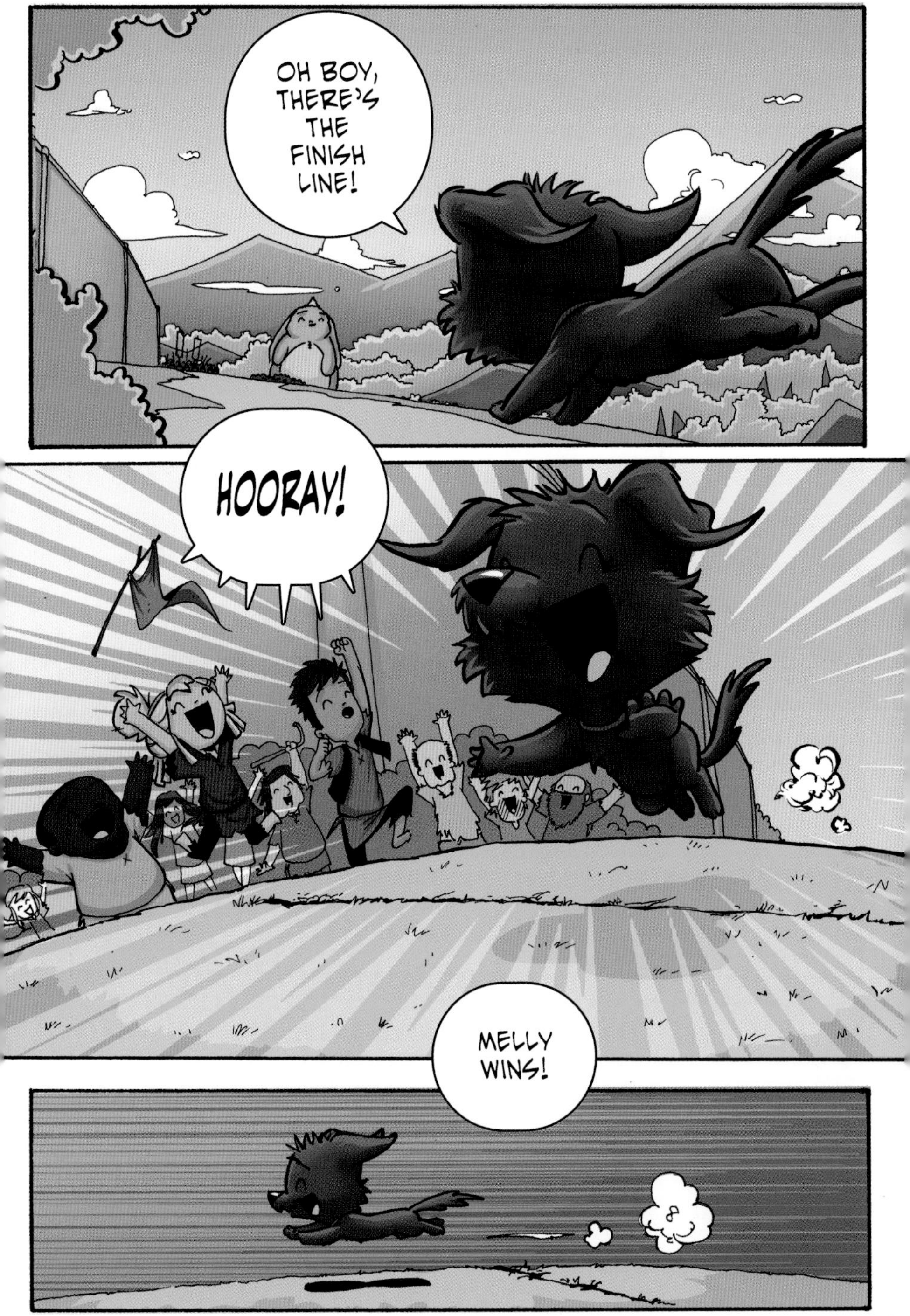
OH BOY, THERE'S THE FINISH LINE!
HOORAY!
MELLY WINS!

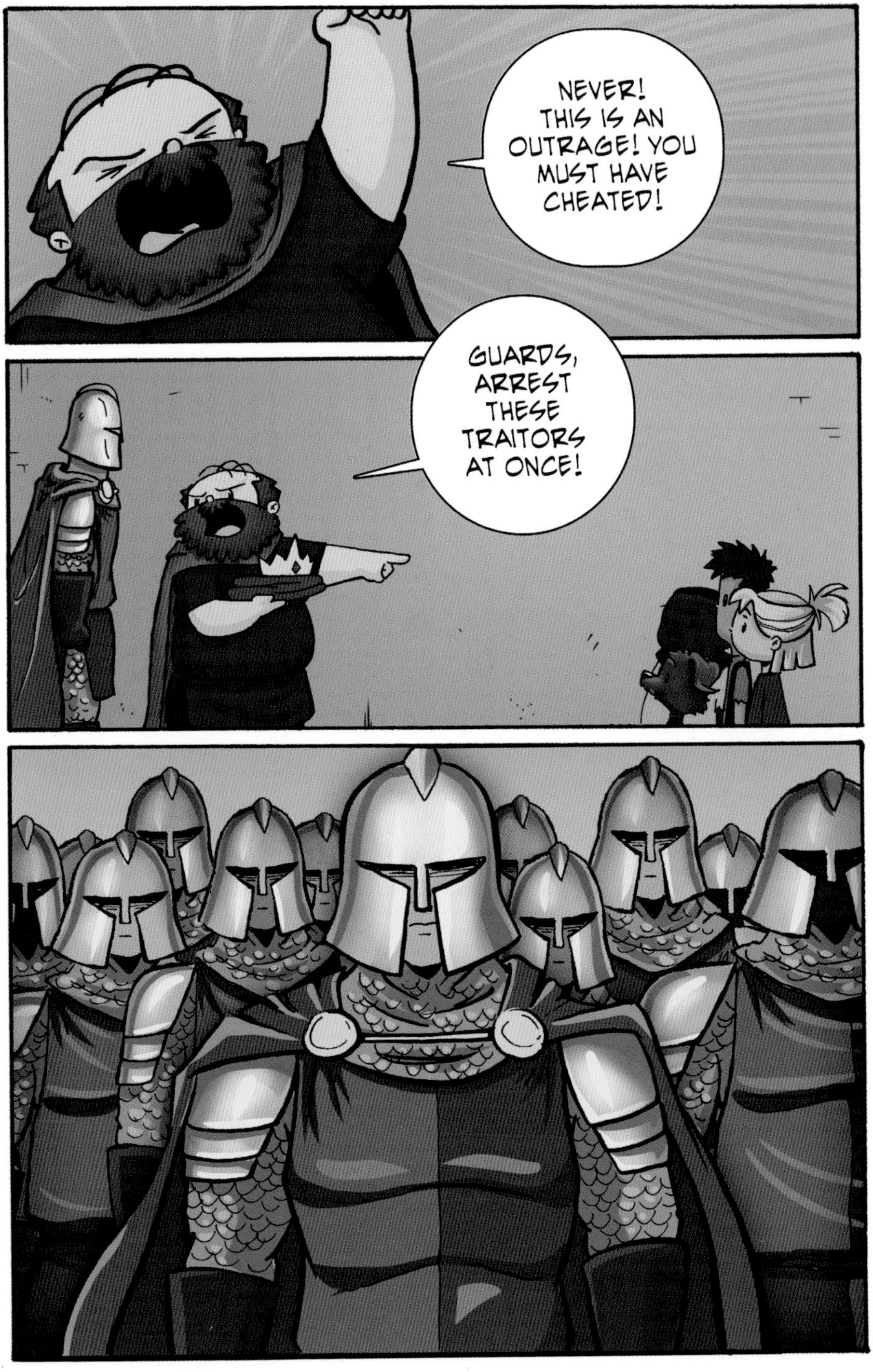
NEVER! THIS IS AN OUTRAGE! YOU MUST HAVE CHEATED!
GUARDS, ARREST THESE TRAITORS AT ONCE!

CHAPTER 8
GIFTS FROM ABOVE

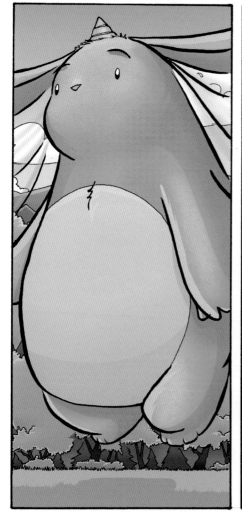

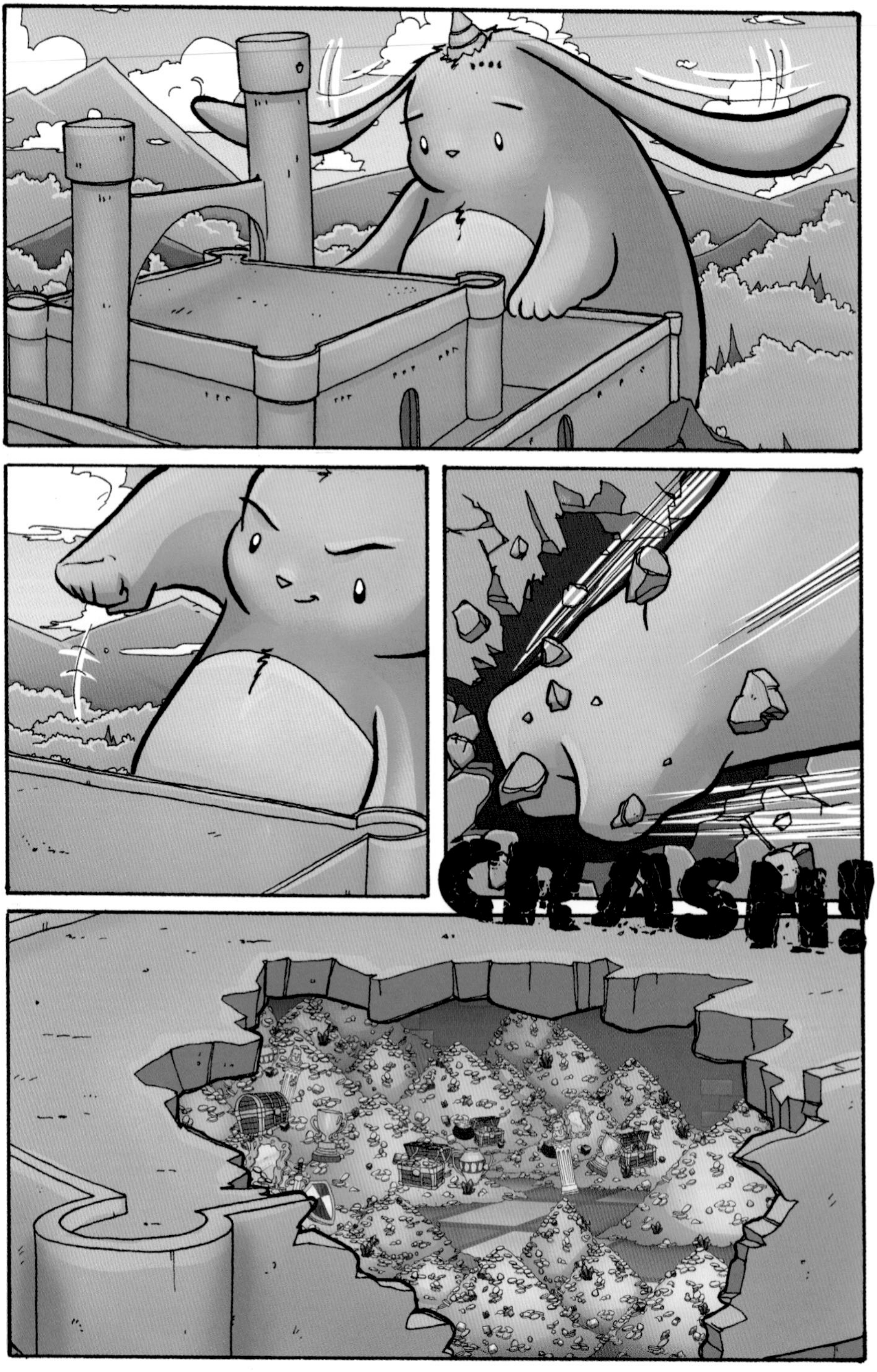
CRASH!

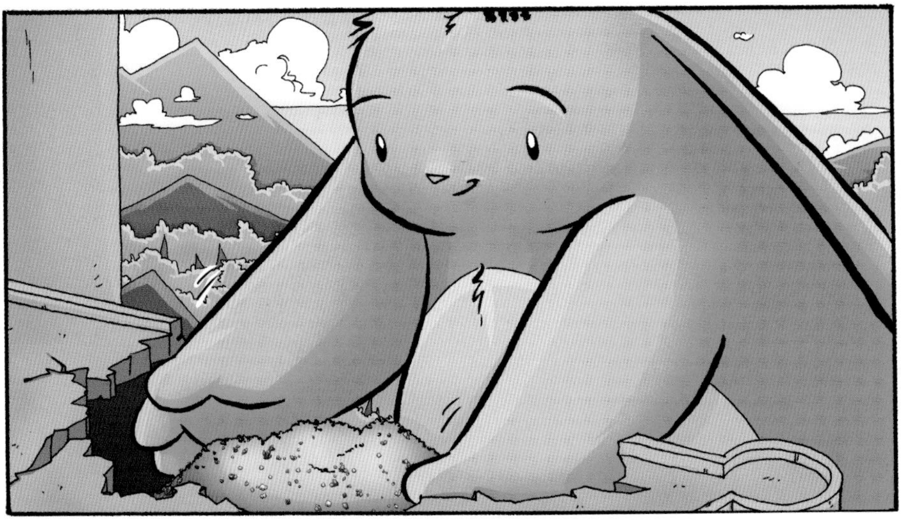

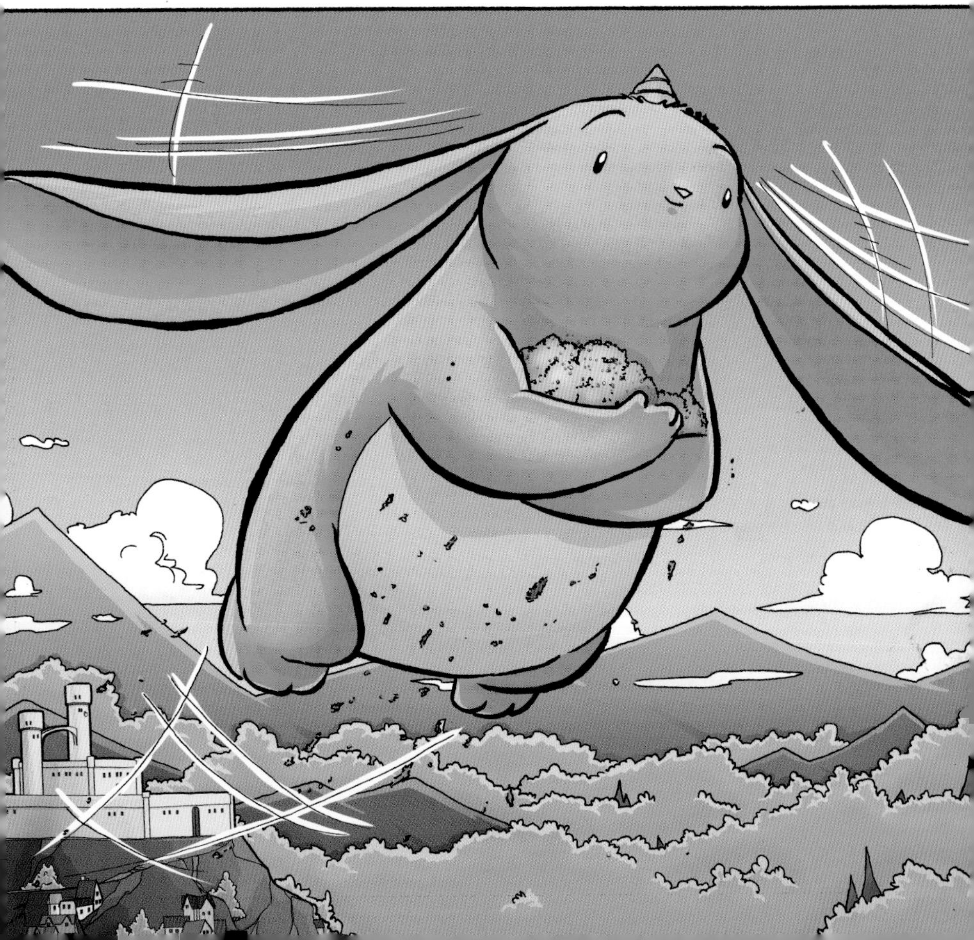

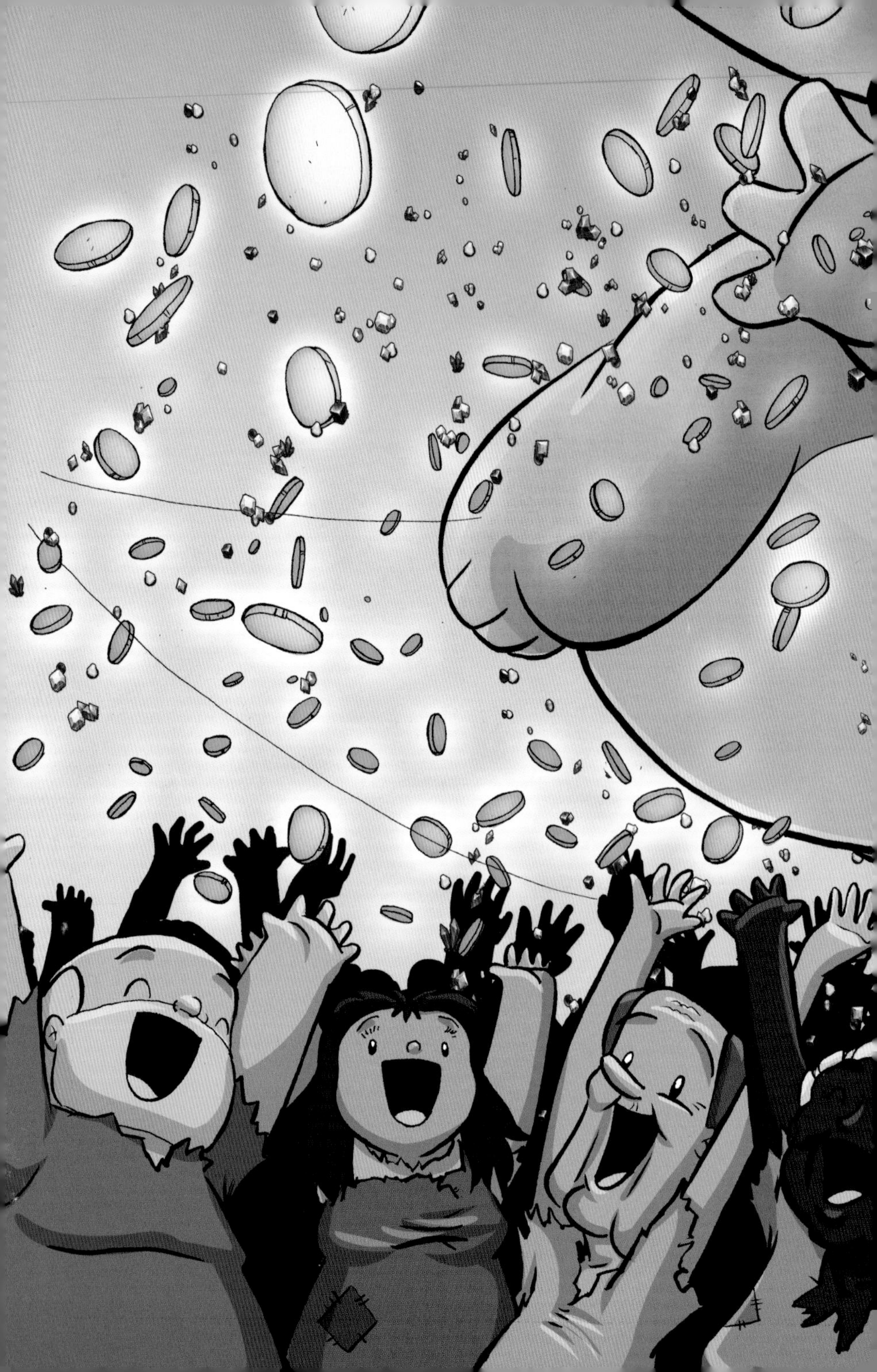

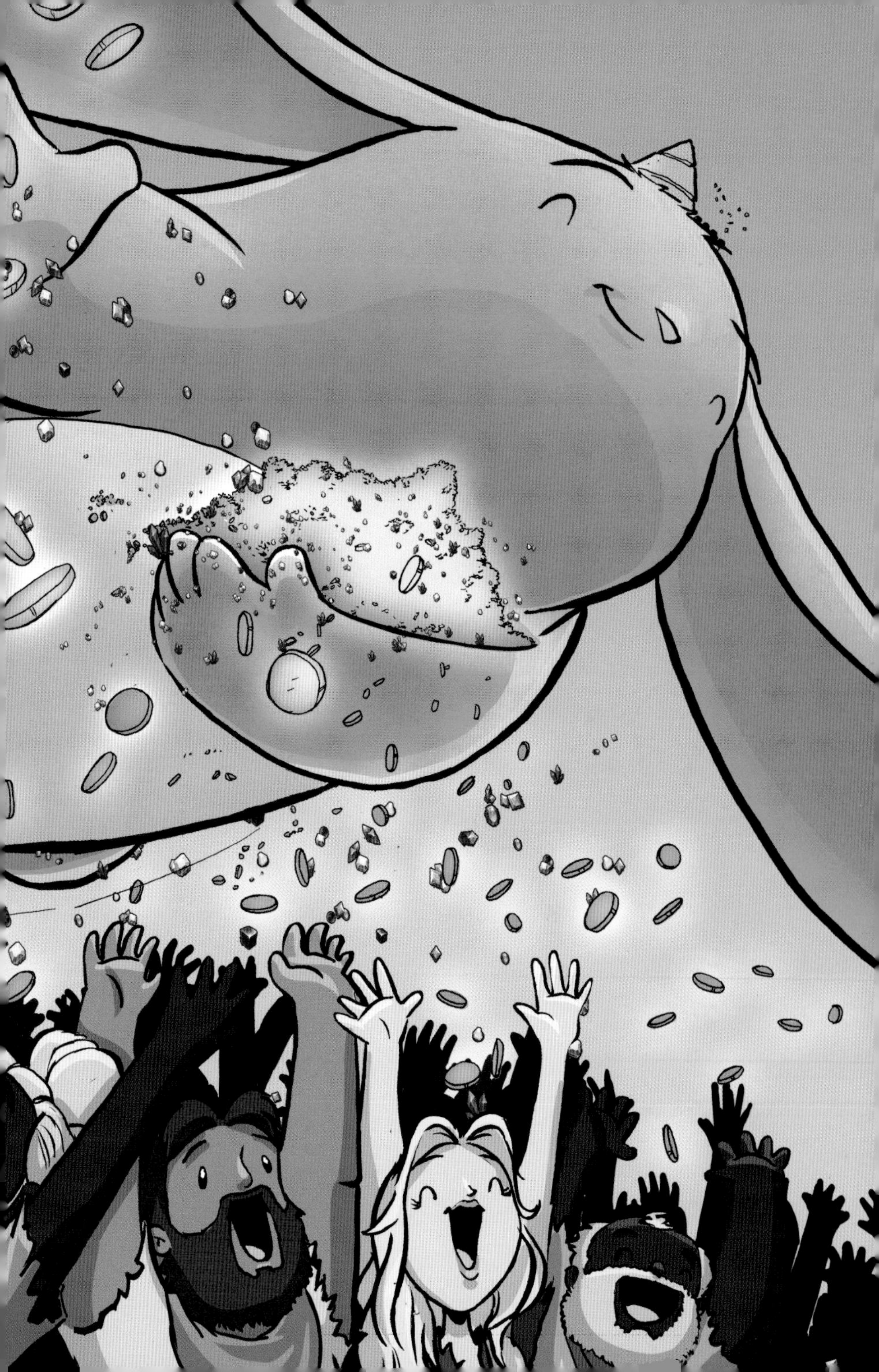

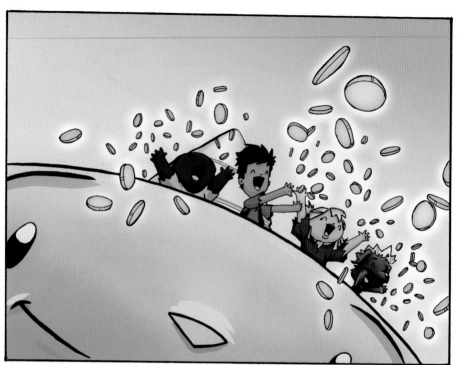

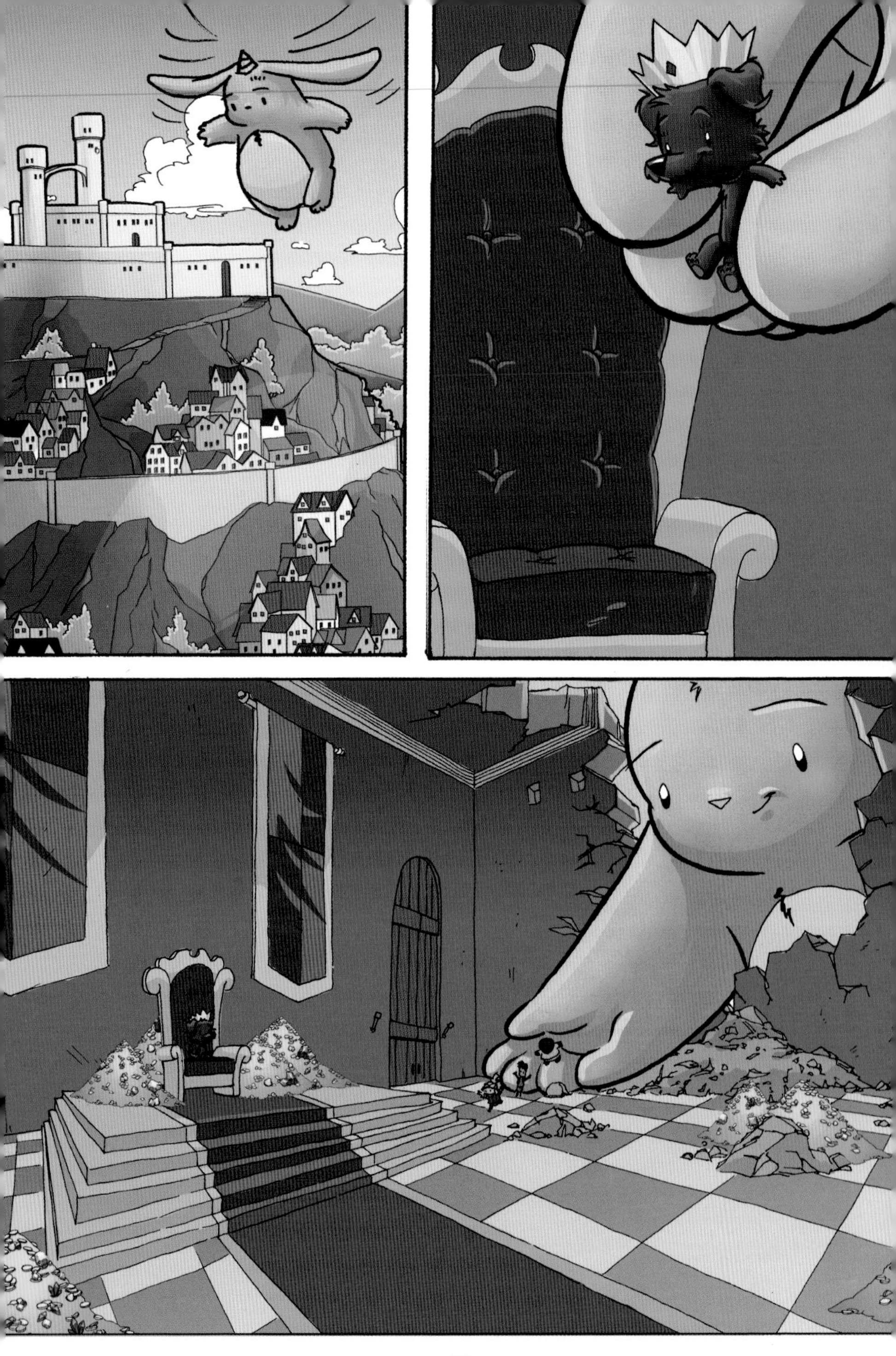

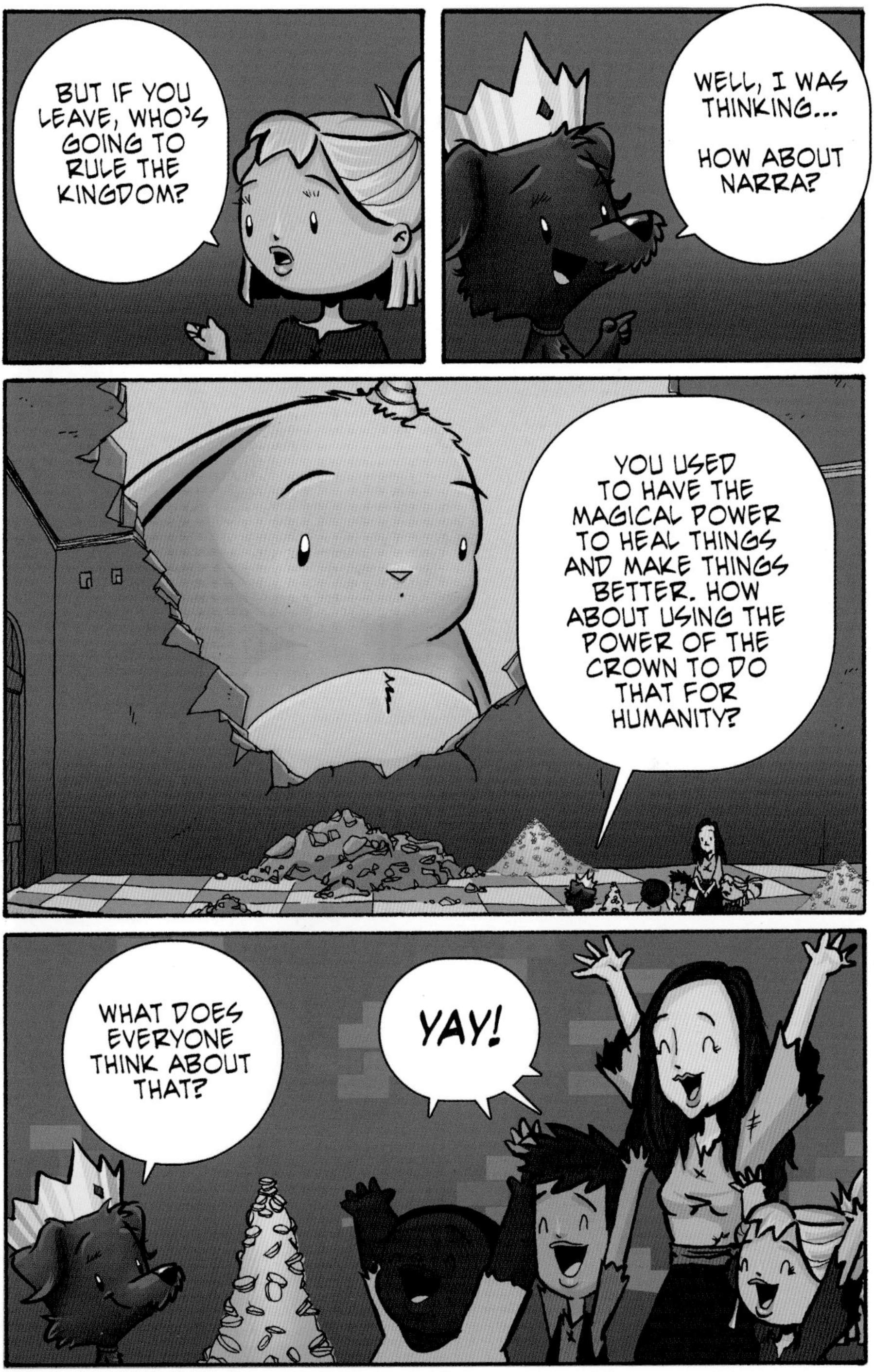
BUT IF YOU LEAVE, WHO'S GOING TO RULE THE KINGDOM?
WELL, I WAS THINKING...
HOW ABOUT NARRA?
YOU USED TO HAVE THE MAGICAL POWER TO HEAL THINGS AND MAKE THINGS BETTER. HOW ABOUT USING THE POWER OF THE CROWN TO DO THAT FOR HUMANITY?
WHAT DOES EVERYONE THINK ABOUT THAT?
YAY!

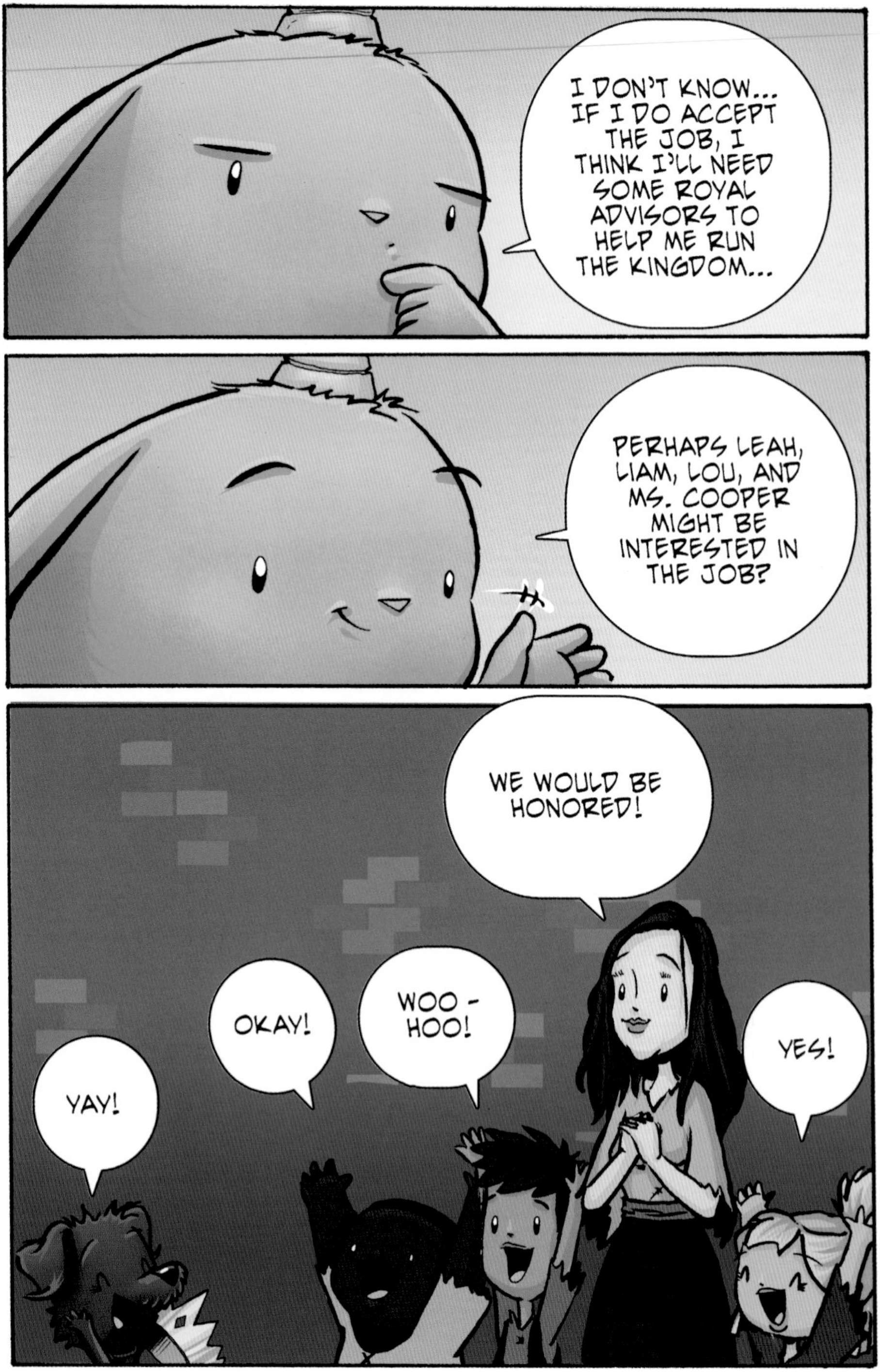
I DON'T KNOW... IF I DO ACCEPT THE JOB, I THINK I'LL NEED SOME ROYAL ADVISORS TO HELP ME RUN THE KINGDOM...
PERHAPS LEAH, LIAM, LOU, AND MS. COOPER MIGHT BE INTERESTED IN THE JOB?
WE WOULD BE HONORED!
YAY!
OKAY!
WOO-HOO!
YES!

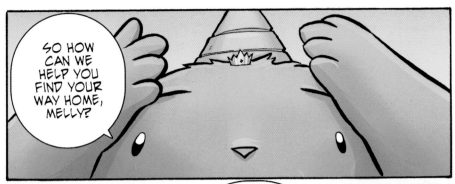

SO HOW CAN WE HELP YOU FIND YOUR WAY HOME, MELLY?

MINE'S THE HOUSE THAT SMELLS LIKE BATHROOM SPRAY AND SOMETIMES CHICKEN NUGGETS...

DOES ANYONE KNOW THAT ONE?

UM... I'M NOT SURE I...

GAK-HURK!

SHOOP!

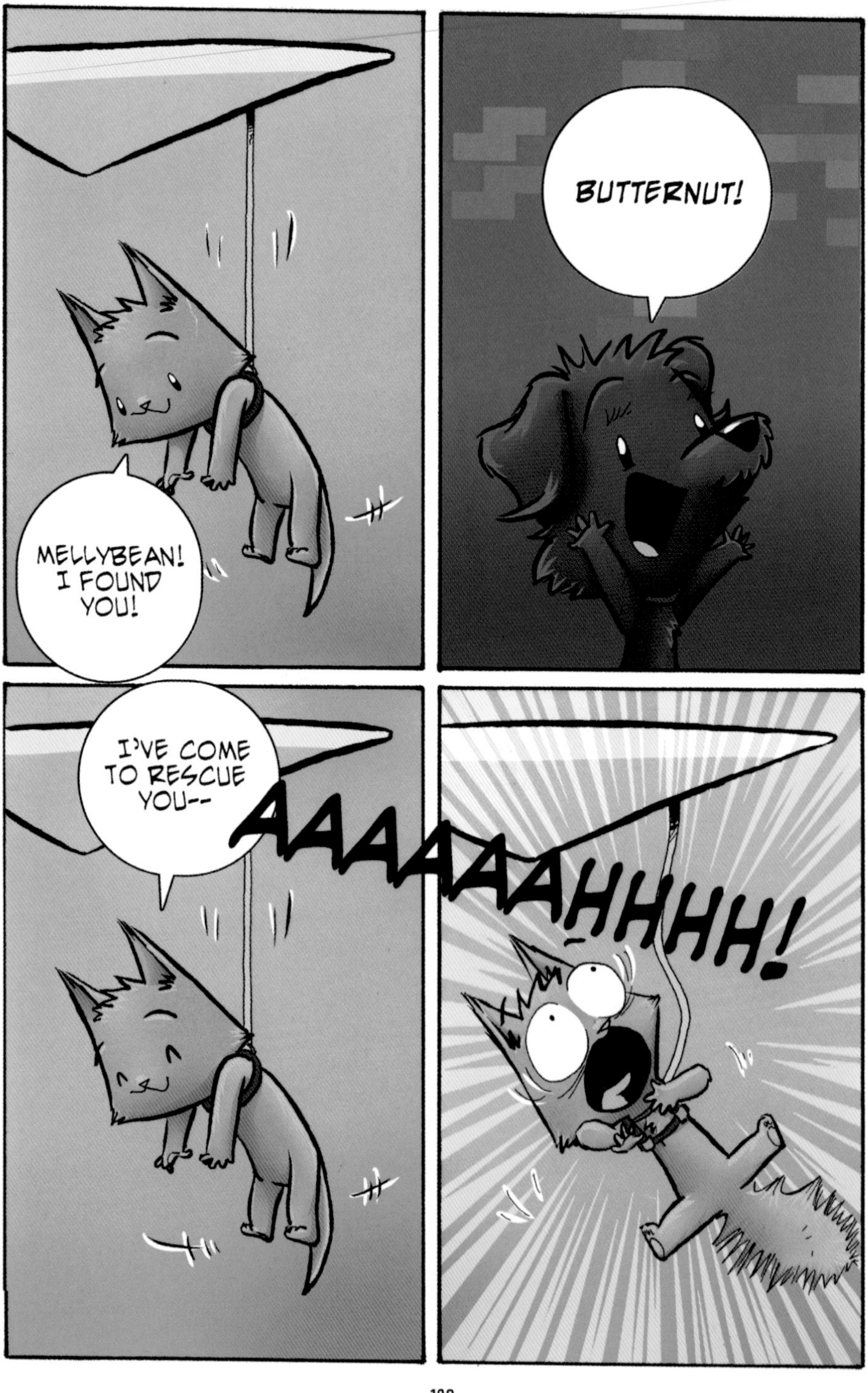
MELLYBEAN! I FOUND YOU!
BUTTERNUT!
I'VE COME TO RESCUE YOU--
AAAAAAAHHHHH!

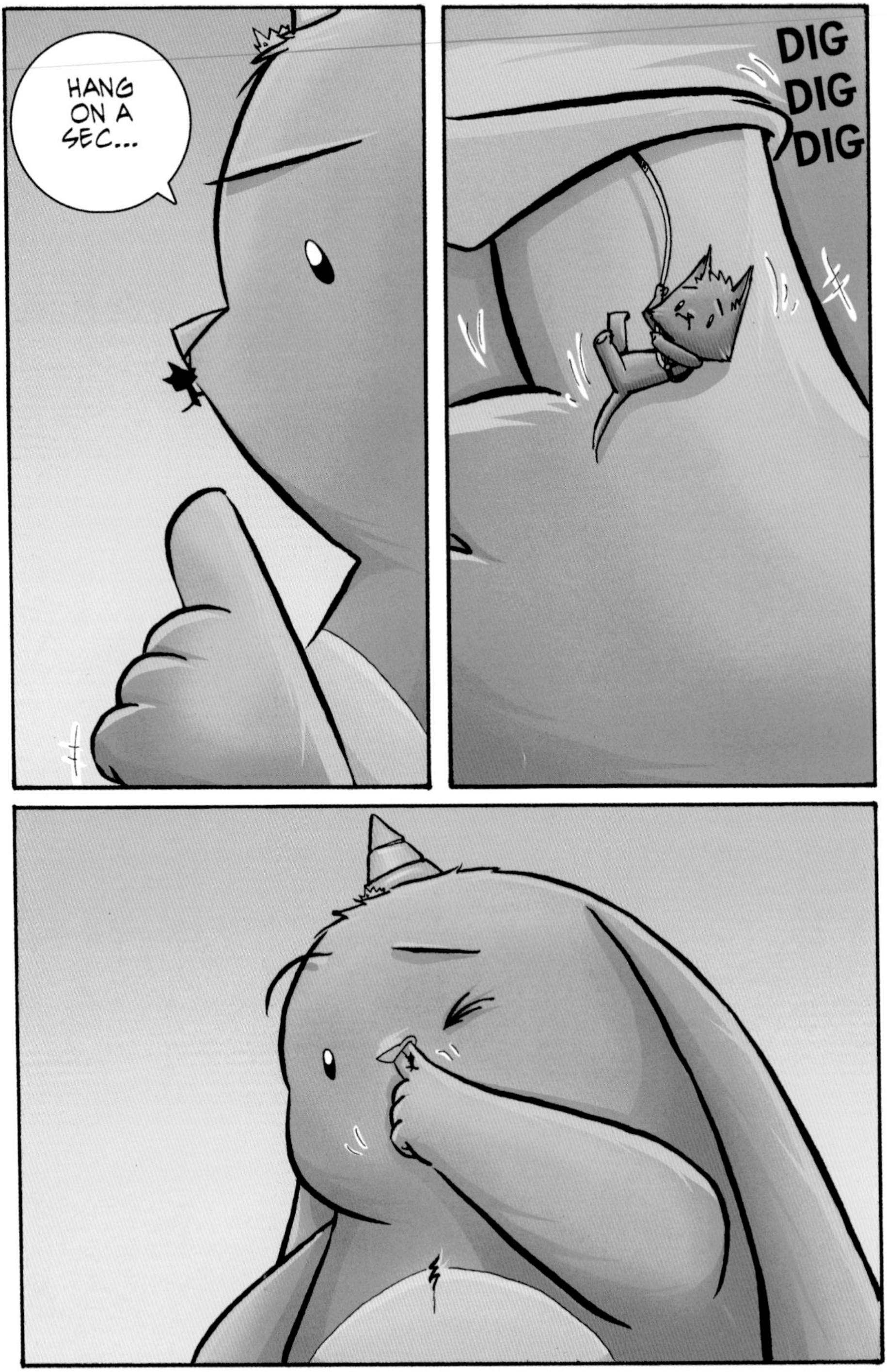
HANG ON A SEC...
DIG DIG DIG

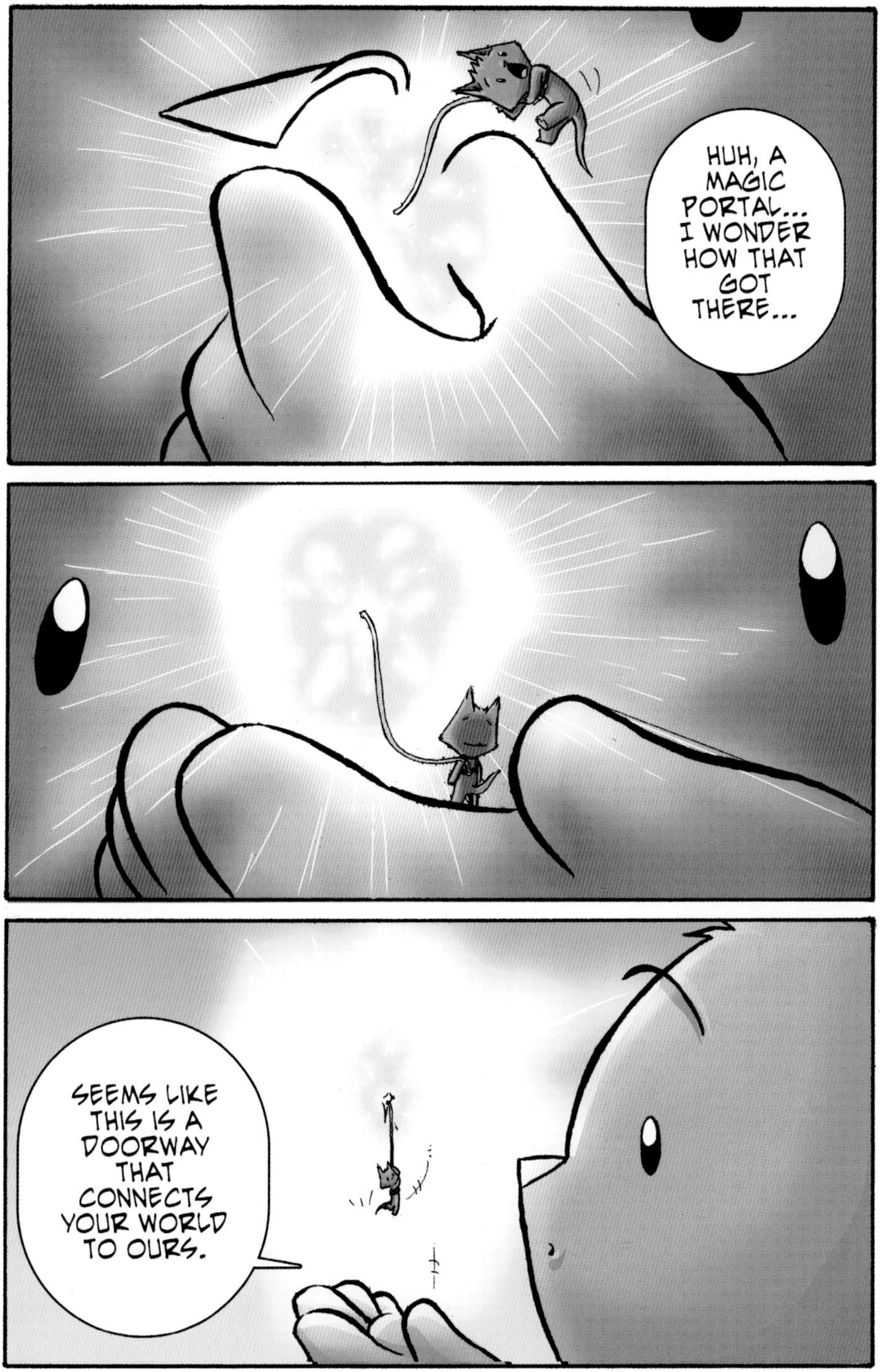
HUH, A MAGIC PORTAL... I WONDER HOW THAT GOT THERE...
SEEMS LIKE THIS IS A DOORWAY THAT CONNECTS YOUR WORLD TO OURS.

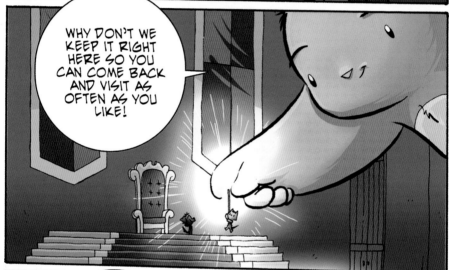

194

CHAPTER 9
NONE THE WISER

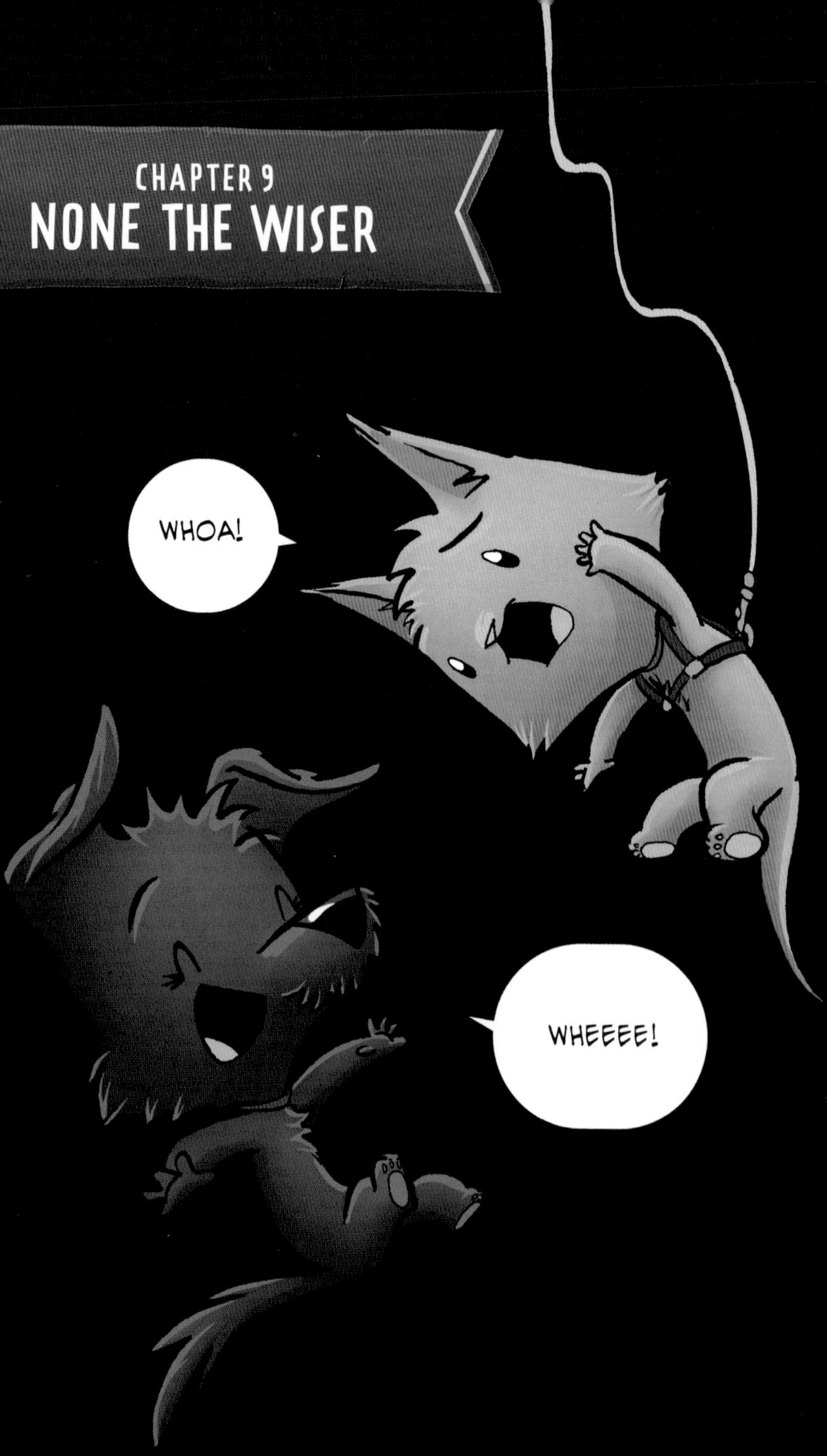

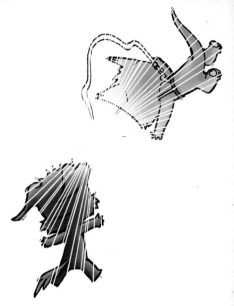

POP!

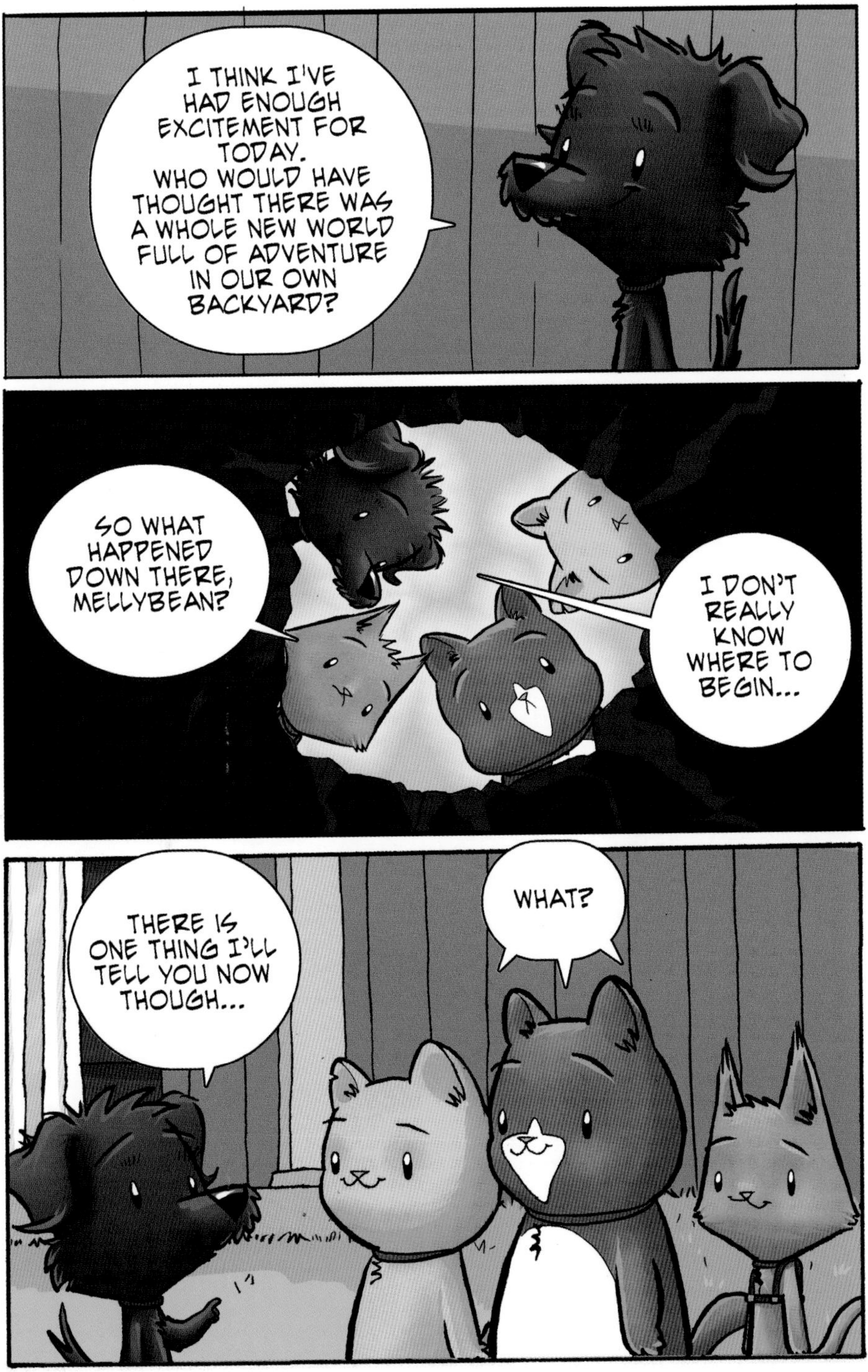
I THINK I'VE HAD ENOUGH EXCITEMENT FOR TODAY. WHO WOULD HAVE THOUGHT THERE WAS A WHOLE NEW WORLD FULL OF ADVENTURE IN OUR OWN BACKYARD?
SO WHAT HAPPENED DOWN THERE, MELLYBEAN?
I DON'T REALLY KNOW WHERE TO BEGIN...
THERE IS ONE THING I'LL TELL YOU NOW THOUGH...
WHAT?

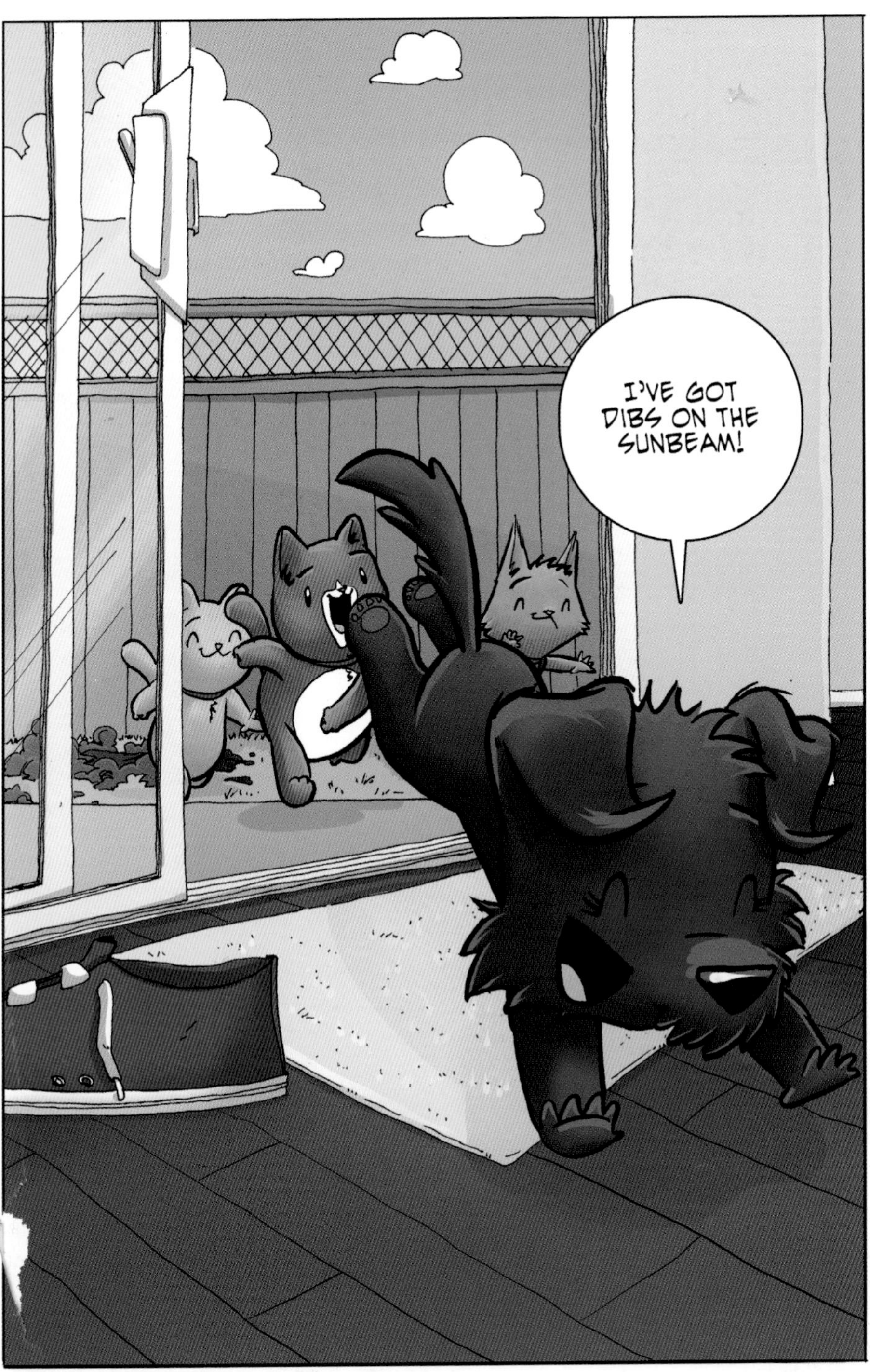
I'VE GOT DIBS ON THE SUNBEAM!

AUTHOR'S NOTE

Ever since I was four years old (learning to draw by tracing *Garfield* comic strips) I wanted to be an author. Now, at age forty, that dream has finally come true, and I couldn't be more grateful to everyone who helped make this possible. So from the bottom of my heart, thank you!

This series is about how one ordinary person (a pup in this case) can make a big difference just by being themselves. You don't have to be the "Chosen One" or "gifted" to make an impact on the world or in someone else's life. Just being you is enough, which is one of the many things my dog Melly has taught me.

That's right! It might be hard to believe, but Melly—and all of her feline friends, actually—are based on my real-life pets. In the summer of 2018, my girlfriend (who's now my fiancée!) and I adopted a two-month-old puppy we named Melody (and affectionately nicknamed Melly or Mellybean). The real Melly will always try to get Butternut, Tugs, and Charlie (Chuck) to play with her—and though she often tries to steal the cat's stinky food, they get along great and all share the love of a good sunbeam. Melly is hands down the most courageous and adventurous one of us, making new friends wherever we go and braving the great outdoors. We're an odd little family of misfits, and having this book to live out magical adventures that we'd never really get to go on is such a treat, and it means a lot to me to get to spend time living with and writing stories about ones I love so much.

Mellybean, both the real dog and the book, has changed my life, and I hope her adventures will bring as much joy to you, reading them, as they have for me writing and drawing them. I can't wait to see where her story will take us to next!